Praise for **Betty Neels**

"Neels is especially good at painting her scenes with choice words, and this adds to the charm of the story."
—*USATODAY.com*'s *Happy Ever After* blog on *Tulips for Augusta*

"Betty Neels surpasses herself with an excellent storyline, a hearty conflict and pleasing characters."
—*RT Book Reviews* on *The Right Kind of Girl*

"Once again Betty Neels delights readers with a sweet tale in which love conquers all."
—*RT Book Reviews* on *Fate Takes a Hand*

"One of the first Harlequin authors I remember reading. I was completely enthralled by the exotic locales... Her books will always be some of my favorites to re-read."
—*Goodreads* on *A Valentine for Daisy*

"I just love Betty Neels!... If you like a good old-fashioned romance...you can't go wrong with this author."
—*Goodreads* on *Caroline's Waterloo*

Romance readers around the world were sad to note the passing of **Betty Neels** in June 2001. Her career spanned thirty years, and she continued to write into her ninetieth year. To her millions of fans, Betty epitomized the romance writer, and yet she began writing almost by accident. She had retired from nursing, but her inquiring mind still sought stimulation. Her new career was born when she heard a lady in her local library bemoaning the lack of good romance novels. Betty's first book, *Sister Peters in Amsterdam*, was published in 1969, and she eventually completed 134 books. Her novels offer a reassuring warmth that was very much a part of her own personality. She was a wonderful writer, and she is greatly missed. Her spirit and genuine talent live on in all her stories.

The Best of BETTY NEELS

'Tis The Season

MILLS & BOON

'TIS THE SEASON © 2022 by Harlequin Books S.A.

A CHRISTMAS ROMANCE
© 1999 by Betty Neels
Australian Copyright 1999
New Zealand Copyright 1999

First Published 1999
Second Australian Paperback Edition 2022
ISBN 978 1 867 26828 4

A HAPPY MEETING
© 1992 by Betty Neels
Australian Copyright 1992
New Zealand Copyright 1992

First Published 1992
Second Australian Paperback Edition 2022
ISBN 978 1 867 26828 4

ALWAYS AND FOREVER
© 2001 by Betty Neels
Australian Copyright 2001
New Zealand Copyright 2001

First Published 2001
Second Australian Paperback Edition 2022
ISBN 978 1 867 26828 4

Except for use in any review, the reproduction or utilisation of this work in whole or in part in any form by any electronic, mechanical or other means, now known or hereafter invented, including xerography, photocopying and recording, or in any information storage or retrieval system, is forbidden without the permission of the publisher.

This book is sold subject to the condition that it shall not, by way of trade or otherwise, be lent, resold, hired out or otherwise circulated without the prior consent of the publisher in any form of binding or cover other than that in which it is published and without a similar condition including this condition being imposed on the subsequent purchaser.

All rights reserved including the right of reproduction in whole or in part in any form. This edition is published in arrangement with Harlequin Books S.A. Cover art used by arrangement with Harlequin Books S.A. All rights reserved.

This is a work of fiction. Names, characters, places, and incidents are either the product of the author's imagination or are used fictitiously, and any resemblance to actual persons, living or dead, business establishments, events, or locales is entirely coincidental.

Published by
Mills & Boon
An imprint of Harlequin Enterprises (Australia) Pty Limited
(ABN 47 001 180 918), a subsidiary of HarperCollins
Publishers Australia Pty Limited (ABN 36 009 913 517)
Level 13, 201 Elizabeth Street
SYDNEY NSW 2000
AUSTRALIA

MIX
Paper | Supporting responsible forestry
FSC® C001695
www.fsc.org

® and ™ (apart from those relating to FSC®) are trademarks of Harlequin Enterprises (Australia) Pty Limited or its corporate affiliates. Trademarks indicated with ® are registered in Australia, New Zealand and in other countries. Contact admin_legal@Harlequin.ca for details.

Printed and bound in Australia by McPherson's Printing Group

CONTENTS

A CHRISTMAS ROMANCE	7
A HAPPY MEETING	79
ALWAYS AND FOREVER	243

A Christmas Romance

CHAPTER ONE

THEODOSIA CHAPMAN, climbing the first of the four flights which led to her bed-sitter—or, as her landlady called it, her studio flat—reviewed her day with a jaundiced eye. Miss Prescott, the senior dietician at St Alwyn's hospital, an acidulated spinster of an uncertain age, had found fault with everyone and everything. As Theodosia, working in a temporary capacity as her personal assistant, had been with her for most of the day, she'd had more than her share of grumbles. And it was only Monday; there was a whole week before Saturday and Sunday...

She reached the narrow landing at the top of the house, unlocked her door and closed it behind her with a sigh of contentment. The room was quite large with a sloping ceiling and a small window opening onto the flat roof of the room below hers. There was a small gas stove in one corner with shelves and a cupboard and a gas fire against the wall opposite the window.

The table and chairs were shabby but there were bright cushions, plants in pots and some pleasant pictures on the walls. There was a divan along the end wall, with a bright cover, and a small bedside table close by with a pretty lamp. Sitting upright in the centre of the divan was a large and handsome ginger cat. He got down as Theodosia went in, trotted to meet her and she picked him up to perch him on her shoulder.

'I've had a beastly day, Gustavus. We must make up for it—we'll have supper early. You go for a breath of air while I open a tin.'

She took him to the window and he slipped out onto the roof to prowl among the tubs and pots she had arranged there. She watched him pottering for a moment. It was dark and cold, only to be expected since it was a mere five weeks to Christmas, but the lamplight was cheerful. As soon as he came in she would close the window and the curtains and light the gas fire.

She took off her coat and hung it on the hook behind the curtain where she kept her clothes and peered at her face in the small square mirror over the chest of drawers. Her reflection stared back at her—not pretty, perhaps, but almost so, for she had large, long-lashed eyes, which were grey and not at all to her taste, but they went well with her ginger hair, which was straight and long and worn in a neat topknot. Her mouth was too large but its corners turned up and her nose was just a nose, although it had a tilt at its tip.

She turned away, a girl of middle height with a pretty figure and nice legs and a lack of conceit about her person. Moreover, she was possessed of a practical nature which allowed her to accept her rather dull life at least with tolerance, interlarded with a strong desire to change it if she saw the opportunity to do so. And that for the moment didn't seem very likely.

She had no special qualifications; she could type and take shorthand, cope adequately with a word processor and a computer and could be relied upon, but none of these added up to much. Really, it was just as well that Miss Prescott used her for most of the day to run errands, answer the phone and act as go-between for that lady and any member of the medical or nursing staff who dared to query her decisions about a diet.

Once Mrs Taylor returned from sick leave then Theodosia supposed that she would return to the typing pool. She didn't like that very much either but, as she reminded herself with her usual good sense, beggars couldn't be choosers. She managed on her salary although the last few days of the month were always dicey and there was very little chance to save.

Her mother and father had died within a few weeks of each other, victims of flu, several years ago. She had been nineteen, on the point of starting to train as a physiotherapist, but there hadn't been enough money to see her through the training. She had taken a business course and their doctor had heard of a job in the typing pool at St Alwyn's. It had been a lifeline, but unless she could acquire more skills she knew that she had little chance of leaving the job. She would be twenty-five on her next birthday...

She had friends, girls like herself, and from time to time she had been out with one or other of the young doctors, but she encountered them so seldom that friendships died for lack of meetings. She had family, too—two great-aunts, her father's aunts—who lived in a comfortable red-brick cottage at Finchingfield. She spent her Christmases with them, and an occasional weekend, but although they were kind to her she sensed that she interfered with their lives and was only asked to stay from a sense of duty.

She would be going there for Christmas, she had received their invitation that morning, written in the fine spiky writing of their youth.

Gustavus came in then and she shut the window and drew the curtains against the dark outside and set about getting their suppers. That done and eaten, the pair of them curled up in the largest of the two shabby chairs by the gas fire and while Gustavus dozed Theodosia read her library book. The music on the radio was soothing and the room with its pink lampshades looked cosy. She glanced round her.

'At least we have a very nice home,' she told Gustavus, who twitched a sleepy whisker in reply.

Perhaps Miss Prescott would be in a more cheerful mood, thought Theodosia, trotting along the wet pavements to work in the morning. At least she didn't have to catch a bus; her bedsitter might not be fashionable but it was handy...

The hospital loomed large before her, red-brick with a great many Victorian embellishments. It had a grand entrance, rows and rows of windows and a modern section built onto one side where the Emergency and Casualty departments were housed.

Miss Prescott had her office on the top floor, a large room lined with shelves piled high with reference books, diet sheets and files. She sat at an important-looking desk, with a computer, two telephones and a large open notebook filled with the lore of her profession, and she looked as important as her desk. She was a big woman with commanding features and a formidable bosom—a combination of attributes which aided her to triumph over any person daring to have a difference of opinion with her.

Theodosia had a much smaller desk in a kind of cubby-hole with its door open so that Miss Prescott could demand her services at a moment's notice. Which one must admit were very frequent. Theodosia might not do anything important—like making out diet sheets for several hundreds of people, many of them different—but she did her share, typing endless lists, menus, diet sheets, and rude letters to ward sisters if they complained. In a word, Miss Prescott held the hospital's stomach in the hollow of her hand.

She was at her desk as Theodosia reached her office.

'You're late.'

'Two minutes, Miss Prescott,' said Theodosia cheerfully. 'The lift's not working and I had five flights of stairs to climb.'

'At your age that should be an easy matter. Get the post opened, if you please.' Miss Prescott drew a deep indignant breath which made her corsets creak. 'I am having trouble with the Women's Medical ward sister. She has the impertinence to disagree with the diet I have formulated for that patient with diabetes and kidney failure. I have spoken to her on the telephone and when I have rewritten the diet sheet you will take it down to her. She is to keep to my instructions on it. You may tell her that.'

Theodosia began to open the post, viewing without relish the prospect of being the bearer of unwelcome news. Miss Prescott, she had quickly learned, seldom confronted any of those who had the temerity to disagree with her. Accordingly, some half an hour later she took the diet sheet and began her journey to Women's Medical on the other side of the hospital and two floors down.

Sister was in her office, a tall, slender, good-looking woman in her early thirties. She looked up and smiled as Theodosia knocked.

'Don't tell me, that woman's sent you down with another diet sheet. We had words…!'

'Yes, she mentioned that, Sister. Shall I wait should you want to write a reply?'

'Did she give you a message as well?'

'Well, yes, but I don't think I need to give it to you. I mean, I think she's already said it all…'

Sister laughed. 'Let's see what she says this time…'

She was reading it when the door opened and she glanced up and got to her feet. 'Oh, sir, you're early…'

The man who entered was very large and very tall so that Sister's office became half its size. His hair was a pale brown, greying at the temples, and he was handsome, with heavy-lidded eyes and a high-bridged nose upon which was perched a pair of half glasses. All of which Theodosia noticed with an interested eye. She would have taken a longer look only she caught his eye—blue and rather cold—and looked the other way.

He wished Sister good morning and raised one eyebrow at Theodosia. 'I'm interrupting something?' he asked pleasantly.

'No, no, sir. Miss Prescott and I are at odds about Mrs Bennett's diet. They sent Theodosia down with the diet sheet she insists is the right one…'

He held out a hand and took the paper from her and read it.

'You do right to query it, Sister. I think that I had better have a word with Miss Prescott. I will do so now and return here in a short while.'

He looked at Theodosia and opened the door. 'Miss—er—Theodosia shall return with me and see fair play.'

She went with him since it was expected of her, though she wasn't sure about the fair play; Miss Prescott usually made mincemeat of anyone disagreeing with her, but she fancied that this man, whoever he was, might not take kindly to such treatment.

Theodosia, skipping along beside him to keep up, glanced up at his impassive face. 'You work here too?' she asked, wanting only to be friendly. 'This is such a big place I hardly ever meet the same person twice, if you see what I mean. I expect you're a doctor—well, a senior doctor, I suppose. I expect you've met Miss Prescott before?'

There were climbing the stairs at a great rate. 'You'll have to slow down,' said Theodosia, 'if you want me to be there at the same time as you.'

He paused to look down at her. 'My apologies, young lady, but I have no time to waste loitering on a staircase.'

Which she considered was a rather unkind remark. She said tartly, 'Well, I haven't any time to waste either.'

They reached Miss Prescott's office in silence and he opened the door for her. Miss Prescott didn't look up.

'You took your time. I shall be glad when Mrs Taylor returns. What had Sister to say this time?'

She looked up then and went slowly red. 'Oh—you need my advice, sir?'

He walked up to her desk, tore the diet sheet he held into several pieces and laid them on the blotter before her. He said quietly, 'Miss Prescott, I have no time to waste with people who go against my orders. The diet is to be exactly as I have asked for. You are a dietician, but you have no powers to overrule the medical staff's requests for a special diet. Be so good as to remember that.'

He went quietly out of the room, leaving Miss Prescott gobbling with silent rage. Theodosia studied her alarmingly puce complexion. 'Shall I make a cup of tea?'

'No—yes. I'm upset. That man...'

'I thought he was rather nice,' said Theodosia, 'and he was very polite.'

Miss Prescott ground her teeth. 'Do you know who he is?'

Theodosia, putting teabags into the teapot, said that no, she didn't.

'Professor Bendinck. He's senior consultant on the medical side, is on the board of governers, has an enormous private practice and is an authority on most medical conditions.'

'Quite a lad!' said Theodosia cheerfully. 'Don't you like him?'

Miss Prescott snorted. 'Like him? Why should I like him? He could get me the sack today if he wanted to.' She snapped her mouth shut; she had said too much already.

'I shouldn't worry,' said Theodosia quietly. She didn't like Miss Prescott, but it was obvious that she had had a nasty shock. 'I'm sure he's not mean enough to do that.'

'You don't know anything about him,' snapped Miss Prescott, and took the proffered cup of tea without saying thank you. Theodosia, pouring herself a cup, reflected that she would rather like to know more about him...

The day was rather worse than Monday had been, and, letting herself into her bed-sitter that evening, she heaved a sigh of relief. A quiet evening with Gustavus for company...

There was another letter from her aunts. She was invited to spend the following weekend with them. They had read in their newspaper that the air in London had become very polluted—a day or two in the country air would be good for her. She was expected for lunch on Saturday. It was more of a command than an invitation and Theodosia, although she didn't particulary want to go, knew that she would, for the aunts were all the family she had now.

The week, which had begun badly, showed no signs of improving; Miss Prescott, taking a jaundiced view of life, made sure that everyone around her should feel the same. As the weekend approached Theodosia wished that she could have spent it quietly getting up late and eating when she felt like it, lolling around with the papers. A weekend with the great-aunts was hardly restful. Gustavus hated it—the indignity of the basket, the tiresome journey by bus and train and then another bus; and, when they did arrive, he was only too aware that he wasn't really welcome, only Theodosia had made it plain that if she spent her weekends with her great-aunts then he must go too...

It was Friday morning when, racing round the hospital collecting diet sheets from the wards, Theodosia ran full tilt into the professor, or rather his waistcoat. He fielded her neatly, collected the shower of diet sheets and handed them back to her.

'So sorry,' said Theodosia. 'Wasn't looking where I was going, was I?'

Her ginger head caught fire from a stray shaft of winter sunshine and the professor admired it silently. She was like a spring morning in the middle of winter, he reflected, and frowned at the nonsensical thought.

'Such a rush,' said Theodosia chattily. 'It's always the same on a Friday.'

The professor adjusted the spectacles on his nose and asked, 'Why is that?'

'Oh, the weekend, you know, patients going home and Sister's weekend, too, on a lot of the wards.'

'Oh, yes, I see.' The professor didn't see at all, but he had a wish to stay talking to this friendly girl who treated him like a human being and not like the important man he was. He asked casually, 'And you, miss...er... Do you also go home for the weekend?'

'Well, not exactly. What I mean is, I do have the weekend

off, but I haven't got a home with a family, if that's what you mean. I've got quite a nice bed-sitter.'

'No family?'

'Two great-aunts; they have me for weekends sometimes. I'm going there tomorrow.'

'And where is "there"?' He had a quiet, rather deliberate voice, the kind of voice one felt compelled to answer.

'Finchingfield. That's in Essex.'

'You drive yourself there?'

Theodosia laughed. 'Me? Drive? Though I can ride a bike, I haven't a car. But it's quite easy—bus to the station, train to Braintree and then the local bus. I quite enjoy it, only Gustavus hates it.'

'Gustavus?'

'My cat. He dislikes buses and trains. Well, of course, he would, wouldn't he?'

The professor agreed gravely. He said slowly, 'It so happens that I am going to Braintree tomorrow. I'd be glad to give you and Gustavus a lift.'

'You are? Well, what a coincidence; that would be...' She stopped and blushed vividly. 'I didn't mean to cadge a lift off you. You're very kind to offer but I think I'd better not.'

'I'm quite safe,' said the professor mildly, 'and since you didn't know that I would be going to Braintree in the morning you could hardly be accused of cadging.'

'Well, if you don't mind—I would be grateful...'

'Good.' He smiled then and walked away and she, remembering the rest of the diet sheets, raced off to the men's ward... It was only as she handed over the rest of the diet sheets to Miss Prescott that she remembered that he hadn't asked her where she lived nor had he said at what time he would pick her up. So that's that, reflected Theodosia, scarcely listening to Miss Prescott's cross voice.

If she had hoped for a message from him during the day she was to be disappointed. Five o'clock came and half an hour later—for, of course, Miss Prescott always found something else for her to do just as she was leaving—Theodosia raced through the hospital, intent on getting home, and was brought up short by the head porter hailing her from his lodge in the entrance hall.

'Message for you, miss. You're to be ready by ten o'clock. You'll be fetched from where you live.'

He peered at her over his spectacles. 'That's what Professor Bendinck said.'

Theodosia had slithered to a halt. 'Oh, thank you, Bowden,' she said, and added, 'He's giving me a lift.'

The head porter liked her. She was always cheerful and friendly. 'And very nice too, miss,' he said. 'Better than them trains and buses.'

Theodosia, explaining to Gustavus that they would be travelling in comfort instead of by the public transport he so disliked, wondered what kind of car the professor would have. Something rather staid, suitable for his dignified calling, she supposed. She packed her overnight bag, washed her hair and polished her shoes. Her winter coat was by no means new but it had been good when she had bought it and she consoled herself with the thought that winter coats didn't change their style too much. It would have to be the green jersey dress...

At ten o'clock the next morning she went down to the front door with Gustavus in his basket and her overnight bag over her shoulder. She would give him ten minutes, she had decided, and if he didn't turn up she would get a bus to Liverpool Street Station.

He was on the doorstep, talking to Mrs Towzer, who had a head crammed with pink plastic curlers and a feather duster in one hand. When she saw Theodosia she said, 'There you are, ducks; I was just telling your gentleman friend here that you was a good tenant. A real lady—don't leave the landing lights on all night and leaves the bath clean...'

Theodosia tried to think of something clever to say. She

would have been grateful if the floor had opened and swallowed her. She said, 'Good morning, Mrs Towzer—Professor.'

'Professor, are you?' asked the irrepressible Mrs Towzer. 'Well, I never...'

Theodosia had to admire the way he handled Mrs Towzer with a grave courtesy which left that lady preening herself and allowed him to stuff Theodosia into the car, put her bag in the boot, settle Gustavus on the back seat with a speed which took her breath and then drive off with a wave of the hand to her landlady.

Theodosia said tartly, 'It would have been much better if I had gone to the hospital and met you there.'

He said gently, 'You are ashamed of your landlady?'

'Heavens, no! She's kind-hearted and good-natured, only there really wasn't any need to tell you about turning off the lights...'

'And cleaning the bath!' To his credit the professor adopted a matter-of-fact manner. 'I believe she was paying you a compliment.'

Theodosia laughed, then said, 'Perhaps you are right. This is a very comfortable car.'

It was a Bentley, dark grey, with its leather upholstery a shade lighter.

'I expect you need a comfortable car,' she went on chattily. 'I mean, you can't have much time to catch buses and things.'

'A car is a necessity for my job. You're warm enough? I thought we might stop for coffee presently. At what time do your great-aunts expect you?'

'If I don't miss the bus at Braintree I'm there in time for lunch. But I'll catch it today; I don't expect it takes long to drive there.'

He was driving north-east out of the city. 'If you will direct me I will take you to Finchingfield; it is only a few miles out of my way.'

She looked at his calm profile uncertainly; without his specs he was really very handsome... 'You're very kind but I'm putting you out.'

'If that were the case I would not have suggested it,' he told her. A remark which she felt had put her in her place. She said meekly, 'Thank you,' and didn't see him smile.

Clear out of the city at last, he drove to Bishop's Stortford and turned off for Great Dunmow, and stopped there for coffee. They had made good time and Theodosia, enjoying his company, wished that their journey were not almost at an end. Finchingfield was only a few miles away and all too soon he stopped in front of the great-aunts' house.

It stood a little way from the centre of the village, in a narrow lane with no other houses nearby; it was a red-brick house, too large to be called a cottage, with a plain face and a narrow brick path leading from the gate to its front door. The professor got out, opened Theodosia's door, collected her bag and Gustavus in his basket and opened the gate and followed her up the path. He put the bag and the basket down. 'I'll call for you at about half past six tomorrow, if that isn't too early for you?'

'You'll drive me back? You're sure it's not disturbing your weekend?'

'Quite sure. I hope you enjoy your visit, Theodosia.'

He went back to the car and got in, and sat waiting until she had banged the door knocker and the door was opened. And then he had gone.

Mrs Trickey, the aunt's daily housekeeper, opened the door. She was a tall, thin woman, middle-aged, with a weather-beaten face, wearing an old-fashioned pinny and a battered hat.

'You're early.' She craned her neck around Theodosia and watched the tail-end of the car disappear down the lane. "Oo's that, then?'

Mrs Trickey had been looking after the aunts for as long as Theodosia could remember and considered herself one of the household. Theodosia said cheerfully, 'Hello, Mrs Trickey; how nice to see you. I was given a lift by someone from the hospital.'

The housekeeper stood aside to let her enter and then went ahead of her down the narrow, rather dark hall. She opened a door at its end, saying, 'Go on in; your aunts are expecting you.'

The room was quite large, with a big window overlooking the garden at the back of the house. It was lofty-ceilinged, with a rather hideous wallpaper, and the furniture was mostly heavy and dark, mid-Victorian, and there was far too much of it. Rather surprisingly, here and there, were delicate Regency pieces, very beautiful and quite out of place.

The two old ladies got up from their places as Theodosia went in. They were tall and thin with ramrod backs and white-haired, but there the resemblance ended.

Great-Aunt Jessica was the elder, a once handsome woman with a sweet smile, her hair arranged in what looked like a bird's nest and wearing a high-necked blouse under a cardigan and a skirt which would have been fashionable at the turn of the century. It was of good material and well made and Theodosia couldn't imagine her aunt wearing anything else.

Great-Aunt Mary bore little resemblance to her elder sister; her hair was drawn back from her face into a neat coil on top of her head and although she must have been pretty when she was young her narrow face, with its thin nose and thin mouth, held little warmth.

Theodosia kissed their proffered cheeks, explained that she had been driven from London by an acquaintance at the hospital and would be called for on the following evening, and then enquired about the old ladies' health.

They were well, they told her, and who exactly was this acquaintance?

Theodosia explained a little more, just enough to satisfy them and nip any idea that Mrs Trickey might have had in the bud. The fact that the professor was a professor helped; her aunts had had a brother, be-whiskered and stern, who had been a professor of something or other and it was obvious that the title conferred respectability onto anyone who possessed it. She was sent away to go to her room and tidy herself and Gustavus was settled in the kitchen in his basket. He didn't like the aunts' house; no one was unkind to him but no one talked to him except Theodosia. Only at night, when everyone was in bed, she crept down and carried him back to spend the night with her.

Lunch was eaten in the dining room, smaller than the drawing room and gloomy by nature of the one small window shrouded in dark red curtains and the massive mahogany sideboard which took up too much space. The old ladies still maintained the style of their youth; the table was covered with a starched white linen cloth, the silver was old and well polished and the meal was served on china which had belonged to their parents. The food didn't live up to the table appointments, however; the aunts didn't cook and Mrs Trickey's culinary skill was limited. Theodosia ate underdone beef, potatoes and cabbage, and Stilton cheese and biscuits, and answered her aunts' questions...

After lunch, sitting in the drawing room between them, she did her best to tell them of her days. Aunt Jessica's questions were always kind but Aunt Mary sometimes had a sharp tongue. She was fond of them both; they had always been kind although she felt that it was from a sense of duty. At length their questions came to an end and the subject of Christmas was introduced.

'Of course, you will spend it here with us, my dear,' said Great-Aunt Jessica. 'Mrs Trickey will prepare everything for us on Christmas Eve as she usually does and I have ordered the turkey from Mr Greenhorn. We shall make the puddings next week...'

'We are so fortunate,' observed Great-Aunt Mary. 'When one thinks of the many young girls who are forced to spend Christmas alone...' Which Theodosia rightly deduced was a remark intended to remind her how lucky she was to have the festive season in the bosom of her family.

At half past four exactly she helped Mrs Trickey bring in the tea tray and the three of them sat at a small table and ate cake and drank tea from delicate china teacups. After the table had been cleared, they played three-handed whist, with an interval so that they could listen to the news. There was no television; the aunts did not approve of it.

After Mrs Trickey had gone home, Theodosia went into the kitchen and got supper. A cold supper, of course, since the aunts had no wish to cook, and once that was eaten she was told quite kindly that she should go to bed; she had had a long journey and needed her rest. It was chilly upstairs, and the bathroom, converted years ago from one of the bedrooms, was far too large, with a bath in the middle of the room. The water wasn't quite hot so she didn't waste time there but jumped into bed, reminding herself that when she came at Christmas she must bring her hot-water bottle with her...

She lay awake for a while, listening to the old ladies going to their beds and thinking about the professor. What was he doing? she wondered. Did he live somewhere near Finchingfield? Did he have a wife and children with whom he would spend Christmas? She enlarged upon the idea; he would have a pretty wife, always beautifully dressed, and two or three charming children. She nodded off as she added a dog and a couple of cats to his household and woke several hours later with cold feet and thoughts of Gustavus, lonely in the kitchen.

She crept downstairs and found him sitting on one of the kitchen chairs, looking resigned. He was more than willing to return to her room with her and curl up on the bed. He was better than a hot-water bottle and she slept again until early morning, just in time to take him back downstairs before she heard her aunts stirring.

Sunday formed a well-remembered pattern: breakfast with Mrs Trickey, still in a hat, cooking scrambled eggs, and then church. The aunts wore beautifully tailored coats and skirts, made exactly as they had been for the last fifty years or so, and felt hats, identical in shape and colour, crowning their heads.

Theodosia was in her winter coat and wearing the small velvet hat she kept especially for her visits to Finchingfield.

The church was beautiful and the flowers decorating it scented the chilly air. Although the congregation wasn't large, it sang the hymns tunefully. And after the service there was the slow progress to the church porch, greeting neighbours and friends and finally the rector, and then the walk back to the house.

Lunch, with the exception of the boiled vegetables, was cold. Mrs Trickey went home after breakfast on Sundays, and the afternoon was spent sitting in the drawing room reading the *Sunday Times* and commenting on the various activities in the village. Theodosia got the tea and presently cleared it away and washed the china in the great stone sink in the scullery, then laid the table for the aunts' supper. It was cold again so, unasked, she found a can of soup and put it ready to heat up.

She filled their hot-water bottles, too, and popped them into their beds. Neither of them approved of what they called the soft modern way of living—indeed, they seemed to enjoy their spartan way of living—but Theodosia's warm heart wished them to be warm at least.

The professor arrived at exactly half past six and Theodosia, admitting him, asked rather shyly if he would care to meet her aunts, and led the way to the drawing room.

Great-Aunt Jessica greeted him graciously and Great-Aunt Mary less so; there was no beard, though she could find no fault with his beautiful manners. He was offered refreshment, which he declined with the right amount of regret, then he assured the old ladies that he would drive carefully, expressed pleasure at having met them, picked up Gustavus's basket and Theodosia's bag and took his leave, sweeping her effortlessly before him.

The aunts, in total approval of him, accompanied them to the door with the wish, given in Great-Aunt Jessica's rather commanding voice, that he might visit them again. 'You will be most welcome when you come again with Theodosia,' she told him.

Theodosia wished herself anywhere but where she was, sitting beside him in his car again. After a silence which lasted too long she said, 'My aunts are getting old. I did explain that I had accepted a lift from you, that I didn't actually know you, but that you are at the hospital...'

The professor had left the village behind, making for the main road. He said impassively, 'It is only natural that they should wish to know who I am. And who knows? I might have the occasion to come this way again.'

Which somehow made everything all right again. In any case she had discovered it was hard to feel shy or awkward with him.

'Did you enjoy your weekend?' she wanted to know.

'Very much. And you? A couple of quiet days away from the hospital can be just what one needs from time to time.'

Perhaps not quite as quiet as two days with the great-aunts, reflected Theodosia, and felt ashamed for thinking it for they must find her visits tiresome, upsetting their quiet lives.

'Shall we stop for a meal?' asked the professor. 'Unless you're anxious to get back? There is a good place at Great Dunmow. I'll have to go straight to the hospital and won't have time to eat.'

'You don't have to work on a Sunday evening?' asked Theodosia, quite shocked.

'No, no, but I want to check on a patient—Mrs Bennett. It will probably be late by the time I get home.'

'Well, of course we must stop,' said Theodosia. 'You can't go without your meals, especially when you work all hours.' She added honestly, 'I'm quite hungry, too.'

'Splendid. I could hardly eat a steak while you nibbled at a lettuce leaf.'

He stopped in the market place at Great Dunmow and ushered her into the Starr restaurant. It was a pleasing place, warm and very welcoming, and the food was splendid. While the professor ate his steak, Theodosia enjoyed a grilled sole, and they both agreed that the bread and butter pudding which followed was perfection. They lingered over coffee until Theodosia said,

'We really ought to go or you'll never get to bed tonight, not if you are going to see your patient when we get back. It's after nine o'clock...'

The professor ignored the time for he was enjoying himself; Theodosia was good company. She was outspoken, which amused him, and, unlike other girls in his acquaintance, she was content with her lot and happy. And she made him laugh. It was a pity that once they got back to London he would probably not see her again; their paths were unlikely to cross.

The rest of their journey went too swiftly; he listened to Theodosia's cheerful voice giving her opinion on this, that and the other, and reflected that she hadn't once talked about herself. When they reached Mrs Towzer's house, he got out, opened her car door, collected Gustavus in his basket and her bag and followed her up the stairs to her attic. He didn't go in—she hadn't invited him anyway—but she offered a hand and thanked him for her supper and the journey. 'I enjoyed every minute of it,' she assured him, looking up at him with her gentle grey eyes. 'And I do hope you won't be too late going to bed. You need your rest.'

He smiled then, bade her a quiet goodnight, and went away, back down the stairs.

CHAPTER TWO

MONDAY MORNING AGAIN, and a cold one. Theodosia, going shivering to the bathroom on the floor below, envied Gustavus, curled up cosily on the divan. And there was a cold sleet falling as she went to work. A cheerful girl by nature, Theodosia was hard put to view the day ahead with any equanimity. But there was something to look forward to, she reminded herself; the hospital ball was to be held on Saturday and she was going with several of the clerical staff of the hospital.

She hadn't expected that she would be asked to go with any of the student doctors or the young men who worked in the wages department. She was on good terms with them all but there were any number of pretty girls from whom they could choose partners. All the same, when she had gone to earlier years' balls, she had had partners enough for she danced well.

She would need a new dress; she had worn the only one she had on three successive years. She pondered the problem during the day. She couldn't afford a new dress—that was quite out of the question—but someone had told her that the Oxfam shops in the more fashionable shopping streets quite often yielded treasures...

On Tuesday, she skipped her midday dinner, begged an extra hour of Miss Prescott and took a bus to Oxford Street.

* * *

The professor, caught in a traffic jam and inured to delays, passed the time glancing idly around him. There was plenty to catch his eye; shoppers thronged the pavement and the shop windows were brilliantly lighted. It was the sight of a gleaming ginger head of hair which caught his attention. There surely weren't two girls with hair that colour…?

The Oxfam lights were of the no-nonsense variety; the shopper could see what he or she was buying. Theodosia, plucking a dove-grey dress off the rails, took it to the window to inspect it better and he watched her as she examined it carefully—the label, the price tag, the seams… It was a pity that the traffic moved at last and he drove on, aware of an unexpected concern that she should be forced to buy someone else's dress.

Theodosia, happily unaware that she had been seen, took the dress home that evening, tried it on and nipped down to the bathroom where there was a full-length mirror. It would do; she would have to take it in here and there and the neck was too low. She brought out her work basket, found a needle and thread and set to. She was handy with her needle but it took a couple of evenings' work till she was satisfied that it would pass muster.

It wasn't as though she was going with a partner, she reminded herself. There would be a great many people there; no one would notice her. Miss Prescott would be going, of course, but any mention of the ball during working hours was sternly rebuked and when Theodosia had asked her what she would be wearing she'd been told not to be impertinent. Theodosia, who had meant it kindly, felt hurt.

She dressed carefully on Saturday evening. The grey dress, viewed in the bathroom looking-glass by the low-wattage bulb, looked all right. A pity she couldn't have afforded a pair of those strappy sandals. Her slippers were silver kid and out of date but at least they were comfortable. She gave Gustavus his supper, made sure that he was warm and comfortable on the divan, and walked to the hospital wrapped in her winter coat and, since it was drizzling, sheltered under her umbrella.

The hospital courtyard was packed with cars for this was an evening when the hospital Board of Governers and their wives, the local Mayor and his wife and those dignitaries who were in some way connected to St Alwyn's came to grace the occasion. Theodosia slipped in through a side door, found her friends, left her coat with theirs in a small room the cleaners used to store their buckets and brooms and went with them to the Assembly Hall where the ball was already under way.

It looked very festive, with paper chains and a Christmas tree in a corner of the stage where the orchestra was. There were balloons and holly and coloured lights and already there were a great many people dancing. Once there, one by one her friends were claimed and she herself was swept onto the dance floor by one of the technicians from the path lab. She didn't know him well and he was a shocking dancer but it was better than hovering on the fringe of the dancers, looking as though dancing was the last thing one wanted to do.

When the band stopped, one of the students with whom she had passed the time of day occasionally claimed her. It was a slow foxtrot and he had time to tell her about the post-mortem he had attended that morning. She listened carefully, feeling slightly sick, but aware that he was longing to talk about it to someone. There were several encores, so that it was possible for him to relate the very last of the horrid details. When the band stopped finally and he offered to fetch her a drink she accepted thankfully.

She had seen the professor at once, dancing with an elegantly dressed woman, and then again with the sister from Women's Medical and for a third time with the Mayor's wife.

And he had seen her, for there was no mistaking that gingery head of hair. When he had danced with all the ladies he was expected to dance with, he made his way round the dancers until he came upon her, eating an ice in the company of the hospital engineer.

He greeted them both pleasantly, and after a few moments of talk with the engineer swept her onto the dance floor.

'You should ask me first,' said Theodosia.

'You might have refused! Are you enjoying yourself?'

'Yes, thank you.' And she was, for he danced well and they were slow foxtrotting again. The hospital dignitaries wouldn't allow any modern dancing; there was no dignity in prancing around waving arms and flinging oneself about...but foxtrotting with a woman you liked was very satisfying, he reflected.

The professor, his eye trained to see details at a glance, had recognised the grey dress. It was pretty in a demure way but it wasn't her size. He could see the tucks she had taken on the shoulders to make a better fit and the neat seams she had taken in at the waist. It would be a pleasure to take her to a good dress shop and buy her clothes which fitted her person and which were new. He smiled at the absurd thought and asked her with impersonal kindness if she was looking forward to Christmas.

'Oh, yes, and it will be three days this year because of Sunday coming in between.' She sounded more enthusiastic than she felt; three days with the aunts wasn't a very thrilling prospect, but she reminded herself that that was ungrateful. She added, by way of apology for thinking unkindly of them, 'The greataunts enjoy an old-fashioned Christmas.'

He could make what he liked of that; it conjured up pictures of a lighted Christmas tree, masses of food and lots of presents; with a party on Boxing Day...

She underestimated the professor's good sense; he had a very shrewd idea what her Christmas would be like. He glanced down at the ginger topknot. It would be a mistake to pity her; she had no need of that. He had never met anyone so content with life and so willing to be happy as she, but he found himself wishing that her Christmas might be different.

He resisted the urge to dance with her for the rest of the evening, handed her back to the engineer and spent the next few moments in cheerful talk before leaving her there.

It was at the end of the evening that he went looking for her amongst the milling crowd making their way out of the hospital. She was on her way out of the entrance when he found her. He touched her arm lightly.

'Come along; the car's close by.'

'There's no need... It's only a short walk... I really don't...' She could have saved her breath; she was propelled gently along away from the crowded forecourt, stuffed tidily into the car and told to fasten her seat belt. It was only as he turned out of the forecourt into the street that she tried again. 'This is quite...'

'You're wasting your breath, Theodosia.' And he had nothing more to say until they reached Mrs Towzer's house. No lights were on, of course, and the rather shabby street looked a bit scary in the dark; walking back on her own wouldn't have been very nice...

He got out, opened her door and took the key she had ready in her hand from her, opened the door silently and switched on the dim light in the hall.

Theodosia held out a hand for the key and whispered, 'Thank you for the lift. Goodnight.' And took off her shoes.

The professor closed the door without a sound, picked up her shoes and trod silently behind her as she went upstairs. She was afraid that he might make a noise but he didn't and she had to confess that it was comforting to have him there. Mrs Towzer, with an eye to economy, had installed landing lights which switched off unless one was nippy between landings.

At her own door he took her key, opened the door and switched on the light, gave her back her key and stood aside for her to pass him.

'Thank you very much,' said Theodosia, still whispering. 'Do be careful going downstairs or you'll be left in the dark, and you will shut the street door?'

The professor assured her in a voice as quiet as her own that he would be careful, and bade her goodnight, pushed her gently into the room and closed the door. Back in his car he wondered why he hadn't kissed her; he had very much wanted to.

As for Theodosia, tumbling into bed presently, hugging a tolerant Gustavus, her sleepy head was full of a jumble of delightful thoughts, all of them concerning the professor.

Going for a brisk walk in Victoria Park the following afternoon, she told herself that he had just happened to be there and that common politeness had forced him to give her a lift back. She went home and had a good tea then went to evensong, to pray there for a happy week ahead!

She wasn't sure if it was an answer to her prayers when she received a letter from Great-Aunt Jessica in the morning. She was asked to go to Fortnum & Mason and purchase the items on the enclosed list. 'And you may bring them down next weekend,' wrote her aunt.

Theodosia studied the list: ham on the bone, Gentleman's Relish, smoked salmon, brandy butter, a Stilton cheese, Bath Oliver biscuits, *marrons glacés*, Earl Grey tea, coffee beans, peaches in brandy... Her week's wages would barely pay for them, not that she could afford to do that. She peered into the envelope in the forlorn hope of finding a cheque or at least a few bank notes but it was empty. She would have to go to the bank and draw out the small amount of money she had so painstakingly saved. If she skipped her midday dinner she would have time to go to the bank. Great-Aunt Jessica would pay her at the weekend and she could put it back into her account.

It wasn't until Wednesday that she had the opportunity to miss her dinner. There was no time to spare, so she hurtled down to the entrance, intent on getting a bus.

The professor, on his way to his car, saw her almost running across the forecourt and cut her off neatly before she could reach the street. She stopped in full flight, unable to get past his massive person.

Theodosia said, 'Hello, Professor,' and then added, 'I can't stop...'

A futile remark with his hand holding her firmly. 'If you're in a hurry, I'll drive you. You can't run to wherever you're going like that.'

'Yes, I can...'

'Where to?'

She had no need to answer his question yet she did. 'The bank and then Fortnum & Mason.'

He turned her round and walked her over to his car. Once inside he said, 'Now tell me why you are in such a hurry to do this.'

He probably used that gentle, compelling voice on his patients, and Theodosia felt compelled once more to answer him. She did so in a rather disjointed manner. 'So, you see, if you don't mind I must catch a bus...'

'I do mind. What exactly do you have to buy?'

She gave him the list. 'You see, everything on it is rather expensive and, of course, Great-Aunt Jessica doesn't bother much about money. She'll pay me at the weekend. That's why I have to go to the bank.'

'That will take up too much time,' said the professor smoothly. 'We will go straight to Fortnum & Mason; I'll pay for these and your aunt can pay me. It just so happens,' he went on in a voice to convince a High Court judge, 'that I am going to Braintree again on Saturday. I'll give you a lift and deliver these things at the same time.'

Theodosia opened her mouth to speak, shut it again and then said, 'But isn't this your lunch hour?'

'Most fortunately, yes; now, let us get this shopping down.'

'Well, if you think it is all right?'

'Perfectly all right and sensible.'

Once there he ushered her in, handed her list over to a polite young man with the request to have the items packed up and ready within the next half an hour or so, and steered her to the restaurant.

'The food department will see to it all,' he told her. 'So much quicker and in the meantime we can have something to eat.'

Theodosia found her tongue. 'But ought I not to choose everything?'

'No, no. Leave everything to the experts; that's what they are here for. Now, what would you like? We have about half an hour. An omelette with French fries and a salad and a glass of white wine?'

It was a delicious meal and all the more delicious because it was unexpected. Theodosia, still breathless from the speed with which the professor had organised everything, and not sure if she hadn't been reckless in allowing him to take over in such a high-handed manner, decided to enjoy herself. This was a treat, something which seldom came her way.

So she ate her lunch, drank the wine and a cup of coffee and followed him back to the food hall, to find a box neatly packed and borne out to the car by the doorman. She was ushered into the car, too, and told to wait while the professor went back to pay the bill and tip the doorman.

'How much was it?' asked Theodosia anxiously as he got in beside her.

'Would it be a good idea,' suggested the professor carefully, 'if I kept this food at my house? There's not any need to unpack it; everything on the list is there and I have the receipted bill.'

'But why should you do that? It may be a great nuisance for you or your wife...'

'I'm not married, and my housekeeper will stow it safely away until Saturday.'

'Well, if it's really no trouble. And how much was it?'

'I can't remember exactly, but your aunt must have a good idea of what the food costs and the bill seemed very reasonable to me. It's in the boot with the food or I would let you have it.'

'No, no. I'm sure it's all right. And thank you very much.'

He was driving back to the hospital, taking short cuts so that she had still five minutes of her dinner hour left by the time he stopped in the forecourt. She spent two of those thanking him in a muddled speech, smiling at him, full of her delightful lunch and his kindness and worry that she had taken up too much of his time.

'A pleasure,' said the professor, resisting a wish to kiss the tip of her nose. He got out of the car and opened her door and suggested that she had better run.

Despite Miss Prescott's sharp tongue and ill temper, the rest of her day was viewed through rose-coloured spectacles by Theodosia. She wasn't sure why she felt happy; of course, it had been marvellous getting her shopping done so easily and having lunch and the prospect of being driven to the aunts' at the weekend, but it was more than that; it was because the professor had been there. And because he wasn't married.

She saw nothing of him for the rest of the week but on Friday evening as she left the hospital there was a message for her. Would she be good enough to be ready at ten o'clock in the morning? She would be fetched as before. This time there was no mistaking the twinkle in the head porter's eye as he told her. Over the years he had passed on many similar messages but never before from the professor.

'We're going to the aunts' again,' Theodosia told Gustavus. 'In that lovely car. You'll like that, won't you?'

She spent a happy evening getting ready for the morning, washing her hair, examining her face anxiously for spots, doing her nails, and putting everything ready for breakfast in the morning. It would never do to keep the professor waiting.

She went down to the front door punctually in the morning to find him already there, leaning against Mrs Towzer's door, listening to that lady's detailed descriptions of her varicose veins with the same quiet attention he would have given any one of his private patients. Mrs Towzer, seeing Theodosia coming downstairs, paused. 'Well, I'll tell you the rest another time,' she suggested. 'You'll want to be on your way, the pair of you.'

She winked and nodded at him and Theodosia went pink as she wished them both a rather flustered good morning, trying not to see the professor's faint smile. But it was impossible to feel put out once she was sitting beside him as he drove off. Indeed she turned and waved to Mrs Towzer, for it seemed wrong to feel so happy while her landlady was left standing at her shabby front door with nothing but rows of similar shabby houses at which to look.

It was a gloomy morning and cold, with a leaden sky.

'Will it snow?' asked Theodosia.

'Probably, but not just yet. You'll be safely at your great-aunts' by then.'

He glanced at her. 'Will you be going to see them again before Christmas?'

'No, this is an unexpected visit so that I could buy all those things.' In case he was thinking that she was angling for another lift she added, 'I expect you'll be at home for Christmas?'

He agreed pleasantly in a voice which didn't invite more questions so she fell silent. When the silence became rather too long, she began to talk about the weather, that great stand-by of British conversation.

But she couldn't talk about that for ever. She said, 'I won't talk any more; I expect you want to think. You must have a lot on your mind.'

The professor debated with himself whether he should tell her that he had her on his mind, increasingly so with every day that passed. But if he did he would frighten her away. Being friendly was one thing but he sensed that she would fight shy of anything more. He was only too well aware that he was considered by her to be living on a different plane and that their paths would never meet. She was friendly because she was a girl who would be friends with anyone. It was in her nature to be kind and helpful and to like those she met and worked with. Even the redoubtable Miss Prescott.

He said now, 'There is no need to make polite conversation with you, Theodosia; do you not feel the same?'

'Well, yes, I do. I mean, it's nice to be with someone and not have to worry about whether they were wishing you weren't there.'

His rather stern mouth twitched. 'Very well put, Theodosia. Shall we have coffee at Great Dunmow?'

They sat a long while over coffee. The professor showed no signs of hurry. His questions were casual but her answers told him a great deal. She wouldn't admit to loneliness or worry about her future; her answers were cheerful and hopeful. She had no ambitions to be a career girl, only to have a steady job and security.

'You wouldn't wish to marry?'

'Oh, but I would—but not to anyone, you understand,' she assured him earnestly. 'But it would be nice to have a husband and a home; and children.'

'So many young women want a career—to be a lawyer, or a doctor, or a high-powered executive.'

She shook her head. 'Not me; I'm not clever to start with.'

'You don't need to be clever to marry?' He smiled a little.

'Not that sort of clever. But being married isn't just a job, is it? It's a way of life.'

'And I imagine a very pleasant one if one is happily married.'

He glanced at his watch. 'Perhaps we had better get on...'

At the great-aunts' house Mrs Trickey, in the same hat, admitted them and ushered them into the drawing room. Aunt Jessica got up to greet them but Aunt Mary stayed in her chair, declaring in a rather vinegary voice that the cold weather had got into her poor old bones, causing her to be something of an invalid. Theodosia kissed her aunts, sympathised with Aunt Mary and hoped that she wasn't expecting to get free medical treatment from their visitor. She had no chance to say more for the moment since Aunt Jessica was asking Theodosia if she had brought the groceries with her.

The professor greeted the two ladies with just the right amount of polite pleasure, and now he offered to fetch the box of food into the house.

'The kitchen?' he wanted to know.

'No, no. We shall unpack it here; Mrs Trickey can put it all away once that is done. You have the receipted bill, Theodosia?'

'Well, actually, Professor Bendinck has it. He paid for everything. I hadn't enough money.' She could see that that wasn't enough to satisfy the aunts. 'We met going out of the hospital. I was trying to get to the bank to get some money. To save time, because it was my dinner hour, he kindly drove me to Fortnum & Mason and gave them your order and paid for it.'

Aunt Mary looked shocked. 'Really, Theodosia, a young girl should not take any money from a gentleman.'

But Aunt Jessica only smiled. 'Well, dear, we are grateful to Professor Bendinck for his help. I'll write a cheque...'

'Perhaps you would let Theodosia have it? She can let me have it later. I shall be calling for her tomorrow evening.'

Aunt Mary was still frowning. 'I suppose you had spent all your money on clothes—young women nowadays seem to think of nothing else.'

Theodosia would have liked to tell her that it wasn't new clothes, more's the pity. It was cat food, and milk, bread and cheese, tea and the cheaper cuts of meat, and all the other necessities one needed to keep body and soul together. But she didn't say a word.

It was the professor who said blandly, 'I don't imagine that Theodosia has a great deal of money to spare—our hospital salaries are hardly generous.'

He smiled, shook hands and took his leave. At the door to the drawing room he bent his great height and kissed Theodosia's cheek. 'Until tomorrow evening.' His smile included all three ladies as he followed Mrs Trickey to the front door.

Great-Aunt Jessica might not have moved with the times—in her young days gentlemen didn't kiss young ladies with such an air, as though they had a right to do so—but she was romantic at heart and now she smiled. It was Great-Aunt Mary who spoke, her thin voice disapproving.

'I am surprised, Theodosia, that you allow a gentleman to kiss you in that manner. Casual kissing is a regrettable aspect of modern life.'

Theodosia said reasonably, 'Well, I didn't allow him, did I? I'm just as surprised as you are, Aunt Mary, but I can assure you that nowadays a kiss doesn't meant anything—it's a social greeting—or a way of saying goodbye.'

And she had enjoyed it very much.

'Shall I unpack the things you wanted?' she asked, suddenly anxious not to talk about the professor.

It was a task which took some time and successfully diverted the old ladies' attention.

The weekend was like all the others, only there was more talk of Christmas now. 'We shall expect you on Christmas Eve,' said Aunt Jessica. 'Around teatime will suit us very nicely.'

That would suit Theodosia nicely, too. She would have to work in the morning; patients still had diets even at Christmas. There would be a tremendous rush getting the diets organised for the holiday period but with luck she would be able to get a late-afternoon train. She must remember to check the times...

In bed much later that night, with Gustavus curled up beside her, she allowed herself to think about the professor. It was, of course, perfectly all right for him to kiss her, she reassured herself, just as she had reassured her aunts: it was an accepted social greeting. Only it hadn't been necessary for him to do it. He was a very nice man, she thought sleepily, only nice wasn't quite the right word to describe him.

It was very cold in church the next morning and, as usual, lunch was cold—roast beef which was underdone, beetroot and boiled potatoes. The trifle which followed was cold, too, and her offer to make coffee afterwards was rejected by the aunts, who took their accustomed seats in the drawing room, impervious to the chill. Theodosia was glad when it was time for her to get the tea, but two cups of Earl Grey, taken without milk, did little to warm her.

She was relieved when the professor arrived; he spent a short time talking to her aunts and then suggested that they should leave. He hadn't kissed her; she hadn't expected him to, but he did give her a long, thoughtful look before bidding his farewells in the nicest possible manner and sweeping her out to the car.

It must have been the delightful warmth in the car which caused Theodosia to sneeze and then shiver.

'You look like a wet hen,' said the professor, driving away from the house. 'You've caught a cold.'

She sneezed again. 'I think perhaps I have. The church was cold, but the aunts don't seem to mind the cold. I'll be perfectly all right once I'm back at Mrs Towzer's.' She added, 'I'm sorry; I do hope I won't give it to you.'

'Most unlikely. We won't stop for a meal at Great Dunmow, I'll drive you straight back.'

'Thank you.'

It was the sensible thing to do, she told herself, but at the same time she felt overwhelming disappointment. Hot soup, a sizzling omelette, piping hot coffee—any of these would have been welcome at Great Dunmow. Perhaps, despite his denial, he was anxious not to catch her cold. She muffled a sneeze and tried to blow her nose soundlessly.

By the time they reached the outskirts of London she was feeling wretched; she had the beginnings of a headache, a running nose and icy shivers down her spine. The idea of getting a meal, seeing to Gustavus and crawling down to the bathroom was far from inviting. She sneezed again and he handed her a large, very white handkerchief.

'Oh, dear,' said Theodosia. She heaved a sigh of relief at his quiet, 'We're very nearly there.'

Only he seemed to be driving the wrong way. 'This is the Embankment,' she pointed out. 'You missed the way...'

'No. You are coming home with me. You're going to have a meal and something for that cold, then I'll drive you back.'

'But that's a lot of trouble and there's Gustavus...'

'No trouble, and Gustavus can have his supper with my housekeeper.'

He had turned into a narrow street, very quiet, lined with Regency houses, and stopped before the last one in the terrace.

Theodosia was still trying to think of a good reason for insisting on going back to Mrs Towzer's but she was given no chance to do so. She found herself out of the car and in through the handsome door and borne away by a little stout woman with grey hair and a round, cheerful face who evinced no surprise at her appearance but ushered her into a cloakroom at the back of the narrow hall, tut-tutting sympathetically as she did so.

'That's a nasty cold, miss, but the professor will have something for it and there'll be supper on the table in no time at all.'

So Theodosia washed her face and tidied her hair, feeling better already, and went back into the hall and was ushered through one of the doors there. The room was large and high-ceilinged with a bow window overlooking the street. It was furnished most comfortably, with armchairs drawn up on each side of the bright fire burning in the steel grate, a vast sofa facing it, more smaller chairs, a scattering of lamp tables and a mahogany rent table in the bow window. There were glass-fronted cabinets on either side of the fireplace and a long case clock by the door.

Theodosia was enchanted. 'Oh, what a lovely room,' she said, and smiled with delight at the professor.

'Yes, I think so, too. Come and sit down. A glass of sherry will make you feel easier; you'll feel better when you have had a meal. I'll give you some pills later; take two when you go to bed and two more in the morning. I'll give you enough for several days.'

She drank her sherry and the housekeeper came presently to

say that supper was on the table. 'And that nice cat of yours is sitting by the Aga as though he lived here, miss. Had his supper, too.'

Theodosia thanked her and the professor said, 'This is Meg, my housekeeper. She was my nanny a long time ago. Meg, this is Miss Theodosia Chapman; she works at the hospital.'

Meg smiled broadly. 'Well, now, isn't that nice?' And she shook the hand Theodosia offered.

Supper was everything she could have wished for—piping hot soup, an omelette as light as air, creamed potatoes, tiny brussels sprouts and little egg custards in brown china pots for pudding. She ate every morsel and the professor, watching the colour creep back into her cheeks, urged her to have a second cup of coffee and gave her a glass of brandy.

'I don't think I would like it...'

'Probably not. I'm giving it to you as a medicine so toss it off, but not too quickly.'

It made her choke and her eyes water, but it warmed her too, and when she had finished it he said, 'I'm going to take you back now. Go straight to bed and take your pills and I promise you that you will feel better in the morning.'

'You've been very kind; I'm very grateful. And it was a lovely supper...'

She bade Meg goodbye and thanked her, too, and with Gustavus stowed in the back of the car she was driven back to Mrs Towzer's.

The contrast was cruel as she got out of the car: the professor's house, so dignified and elegant, and Mrs Towzer's, so shabby and unwelcoming. But she wasn't a girl to whinge or complain. She had a roof over her head and a job and the added bonus of knowing the professor.

He took the key from her and went up the four flights of stairs, carrying her bag and Gustavus in his basket. Then he opened her door and switched on the light and went to light the gas fire. He put the pills on the table and then said, 'Go straight to bed, Theodosia.' He sounded like an uncle or a big brother.

She thanked him again and wished him goodnight and he went to the door. He turned round and came back to where she was standing, studying her face in a manner which disconcerted her. She knew that her nose was red and her eyes puffy; she must look a sight...

He bent and kissed her then, a gentle kiss on her mouth and quite unhurried. Then he was gone, the door shut quietly behind him.

'He'll catch my cold,' said Theodosia. 'Why ever did he do that? I'll never forgive myself if he does; I should have stopped him.'

Only she hadn't wanted to. She took Gustavus out of his basket and gave him his bedtime snack, put on the kettle for her hot-water bottle and turned the divan into a bed, doing all these things without noticing what she was doing.

'I should like him to kiss me again,' said Theodosia loudly. 'I liked it. I like him—no, I'm in love with him, aren't I? Which is very silly of me. I expect it's because I don't see many men and somehow we seem to come across each other quite often. I must stop thinking about him and feeling happy when I see him.'

After which praiseworthy speech she took her pills and, warmed by Gustavus and the hot-water bottle, presently went to sleep—but not before she had had a little weep for what might have been if life had allowed her to tread the same path as the professor.

CHAPTER THREE

THEODOSIA FELT BETTER in the morning; she had a cold, but she no longer felt—or looked—like a wet hen. She took the pills she had been given, ate her breakfast, saw to Gustavus and went to work. Miss Prescott greeted her sourly, expressed the hope that she would take care not to pass her cold on to her and gave her enough work to keep her busy for the rest of the day. Which suited Theodosia very well for she had no time to think about the professor. Something, she told herself sternly, she must stop doing at once—which didn't prevent her from hoping that she might see him as she went around the hospital. But she didn't, nor was his car in the forecourt when she went home later that day.

He must have gone away; she had heard that he was frequently asked to other hospitals for consultations, and there was no reason why he should have told her. It was during the following morning, on her rounds, that she overhead the ward sister remark to her staff nurse that he would be back for his rounds at the end of the week. It seemed that he was in Austria.

Theodosia dropped her diet sheets deliberately and took a long time picking them up so that she could hear more.

'In Vienna,' said Sister, 'and probably Rome. Let's hope he gets back before Christmas.'

A wish Theodosia heartily endorsed; the idea of him spending Christmas anywhere but at his lovely home filled her with unease.

She was quite herself by the end of the week; happy to be free from Miss Prescott's iron hand, she did her shopping on Saturday and, since the weather was fine and cold, decided to go to Sunday's early-morning service and then go for a walk in one of the parks.

It was still not quite light when she left the house the next morning and there was a sparkle of frost on the walls and rooftops. The church was warm, though, and fragrant with the scent of chrysanthemums. There wasn't a large congregation and the simple service was soon over. She started to walk back, sorry to find that the early-morning sky was clouding over.

The streets were empty save for the occasional car and an old lady some way ahead of her. Theodosia, with ten minutes' brisk walk before her, walked faster, spurred on by the thought of breakfast.

She was still some way from the old lady when a car passed her, going much too fast and swerving from side to side of the street. The old lady hadn't a chance; the car mounted the kerb as it reached her, knocked her down and drove on.

Theodosia ran. There was no one about, the houses on either side of the street had their curtains tightly pulled over the windows, and the street was empty; she wanted to scream but she needed her breath.

The old lady lay half on the road, half on the pavement. She looked as though someone had picked her up and tossed her down and left her in a crumpled heap. One leg was crumpled up under her and although her skirt covered it Theodosia could see that there was blood oozing from under the cloth. She was conscious, though, turning faded blue eyes on her, full of bewilderment.

Theodosia whipped off her coat, tucked it gently under the

elderly head and asked gently, 'Are you in pain? Don't move; I'm going to get help.'

'Can't feel nothing, dearie—a bit dizzy, like.'

There was a lot more blood now. Theodosia lifted the skirt gently and looked at the awful mess under it. She got to her feet, filling her lungs ready to bellow for help and at the same time starting towards the nearest door.

The professor, driving himself back from Heathrow after his flight from Rome, had decided to go first to the hospital, check his patients there and then go home for the rest of the day. He didn't hurry. It was pleasant to be back in England and London—even the shabbier streets of London—was quiet and empty. His peaceful thoughts were rudely shattered at the sight of Theodosia racing across the street, waving her arms like a maniac.

He stopped the car smoothly, swearing softly, something he seldom did, but he had been severely shaken...

'Oh, do hurry, she's bleeding badly,' said Theodosia. 'I was just going to shout for help for I'm so glad it's you...'

He said nothing; there would be time for words later. He got out of the car and crossed the street and bent over the old lady.

'Get my bag from the back of the car.' He had lifted the sodden skirt. When she had done that he said, 'There's a phone in the car. Get an ambulance. Say that it is urgent.'

She did as she was told and went back to find him on his haunches, a hand rummaging in his bag, while he applied pressure with his other hand to the severed artery.

'Find a forceps,' he told her. 'One with teeth.'

She did that too and held a second pair ready, trying not to look at the awful mess. 'Now put the bag where I can reach it and go and talk to her.' He didn't look up. 'You got the ambulance?'

'Yes, I told them where to come and that it was very urgent.'

She went and knelt by the old lady, who was still conscious but very pale.

'Bit of bad luck,' she said in a whisper. 'I was going to me daughter for Christmas...'

'Well, you will be well again by then,' said Theodosia. 'The doctor's here now and you're going to hospital in a few minutes.'

'Proper Christmas dinner, we was going ter 'ave. Turkey and the trimmings—I like a bit of turkey...'

'Oh, yes, so do I,' said Theodosia, her ears stretched for the ambulance. 'Cranberry sauce with it...'

'And a nice bit of stuffing.' The old lady's voice was very weak. 'And plenty of gravy. Sprouts and pertaters and a good bread sauce. Plenty of onion with it.'

'Your daughter makes her own puddings?' asked Theodosia, and thought what a strange conversation this was—like a nightmare only she was already awake.

'Is there something wrong with me leg?' The blue eyes looked anxious.

'You've cut it a bit; the doctor's seeing to it. Wasn't it lucky that he was passing?'

'Don't 'ave much ter say for 'imself, does 'e?'

'Well, he is busy putting a bandage on. Do you live near here?'

'Just round the corner—Holne Road, number six. Just popped out ter get the paper.' The elderly face crumpled. 'I don't feel all that good.'

'You'll be as bright as a button in no time,' said Theodosia, and heard the ambulance at last.

Things moved fast then. The old lady, drowsy with morphia now, was connected up to oxygen and plasma while the professor tied off the torn arteries, checked her heart and with the paramedics stowed her in the ambulance.

Theodosia, making herself small against someone's gate, watched the curious faces at windows and doors and wondered if she should go.

'Get into the car; I'll drop you off. I'm going to the hospital.'

He stared down at her unhappy face. 'Hello,' he said gently, and he smiled.

He had nothing more to say and Theodosia was feeling sick. He stopped at Mrs Towzer's just long enough for her to get out and drove off quickly. She climbed the stairs and, once in her room, took off her dirty, blood-stained clothes and washed and dressed again, all the while telling Gustavus what had happened.

She supposed that she should have breakfast although she didn't really want it. She fed Gustavus and put on the kettle. A cup of tea would do.

When there was a knock on the door she called, 'Come in,' remembering too late that she shouldn't have done that before asking who was there.

The professor walked in. 'You should never open the door without checking,' he said. He turned off the gas under the kettle and the gas fire and then stowed Gustavus in his basket.

'What are you doing?' Theodosia wanted to know.

'Taking you back for breakfast—you and Gustavus. Get a coat—something warm.'

'My coat is a bit—that is, I shall have to take it to the cleaners. I've got a mac.' She should have been annoyed with him, walking in like that, but somehow she couldn't be bothered. Besides, he was badly in need of the dry cleaners, too. 'Is the old lady all right?'

'She is in theatre now, and hopefully she will recover. Now, hurry up, dear girl.'

She could refuse politely but Gustavus was already in his basket and breakfast would be very welcome. She got into her mac, pulled a woolly cap over her bright hair and accompanied him downstairs. There was no one about and the street was quiet; she got into the car when he opened the door for her, mulling over all the things she should have said if only she had had her wits about her.

As soon as they had had their breakfast she would tell him that she was having lunch with friends... She discarded the idea. To tell him fibs, even small, harmless ones, was something she found quite impossible. She supposed that was because she loved him. People who loved each other didn't have secrets. Only he didn't love her.

She glanced sideways at him. 'You've spoilt your suit.'

'And you your coat. I'm only thankful that it was you who were there. You've a sensible head under that bright hair; most people lose their wits at an accident. You were out early?'

'I'd been to church. I planned to go for a long walk. I often do on a Sunday.'

'Very sensible—especially after being cooped up in the hospital all week.'

Meg came to meet them as they went into the house. She took Theodosia's mac and cap and said firmly, 'Breakfast will be ready just as soon as you've got into some other clothes, sir. Miss Chapman can have a nice warm by the fire.'

She bustled Theodosia down the hall and into a small, cosy sitting room where there was a bright fire burning. Its window overlooked a narrow garden at the back and the round table by it was set for breakfast.

'Now just you sit quiet for a bit,' said Meg. 'I'll get Gustavus.'

The cat, freed from his basket, settled down before the fire as though he had lived there all his life.

The professor came presently in corduroys and a polo-necked sweater. Cashmere, decided Theodosia. Perhaps if she could save enough money she would buy one instead of spending a week next summer at a bed and breakfast farm.

Meg followed him in with a tray of covered dishes; Theodosia's breakfasts of cornflakes, toast and, sometimes, a boiled egg paled to oblivion beside this splendid array of bacon, eggs, tomatoes, mushrooms and kidneys.

He piled her plate. 'We must have a good breakfast if we are to go walking, too,' he observed.

She stared at him across the table. 'But it is me who is going walking...'

'You don't mind if I come, too? Besides, I need your help. I'm going to Worthing to collect a dog; he'll need a good walk before we bring him back.'

'A dog?' said Theodosia. 'Why is he at Worthing? And you don't really need me with you.'

He didn't answer at once. He said easily, 'He's a golden Labrador, three years old. He belongs to a friend of mine who has gone to Australia. He's been in a dog's home for a week or so until I was free to take him over.'

'He must be unhappy. But not any more once he's living with you. If you think it would help to make him feel more at home if I were there, too, I'd like to go with you.' She frowned. 'I forgot, I can't. Gustavus...'

'He will be quite happy with Meg, who dotes on him.' He passed her the toast. 'So that's settled. It's a splendid day to be out of doors.'

They had left London behind them and were nearing Dorking when he said, 'Do you know this part of the country? We'll leave the main road and go through Billingshurst. We can get back onto the main road just north of Worthing.'

Even in the depths of winter, the country was beautiful, still sparkling from the night frost and the sun shining from a cold blue sky. Theodosia, snug in the warmth and comfort of the car, was in seventh heaven. She couldn't expect anything as delightful as this unexpected day out to happen again, of course. It had been a kindly quirk of fate which had caused them to meet again.

She said suddenly, 'That old lady—it seems so unfair that she should be hurt and in hospital while we're having this glorious ride—' She stopped then and added awkwardly, 'What I mean is, I'm having a glorious ride.'

The professor thought of several answers he would have liked to make to that. Instead he said casually, 'It's a perfect day, isn't it? I'm enjoying it, too. Shall we stop for a cup of coffee in Billingshurst?'

When they reached Worthing, he took her to one of the splendid hotels on the seafront where, the shabby raincoat hidden out of sight in the cloakroom, she enjoyed a splendid lunch with him, unconscious of the glances of the other people there, who were intrigued by the vivid ginger of her hair.

It was early afternoon when they reached the dog's home. He was ready and waiting for them, for he recognized the professor as a friend of his master and greeted him with a dignified bark or two and a good deal of tail-wagging. He was in a pen with a small dog of such mixed parentage that it was impossible to tell exactly what he might be. He had a foxy face and bushy eyebrows, a rough coat, very short legs and a long thin tail. He sat and watched while George the Labrador was handed over and Theodosia said, 'That little dog, he looks so sad...'

The attendant laughed. 'He's been George's shadow ever since he came; can't bear to be parted from him. They eat and sleep together, too. Let's hope someone wants him. I doubt it—he came in off a rubbish dump.'

The professor was looking at Theodosia; he knew with resigned amusement that he was about to become the owner of the little dog. She wasn't going to ask, but the expression on her face was eloquent.

'Then perhaps we might have the little dog as well since they are such friends. Has he a name?'

He was rewarded by the happiness in her face. 'He may come, too?' She held out her arms for the little beast, who was shivering with excitement, and he stayed there until the professor had dealt with their payment, chosen a collar and lead for him and they had left the home.

'A brisk walk on the beach will do us all good,' said the professor. 'We must have a name,' he observed as the two dogs ran to and fro. They had got into the car without fuss and now they were savouring their freedom.

'Max,' said Theodosia promptly. 'He's such a little dog and I don't suppose he'll grow much more so he needs an important name. Maximilian—only perhaps you could call him Max?'

'I don't see why not,' agreed the professor. He turned her round and started to walk back to the car. He whistled to the dogs. 'George, Max...'

They came running and scrambled into the car looking anxious.

'It's all right, you're going home,' said Theodosia, 'and everyone will love you.' She remembered then. 'Gustavus—he's not used to dogs; he never sees them...'

'Then it will be a splendid opportunity for him to do so. We will put the three of them in the garden together.'

'We will? No, no, there's no need. If you'll give me time to pop him into his basket, I can take him with me.'

The professor was driving out of Worthing, this time taking the main road to Horsham and Dorking. The winter afternoon was already fading into dusk and Theodosia reflected on how quickly the hours flew by when one was happy.

He hadn't answered her; presumably he had agreed with her. There would be buses, but she would have to change during the journey back to her bed-sitter. She reminded herself that on a Sunday evening with little traffic and the buses half empty she should have an easy journey.

They talked from time to time and every now and then she turned round to make sure the dogs were all right. They were sitting upright, close together, looking uncertain.

'Did you have a dog when you were a little girl?' asked the professor.

'Oh, yes, and a cat. I had a pony, too.'

'Your home was in the country?' he asked casually.

She told him about the nice old house in Wiltshire and the school she had gone to and how happy she had been, and then said suddenly, 'I'm sorry, I must be boring you. It's just that I don't get the chance to talk about it very often. Of course, I think about it whenever I like.' She glanced out of the window into the dark evening. 'Are we nearly there?'

'Yes, and you have no need to apologize; I have not been bored. I have wondered about your home before you came to London, for you are so obviously a square peg in a round hole.'

'Oh? Am I? I suppose I am, but I'm really very lucky. I mean, I have the great-aunts and a job and I know lots of people at the hospital.'

'But perhaps you would like to do some other work?'

'Well, I don't think I'm the right person to have a career, if you mean the sort who wear those severe suits and carry briefcases...'

He laughed then, but all he said was, 'We're almost home.'

If only it were home—her home, thought Theodosia, and then told herself not to be a silly fool. She got out when he opened her door and waited while he took up the dogs' leads and ushered them to the door. When she hesitated he said, 'Come along, Theodosia. Meg will have tea waiting for us.'

Much later, lying in bed with Gustavus curled up beside her, Theodosia thought over her day, minute by minute. It had been like a lovely dream, only dreams were forgotten and she would never forget the hours she had spent with the professor. And the day had ended just as he had planned it beforehand; they had had tea by the fire with the two dogs sitting between them as though they had lived there all their lives. Although she had been a bit scared when the professor had fetched Gustavus and introduced him to the dogs, she had said nothing. After a good deal of spitting and gentle growling the three animals had settled down together.

She had said that she must go back after tea, but somehow he'd convinced her that it would be far better if she stayed for supper. 'So that Gustavus can get used to George and Max,' he had explained smoothly. She hated leaving his house and her bed-sitter was cold and uninviting.

The professor had lighted the gas fire for her, drawn the curtains over the window and turned on the table lamp, before going to the door, smiling at her muddled thanks and wishing her goodnight in a brisk manner.

There was no reason why he should have lingered, she told herself sleepily. Perhaps she would see him at the hospital—not to talk to, just to get a glimpse of him would do, so that she knew that he was still there.

In the morning, when she woke, she told herself that any foolish ideas about him must be squashed. She couldn't pretend that she wasn't in love with him, because she was and there was nothing she could do about that, but at least she would be sensible about it.

This was made easy for her since Miss Prescott was in a bad mood. Theodosia had no time at all to think about anything but the endless jobs her superior found for her to do, but in her dinner hour she went along to the women's surgical ward and asked if she might see the old lady.

She was sitting propped up in bed, looking surprisingly cheerful. True, she was attached to a number of tubes and she looked pale, but she remembered Theodosia at once.

'I'd have been dead if you hadn't come along, you and that nice doctor. Patched me up a treat, they have! My daughter's been to see me, too. Ever so grateful, we both are.'

'I'm glad I just happened to be there, and it was marvellous luck that Professor Bendinck should drive past...'

'Professor, is he? A very nice gentleman and ever so friendly. Came to see me this morning.'

Just to know that he had been there that morning made Theodosia feel happy. Perhaps she would see him too...

But there was no sign of him. The week slid slowly by with not so much as a glimpse of him. Friday came at last. She bade Miss Prescott a temporary and thankful goodbye and made her way through the hospital. It had been raining all day and it was cold as well. A quiet weekend, she promised herself, making for the entrance.

The professor was standing by the main door and she saw him too late to make for the side door. As she reached him she gave him a cool nod and was brought to a halt by his hand.

'There you are. I was afraid that I had missed you.'

'I've been here all this week,' said Theodosia, aware of the hand and filled with delight, yet at the same time peevish.

'Yes, so have I. I have a request to make. Would you be free on Sunday to take the dogs into the country? George is very biddable, but Max needs a personal attendant.' He added, most unfairly, 'And since you took such an interest in him...'

She felt guilty. 'Oh, dear. I should have thought... It was my fault, wasn't it? If I hadn't said anything... Ought he to go back to Worthing and find another owner?'

'Certainly not. It is merely a question of him settling down. He is so pleased to be with George that he gets carried away. They couldn't be separated.' He had walked her through the door. 'I'll drive you home...'

'There's no need.'

Which was a silly remark for it was pouring with rain, as well as dark and cold.

She allowed herself to be stowed in the car and when they got to Mrs Towzer's house he got out with her. 'I'll be here at ten o'clock on Sunday,' he told her, and didn't wait for her answer.

'Really,' said Theodosia, climbing the stairs. 'He does take me for granted.'

But she knew that wasn't true. He merely arranged circumstances in such a way that he compelled her to agree to what he suggested.

She was up early on Sunday morning, getting breakfast for herself and Gustavus, explaining to him that she would have to leave him alone. 'But you shall have something nice for supper,' she promised him. The professor hadn't said how long they would be gone, or where. She frowned. He really did take her for granted; next time she would have a good excuse...

It was just before ten o'clock when he knocked on her door. He wished her good morning in a casual manner which gave her the feeling that they had known each other all their lives. 'We'll take Gustavus, if you like. He'll be happier in the car than sitting by himself all day.'

'Well, yes, perhaps—if George and Max won't mind and it's not too long.'

'No distance.' He was settling Gustavus in his basket. 'A breath of country air will do him good.'

Mrs Towzer wasn't in the hall but her door was just a little open. As the professor opened the door he said, 'We shall be back this evening, Mrs Towzer,' just as her face appeared in the crack in the door.

'She's not being nosy,' said Theodosia as they drove away. 'She's just interested.'

She turned her head a little and found George and Max leaning against her seat, anxious to greet her and not in the least bothered by Gustavus in his basket. She was filled with happiness; it was a bright, cold morning and the winter sun shone, the car was warm and comfortable and she was sitting beside the man she loved. What more could a girl want? A great deal, of course, but Theodosia, being the girl she was, was content with what she had at the moment.

'Where are we going?' she asked presently. 'This is the way to Finchingfield.'

'Don't worry, we are not going to your great-aunts'. I have a little cottage a few miles from Saffron Walden; I thought we could go there, walk the dogs and have a picnic lunch. Meg has put something in a basket for us.'

He didn't take the motorway but turned off at Brentwood and took the secondary roads to Bishop's Stortford and after a few miles turned off again into a country road which led presently to a village. It was a small village, its narrow main street lined with small cottages before broadening into a village green ringed by larger cottages and several houses, all of them overshadowed by the church.

The professor turned into a narrow lane leading from the green and stopped, got out to open a gate in the hedge and then drove through it along a short paved driveway, with a hedge on one side of it and a fair-sized garden on the other, surrounding a reed-thatched, beetle-browed cottage with a porch and small latticed windows, its brick walls faded to a dusty pink. The same bricks had been used for the walls on either side of it which separated the front garden from the back of the house, pierced by small wooden doors.

The professor got out, opened Theodosia's door and then released the dogs.

'Gustavus...' began Theodosia.

'We will take him straight through to the garden at the back. There's a high wall, so he'll be quite safe there and he can get into the cottage.'

He unlocked one of the small doors and urged her through with the dogs weaving themselves to and fro and she could see that it was indeed so; the garden was large, sloping down to the fields and surrounded by a high brick wall. It was an old-fashioned garden with narrow brick paths between beds which were empty now, but she had no doubt they would be filled with rows of orderly vegetables later on. Beyond the beds was a lawn with fruit bushes to one side of it and apple trees.

'Oh, how lovely—even in winter it's perfect.'

He sat Gustavus's basket down, opened it and presently Gustavus poked out a cautious head and then sidled out.

'He's not used to being out of doors,' said Theodosia anxiously, 'only on the roof outside my window. At least, not since I've had him. He was living on the streets before that, but that's not the same as being free.'

She had bent to stroke the furry head and the professor said gently, 'Shall we leave him to get used to everything? The dogs won't hurt him and we can leave the kitchen door open.'

He unlocked the door behind him and stood aside for her to go inside. The kitchen was small, with a quarry-tiled floor, pale yellow walls and an old-fashioned dresser along one wall. There was an Aga, a stout wooden table and equally stout chairs and a deep stone sink. She revolved slowly, liking what she saw; she had no doubt that the kitchen lacked nothing a housewife would need, but it was a place to sit cosily over a cup of coffee, or to come down to in the morning and drink a cup of tea by the open door...

'Through here,' said the professor, and opened a door into the hall.

It was narrow, with a polished wooden floor and cream-painted walls. There were three doors and he opened the first one. The living room took up the whole of one side of the cottage, with little windows overlooking the front garden and French windows opening onto the garden at the back. It was a delightful room with easy chairs, tables here and there and a wide inglenook. The floor was wooden here, too, but there were rugs on it, their faded colours echoing the dull reds and blues of the curtains. There were pictures on the walls but she was given no chance to look at them.

'The dining room,' said the professor as she crossed the hall. It was a small room, simply furnished with a round table, chairs and a sideboard, and all of them, she noted, genuine pieces in dark oak.

'And this is my study.' She glimpsed a small room with a desk and chair and rows of bookshelves.

The stairs were small and narrow and led to a square landing. There were three bedrooms, one quite large and the others adequate, and a bathroom. The cottage might be old but no expense had been spared here. She looked at the shelves piled with towels and all the toiletries any woman could wish for.

'Fit for a queen,' said Theodosia.

'Or a wife...'

Which brought her down to earth again. 'Oh, are you thinking of getting married?'

'Indeed, I am.'

She swallowed down the unhappiness which was so painful that it was like a physical hurt. 'Has she seen this cottage? She must love it...'

'Yes, she has seen it and I think that she has found it very much to her taste.'

She must keep on talking. 'But you won't live here? You have your house in London.'

'We shall come here whenever we can.'

'The garden is lovely. I don't suppose you have much time to work in it yourself.'

'I make time and I have a splendid old man who comes regularly, as well as Mrs Trump who comes every day when I'm here and keeps an eye on the place when I'm not.'

'How nice,' said Theodosia inanely. 'Should I go and see if Gustavus is all right?'

He was sitting by his basket looking very composed, ignoring the two dogs who were cavorting around the garden.

'It's as though he's been here all his life,' said Theodosia. She looked at the professor. 'It's that kind of house, isn't it? Happy people have lived in it.'

'And will continue to do so. Wait here; I'll fetch the food.'

They sat at the kitchen table eating their lunch; there was soup in a Thermos; little crusty rolls filled with cream cheese and ham, miniature sausage rolls, tiny buttery croissants and piping hot coffee from another Thermos. There was food for the animals as well as a bottle of wine. Theodosia ate with the pleasure of a child, keeping up a rather feverish conversation. She was intent on being cool and casual, taking care to talk about safe subjects—the weather, Christmas, the lighter side of her work at the hospital. The professor made no effort to change the subject, listening with tender amusement to her efforts and wondering if this would be the right moment to tell her that he loved her. He decided it was not, but he hoped that she might begin to do more than like him. She was young; she might meet a younger man. A man of no conceit, he supposed that she thought of him as a man well past his first youth.

They went round the garden after lunch with Gustavus in Theodosia's arms, the dogs racing to and fro, and when the first signs of dusk showed they locked up the little house, stowed the animals in the car and began the drive back to London.

They had reached the outskirts when the professor's bleeper disturbed the comfortable silence. Whoever it was had a lot to say but at length he said, 'I'll be with you in half an hour.' Then he told Theodosia, 'I'll have to go to the hospital. I'll drop you off on the way. I'm sorry; I had hoped that you would have stayed for supper.'

'Thank you, but I think I would have refused; I have to get ready for work tomorrow—washing and ironing and so on.' She added vaguely, 'But it's kind of you to invite me. Thank you for a lovely day; we've enjoyed every minute of it!' Which wasn't quite true, for there had been no joy for her when he'd said that he was going to get married.

When they reached Mrs Towzer's she said, 'Don't get out; you mustn't waste a moment...'

He got out all the same without saying anything, opened the door for her, put Gustavus's basket in the hall and then drove away with a quick nod.

'And that is how it will be from now on,' muttered Theodosia, climbing the stairs and letting herself into her cold bed-sitter. 'He's not likely to ask me out again, but if he does I'll not go. I must let him see that we have nothing in common; it was just chance meetings and those have to stop!'

She got her supper—baked beans on toast and a pot of tea—fed a contented Gustavus and presently went to bed to cry in comfort until at last she fell asleep.

CHAPTER FOUR

THE WEEK BEGAN BADLY. Theodosia overslept; Gustavus, usually so obedient, refused to come in from the roof; and the coil of ginger hair shed pins as fast as she stuck them in. She almost ran to work, to find Miss Prescott, despite the fact that it would be Christmas at the end of the week, in a worse temper than usual. And as a consequence Theodosia did nothing right. She dropped things, spilt things, muddled up diet sheets and because of that went late to her dinner.

It was cottage pie and Christmas pudding with a blindingly yellow custard—and on her way back she was to call in at Women's Medical and collect two diet sheets for the two emergencies which had been admitted. Because it was quicker, although forbidden, she took the lift to the medical floor and when it stopped peered out prudently before alighting; one never knew, a ward sister could be passing.

There was no ward sister but the professor was standing a few yards away, his arm around a woman. They had their backs to her and they were laughing and as Theodosia looked the woman stretched up and kissed his cheek. She wasn't a young woman but she was good-looking and beautifully dressed.

Theodosia withdrew her head and prayed hard that they would go away. Which presently they did, his arm still around the woman's shoulders, and as she watched, craning her neck, Women's Medical ward door opened, Sister came out and the three of them stood talking and presently went into the ward.

Theodosia closed the lift door and was conveyed back to Miss Prescott's office.

'Well, let me have those diet sheets,' said that lady sharply.

'I didn't get them,' said Theodosia, quite beside herself, and, engulfed in feelings she hadn't known she possessed, she felt reckless. 'I went late to dinner and I should have had an hour instead of the forty minutes you left me. Someone else can fetch them. Why don't you go yourself, Miss Prescott?'

Miss Prescott went a dangerous plum colour. 'Theodosia, can I believe my ears? Do you realise to whom you speak? Go at once and get those diet sheets.'

Theodosia sat down at her desk. There were several letters to be typed, so she inserted paper into her machine and began to type. Miss Prescott hesitated. She longed to give the girl her notice on the spot but that was beyond her powers. Besides, with all the extra work Christmas entailed she had to have help in her office. There were others working in the department, of course, but Theodosia, lowly though her job was, got on with the work she was familiar with.

'I can only assume that you are not feeling yourself,' said Miss Prescott. 'I am prepared to overlook your rudeness but do not let it occur again.'

Theodosia wasn't listening; she typed the letters perfectly while a small corner of her brain went over and over her unexpected glimpse of the professor. With the woman he was going to marry, of course. He would have been showing her round the hospital, introducing her to the ward sisters and his colleagues, and then they would leave together in his car and go to his home...

As five o'clock struck she got up, tidied her desk, wished an astonished Miss Prescott good evening and went home. The bed-sitter was cold and gloomy; she switched on the lamps, turned on the fire, fed Gustavus and made herself a pot of tea. She was sad and unhappy but giving way to self-pity wasn't going to help. Besides, she had known that he was going to marry; he had said so. But she must avoid him at the hospital...

She cooked her supper and presently went to bed. She had been happy, allowing her happiness to take over from common sense. She had no doubt that sooner or later she would be happy again; it only needed a little determination.

So now, instead of hoping to meet him as she went round the hospital, she did her rounds with extreme caution. Which took longer than usual, of course, and earned Miss Prescott's annoyance. It was two days later, sharing a table with other latecomers from the wards and offices, that the talk became animated. It was a student nurse from Women's Medical who started it, describing in detail the companion Professor Bendinck had brought to see the ward. 'She was gorgeous, not very young, but then you wouldn't expect him to be keen on a young girl, would you? He's quite old...'

Theodosia was about to say that thirty-five wasn't old—a fact she had learned from one of her dancing partners at the ball—and even when he was wearing his specs he still looked in his prime. But she held her tongue and listened.

'She was wearing a cashmere coat and a little hat which must have cost the earth, and her boots...!' The nurse rolled expressive eyes. 'And they both looked so pleased with themselves. He called her "my dear Rosie", and smiled at her. You know, he doesn't smile much when he's on his rounds. He's always very polite, but sort of reserved, if you know what I mean. I suppose we'll be asked to fork out for a wedding present.'

A peevish voice from the other end of the table said, 'Those sort of people have everything; I bet he's loaded. I wonder where he lives?'

Theodosia wondered what they would say if she told them.

'Oh, well,' observed one of the ward clerks. 'I hope they'll be happy. He's nice, you know—opens doors for you and says good morning—and his patients love him.'

Someone noticed the time and they all got up and rushed back to their work.

Two more days and it would be Christmas Eve and she would be free. Her presents for the aunts were wrapped, her best dress brushed and ready on its hanger, her case already half packed with everything she would need for the weekend, Gustavus's favourite food in her shoulder bag. She should be able to catch a late-afternoon train, and if she missed it there was another one leaving a short while later. She would be at the aunts' well before bedtime.

She was almost at the hospital entrance on her way home that evening when she saw the professor. And he had seen her, for he said something to the house doctor he was talking to and began to walk towards her.

Help, thought Theodosia. She was so happy to see him that if he spoke to her she might lose all her good sense and fling herself at him.

And help there was. One of the path lab assistants, the one who had danced with her at the ball, was hurrying past her. She caught hold of his arm and brought him to a surprised halt.

'Say something,' hissed Theodosia. 'Look pleased to see me, as though you expected to meet me.'

'Whatever for? Of course I'm pleased to see you, but I've a train to catch...'

She was still holding his sleeve firmly. The professor was very close now, not hurrying, though; she could see him out of the corner of her eye. She smiled up at her surprised companion. She said very clearly, 'I'll meet you at eight o'clock; we could go to that Chinese place.' For good measure she kissed his cheek and, since the professor was now very close, wished him good evening. He returned her greeting in his usual pleasant manner and went out to his car.

'Whatever's come over you?' demanded the young man from

the path lab. 'I mean, it's all very well, but I've no intention of taking you to a Chinese restaurant. For one thing my girl wouldn't stand for it and for another I'm a bit short of cash.' He goggled at her. 'And you kissed me!'

'Don't worry, it was an emergency. I was just pretending that we were keen on each other.'

He looked relieved. 'You mean it was a kind of joke?'

'That's right.' She looked over his shoulder and caught a glimpse of the Bentley turning out of the forecourt. 'Thanks for helping me out.'

'Glad I could help. A lot of nonsense, though.'

He hurried off and Theodosia walked back to her bed-sitter, then told Gustavus all about it. 'You see,' she explained, 'if he doesn't see me or speak to me, he'll forget all about me. I shan't forget him but that's neither here nor there. I daresay he'll have a holiday at Christmas and spend it with her. She's beautiful and elegant, you see, and they were laughing together...' Theodosia paused to give her nose a good blow. She wasn't going to cry about it. He would be home by now, sitting in his lovely drawing room, and Rosie would be sitting with him.

Which is exactly what he was doing, George and Max at his feet, his companion curled up on a sofa. They were both reading, he scanning his post, she leafing through a fashion magazine. Presently she closed it. 'You have no idea how delightful it is to have the whole day to myself. I've spent a small fortune shopping and I can get up late and eat food I haven't cooked myself. It's been heaven.'

The professor peered at her over his specs. 'And you're longing to see James and the children...'

'Yes, I am. It won't be too much for you having us all here? They'll give you no peace—it will be a houseful.' She added unexpectedly, 'There's something wrong, isn't there? You're usually so calm and contained, but it's as though something— or someone?—has stirred you up.'

'How perceptive of you, my dear. I am indeed stirred—by a pair of grey eyes and a head of ginger hair.'

'A girl. Is she pretty, young? One of your house doctors? A nurse?'

'A kind of girl Friday in the diet department. She's young—perhaps too young for me—perhaps not pretty but I think she is beautiful. And she is gentle and kind and a delight to be with.' He smiled. 'And her hair really is ginger; she wears it in a bunch on top of her head.'

His sister had sat up, the magazine on the floor. 'You'll marry her, Hugo?'

'Yes, if she will have me. She lives in a miserable attic room with a cat and is to spend Christmas with her only family—two great-aunts. I intend to drive her there and perhaps have a chance to talk...'

'But you'll be here for Christmas?'

'Of course. Perhaps I can persuade her to spend the last day of the holiday here.'

'I want to meet her. Pour me a drink, Hugo, and tell me all about her. How did you meet?'

The following day the professor did his ward rounds, took a morning clinic, saw his private patients in the afternoon and returned to the hospital just before five o'clock. He had made no attempt to look for Theodosia during the morning—he had been too busy—but now he went in search of her. He hadn't been unduly disturbed by the sight of her talking to the young fellow from the path lab. After all, she was on nodding terms with almost everyone in the hospital, excluding the very senior staff, of course. But he had heard her saying that she would meet him that evening; moreover, she had kissed him. He had to know if she had given her heart to the man; after all, he was young and good-looking and she had never shown anything other than friendliness with himself.

He reviewed the facts with a calm logic and made his way to the floor where Theodosia worked.

She came rushing through the door then slithered to a halt because, of course, he was standing in her way. Since he was a big man she had no way of edging round him.

'Oh, hello,' said Theodosia, and then tried again. 'Good evening, Professor.'

He bade her good evening, too, in a mild voice. 'You're looking forward to Christmas? I'll drive you to Finchingfield. The trains will be packed and running late. Could you manage seven o'clock?'

She had time to steady her breath; now she clutched at the first thing that entered her head. On no account must she go with him. He was being kind again. Probably he had told his fiancée that he intended to drive her and Rosie had agreed that it would be a kindness to take the poor girl to these aunts of hers. She shrank from kindly pity.

'That's very kind of you,' said Theodosia, 'but I'm getting a lift—he's going that way, staying with friends only a few miles from Finchingfield.' She was well away now. 'I'm going to a party there—parties are such fun at Christmas, aren't they?' She added for good measure, 'He'll bring me back, too.'

She caught the professor's eye. 'He works in the path lab...'

If she had hoped to see disappointment on his face she was disappointed herself. He said pleasantly, 'Splendid. You're well organised, then.'

'Yes, I'm looking forward to it; such fun...' She was babbling now. 'I must go—someone waiting. I hope you have a very happy Christmas.'

She shot away, racing down the stairs. He made no attempt to follow her. That he was bitterly disappointed was inevitable but he was puzzled, too. Theodosia had been altogether too chatty and anxious to let him know what a splendid time she was going to have. He could have sworn that she had been making it up as she went along... On the other hand, she might have been feeling embarrassed; she had never been more than friendly but she could possibly be feeling awkward at not having mentioned the young man from the path lab.

He went back to his consulting rooms, saw his patients there and presently went home, where his manner was just as usual, asking after his sister's day, discussing the preparations for Christmas, for Rosie's husband and the two children would be arriving the next morning. And she, although she was longing to talk about Theodosia, said nothing, for it was plain that he had no intention of mentioning her.

And nor did he make any attempt to seek her out at the hospital during the following day. There was a good deal of merriment; the wards looked festive, the staff were cheerful—even those who would be on duty—and those who were able to left early. The professor, doing a late round, glanced at his watch. Theodosia would have left by now for it was almost six o'clock. He made his way to the path lab and found the young man who had been talking to Theodosia still there.

'Not gone yet?' he asked. 'You're not on duty over the weekend, are you?'

'No, sir, just finishing a job.'

'You live close by?' asked the professor idly.

'Clapham Common. I'm meeting my girlfriend and we'll go home together. I live at home but she's spending Christmas with us.'

'Ah, yes. There's nothing like a family gathering. You're planning to marry.'

'Well, as soon as Dorothy's sold her flat—her parents are dead. Once it's sold we shall put our savings together and find something around Clapham.'

'Well, I wish you the best of luck and a happy Christmas!'

The professor went on his unhurried way, leaving the young man with the impression that he wasn't such a bad old stick after all, despite his frequent requests for tests at a moment's notice.

The professor went back to his office; ten minutes' work

would clear up the last odds and ends of his work for the moment. He had no idea why Theodosia had spun such a wildly imaginative set of fibs but he intended to find out. Even if she had left at five o'clock she would hardly have had the time to change and pack her bag and see to Gustavus.

He was actually at the door when he was bleeped…

Theodosia hurried home. Miss Prescott, true to form, had kept her busy until the very last minute, which meant that catching the early train was an impossibility. She would phone the aunts and say that she would be on the later train. Once in her room she fed an impatient Gustavus, changed into her second-best dress, brushed her coat, found her hat and, since she had time to spare, put on the kettle for a cup of tea. It would probably be chilly on the train and there would be a lot of waiting round for buses once she got to Braintree.

She was sipping her tea when someone knocked on the door, the knock followed by Mrs Towzer's voice. Theodosia asked her in, explaining at the same time that she was just about to leave for her train.

'Won't keep you then, love. Forgot to give you this letter—came this morning—in with my post. Don't suppose it's important. 'Ave a nice time at your auntys'. 'Aving a bit of a party this evening; must get meself poshed up. The 'ouse'll be empty, everyone off 'ome.' They exchanged mutual good wishes and Mrs Towzer puffed her way down the stairs.

The letter was in Great-Aunt Mary's spidery hand. Surely not a last-minute request to shop for some forgotten article? Unless it was something she could buy at the station there was no time for anything else.

Theodosia sat down, one eye on the clock, and opened the letter.

She read it and then read it again. Old family friends, an archdeacon and his wife, had returned to England from South America, wrote Aunt Mary. Their families were in Scotland

and they did not care to make such a long journey over the holiday period.

'Your aunt Jessica and I have discussed this at some length and we have agreed that it is our duty to give these old friends the hospitality which our Christian upbringing expects of us. Christmas is a time for giving and charity,' went on Aunt Mary, and Theodosia could almost hear her vinegary voice saying it. As Theodosia knew, continued her aunt, the accommodation at the cottage was limited, and since she had no lack of friends in London who would be only too glad to have her as a guest over Christmas they knew she would understand. 'We shall, of course, miss you...'

Theodosia sat quite still for a while, letting her thoughts tumble around inside her head, trying to adjust to surprise and an overwhelming feeling that she wasn't wanted. Of course she had friends, but who, on Christmas Eve itself, would invite themselves as a guest into a family gathering?

Presently she got up, counted the money in her purse, got her shopping bag from behind the door, assured Gustavus that she would be back presently and left the house. There was no one around; Mrs Towzer was behind closed doors getting ready for the party. She walked quickly to a neighbouring street where there was a row of small shops. There was a supermarket at its end but she ignored it; there the shops would stay open for another hour or so, catching the last-minute trade. Although she had the money she had saved for her train ticket she needed to spend it carefully.

Tea, sugar, butter and a carton of milk, cheese, food for Gustavus and a bag of pasta which she didn't really like but which was filling, baked beans and a can of soup. She moved on to the butcher, and since it was getting late and he wouldn't be open again for three days he let her have a turkey leg very cheap. She bought bacon, too, and eggs, and then went next door to the greengrocer for potatoes and some apples.

Lastly she went to the little corner shop at the end of the row, where one side was given over to the selling of bread, factory-baked in plastic bags, and lurid iced cakes, the other side packed with everything one would expect to find in a bazaar.

Theodosia bought a loaf and a miniature Christmas pudding and then turned her attention to the other side of the shop. She spent the last of her money on a miniature Christmas tree, which was plastic, with a few sprigs of holly, and very lastly a small box of chocolates.

Thus burdened she went back to Mrs Towzer's. The front door was open; there were guests for the party milling about in the hall. She passed them unnoticed and climbed the stairs.

'We are going to have a happy Christmas together,' she told Gustavus. 'You'll be glad, anyway, for you'll be warm here, and I've bought you a present and you've bought me one, too.'

She unpacked everything, stowed the food away and then set the Christmas tree on the table. She had no baubles for it but at least it looked festive. So did the holly and the Christmas cards when she had arranged them around the room.

Until now she hadn't allowed her thoughts to wander but now her unhappiness took over and she wept into the can of soup she had opened for her supper. It wasn't that she minded so very much being on her own; it was knowing that the great-aunts had discarded her in the name of charity. But surely charity began at home? And she could have slept on the sofa...

She ate her soup, unpacked the weekend bag she had packed with such pleasure, and decided that she might as well go to bed. And for once, since there was no one else to dispute her claim, she would have a leisurely bath...

It was half past eight before the professor left the hospital and now that he was free to think his own thoughts he gave them his full attention. Obviously he had nothing to fear from the lad in the path lab. For reasons best known to herself, Theodosia had embarked on some rigmarole of her own devising—a ploy to warn him off? She might not love him but she liked him. A man of no conceit, he was aware of that. And there was something wrong somewhere.

He drove himself home, warned his sister and brother-in-law that he might be late back, sought out Meg in the kitchen and told her to get a room ready for a guest he might be bringing back with him. Then he got into his car, this time with George and Max on the back seat, and drove away.

His sister, at the door to see him off, turned to see Meg standing beside her.

'It'll be that nice young lady with the gingery hair,' said Meg comfortably. 'Dear knows where she is but I've no doubt he'll bring her back here.'

'Oh, I do hope so, Meg; she sounds just right for him. Should we wait for dinner any longer?'

'No, ma'am, I'll serve it now. If they're not back by midnight I'll leave something warm in the Aga.'

Once he had left the centre of the city behind, the streets were almost empty. The professor reached Bishop's Stortford in record time and turned off to Finchingfield.

There were lights shining from the windows of the great-aunt's house. He got out with a word to the dogs and thumped the knocker.

Mrs Trickey opened the door, still in her hat. She said, 'You're a bit late to come calling; I'm off home.'

The professor said in his calm way, 'I'd like to see Miss Theodosia.'

'So would I. She's not here, only that archdeacon and his wife wanting hot water and I don't know what—a fire in their bedroom, too. You'd best come in and speak to Miss Chapman.'

She opened the door into the drawing room. 'Here's a visitor for you, Miss Chapman, and I'll be off.'

Great-Aunt Jessica had risen from her chair. 'Professor, this is unexpected. May I introduce Archdeacon Worth and Mrs Worth, spending Christmas with us...?'

The professor's manners were beautiful even when he was

holding back impatience. He said all the right things and then, 'I came to see Theodosia...'

It was Aunt Mary who answered him.

'These old family friends of ours are spending Christmas with us. Having just returned from South America, they had no plans for themselves. We were delighted to be able to offer them hospitality over the festive season.'

'Theodosia?' He sounded placid.

'I wrote to her,' said Aunt Mary. 'A young gel with friends of her own age—I knew that she would understand and have no difficulty in spending Christmas with one or other of them.'

'I see. May I ask when she knew of this arrangement?'

'She would have had a letter—let me see, when did I post it? She must have had it some time today, certainly. We shall, of course, be delighted to see her—when something can be arranged.'

He said pleasantly, 'Yes, we must certainly do that once we are married. May I wish you all a happy Christmas.' He wasn't smiling. 'I'll see myself out.'

He had driven fast to Finchingfield, and now he drove back to London even faster. He was filled with a cold rage that anyone would dare to treat his Theodosia with such unkindness! He would make it up to her for the rest of her life; she should have everything she had ever wanted—clothes, jewels, and holidays in the sun... He laughed suddenly, knowing in his heart that all she would want would be a home and children and love. And he could give her those, too.

The house was quiet as Theodosia climbed the stairs from the bathroom on the floor below. All five occupants of the other bed-sitters had gone home or to friends for Christmas. Only Mrs Towzer was in her flat, entertaining friends for the evening. She could hear faint sounds of merriment as she unlocked her door.

The room looked welcoming and cheerful; the holly and the Christmas cards covered the almost bare walls and the Christmas tree, viewed from a distance, almost looked real. The cat food, wrapped in coloured paper, and the box of chocolates were arranged on each side of it and she had put the apples in a dish on the table.

'Quite festive,' said Theodosia to Gustavus, who was washing himself in front of the gas fire. 'Now I shall have a cup of cocoa and you shall have some milk, and we'll go to bed.'

She had the saucepan in her hand when there was a knock on the door. She remembered then that Mrs Towzer had invited her to her party if she wasn't going away for Christmas. She had refused, saying that she would be away, but Mrs Towzer must have seen her coming in with the shopping and come to renew her invitation.

How kind, thought Theodosia, and opened the door. The professor, closely followed by George and Max, walked in.

'Always enquire who it is before opening your door, Theodosia,' he observed. 'I might have been some thug in a Balaclava helmet.'

She stared up at his quiet face. And even like that, she thought, I would still love him... Since he had walked past her into the room there was nothing for it but to shut the door.

'I was just going to bed...' She watched as the two dogs sat down side by side before the fire, taking no notice of Gustavus.

'All in good time.' He was leaning against the table, smiling at her.

'How did you know I was here?' She was pleased to hear that her voice sounded almost normal, although breathing was a bit difficult.

'I went to see your aunts.'

'My aunts, this evening? Surely not...?'

'This evening. I've just come from them. They are entertaining an archdeacon and his wife.'

'Yes, I know. But why?'

'Ah, that is something that I will explain.'

He glanced around him, at the tree and the holly and the cards and then at the tin of cocoa by the sink. Then he studied her silently. The shapeless woolly garment she was wearing did nothing to enhance her appearance but she looked, he considered, beautiful; her face was fresh from soap and water, her hair hanging around her shoulders in a tangled gingery mass.

He put his hands in his pockets and said briskly, 'Put a few things in a bag, dear girl, and get dressed.'

She goggled at him. 'Things in a bag? Why?'

'You are spending Christmas with me at home.'

'I'm not. I have no intention of going anywhere.' She remembered her manners. 'Thank you for asking me, but you know as well as I that it's not possible.'

'Why not—tell me?'

She said wildly, 'I saw you at the hospital. I wasn't spying or anything like that but I got out of the lift and saw you both standing there. You had your arm round her and she was laughing at you. How could you possibly suggest...?' She gave a great gulp. 'Oh, do go away,' she said, and then asked, 'Does she know you are here? Did she invite me, too?'

The professor managed not to smile. 'No, she doesn't but she expects you. And Meg has a room ready for you...'

'It is most kind of you,' began Theodosia, and put a hand on his arm. This was a mistake, for he took it, turned it over and kissed the palm.

'Oh, no,' said Theodosia in a small voice as he wrapped his great arms round her.

She wriggled, quite uselessly, and he said gently, 'Keep still, my darling; I'm going to kiss you.'

Which he did at some length and very thoroughly. 'I have been wanting to do that for a long time. I've been in love with you ever since we first met. I love you and there will be no reason for anything I do unless you are with me.'

Somewhere a nearby church clock struck eleven. 'Now get some clothes on, my love, and we will go home.'

Theodosia dragged herself back from heaven. 'I can't— Oh, Hugo, you know I can't.'

He kissed her gently. 'You gave me no chance to explain; indeed you flung that lad from the path lab in my face, did you not? My sister, Rosie, and her husband and children are spending Christmas with me. It was she you saw at the hospital and you allowed yourself to concoct a lot of nonsense.'

'Yes, well...' She smiled at him. 'Do you really want to marry me?'

'More than anything in the world.'

'You haven't asked me yet.'

He laughed then and caught her close again. 'Will you marry me, Theodosia?

'Yes, yes, of course I will. I did not try to fall in love with you but I did.'

'Thank heaven for that. Now find a toothbrush and take off that woolly thing you are wearing and get dressed. You can have fifteen minutes. Gustavus and the dogs and I will doze together until you are ready.'

'I can't leave him.'

'Of course not; he is coming too.'

The professor settled in a chair and closed his eyes.

It was surprising how much one could do in a short time when one was happy and excited and without a care in the word. Theodosia was dressed, her overnight bag packed after a fashion, her hair swept into a topknot and the contents of her handbag checked in something like ten minutes. She said rather shyly, 'I'm ready...'

The professor got to his feet, put Gustavus into his basket, fastened the window, turned off the gas and went to look in the small fridge. He eyed the morsel of turkey and the Christmas pudding, but said merely, 'We'll turn everything off except the fridge. We can see to it in a few days; you won't be coming back here, of course.'

'But I've nowhere else—the aunts...'

'You will stay with me, and since you are an old-fashioned girl Meg shall chaperon you until I can get a special licence and we can be married.' He gave her a swift kiss. 'Now come along.'

He swept her downstairs and as they reached the hall Mrs Towzer came to see who it was.

'Going out, Miss Chapman? At this time of night?' She eyed the professor. 'You've been here before; you seemed a nice enough gent.' She stared at him severely. 'No 'anky-panky, I 'ope.'

The professor looked down his splendid nose at her. 'Madam, I am taking my future wife to spend Christmas at my home with my sister and her family. She will not be returning here, but I will call after Christmas and settle any outstanding expenses.'

'Oh, well, in that case... 'Appy Christmas to you both.' She looked at George and Max and Gustavus's whiskery face peering from his basket. 'And all them animals.'

Stuffed gently into the car, Theodosia said, 'You sounded just like a professor, you know—a bit stern.'

'That is another aspect of me which you will discover, dear heart, although I promise I will never be stern with you.' He turned to look to her as he started the car. 'Or our children.'

She smiled and wanted to cry, too, for a moment. From happiness, she supposed. 'What a wonderful day to be in love and be loved. I'm so happy.'

As they reached his house, the first strokes of midnight sounded from the church close by, followed by other church bells ringing in Christmas Day. The professor ushered his small party out of the car and into his house. The hall was quiet and dimly lit and George and Max padded silently to the foot of the stairs where they sat like statues. He closed the door behind him, set Gustavus in his basket on the table and swept Theodosia into his arms. 'This is what I have wanted to do—to wish you a happy Christmas in my own home—your home, too, my dearest.'

Theodosia, after being kissed in a most satisfactory manner, found her breath. 'It's true, it's all true? Dearest Hugo, Happy Christmas.' She stretched up and kissed him and then kissed him again for good measure.

* * * * *

A Happy Meeting

CHAPTER ONE

THE DAY HAD been warm for early October but now the sun was low on the horizon and there was a chilly breeze. The quiet country road running between the trees was full of shadows; in an hour or so it would be dusk. The girl sitting on the grass verge shivered a little and put her arm around the lean, unkempt animal beside her: a half-grown dog in a deplorable condition, the rope which had held him fast to a tree still dangling from his scraggy neck. It was when she had found him not an hour earlier and struggled to free him that he had knocked her down. She had fallen awkwardly and twisted her ankle, and getting herself as far as the road had been a nightmare that she was relieved to have done with. Now she sat, more or less patiently, hoping for help. Two cars had gone past since she had dragged herself and the dog to the road but although she had waved and shouted neither of them had stopped. She studied her ankle in the dimming light; it had swollen alarmingly and she hadn't been able to get her shoe off; there was nothing to do but wait for help, although, since the road was not much more than a country lane connecting two villages, there didn't seem much chance of that before early morning when the farm tractors would begin their work.

'We may have to spend the night,' she told the animal beside her, for the sound of her voice was a comfort of sorts, 'but I'll look after you, although I'm not sure how.' The animal cowered closer; she could feel its ribs against her side, and she gave it a soothing pat. 'It's nice to have company, anyway,' she assured him.

Dusk had fallen when she heard a car coming and presently its headlights swept over them as it passed.

'That's that,' said the girl. 'You can't blame anyone for not stopping...'

However, the car was coming back, reversing slowly until it was level with them and then stopping. The man who got out appeared to her nervous eyes to be a giant and she felt a distinct desire to get up and run, only she couldn't. He came towards her slowly and somehow when he spoke his voice was reassuringly quiet and calm.

'Can I help?' he asked, and his voice was kind too. 'You're hurt?'

He stood for a moment looking down at her; a small girl with no looks, too thin, but even in the deepening dusk her eyes were beautiful.

'Well, not really hurt, but I twisted my ankle and I can't walk.' She studied him carefully and liked what she saw. This was no young man out for an evening's ride but a soberly clad man past his first youth, his pale hair silvered at the temples. He was good-looking too, though that did not matter. 'I would be very grateful for a lift as far as Minton Cracknell; it's only a couple of miles along the road. I live there.'

'Of course, but may I look at your ankle first? I'm a doctor and it looks as though it needs attention.'

He squatted down beside her, and, when the dog growled, put out a large hand for the beast to sniff. 'We must have that shoe off,' he told her, and got out a pocket knife and cut the laces.

'I'm going to hurt you,' he said, and did despite his gentleness. 'Good girl. Catch your breath while I get some bandage from the car.'

He was gone and back again before she had had the time to wipe away the tears on her cheeks; she hadn't said a word while the shoe was coming off but she hadn't been able to stop the tears. He handed her a handkerchief without a word and said cheerfully, 'It will feel much better once I've strapped it up. You will have to get it X-rayed tomorrow and rest it for a day or two.'

He got to his feet. 'The dog is yours?' he asked.

'Well, no—I—I heard him barking as I came along the road and he'd been tied to a tree and left to starve; he accidentally tripped me up as I was freeing him...'

'Poor beast, but lucky for him that you heard him. Will you adopt him?'

He was talking idly, giving her time to pull herself together.

'Well, I don't think I can—my stepmother doesn't like dogs—but I can give him a bed and a meal and see if there's anyone in the village...'

'Well, let's get you home,' he said kindly, and scooped her up with a word to the dog, who needed no encouragement but climbed into the back of the car after the girl had been settled in the front seat.

'He'll make an awful mess,' she said apologetically, 'and it's a Bentley, isn't it?'

The man looked amused. 'I don't suppose there will be any lasting damage,' he observed. 'Where do you live exactly?'

'If you go through the village it's the house on the right behind a high brick wall. It's called the Old Rectory. My father inherited it from his father; it's been in the family for years...'

She glanced at his profile. 'You've been very kind.'

'I'm glad that I happened to pass by, Miss...?'

'Preece, Cressida Preece.' She added shyly, 'You're not English, are you?'

'Dutch. Van der Linus—Aldrik van der Linus.'

She said politely, 'Your English is quite perfect. Oh, here's the village.'

The narrow main street of the little place was empty; it was the hour of high tea and lights shone from windows as they passed the small houses lining it.

'It's just along here, past the church...'

The houses had petered out and the car's lights touched on the brick wall and an open gate. The drive was short, ending in a small sweep before a nice old house, not over large but solidly built. The man got out but before he reached the door it was opened by a severe-looking woman with iron-grey hair drawn back into a bun. She had a long thin face and sharp, very dark eyes, and she was dressed in a shabby dress under a white apron.

She looked at the man with a belligerence which he ignored.

'I have brought Miss Preece home,' he told her. 'She has damaged her ankle. If you will tell me where her room is, I will carry her indoors. I think there is no lasting damage but she should rest it for a few days.'

The woman didn't answer him but brushed past him and out to the car.

'Miss Cressida, what has happened? Are you hurt? You must get to your bed...'

The girl spoke matter-of-factly, 'Moggy, dear, I'm quite all right, just sprained an ankle. Mother's not back?' There was a hint of anxiety in her voice, and the man, who had come to stand by the car, frowned.

'No, thank the lord. We'll get you indoors.' Moggy heard a faint growl from the back seat and exclaimed 'What's that—an animal...?'

'A dog, Moggy. I found him tied to a tree. We'll have to hide him tonight and tomorrow I'll go to the village and try and find a home for him.' Cressida undid her seat belt. 'He must have a meal, he's starved.'

'She'll not allow it. We'll get you to your room and I'll feed him and take him down to old Mr Fellows and ask if he will keep the beast in his shed...'

'It might be advisable to get Miss Preece up to her bed,' said the man gently, 'and since I gather the dog is not welcome here

I'll take him with me. I'm going in to Yeovil; there's a good vet there.'

'A vet?' said Cressida sharply. 'He's not to be put to sleep...'

'Certainly not. And now, if I may, I'll carry you indoors and perhaps when we have you settled this animal might be given a small meal.' And at her look of doubt, 'I give you my word that he'll be properly looked after.' He had spoken quietly but Moggy stood back without a word and allowed him to lift Cressida from the car and carry her into the house.

'Up the stairs,' she told him gruffly, 'and down that passage beyond the landing.'

He went up the wide oak staircase unhurriedly, carrying Cressida with no effort, and waited while Moggy went ahead of them and opened a door at the end of the passage.

The room was small and plainly furnished and Dr van der Linus frowned again, for it seemed to him that it was a room suitable to a servant, not the daughter of the house. He laid her gently on the bed and stooped to take a look at the ankle.

'I suggest that you take a couple of paracetamol before you settle for the night,' he observed, 'and be sure and get your doctor to come and look at it in the morning. He may wish to re-strap it and give you instructions as to treatment. You will need to keep off your feet for a few days but he will do what is necessary.' He stood looking down at her. 'Have you paracetamol? Take two as soon as possible with a drink.'

He took her hand in his large one. 'A most unfortunate accident, but you will be quite all right again very shortly. And don't worry about the dog, I'll see that it comes to no harm. Goodbye, Miss Preece.'

She didn't want him to go; a sensible girl, inured to accepting what life had to offer her, she wished very much that he would stay. But that, of course, was impossible; he was a complete stranger who had happened to turn up just when he was most needed. Then she thanked him in a polite voice tight with pain and watched his vast back go through the door with regret. At least the dog would be safe and her stepmother had been away from home. She comforted herself with that.

Dr van der Linus trod slowly down the staircase with Moggy leading the way. In the hall he stood still. 'You will look after Miss Preece? She is in a good deal of pain, but get her into bed with a warm drink and the paracetamol and she should sleep. Her own doctor will prescribe what he thinks fit.' He smiled down at the severe face. 'Could I bother you for some water for the dog, and perhaps a slice of bread?' And at her nod, 'May I know your name?'

'Mogford—Miss, but Miss Cressy always calls me Moggy, since she was knee-high.' She went ahead of him. 'I've some soup on the stove; perhaps a drop of that would do the beast some good, then I'll go and see to Miss Cressy.'

She led the way into the kitchen and poured soup into a bowl and broke some bread into it. 'You won't be long?' she asked anxiously. 'Mrs Preece doesn't hold with animals. It's a mercy that she's out...there'll be a fuss enough over Miss Cressy.'

'Yes. I'm sure your mistress will be upset,' observed Dr van der Linus smoothly.

'Upset? Oh, she'll be upset, all right.' She glanced at the clock. 'She'll be back in twenty minutes or so, you'd best hurry.'

Dr van der Linus's eyebrows rose but all he said was, 'I'll be very quick. Shall I leave the bowl behind a bush for you to collect later?'

His companion nodded. 'Thank you for your trouble. You've been most kind.'

She shut the front door upon him and he went to the car, let the dog out while it ate and drank hungrily and then ushered it back in. He had driven a couple of miles and was almost at Templecombe when a car flashed past him. There was a woman driving. Probably Mrs Preece, he reflected as he turned off the road to take the short cut to Yeovil and the vet.

That gentleman, roused from his comfortable chair by the

fire, peered at the dog standing dejectedly on the end of its rope. 'My dear Aldrik, what on earth have you here?'

'A dog, John. I have acquired him from his rescuer who is unable to offer food and shelter. Found tied to a tree on the other side of Minton Cracknell.'

'Want me to have a look? He's in pretty poor shape.' He patted the dog's matted head. 'I didn't know you were over here. Staying with Lady Merrill? You must come and dine one evening before you go back.'

He led the way through the house and out again into a yard at the back to his surgery. 'How is the old lady?'

'In splendid form. Her years sit lightly on her.' He heaved the reluctant dog on to the examination table, gentling him with a steady hand.

'Over here on holiday or doing some work?'

'Oh, a little of both. I've had a week in Edinburgh; I'm going on to Bristol to give a series of lectures and then back to London before I go home.'

'Well, dine with us before you leave. Molly will be disappointed if you don't. How about one evening next week? Any evening, take pot luck.'

'I should like that. May I give you a ring?'

The vet was bending over the dog. 'He hasn't anything broken as far as I can see. Half starved—more than half—and ill-treated—look at these sores. Do you want me to get him fit, or...?'

'Get him fit, will you? I promised his rescuer; a dab of a girl with huge brown eyes.'

John looked up. 'You say he was found near Minton Cracknell? That would be Cressida Preece. She brought me a cat a month or two ago—in a bad way, paid to have her cured of burns, quite nasty ones as a result of some lout tying a squib to her tail. She's still paying me, a bit at a time.'

'And yet she lives in a pleasant house...?'

'Yes but I fancy her life isn't as pleasant. Her father died some months ago; she lives with her stepmother. Unfortunately he left everything to her under the impression, one presumes, that she would provide for his daughter.'

Dr van der Linus stroked the trembling dog's head. 'Surely in this day and age the girl can leave home and get a job?'

'One would think so, though I don't imagine she's trained for anything. What shall I do? Get this beast fit and let her know?'

'No. I've taken rather a fancy to him. I'll take him with me when I go back to Holland. May I leave him with you? My grandmother will be wondering where I have got to.'

'Give me a ring in the morning, and we'll see how he is after some food and a night's sleep.'

The doctor got back into his car and drove away from the town, going north and presently turning into a maze of sideroads which brought him eventually to a small village lying between hilly country. It was indeed a small place, with a church, a handful of cottages, and a handsome vicarage, a shop and a duck pond. He drove through it before turning in between redbrick pillars surmounted by weatherbeaten lions and following a drive between thick undergrowth. It ended in a wide gravel sweep before a red-brick house of the Queen Anne period, light streaming from its windows and ringed around by trees. Dr van der Linus, getting out of his car, thought how welcoming it was. The door was opened as he reached it and a dignified old man, rather shaky on his legs, wished him a good evening and offered the information that Lady Merrill was in the small drawing-room.

'I'm late, Baxter—I got held up. Give me ten minutes before you serve dinner, will you?' He clapped the old man gently on the shoulders and crossed the hall to one of the open doors.

The room was a pleasant one, a little old-fashioned but light and airy with some rather massive furniture and thickly carpeted. The doctor crossed to a chair by the fire and the old lady sitting in it turned a smiling face to him as two Pekinese dogs hurried to meet him. He bent to pat them before stooping to kiss his grandmother.

'My apologies for being late, my dear. I was unexpectedly delayed.'

'Did the lecture not go well?'

'Oh, very well. I was forced to stop on my way...'

'Pour yourself a drink and tell me about it.'

Which he did. 'Was she pretty, this girl?'

'Pretty? To tell you the truth, I can't remember how she looked. She had nice eyes and a very pleasant voice.' He sounded indifferent and presently they talked of other things. He didn't think of the girl again.

Cressida, with Miss Mogford's help, had got herself into bed. Her ankle hurt abominably but the paracetamol was beginning to take effect. Moggy had arranged a small footstool in the bed so that her foot was free of the bedclothes and perhaps by the morning it would be better. Staying in bed was a luxury her stepmother disapproved of. Hopefully she wouldn't come home until late and need know nothing about it until the morning. She drank the tea Miss Mogford brought her and was urged to go to sleep, and she did as she was bid. She was awakened half an hour later by the entrance of Mrs Preece, a woman who in her youth had been enchantingly pretty and now in middle age, by dint of dieting ruthlessly, going to the best hairdressers so that her once golden hair should show no hint of grey, using every aid to beauty which caught her eye in the glossy magazines she favoured and wearing the floating draperies which gave her the look of helpless femininity which hid a nature as cold and hard as steel, preserved the illusion of sweetness of character.

'What is all this nonsense I hear from Miss Mogford?' she wanted to know. 'And why are you in bed? It's barely nine o'clock? Really, Cressida, I hardly expect a healthy girl of four and twenty to loll around like this.'

Cressida, used to her stepmother's manner towards her, sat

up in bed. 'I'm in bed because I can't stand on my foot and it's very painful. I dare say it will be all right by the morning.'

'It had better be—I've the Worthingtons coming to dinner and I want the flowers done and the silver epergne properly polished.' She sighed heavily. 'I've a splitting headache; I was forced to come away early from the party. I shall go to bed and can only hope that Miss Mogford will spare the time to bring me a hot drink and run my bath.'

She went away without saying goodnight and Cressida wriggled down into her bed again, wide awake now and aware that her ankle was hurting. It was too soon to take any more paracetamol. She tugged her pillows into comfort and allowed her thoughts to roam.

The man who had brought her home had been nice; not just nice, he had treated her...she sought for words—as though she mattered; and since she knew only too well that her looks were negligible she had appreciated that. He had been surprised when he'd seen her room, she had noticed that at once, but since she wasn't going to see him again she didn't think that mattered. She knew that the few friends she had in the village were at a loss to understand why she stayed at home when it was so obvious that she wasn't welcome there now that her father was dead. She had never told anyone that she stayed there because of Moggy. Moggy had no home of her own; she had worked all her life for Cressida's parents, never able to save because she had a married sister whose husband had become paralysed soon after they had married and had lived for many years, a helpless wreck, his life made bearable by the extras Moggy's earnings had helped to buy. Now at fifty-eight years, she had two more years before she could draw her pension and receive the annuity Mr Preece had left her. Until then there was nothing else she could do but stay with Mrs Preece, since that lady had led her to understand that unless she remained in her employ until her sixtieth birthday her annuity would be cancelled. Since Miss Mogford, for all her severe appearance, was afraid that no one else would employ her in any case, and, over and above that, had set her heart on going to live with her now widowed sister where she would enjoy a snug retirement, she stayed on, managing the house with the help of girls from the village and Cressida. It was only because Cressida understood Moggy's situation that she stayed. Two years, she told herself repeatedly, would soon pass, and once Moggy was safely ensconced with her sister she herself would feel free to go away. She had no idea what she would do, she hadn't been trained for anything but she was handy about the house and even in this day and age there were old ladies who needed companions. A roof over her head and some money to spend was all she expected until she had found her feet.

It was a great pity that her father, that most trusting of men, had left everything to her stepmother, under the impression that she would give Cressida an allowance. Instead of that, Mrs Preece had lost no time in making it quite clear that that was out of the question. Cressida would have to help Miss Mogford and in return she would be clothed and fed and be given pocket money.

Cressida, after a number of indignant protests, had had every intention of leaving, only to be stymied by being told of Moggy's situation. She had plenty of common sense, added to which she was a girl of spirit, but Moggy had been a faithful and loving employee and a pleasant retirement was almost within her grasp. Cressida stayed and those who knew her thought silently that she should have shown more spirit.

She confided in no one, even her closest friends, and since Mrs Preece was always charmingly maternal towards her when there was anyone around they began to think that Cressida liked the way she lived. She was always cheerful and showed no envy when friends became engaged or got themselves good jobs away from the village, and they weren't to know of the long hours she spent planning her future. She didn't brood, for she despised self-pity, but now and then she wished that she had even a modicum of good looks; a pretty face, she was sure, would be a great help in getting a job.

She dozed off, to wake in the night from the throbbing of her ankle.

Moggy came to see how she was in the morning, took one look at her white face and told her to stay where she was.

'I can't,' said Cressida, 'there are the flowers to arrange and some silver to polish.' So saying she got out of bed, set her injured foot floor and did something she had never done before in her life. She fainted.

Moggy picked her up and put her on the bed and marched down to Mrs Preece's bedroom. Regardless of the fact that it was still two hours short of her usual entry with a tray of tea, she roused her mistress briskly.

'Miss Cressida's fainted, on account of her trying to get up because you told her to,' said Miss Mogford with a snap. 'You'd best get the doctor to her.'

Mrs Preece sat up in bed. 'For a sprained ankle? Probably she's only wrenched it badly. Certainly not, but I suppose she'd better stay in bed for the time being. What a nuisance this is and now I shall have a headache being wakened so abruptly. Really, you might consider my nerves.'

She sank back on her pillows. 'Go away and bring my tea at the usual time.'

Miss Mogford went away, muttering darkly to herself once the door was shut. Things couldn't go on like this; something would have to be done, although she had no idea what it was. She went to the kitchen and made a pot of tea and bore it upstairs to Cressida's room and shared it with her. It was hot and strong, and, lulled by the paracetamol, Cressida felt better.

'I could get up,' she suggested, 'if I had a stick...'

'Nonsense, you'll do no such thing. That nice doctor who brought you home would be very annoyed if he knew.'

'He doesn't know,' said Cressida, and felt a pang of regret because of that. She was a sensible girl, concealing a romantic nature beneath her ordinary appearance; no good would come of wanting something she couldn't have. She contrived to wash with Moggy's aid, brushed her hair, which was long and mousy, and plaited it and set about persuading Moggy to bring the silver epergne upstairs. 'With an old newspaper,' she urged, 'and the polish and cloths. I can do it easily and it will keep me occupied.'

'All right,' Moggy was grudging, 'but only when you've had your breakfast.'

'I'm not hungry...'

'You'll eat what I bring you,' said Moggy.

Dr van der Linus was up early, to walk in the garden with the dogs and enjoy the crisp sunshine of the morning. He had slept soundly but he was aware of uneasiness; although he could barely remember what the girl he had helped on the previous evening looked like, he was unable to shake off the feeling that he ought to do something about her. He hadn't liked the vague air of disquiet which she and the woman who admitted them had had and he had been puzzled at the bare little room which was surely unsuitable for a daughter of the house. The housekeeper had been anxious for him to leave, too.

He went indoors to his breakfast. It might be a good idea to get the name of the local doctor and give him a ring; on the other hand, that smacked of officiousness. He sighed and poured himself some more coffee. It would be better if he were to call and enquire. He was to lunch with friends at Castle Cary and need not go much out of his way.

He went upstairs to his grandmother's room presently. She was sitting up in bed, her breakfast on a tray before her.

'Come in and finish this toast,' she begged him. 'Mrs Wiffin has this passion for feeding me up! Aren't you going over to Castle Cary to the Colliers'? Is Jenny at home?'

He smiled slowly. 'Matchmaking, Grandmother? I don't

know if she's at home. In any case...' He paused. 'It is time I married, but not Jenny.'

'You've found the girl?' asked Lady Merrill eagerly.

'I'm not sure. She's very suitable. Her name is Nicola van Germert—you've met her. The daughter of one of the professors at Leiden University. We know all the same people and share a similar lifestyle.'

Lady Merrill bit into her toast. 'Not good reasons for marriage, my dear, but you're old enough and wise enough to know what you want. Most men want love as well,' she added drily.

He got up. 'Well, I suppose we aren't all lucky enough to find it. Will you be at home at teatime? We can sit in the garden, if it's warm enough, and gossip.' He bent to kiss her cheek. 'Staying here with you is something I always look forward to.'

'So do I, my dear. But you would be lost without your work. Don't you miss the hospitals and clinics and patients?'

'Oh, yes, very much. They are the most important things in my life, Grandmother.'

'Part of your life, Aldrik. Now run along and enjoy yourself.'

At the door he turned. 'I thought I'd call in on my way and see how that girl is getting on. I must find out about the dog too and let her know.'

'That would be kind.' Lady Merrill watched his vast back disappear through her door. She looked thoughtful. Considering the girl was so uninteresting that he couldn't remember what she looked like Aldrik was being very kind. But, of course, he was a kind man.

He drove away in the Bentley presently. Minton Cracknell wasn't all that distance away but there was no direct road to it. He needed to go considerably out of his way to reach it but since it was less than ten miles to Castle Cary from there and for most of the way a main road he would have time to make his call.

The house looked pleasant enough as he got out of the car but the housekeeper's face bore a look of gloomy indignation. The doctor was used to dealing with every kind of person; his 'good morning' was briskly friendly with strong overtones of authority.

'I've called to enquire after Miss Preece. I'm on my way to friends and had to pass the door.'

'She's in bed but that ankle's that swollen, I don't like the look of it...'

'The doctor is calling?'

She shook her head, speaking softly. 'Mrs Preece says it's not necessary.'

'Perhaps I might have a word with her? I know it isn't my business but perhaps I might persuade her.'

Miss Mogford's stern visage crumpled. 'Oh, sir, if you would. I don't know what to do...'

She stood aside to allow him to enter and left him in the hall while she went to find Mrs Preece.

She came back presently. 'If you'd come this way, sir...'

Mrs Preece was sitting by a briskly burning fire, a tray of coffee beside her, and she didn't get out of her chair.

'You must forgive me for not getting up,' she said in a small plaintive voice. 'I'm not very strong. I understand that you were so kind as to bring Cressida home yesterday. Do sit down—it is most kind of you to call too.' She said sharply to Miss Mogford hovering at the door, 'Bring some more coffee, will you? This is cold...'

The doctor sat, accepted the coffee when it came, listened with apparent sympathy to his hostess's light voice describing various aspects of her ill health, put down his cup and said in a gentle voice, 'I should like to see your stepdaughter's ankle; just to check on the strapping. She will be going for an X-ray some time today, I expect?'

Mrs Preece gave a tinkling laugh. 'Good heavens, no, Doctor, it's only a sprain. She should be up and about in no time. So vexing that she should have to stay in bed but she has never fainted before, the silly girl. And I have guests for dinner this evening too.'

'But you have no objection to my seeing her?' asked the doctor, and something in his voice made her shrug her shoulders and give a reluctant consent.

'Do encourage her to get up—she will be much better on her feet, will she not?' Mrs Preece gave him a charming smile, her head a little on one side. Really, she thought, he was so good-looking and charming that one would agree to anything that he might say.

'No, she would be much worse,' said Dr van der Linus. He spoke with such calm charm that she didn't realise that he had contradicted her flatly.

'Well, Miss Mogford shall take you to her room,' said Mrs Preece, 'I find the stairs trying—I have to be careful.'

She sounded wistful and long-suffering and if she expected the doctor to enquire sympathetically as to the reason she was to be disappointed.

Miss Mogford, summoned, led him up the stairs in silence. Only at Cressida's door she paused to look at him. She still said nothing, though she tapped on the door and opened it for him to go into the room.

Cressida was sitting up in bed, her small person surrounded by sheets of newspaper upon which rested the silver epergne which she was polishing. There was nothing beautiful about her; her hair hung in its long plait over one shoulder, her face, un-made-up, shone with her exertions, and she had a smear on one cheek and both hands were grimed with silver polish. The doctor, a kind man, eyed her with much the same feelings which he would have displayed if he had encountered a kitten or a puppy in need of help.

His, 'Good morning, Miss Preece,' was uttered with impersonal courtesy, and, since she was staring at him, open-mouthed, he said, 'I happened to be passing and felt that the least I could do was to enquire about your ankle.'

Cressida shut her mouth with a snap. She said politely, 'How kind of you. I'm fine, thank you.' She gave him a small smile. 'Isn't it a lovely morning?'

'Splendid. May I look at your ankle? It is of course, none of my business, but I feel that it should be X-rayed.'

'Well, I'm not sure,' began Cressida, to be told by Moggy to hush.

'The doctor knows best,' said that lady sternly. 'Just you lie still, Miss Cressida, and let him take a look.'

The doctor bent his great height and examined the ankle. When he had looked his fill he straightened up again. 'I'm not your doctor so I can do very little to help you, but I will do my best to advise your stepmother to allow the doctor to see you. It is a nasty sprain. It will get better quickly enough, though, provided it receives the right treatment.'

'And if it doesn't?' asked Cressida in a matter-of-fact voice.

'You will hobble around for a long time—a painful time too.'

'Well, thank you. It was very kind of you to come. I suppose you don't know what happened to that poor dog?'

'He needs only good food and rest and good care.' He smiled down at her. 'I shall take him back with me when I go to Holland.'

Her ordinary face was transformed by delight. 'Oh, how absolutely super! I'm sure he'll be a very handsome beast when he's fully grown.'

The doctor concealed his doubts admirably. 'I have no doubt of that.'

He put out a hand and engulfed hers in its firm grasp.

'You'll have to wash your hand,' said Cressida in her sensible way, 'it's covered in polish.' And then she added, 'I hope you have a good journey home.'

After he had gone she sat in her bed, the epergne forgotten, feeling lonely and somehow bereft.

Beyond registering his opinion that Cressida should have her ankle X-rayed, the doctor didn't waste time with Mrs Preece. He pleaded an urgent engagement and drove away.

In the village he stopped, enquired as to where the doctor lived and presented himself at the surgery door. Dr Braddock was on the point of leaving on his rounds.

'Van der Linus...' he said. 'I know that name. You wrote an article in the *Lancet* last month about neutropenia—a most interesting theory. Come in, come in, I'm delighted to meet you.'

'I've been poaching on your preserves,' said Dr van der Linus. 'If I might explain...'

Dr Braddock heard him out. 'I'll go this morning. I know—we all know—that things aren't right at the Old Rectory. Little Cressida is a dear child but one cannot interfere—though I will do my best to get her into hospital for a few days for she will never be able to get the proper rest she needs if she is at home...'

'It puts me in mind of Cinderella and her stepmother,' observed Dr van der Linus.

Dr Braddock nodded. 'Ridiculous, isn't it, in this day and age? There is obviously some reason which is keeping Cressida at home but she isn't going to tell anyone what it is.'

Dr van der Linus went on his way presently; he was going to be late for lunch at the Colliers'. As indeed he was, but he was an old friend and readily forgiven and moreover Jenny was an amusing companion. He told himself that he had done all that he could for Cressida Preece; she was a grown woman and should be capable of arranging her own life.

On his way back to his grandmother's house he reflected that she had seemed quite content with her lot. Probably things would improve. He frowned, aware that he was finding it difficult to forget her. 'Which is absurd,' he muttered. 'I can't even remember what she looks like.'

CHAPTER TWO

CRESSIDA, PUTTING A final polish on the table silver, was astonished when Moggy opened the door to admit Dr Braddock.

He wished them a good morning, patted her on the shoulder and signified his intention of examining her ankle.

'However did you know about it?' asked Cressida and tried not to wince as he prodded it gently.

'Dr van der Linus very correctly informed me. How fortunate that he should have found you, my dear. I couldn't better the strapping myself but you must have it X-rayed. I've got my car outside. I'll run you in to Yeovil now and get it done...'

'Must you? I mean, Stepmother's got a dinner party this evening...'

'There is no need for her to come with you,' said Dr Braddock testily. He turned to Miss Mogford. 'Do you suppose we could give her a chair downstairs? Just get her into a dressing-gown.'

'How shall I get back here?' asked Cressida sensibly.

'Well, I have to come home, don't I?' He went to the door. 'I'll go and see your stepmother while Miss Mogford gets you ready, and don't waste time.'

'The silver,' said Cressida urgently, watching Moggy bundling it up, 'I haven't quite finished it.'

'Pooh,' said Miss Mogford, 'that's of no importance. Here's your dressing-gown.'

Doctor Braddock came back presently and between them he and Miss Mogford carried Cressida down to the hall and out of the door, into his car. Mrs Preece came after them, on the verge of tears. 'What am I to do?' she asked pathetically. 'There's the table to arrange and the drinks and the flowers to do. Really, Cressida, I do think you're being very selfish...'

No one answered her. The doctor and Moggy were too occupied in conveying Cressida as painlessly as possible and Cressida was gritting her teeth against the pain.

Dr Braddock drove off and as soon as she had control of her voice again she asked, 'They won't keep me long? I really should get back to help as quickly as I can. If I could be back by lunchtime? You're awfully kind having given me a lift, Dr Braddock, but I expect you have to come back home for lunch.'

She wasn't back for lunch, however; instead she found herself in one of the side-wards, comfortably in bed with a cradle over the injured ankle and the prospect of several days' rest.

'I really can't,' she explained to the cheerful house doctor who came to see her after she was warded. 'I haven't anything with me and there is a great deal I must do at home...'

'Well, if you don't rest that foot for a few days you won't be doing anything at all at home or anywhere else. Dr Braddock is going to call and see your stepmother on his way home. I dare say she will come and see you and bring you anything you need.'

The very last thing that lady would do, but there was no point in saying so. Cressida murmured suitably and since the bed was comfortable and she had had an irksome morning she closed her eyes and took a nap.

Miss Mogford came that evening, carrying a small holdall with what she considered necessary for Cressida's comfort while she was in hospital.

Cressida was delighted to see her, but worried too. 'Moggy,

however did you get away? It's the dinner party too...is Stepmother very cross?'

'Livid,' said Miss Mogford, succinctly, 'but Dr Braddock was quite sharp with her, told her she was responsible for you and I don't know what else—I just happened to be passing through the hall and the door wasn't quite closed—so when he'd gone she phoned a catering firm and they're there now, seeing to everything. She told me to bring you what you needed here and I got the baker's van to bring me.'

'How will you get back?'

'The van's going back in an hour—the driver's got the day off tomorrow.'

'I don't know how long I'm here for...'

'I heard Dr Braddock say a couple of days, so you have a nice rest, Miss Cressida, and you'll have to take things easy when you come home.'

'Is my stepmother very annoyed?'

'Well, she's put out,' said Miss Mogford, uttering the understatement of a lifetime.

It was surprising what two days at the hospital did for Cressida. Of course there were the painful physiotherapy sessions, but for a good deal of each day she sat, the injured ankle resting on a stool, reading the discarded magazines and newspapers of the other patients, racing through the romantic fiction the lady from the hospital library was kind enough to bring her. She didn't turn up her unassuming nose at the food either; by the end of the second day she had colour in her cheeks and had put on a much-needed pound or two.

It was after breakfast on the following morning that the orthopaedic registrar came to tell her that she was fit enough to go home. 'You must wear an elastic stocking for a couple of weeks and keep off your feet as much as possible, and mind you rest the ankle properly. Sister phoned your stepmother and she assures us that you will be well looked after. We'll arrange for the hospital car service to pick you up after midday dinner today.'

Cressida thanked him and reflected that with a stocking and a stick she would be able to manage well enough. Indeed, she would have to...

She was sitting dressed and ready to leave, her ankle resting on the stool before her, when the door opened and Dr van der Linus walked in.

His greeting was genial. 'I had to have a word with someone here and thought I would call and see how you are getting on. I hear you're going home?'

'Yes. I'm waiting for transport. I'm quite better again.' She gave him a steady smile. 'I'm most grateful for everything you did for me.'

'Think nothing of it. I'm going past your home; I'll take you if you're ready to go. Just let me have a word with Sister...' He had gone before she could answer.

On the way back he told her that he was going to London on the following day and then back to Holland. 'I don't expect to be back here for some time,' he told her, and then casually, 'Have you any plans for your future?'

'No, none,' said Cressida bleakly. Her look was sad. 'At least not for some time.'

'Ah, well,' said the doctor easily, 'I dare say you have your reasons for staying at home.'

'Yes, I have. What will happen to the dog while you're in London?'

He accepted the change of subject without demur. 'He's to stay at the vet's. I will collect him when I leave England. He looks quite handsome, you know, although I'm not quite sure what he is. He's young still, about six months, and still going to grow.'

'You'll have room for him at your home?'

'Oh, yes.' He stopped in front of her house and got out to help her.

'Thank you very much,' she said. 'Would you like to come in and see my stepmother?'

The doctor smiled a little; it was obvious that she hoped that he would refuse. 'Why not?' he said cheerfully, and took her arm. 'Use your stick,' he counselled her, and, 'Put your weight on your good foot and for heaven's sake don't stand about; sit when you can and keep your foot up.'

Miss Mogford had been on the watch for Cressida's return. She opened the door wide, and her severe features softened into a smile. 'There, that's better. My goodness, a couple of days in hospital have done you a power of good, Miss Cressy—I swear you've put on a pound or two.'

'Is my stepmother in?' asked Cressida. 'I'm sure Dr van der Linus—'

The rest of her words were lost in Mrs Preece's voice, 'Is that you, Cressida? And about time too. All this rubbish I've been hearing about this ankle of yours...' A half-open door was thrust open and she came into the hall, caught sight of the doctor's vast person and went on smoothly, 'You poor child, have you had a lot of pain? I didn't come to visit you for you know how sensitive I am about illness.' She smiled at Dr van der Linus. 'My nerves, you know—I'm a martyr to them.' She turned to Cressida. 'Run along upstairs, dear, I dare say you would like a rest. Miss Mogford shall bring you your tea presently.'

She turned her back on Cressida, 'Tea is just made,' she said to the doctor. 'Do have a cup with me. I see so few people and you must tell me about Cressida's ankle.'

He refused with a charm as smooth as her own. 'I have an evening appointment and have still some distance to drive. Miss Preece should be all right now—a week or two keeping off the ankle and plenty of rest. But, of course, you will know what to do.'

He shook hands again and then turned to Cressida standing so quietly close by. 'I am sure that Dr Braddock will be over to see you shortly. I'm glad that the damage wasn't worse. I'll take care of the dog.'

She smiled. 'I'm sure you will and it's very kind of you to have him. I hope you have a good journey home.'

He stared down at her—such a plain little face but such beautiful eyes, and despite her smile she was unhappy. Not surprisingly, he considered; he had a poor view of Mrs Preece.

Sitting opposite his grandmother that evening, he voiced his vague disquiet about Cressida. 'The girl seems sensible enough,' he observed, 'and really one hardly expects the modern young woman to behave like Cinderella. Mrs Preece is someone that anyone with an ounce of good sense would get away from as quickly as possible.'

'Then there must be a good reason for the girl to remain there. Have you any idea what it might be?'

'None.' He added, 'I suppose there is no way of finding out?'

'Well, of course there is; ask her.'

'Perhaps I will. I must go up to town tomorrow but I'll come down to say goodbye before I go over to Holland, my dear, and I'll make time to see her then.' He frowned. 'Do you think I'm making a mountain out of a molehill? Probably I shall get short shrift...'

'In that case you need do no more about it. On the other hand she may be longing to confide in someone.'

It was a week later when he came back to Lady Merrill's and on a sudden impulse turned off the main road to go to Minton Cracknell. He was within half a mile of the village when he saw Cressida, walking awkwardly with a stick, going in the same direction as he was. He drew up beside her, and opened the door. His 'Hello, can I give you a lift?' was casually uttered and when she turned to look at him he was careful to stay casual. She had been crying, although she smiled now and thanked him politely.

'That's kind of you, but I walk a little way each day, you know—it's good for me.'

The doctor said, 'Get in, Cressida,' in a gentle voice which none the less she felt compelled to obey. She got in.

'Is your stepmother at home?'

She shook her head. 'No. She goes to Bath to have her hair done. Did you want to see her?'

'No. Why have you been crying, Cressida?' He leaned across her and closed the door. 'Supposing you tell me what is wrong? And I must beg you not to tell me that there is nothing wrong, because that is merely wasting time. Possibly you do not wish to confide in a friend but since we are unlikely to meet again you can safely unburden yourself to me.'

'I don't think,' began Cressida doubtfully, 'actually, that it would be of any interest to you.'

'You are politely telling me that it is none of my business. Quite right, and all the more reason to talk to me. Since it is none of my business I shall give you no advice, nor shall I read you a lecture or tell you that none of it matters.' He laid a great arm along the seat behind her shoulders. 'Now let's have it...'

It was hard to start, it had been all bottled up for so long, but once started Cressida was unable to stop. It all came pouring out. 'It's Moggy, you see,' she explained. 'If she leaves before she's sixty she can't have Father's legacy and she depends on that for her old age...'

'Have you seen the will...?'

'No. Mr Tims, the solicitor, read it out to us but it was full of heretofores and those long words they use.'

'Just supposing that there had been a misunderstanding about the terms of the legacy, Miss Mogford would be able to leave, would she not? And you would be free to leave home, knowing that her future was secure.'

Cressida gave a great sniff and he glanced at her. She hardly looked her best, her hair was all over the place, as far as he could judge she had no make-up on and her clothes were deplorable. He said very kindly, 'It is likely that Miss Mogford hasn't understood the conditions of the legacy. If that could be looked into she might find herself free to leave before she is sixty. Who exactly told her of this condition?'

'My stepmother.'

The doctor frowned. Tiresome woman, and how on earth had he come to get involved in the business? All the same it seemed to him that he was the only one with a pair of scissors to cut the tangle. A pity that he would be leaving the country so soon...

'Feel better?' he asked.

'Yes, thank you.' She put a hand on the door-handle. 'You've been very kind. I won't keep you.'

His hand came down on hers, firm and warm. 'The rest of the day is my own. I'll drive you home.'

At the gates she asked him, 'Would you like to come in? Moggy will make a pot of tea...'

He had got out of the car too and stood looking down at her. 'I should have liked that but I'm going into Yeovil to collect the dog. Have you any ideas about a name?'

'Well, no. Oughtn't he to have a Dutch name since he's to live in Holland?'

'He is English; he should have a name which is common to both countries.'

'Caesar?'

'That would do very nicely. It will suit him, too; he bids fair to be a large beast when he is grown.'

Cressida put out a hand. 'I'm so glad he's going to be looked after. That's wonderful; thank you again for all you've done. Goodbye.'

The hand holding hers felt reassuringly large and secure. She wished very much that the doctor wasn't going away. He would forget her, of course, but knowing him even for such a short time had been pleasant.

He waited by the car until she reached the door and went inside, turning to give a final wave as she did so.

She didn't tell Moggy about the will. First she would write to Mr Tims; it would never do to raise the dear soul's hopes until she had heard from him. Over their tea they talked about the dog and the splendid home he would have when he travelled to Holland.

'Lucky beast,' said Miss Mogford with a good deal of feeling.

Dr van der Linus found his grandmother sitting in her high-backed armchair by a brisk fire. The weather was still fine and sunny, but, as she pointed out cheerfully, arthritis and old age needed warmth.

He bent to kiss her cheek. 'My dear, you are one of those lucky people who never grow old; you're really a very pretty lady, you know.'

'Go on with you! Buttering me up... What have you been doing with yourself?'

'Working.' He sat down opposite her. 'Grandmother, do you know of a Mr Tims of Sherborne?'

'Of course I do. He is my solicitor, has been for years—must be all of seventy.'

'Do you suppose he would allow me the sight of Mr Preece's will?'

'Been to see that girl again, have you?' Lady Merrill's old eyes twinkled with amusement.

'I met her on the road as I was coming here. She looked like a small wet hen. I gave her a lift home and got her to talk. I fancy Mrs Preece has—shall we say?—misunderstood the terms of the will...' He explained briefly and his grandmother nodded in quick understanding.

'So if she has been misleading the girl and the housekeeper things can be put right, the housekeeper can leave and the girl will be free to find herself a job.' Her old face puckered in thought. 'What kind of a job would a wet hen be able to get?'

The doctor laughed. 'I think that if she were free and independent she might begin to look like any other girl. Have you any ideas?'

'I'll think about it. Go and phone George Tims and then come and play cribbage?'

Mr Tims was co-operative. The doctor might pop in any time he chose during the next day. Dr van der Linus went back to the drawing-room and bent his powerful mind to the problem of allowing his grandmother to win without her suspecting it.

Undoubtedly there had been a misunderstanding, Mr Tims assured the doctor the following morning; Miss Mogford was free to leave when she wished and would receive her legacy without delay. 'Mrs Preece will miss her; she has been with the family for many years and will be hard to replace. Mrs Preece is a delicate lady, unable to do a great deal, but of course she will have Cressida—such a sensible girl.'

The doctor agreed blandly and drove back to the house. The little wet hen deserved a chance. She was, he supposed, possessed of the normal skills of a well-educated girl; she should have no difficulty in getting herself a job, but what as? She knew nothing about computers; he felt sure of that. Probably she couldn't type or do shorthand, and she would be no good as a nurse; far too small for a start and with far too soft a heart. Not that he approved of nurses who didn't have soft hearts, that was a vital part of being a decent nurse—but he suspected that she would allow personal sympathy with the patient to supplant nursing expertise. It would have to be something around the house, he thought vaguely. Were there companions nowadays? He wasn't sure, but there were au pairs from whom all that was required was common sense, an ability to do chores around the house, like children and animals and be willing to babysit. He knew that; various of his married friends had them. She would have a roof over her head too...

He was turning in at Lady Merrill's gate when he found the answer.

Over dinner he told his grandmother what he had in mind. 'I shall want your help, my dear,' he added.

Lady Merrill listened carefully. 'This is really rather fun.

You do realise that I shall have to do this through a third person? I cannot appear on Mrs Preece's doorstep out of the blue. Let me see, Audrey Sefton knows her. Leave it to me, Aldrik. Is the girl presentable?'

He leaned back in his chair. 'She has a pretty voice and nice manners. Beautiful eyes and no looks. I suppose dressed in the right clothes she would do very well in the most exacting of households.'

'Yes, dear—but how does she get these clothes if she has no money?'

'I'll see Mr Tims. A small sum held in some sort of reserve for her use or something similar.'

His grandmother gave him a sharp look. 'You're going to a great deal of trouble, my dear. She would probably get herself some sort of work if she were left to do so.'

'Oh, I'm sure she would. I shall be going up to Friesland in any case and I'll see Charity and Tyco. Charity might like company for a few months, at least until the baby is born, and that will give Cressida time to look around and decide what she wants to do.'

'Yes, dear? Will you stay up there?'

'I've no appointments there until the middle of the month. I'm tied up in Leiden almost as soon as I get back. That will give me a chance to see something of Nicola...'

'I'm sure she will be pleased to see you again. There's nothing definite, I suppose, dear?'

'No, Grandmother. We are both sensible people; a deep regard and a full knowledge of each other's character seems to me to be essential before marrying.' It sounded pompous but he disarmed her with a grin.

His grandmother gave him a loving look. He was her very favourite grandchild and she wanted him to be happy. He loved his work as a consultant physician and he was very successful. He had money, friends, and those who worked for him liked him. All very well, she thought, but he has no idea what it is like to be in love. Nicola was a cold fish, elegant and witty and wanting, Lady Merrill suspected, only a secure place in her comfortable world, never mind the romance.

He left the next day, promising to come and see her as soon as he could spare a few days. 'I'll be driving Mama over before Christmas,' he promised her.

Two days later Mrs Preece came down to breakfast looking annoyed. 'So vexing—I had planned to go into Yeovil and do some shopping; now that wretched Mr Tims wants to call this morning. Hurry up and eat your breakfast, Cressida, and get a tray ready. If he doesn't stay I'll still have time to go. Bring the coffee as soon as he gets here.'

Cressida went to the kitchen, laid a tray for coffee and told Miss Mogford, 'Half-past ten, he said in his letter. She didn't tell me why, papers to sign, I expect.'

Mr Tims arrived punctually and Mrs Preece, eager to get to Yeovil, didn't keep him waiting. Cressida carried in the coffee, wished him a cheerful good morning and made for the door.

'What I have to say concerns both Cressida and Miss Mogford, Mrs Preece. I should like them both to be here if you would be so kind.'

Mrs Preece flashed him a look quite lacking in kindness. 'Really, Mr Tims, is this necessary? They are both busy around the house.'

Mr Tims looked at her over his spectacles. 'It is necessary, Mrs Preece.'

So Cressida fetched Miss Mogford and they sat awkwardly side by side on one of the big sofas, wondering what on earth was going to happen next.

Mr Tims cleared his throat and opened his briefcase. 'I was looking through Mr Preece's papers very recently and it occurs to me that there may have been a misunderstanding concerning Miss Mogford's legacy. According to the will she is entitled to claim it whenever she wishes; she may in fact leave as soon as she wants and the money will be paid to her. There is no question of her having to remain in service until she is sixty. I believe that was the impression given her at the time of the reading of the will; mistakenly of course.'

Miss Mogford said gruffly. 'You really mean that? I can pack my bags and go and still have the legacy?' She looked at Mrs Preece. 'Madam told me that I would have to stay or I wouldn't get the money.'

Mrs Preece hastily adjusted her features into a look of apologetic regret. 'Oh, dear, I'm sure that was never intended. Silly me, I never have been any good at this kind of thing.'

She smiled charmingly at Mr Tims, who said politely, 'Well, no harm done, I imagine.' He turned to Cressida. 'If at any future time you should decide to leave home, I am entrusted with a small sum of money, sufficient, I trust, to start you off in whatever venture you may consider.'

'Oh, Cressida would never dream of leaving me,' said Mrs Preece quickly. 'My nerves, you know. It is essential that I have someone to take care of me and she is very used to that.'

Cressida said nothing, merely thanked Mr Tims and offered him more coffee. He refused, and said that he had another client to see in the neighbourhood, and Miss Mogford got up to show him out. Mrs Preece bade him goodbye in a cold voice—he hadn't shown her the sympathy she had expected—and Cressida shook hands, saying nothing but looking at him with eyes alight with damped-down excitement. By jove, thought Mr Tims, those lovely eyes of hers made a man forget her ordinary looks.

When he had gone Mrs Preece said sharply, 'Of course there is no question of your going, Miss Mogford. I'm quite prepared to give you a bigger wage, and after all this has been your home for years.'

Moggy's severe features became even more severe. 'You pay me weekly, Mrs Preece. I'm giving you a week's notice as from today.'

She turned on her heel and marched briskly back to the kitchen, leaving Mrs Preece speechless. But not for long!

'The wretch, after all I've done for her. Go after her, Cressida, and tell her she must stay. What am I to do without a housekeeper?' Tears of self-pity rolled down her carefully made-up cheeks.

Cressida, a-fire with the prospect of freedom, sat down on the arm of a chair. 'No, I won't tell Moggy anything of the sort,' she said calmly. 'You've never done anything for her and you can get another housekeeper.'

Mrs Preece's eyes bulged. 'Cressida, have you taken leave of your senses? How dare you talk to me like that, after all I've…?'

She stopped because Cressida was smiling. 'I'm going too, Stepmother.'

'Don't be ridiculous. What will you do? And you've no money.'

'I'm very experienced in housework and Mr Tims said that there was a little money.'

'Rubbish. No one will employ you.' Mrs Preece changed her tactics. 'If you will stay, Cressida, I'll make you an allowance. I'll get another housekeeper and you can train her. I simply cannot manage without someone to run this house. My nerves…' She gave Cressida a wan smile. 'What would your father have said?'

'He would have told me to pack my bags and go,' said Cressida promptly.

Cressida lay awake for a long time that night. She intended to leave at the same time as Moggy although just for the moment she had no idea as to what she would do. London, she supposed vaguely; surely there would be work of some sort there. If she had a roof over her head she could save most of her wages and then train for something, she wasn't sure what. But to be free and live her own life—she uttered a sigh of pure content and fell asleep.

In the light of early morning she lost some of the euphoria. She wasn't sure if she had enough money to get to London, for a start—she would have to see Mr Tims—and when she got there, then where would she go? This was something which would have to be settled before she left home; she was a practical girl; to arrive in London with no notion of where she was to lay her head that night was bird-witted. Something would have to be done about that.

Something was. Mrs Preece, sitting languidly in her drawing-room, refusing to do anything about rearranging her household, declaring that she felt ill enough to take to her bed, was forced to pull herself together when Miss Mogford came to tell her that she had a caller: Mrs Sefton, who lived some miles from Minton Cracknell but whom she had met on various occasions at other people's houses. She didn't like the lady overmuch; overbearing, she considered, with an amused contempt for weak nerves and women who couldn't do the washing-up for themselves. That she lived in a large house, well-staffed and well-run, had nothing to say to the matter; Mrs Sefton was perfectly capable of running the place single-handed if it were necessary and that without a single grumble.

She breezed into the room now and bade her reluctant hostess good morning. Her voice wasn't loud but had a penetrating ring to it, so that Mrs Preece closed her eyes for a moment.

'A lovely morning,' declared Mrs Sefton. 'You should be out. There's the autumn fête at Watly House this afternoon—aren't you going?'

Mrs Preece said faintly that no, she didn't think she felt well enough.

'Well, you look all right,' said Mrs. Sefton.

'My nerves, you know.'

Mrs Sefton, who had never quite discovered what nerves, when mentioned by their possessor, meant, ignored this.

'I'm here to ask a favour. That gel of yours, Cressida, I've a job for her...'

'She doesn't need a job,' said Mrs Preece, sitting up smartly.

'I know someone who needs her—an old friend of mine, Lady Merrill, desperately needs a companion for a few weeks while her permanent companion has a holiday.' Mrs Sefton, pleased with her fabrication, added in ringing tones, 'Not much to do you know—just a few chores. She's just the one for it. I'm sure you can manage without her—I don't suppose you see much of her anyway, she goes out a good deal I dare say.'

'Cressida likes to stay at home with me,' said Mrs. Preece sourly.

'Does she? In that case she'll know just what to do for Lady Merrill. She lives north of Sherborne, quite easy to get at—just the other side of Charlton Horethorne.'

Miss Mogford came in with the coffee and Mrs Preece poured it with a shaking hand. 'I'm quite sure that Cressida won't wish to leave me,' she said in a die-away voice.

'Well, let's have her in to speak for herself,' said Mrs Sefton. She stopped Moggy on her way to the door. 'Ask Miss Preece to come here, will you?'

Mrs Preece opened her mouth to say something tart about guests giving orders in someone else's house and then thought better of it. Mrs Sefton was well known and liked in the county and she was known to give her unvarnished opinion of anyone or anything she didn't approve of. Moggy hurried back to the kitchen where Cressida was making the junket Mrs Preece ate each day—it was supposed to keep the skin youthful, she had been told.

'Drop that, Miss Cressida,' said Moggy urgently, 'you're to go to the drawing-room, there's a Mrs Sefton there, wants to see you.'

'Why?' asked Cressida. 'The junket will curdle...'

'Drat the junket. Your stepmother is in a rage so be careful.'

Cressida might be a plain girl but she was graceful and self-possessed. She greeted Mrs Sefton, grudgingly introduced by Mrs Preece, in a quiet voice, and sat down.

'I've a job for you, my dear,' said Mrs Sefton, not beating about the bush. 'An old lady—a great friend of mine—is in need of a companion for a few weeks and I thought of you. Would you care to take it on?'

'You can't leave me, Cressida,' said Mrs. Preece in a fading voice, 'I shall be ill; besides, it is your place to stay here with me.'

Cressida gave her a thoughtful look and turned sparkling blue eyes upon their visitor. 'I should like to come very much,' she said composedly. 'I have been planning to find a job now that our housekeeper is leaving. When would this lady want me to start?'

Mrs Sefton, primed as to when Miss Mogford was leaving, was ready with an answer. 'Would Thursday be too soon?'

'That is quite impossible,' observed Mrs Preece. 'I have had no replies to my advertisement for a housekeeper and Miss Mogford leaves on the same day. Cressida must stay until I find someone to run the house for me.'

'Oh, surely you can manage to do that yourself?' asked Mrs Sefton. 'I dare say you have outside help from the village?'

Mrs Preece had to admit that she had.

'Well, then, get them to come more often,' said Mrs Sefton cheerfully. 'I dare say you might feel much better if you had something to do.' She smiled in a condescending manner at her hostess. 'And do come to the fête; there's nothing like having an outside interest, you know.'

She got to her feet. 'So be ready on Thursday, Cressida—you don't mind if I call you that? Someone will fetch you directly after lunch.'

She looked at Mrs Preece who wished her a feeble goodbye. 'You must excuse me from getting up,' she whispered dramatically. 'The shock, you know...'

'Well, I don't know,' said Mrs Sefton, 'for I didn't realise that you'd had one. I dare say we shall meet. Do you go out at all socially? I have seen you on several occasions at dinner parties and were you not in Bath last week? At the Royal Crescent, dining with the Croftons? Cressida was not with you?'

'Oh, yes—a long-standing engagement. Cressida hates going out, she is very much a home girl.'

Mrs Sefton raised her eyebrows. 'Then in that case, this little job will give her a taste of the outside world, will it not?'

With which parting shot Mrs Sefton took herself off.

Mrs Preece wept and cajoled and threatened for the rest of that day but to no good purpose. Moggy was adamant about leaving, she packed her things and then went to help Cressida with hers. 'I can't think why you stayed, Miss Cressida, you could have gone months ago...'

'I wasn't going to leave you here, Moggy,' was all Cressida would say.

Miss Mogford stared at her, her arms full of clothes. 'So that's why you've put up with your stepmother's tantrums. I'll not forget that, love. If ever you need help or a home or just someone to talk to, I'll be there waiting and don't you forget it.'

Cressida put down the shoes she was polishing and cast her arms around Miss Mogford. 'Moggy, you are a darling, and I'll remember that and I promise that I'll come to you if I need help or advice or a bed. I shall miss you.'

Moggy's stern countenance softened. 'I shall miss you too after all this time. It hasn't been easy, has it? But everything'll come right now. You really want to go to this old lady?'

'Yes, oh, yes, I do. It's a start, I can get a reference from her and I suppose I'll get paid—I forgot to ask—I'll save all I can and besides Mr Tims said there was a little money for me. I'd better go and see him tomorrow... No, I'll phone, he can send the money here.'

She wrapped her shoes carefully and put them into the shabby suitcase. 'We'd better go and start dinner. Stepmother's alone this evening.'

'Well, don't let her put upon you,' advised Miss Mogford firmly.

Cressida turned eyes shining like stars upon her companion. 'I won't, Moggy, never again.'

CHAPTER THREE

BY LUNCHTIME ON Thursday Cressida could feel nothing but relief at leaving her home. Mrs Preece had tried every gambit known to her in her efforts to make Cressida and Miss Mogford change their minds. She had had no success and had resorted to bad temper and reproaches, despite which Cressida had been to the village and arranged for one of the women who came to help in the house to move in temporarily until a new housekeeper could be engaged. She had met the postman on the way and he had given her a letter from Mr Tims—a registered letter containing a hundred pounds and a note—couched in dry-as-dust terms, wishing her well and advising her to use the money prudently until such time as she had a permanent job. Cressida, who hadn't laid hands on anything like that sum for some time, skipped all the way home—rather clumsily because her ankle still pained her at times.

No sooner had she entered the house than her stepmother called to her from the drawing-room. 'Since you're not going until after lunch you might as well get it ready. I'm far too upset to eat much; I'll have an omelette and some thin toast and my usual junket. You had better open a bottle of white wine too.' She picked up the novel she was reading. 'And don't bother to say goodbye, you ungrateful girl. I'll have a tray here.'

Cressida went to the kitchen and found Miss Mogford in the process of getting ready to leave. The baker's van would be calling shortly and the driver was giving her a lift to Templecombe where her sister had a small cottage. Her old-fashioned trunk and cardboard suitcase were already in the hall and as she sat at the kitchen table, wearing her best coat and a rather terrifying hat, she looked as stern as usual but when Cressida joined her her face crumpled.

'That it should come to this—you being turned out of your own home...'

'Well, I've turned myself out, haven't I, Moggy? I hate leaving and so do you but we shall both be a lot happier. After all, it hasn't been much fun since Father died. Has Stepmother paid you your wages?'

Miss Mogford nodded. 'I had to ask her for them. And what about you, Miss Cressy? Will you be all right? Supposing this old lady is too much of a handful?'

'Old ladies, on the whole, are rather nice, Moggy, and in any case it's only for a few weeks then I can pick and choose.' Cressida spoke bracingly because Moggy sounded worried, but she felt uncertain of the future, although she had every intention of making a success of whatever she ended up doing. Leaving her home was a sadness she hadn't quite realised, but to stay forever, pandering to her stepmother's whims, was something no longer to be borne. She had been longing for something to happen and now it had and she would make the very best of it.

'There's the baker,' she said, and bustled her old friend out into the hall. 'Now you've got my address and I've got yours, we'll write regularly and as soon as we can we'll have a few hours together.' She put her arms round Moggy's spare frame and hugged her. 'I'm going to miss you dreadfully but you're going to be happy and so am I.' She planted a kiss on the housekeeper's cheek. 'Now off you go. I'll be leaving in an hour or two...'

Miss Mogford spoke gruffly. 'If your poor pa could see you now, he'd turn in his grave. This isn't what he intended.'

'Well, never mind that, Moggy, we're both getting a chance, aren't we? It's rather exciting...'

She walked Miss Mogford out to the van and found that the driver had stowed the luggage in the back, and was waiting to settle his passenger into the front seat. The last Cressida saw of Moggy was her elderly face rigid with suppressed feelings staring out from under that hat.

In the kitchen, warming the milk for the junket, Cressida shed a few tears. She hadn't meant to, they had oozed out from under her lids and she had wiped them away at once. She was going to miss Moggy, she was going to miss her home too and those of her friends whom she saw from time to time, but, she told herself firmly, this was something she had wished for and now it had happened and she must make the most of it. She made the junket, then beat the eggs for the omelette and cut herself a sandwich, for there wouldn't be time for anything more.

Her stepmother was making things as difficult as possible—she wanted fruit and more coffee and a novel she had put down somewhere and simply had to have. Cressida attending to these wants, gobbled her sandwich as she tidied the kitchen just in time to get her elderly tweed coat as a car drew up before the house. Her stepmother's tray hadn't been cleared and nothing had been done about dinner that evening; Cressida, feeling guilty, didn't mind. She went quietly from the old house with her two shabby suitcases and was met on the doorstep by an elderly man with a weatherbeaten face who wished her good day in a friendly voice and stowed her luggage in the boot of the elderly Daimler.

She had gone to the drawing-room on her way out, and, despite Mrs Preece's wish, had been determined to bid her goodbye.

'I told you not to come, Cressida, and as far as I'm concerned you need not bother to return. I wash my hands of you.'

So Cressida got into the car beside the driver and didn't look back, telling herself firmly that she had gone through one of life's doors and shut it behind her.

The driver was friendly and disposed to talk. He was the gardener at Lady Merrill's place, he explained, and besides that he drove the car when it was wanted and did odd jobs around the place. 'Do you drive, miss?' he wanted to know and when Cressida said that yes, she did, although she had seldom had the chance, he gave the opinion that it would be a good thing if she could drive the car sometimes, 'For Lady Merrill doesn't go out often, but when she does I have to leave my garden,' he explained.

'Does her permanent companion drive?' asked Cressida.

He didn't answer at once. 'Er—well, no. You'll be a real blessing.'

'Well, I do hope so. I haven't been a companion before. Will you tell me your name, please?'

'Bert, Miss. There's Mr Baxter, the butler, 'e's old, and Mrs Wiffin the cook and Elsie the parlourmaid, they've all been there, same as me, for nigh on thirty years and no notion of leaving, neither.'

'Lady Merrill is elderly, isn't she? I don't mean to gossip about her, but I don't really know very much about the job.'

'Well, now, Lady Merrill is what you might call elderly, all of eighty-three, but very spry and nothing wrong in the head as you might say. She'll be glad to have someone young around the place.'

'I hope I won't be too young; is her companion elderly?'

'Elderly, oh, yes, miss. Like dogs, do you?'

'Very much.'

'Two Pekinese we've got. Muff and Belle, nice little beasts.'

Cressida was soothed by his amiable talk. By the time they reached Lady Merrill's house she was in good spirits, sustained by the fatherly attitude of Baxter when he opened the door to her.

'Lady Merrill rests in the afternoon,' he told her as he showed her into the hall, 'but Elsie will take you to your room so that you can unpack if you wish. Perhaps a tray of tea? She will let you know when Lady Merrill is awake.'

Elsie was nice too; elderly and thin and wearing an old-fashioned black dress and a white apron. 'You come with me, miss, and I'll bring you a nice pot of tea presently,' she observed, guiding Cressida up the oak staircase at the back of the hall.

The room into which she was shown was charming, not over large but furnished in great comfort. Her case was already there and Elsie said comfortably, 'You just unpack, miss, and I'll be up with your tea in a brace of shakes.'

Left to herself, Cressida peered into cupboards and drawers, put her head round a door to find a small but luxuriously equipped bathroom, and then started to unpack. She hadn't finished when Elsie came back with the tea, nicely arranged on a tray; paper-thin china and a plate of fairy cakes arranged round a small silver teapot. Cressida thanked her and settled down to enjoy the dainty meal; it was a long time since anyone had served her tea on a tray...

An hour later she was led to a room at the front of the house and ushered in by Elsie. 'It's the young lady, my lady,' said Elsie cheerfully. Plainly the staff weren't afraid of their mistress; they weren't familiar either, Cressida had the impression that they were devoted to her.

Lady Merrill was on a day bed, propped up by pillows and cushions and covered with a gossamer fine rug. She looked older than Cressida had expected but there was nothing elderly about her bright eyes and brisk voice.

'Come over here, my dear, where I can see you,' and, when Cressida did so, she examined her from head to foot. 'I hope you will be happy while you are here. Mrs Sefton was so delighted to arrange for you to come here. I believe she knows your stepmother?'

Cressida said cautiously, 'They met at dinner parties and

other people's houses. I've met her several times at fêtes and church bazaars.'

'A good-hearted woman! I shall call you Cressida.'

'I should like that, Lady Merrill. Could you tell me what you would like me to do? I—I haven't been a companion before and I'm not sure...'

'Well, now, let me see. I shan't need you until ten o'clock each morning; I breakfast in bed and Elsie helps me dress. I like to read my letters and I expect you to answer them for me, run errands, read to me—my sight isn't very good—and talk. I like to talk. Do you watch television?'

'Well, no, very seldom.' Cressida reflected that there had never been much opportunity for her to do so and the only TV had been in the drawing-room where she had seldom had the time to sit.

'I watch the news,' said Lady Merrill, 'and anything which I consider worthwhile. You shall read the programmes to me each morning so that I can decide if there is anything in which I am interested. You will have your meals with me. Do you play cards or chess?—or cribbage? I enjoy patience...'

'Well, yes, I play chess, not very well and cribbage—I used to play with my father. I'm no good at Bridge.'

'Never mind that—we need four to make a game and I've better things to do than sit around a table bickering over the wrong cards I played.' The old lady nodded. 'You'll do, Cressida.'

Elsie came in with the tea-tray and Lady Merrill said, 'Pour me a cup, my dear, and sit down and have your tea with me.' Nothing loath, Cressida did as she was bid, to be questioned at length as to her life at home and her plans for the future. The questions were put in such a kindly manner that she found herself saying rather more than she intended, although thinking about it afterwards she comforted herself with the thought that since she was unlikely to see Lady Merrill once she had left the house it didn't really matter, and in any case she gave vague and evasive answers which, while not misleading, weren't absolutely true.

She was told to go away and unpack her things and return when the gong sounded for dinner, a meal taken in the old lady's company in a rather dark room, massively furnished. The food was delicious and Lady Merrill, despite her age, an excellent talker. Later, getting ready for bed, Cressida standing at her window, warmly wrapped in her dressing-gown against the chill of the night, watched the moon's fitful beams between the clouds and breathed a great gusty sigh of thankfulness. She surely missed her home and Moggy, but she felt in her bones at the same time that she would be happy in this nice old house. For her first job away from home she hadn't done so badly, she reflected; it was a good omen for the future. She got into bed and her last waking thought was that it was a pity she couldn't let Dr van der Linus know that she had fallen on her feet. He had been very kind...she wondered sleepily where he was.

Dr van der Linus was sitting in the drawing-room of a patrician house in Leiden, listening to Nicola van Germert describing a visit she had paid to friends in Amsterdam. She had an amusing way of talking although there was a hint of malice, but he supposed that she could be forgiven that for it spiced her account just enough to make those listening to her smile and from time to time laugh outright. He sat watching her now: a pretty young woman in her late twenties, self-assured, well dressed and confident of her place in society. She would make a good wife, for she had all the attributes of a good hostess and would have no difficulty in managing his home in Friesland. They had known each other for some time now and although nothing had been said their friends were beginning to take it for granted that they would marry. Indeed, he had taken it for granted himself; he was thirty-five, time to settle down, although up until now he had been too immersed in his work to think of marriage. He supposed that if he had met a girl and fallen in love...but he hadn't. Perhaps he was getting too old. He roused himself from his thoughts and joined in the laughter at one of Nicola's witty remarks, and she smiled at him with a faintly possessive air.

The party broke up shortly after that and he drove himself back to the elegant little house he lived in when he was working in Leiden. He had forgotten Nicola, his mind already busy with the next day's patients. He let himself in thankfully and went straight to his study, telling his housekeeper to go to bed as he was greeted boisterously by Caesar and a St Bernard dog of immense size. They followed him into the study and settled down by his desk as he picked up his pen. He hadn't written half a dozen words when he put it down again and looked at his watch. It was almost eleven o'clock; his grandmother seldom slept before midnight and there was a telephone by her bed. He dialled her number.

Her voice with its elderly quaver came strongly over the wires. 'Aldrick—I expected you to telephone; you want to know about Cressida?'

'Merely to ask if she has arrived and is settled safely. You don't find her too much of a burden, my dear?'

'On the contrary, she is a charming girl and so anxious to please. She has volunteered no information as to her departure from her home and I think it is unlikely that she will do so—I imagine she has remained silent for so long about her home life that she is unlikely to speak of it to anyone.'

'I shall be going to Friesland in a couple of days, I'll call in on Charity and Tyco and see if they can suggest something. I am most grateful for your help, Grandmother, but the sooner she is settled in a job the better.'

'You think that she will be happy out of England?' Lady Merrill sounded doubtful. 'She seems rather a shy girl.'

'I believe that she will feel safe, at least until she has found her feet. Once she realises that she is free of her stepmother she will probably train for some specific skill, and make a life for herself in England if she wishes.'

'Yes, dear. I'm sure you're right. You've done a good deal for the girl and she is sensible enough to make her own way in the world. She hasn't a boyfriend? Marriage would solve all her problems for her, wouldn't it?'

The doctor frowned. 'I hope that she doesn't meet some unsuitable fellow and imagine herself in love...'

His grandmother, sitting up in bed, turned a chuckle into a cough. 'She is hardly attractive enough for that, Aldrik, though I dare say a visit to the hairdresser and some new clothes will help to improve her appearance.'

'My dear—of course she must be paid. Will you decide on a suitable wage and let me know?'

'Yes, of course. Weekly, I think. I suspect that she has very little money.'

'Yes, well, I'll leave that to you.'

'Yes, dear.' She bade him goodnight and he put the receiver down. 'That's settled,' he told the dogs. 'Now I can forget about her.' Charity was bound to know of someone who would employ the girl...

He had a teaching round in the morning, private patients to see in the early afternoon and an outpatients clinic afterwards. He was pleasantly tired when he got home again; an hour at his desk and then he would drive himself and the dogs out of Leiden and walk for an hour. He opened his front door, called to his housekeeper that he was home and waited while she came to meet him. Mies was elderly, rather bony, and despite this she contrived to look cosy. She said now, 'You've had a long day—you'll be tired. There's Juffrouw van Germert waiting for you in the drawing-room—I'll bring a pot of coffee.'

He gave her a smiling reply, fending off the two dogs. He had been looking forward to a quiet evening but good manners forbade him from saying so. He went into his drawing-room with the dogs and Nicola called across the room from the chair where she was sitting. 'I thought you might like company after your busy day. All those people and so uninteresting and dull I dare say.'

She didn't get up but held up a hand. 'How about taking me to the Hague for a meal? I've had such a boring day...'

He sat down in his winged chair opposite to her. 'Tell me about it,' he invited.

'Well, that's just it, there's nothing to tell—I did some shopping and had coffee with friends and this afternoon I went to the hairdressers.'

'Perhaps if you had some kind of a job you would find the days pass more quickly?'

She opened her eyes wide. 'Work? Aldrik, I couldn't possibly. To sit in an office all day would be so boring and I'm far too sensitive to be any good at social work of any kind. Besides I don't need—' She was interrupted by the telephone ringing, and the doctor picked up the receiver.

It was Lady Merrill, telling him that she had had a splendid day, that Cressida had been a delightful companion and that they were making plans to drive around the countryside each day while the weather was fine. 'Such an industrious girl, too,' said his grandmother. 'Baxter is enchanted by her and Elsie is so relieved to have someone young to run up and down stairs when I forget something...'

The doctor laughed. 'She sounds a treasure. You think I've done the right thing! I'll see Charity and Tyco very shortly and you can sound her out about coming over here?' He put the phone down presently and turned to find Nicola looking at him intently. She smiled at once, though, and said at her most charming, 'Who is this mysterious girl and why must you talk to the van der Bronses? They live near your place in Friesland, don't they? Is she an au pair?'

Dr van der Linus sat down in his chair again. Nicola looked interested and for some reason he wanted to talk about Cressida. He told her how he had met her and the chain of events which had led him to engineer her escape from what had become an untenable life. 'She is a charming girl, no looks to speak of but beautiful eyes and a gentle voice. My grandmother is delighted with her but of course she can't stay there for long; she supposes that she is filling a gap while my grandmother's companion is on holiday. My idea was to find her a job away from that stepmother of hers where she can feel safe, save some money and decide what she wants to do. The van der Bronses know any number of people; I'm sure they could help.'

Nicola had listened without interrupting at all, her face half turned away so that he didn't see the thoughtful suspicion on it. She had been sure of him and a delightful carefree future; it only needed a small push on her part at the right moment—but now there was a tiny cloud on her horizon: this girl, this plain girl with the eyes was obviously taking more than a fair share of his thoughts and if she went to Friesland he would probably see her frequently. She thought fast.

'Aldrik,' she turned an eager sympathetic face to him, 'never mind the van der Bronses, I know the very thing for this nice girl. Tante Clotilde, remember her? Jonkvrouw van Germert— she lives in Noordwijk-aan-Zee. Near enough for you to keep on eye on her; besides there are any number of English living there and she'll quickly make friends. Tante Clotilde was only saying last week that she wanted a companion, and having an English girl would make it so much more interesting for her.'

She saw the doubt on his face. 'Can you spare the time to go with me and see her soon? There's no need to say anything about this girl until you're satisfied that she might like the job. What is her name?'

'Cressida, Cressida Preece.'

'A pretty name—Shakespeare, isn't it? I wonder why?'

'I've no idea. It might be a good idea. I'm going up to Friesland in a day or two but when I come back—in a week's time—we might visit your aunt. I should feel happier if I knew Cressida was settled somewhere where I can see her from time to time. I feel responsible for her although I am not sure why.'

Nicola allowed herself a sweet smile as she began making plans. She was a clever young woman; she didn't see Aldrik again before he went to his home, but once he had gone she got into her sports car and roared the short distance to Noordwijk-aan-Zee and spent an hour with her aunt...

The doctor drove himself and the dogs north. It was a cold evening and already getting dark and there was little to see of the country through which he travelled, only the dim outline of farms with their great barns attached to them and the gleam of the water from time to time. He had gone over the Afsluitdijk and taken the road towards Leeuwarden, turned north again before he reached the town and joined the road to Dokkum, to turn off again, this time on to a narrow brick road which led him at length to a small village, seven or eight miles from the Waddenzee: a cluster of small houses, a large, austere church and a small school building, all shrouded in darkness, and half a mile beyond the wrought-iron gates which were the entrance to his home.

Wester was waiting for him, a stoutly built, very tall man with a rugged face and blond hair with a heavy sprinkling of grey. He had the door of the house open before the doctor reached it and the two men shook hands. Wester was the best part of ten years older than the doctor and they had known each other since boyhood; Wester's father had been house steward to the doctor's father and when his own father had died he had stepped into his shoes, and since he had married the doctor's cook some five years previously and had two sons it stood to reason that when their time came one or other of them would take over from his father, an arrangement which was satisfactory to everyone concerned.

They stood in the open doorway for a few minutes while the dogs roamed free and the doctor slipped naturally into the language of his youth and spoke Fries, looking around him at the large hall beyond the vestibule where the portraits of his ancestors hung on its white walls, and the wide staircase swept up to the gallery above his head. It was good to be home, he reflected, and the unbidden thought that Cressida would like it crossed his mind. She would like the house in Leiden too, he conceded, small compared with this but charming and old and splendidly furnished. He frowned, whistled to the dogs and went inside while Wester fetched his case from the car and then drove it round to the garage at the back of the house.

He was halfway across the hall when Tyske, Wester's wife, came through the door at the back of the hall to meet him. She was a tall strongly built woman with mild blue eyes and a wide smile, and she broke into speech when she saw him; it was a delight to have him home again and there was a splendid supper waiting for him, he had only to say...

He flung a great arm round her shoulders and lapsed into Fries once more, asking her about the children and whether the cat and the pet rabbits were well, and presently he crossed the hall to his drawing-room, a vast room with a lofty ceiling and tall wide windows draped in russet velvet. There was a stone fireplace, hooded, at one end of the room and some magnificent bow-fronted display cabinets filled with pretty porcelain and silver. The chairs and sofas were large and comfortable, there were lamp tables and a vast rent table between the windows and amber shaded lamps. A log fire burned brightly and the lamplight cast shadows on the silk-panelled walls hung with more portraits and landscapes. The doctor stood a moment, enjoying the room, and then went to sit by the fire; this was his home, he had been born there and lived in it as a boy and although he traveled a good deal nowadays he came back to it with content.

It was a large house and very old, with its steepled roof and odd little towers, rows of small windows under the tiles and chimneys, too large for a man to live in alone, but his father had died within the last few years and his mother was on a long visit to one of his sisters in France, and when she returned, she had told him, if he were to marry, she would prefer to live in the house at Dokkum which she had inherited from her father. 'I hope you will marry soon, my dear,' she had told him. He had smiled and said that at the moment he had no wish to marry; his work took him to major hospitals in his own country as well as in Europe and beyond, true, he was a lecturer at Leiden Medical School and had a number of beds at the hospital, he lectured in Groningen too and he had beds at Leeuwarden, but he went frequently to England for consultations, and, indeed, had travelled on various occasions to America, the Far East and Russia; none the less most of his work was in Holland, a small enough country for him to live, if he wished, here, in his house, and travel with ease to Leiden, Amsterdam and den Haag.

He was summoned presently by Wester and crossed the hall to have his supper in the small room he used as a dining-room unless he had guests. It was cosy, with an old-fashioned stove, a round table and a small sideboard, lighted by wall sconces. He ate an excellent meal, a dog on either side of him, and then went to his study, a room at the back of the house overlooking the gardens, bare now at the approach of winter, merging into the polder land beyond. Here he settled down to work, preparing for a series of lectures that he was to give in Groningen and checking his appointments in Leeuwarden. It was late when he went upstairs to bed and the house was very quiet, the dogs, coming in from a last run in the grounds, settled down in their baskets in the warm kitchen. Wester and Tyske had long since gone to bed and the wind sighed in the trees and when he opened his window the air was crisp and very cold. Winter could be hard in Friesland but the doctor liked it that way. He slept the sleep of a tired man without thinking once of Nicola. He did, however, dream of Cressida.

Cressida didn't dream of him, but she did think of him quite a lot. She had settled down very nicely to her duties, none of them heavy—most of them weren't duties, anyway; she didn't consider that taking the dogs for a walk was a duty, and since she shared Lady Merrill's taste in literature reading out loud was a pleasure. Here were all the books she had never had the time to read during the last two years and in variety. Lady Merrill's taste was catholic; Cressida read Trollope, P.D. James, Alastair Maclean and then large chunks of John Donne, Herrick and Keats and then back to romance—Mary Stewart, and odd chapters of *Jane Eyre* interlarded with books on antiques, about which Lady Merrill knew a great deal, and when these palled Cressida was bidden to fetch the heavy leather-covered albums filled with photos of Lady Merrill's youth.

They talked too, long conversations about clothes, the theatre and how to put the world to rights, but none of their talks revealed anything of Lady Merrill's own family and Cressida was too polite to ask.

She hadn't been so happy for a long time; her days were nicely filled, she was being useful but she wasn't being browbeaten, meals were delicious and Baxter and the rest of the staff were kind. She lost her thinness after the first week and her cheeks were delicately pink. In her purse she had a week's wages as well as the hundred pounds and in response to Lady Merrill's delicate hints she took herself off to Yeovil and bought a tweed skirt, a couple of blouses and a pretty woollen jumper and, since she had become sensitive about the only decent dress she owned and which she donned each evening to compliment Lady Merrill's dark silks and velvets, she went to Laura Ashley and bought a dark red velvet dress, long-sleeved and simple but suitable for the dinner table. She spent rather more than she had meant to but she consoled herself with the thought that when she left Lady Merrill's she would have the nucleus of a suitable wardrobe for the kind of job she could do. She suspected that not all companion's jobs would be as pleasant as this one, but she would have a roof over her head and money in her pocket.

Studying her much improved reflection in her bedroom looking-glass, Cressida allowed herself to think about Dr van der Linus. It was a pity that he couldn't see her now in the red dress. The suspicion that he had pitied her rankled rather; she would have liked to show him that she wasn't normally a wispy creature with a sprained ankle...

Which wasn't how Lady Merrill described her a few nights later, sitting up in bed, chatting with the doctor on the phone. 'Of course I'm not asleep, dear,' she protested, 'you know that I never sleep so early in the night. You want to know about Cressida?' She rearranged her bedjacket and smiled to herself. 'Yes, I quite understand that you still feel responsible for her. She is well and, I believe, happy. She is a delightful companion and such a help to us all. She seemed to me to be a plain girl but she has improved in looks during these last few days. A good thing; she has a far better chance of finding employment now that she has a little colour in her cheeks and is putting on weight. It is surprising what good food does for one.'

'I'm grateful to you, Grandmother, and I hope you will shortly be able to go back to your usual way of life. I mentioned her to Nicola and she tells me that she knows just the person to employ Cressida. An aunt of hers, lives at Noordwijk-aan-Zee and needs a companion. She sounds just what is needed and so much more satisfactory if she is someone who is known to Nicola. You don't think that I am interfering with Cressida's future? I should like to think that she had a good job...'

'Well, Aldrik, the alternative is to cast the girl loose into the world to find her own way. She might be lucky; on the other hand she might not. At least we shall know where she is.' Lady Merrill frowned thoughtfully. 'This aunt, have you met her?'

'Not yet, but I shall go and see her with Nicola when I get back to Leiden. I've a clinic there next week.'

'You will write and let her know?'

'No. I fancy that if she knew what we have contrived she might well refuse. How about getting hold of Mrs Sefton again?'

'A good idea—mutual friends in Holland and so on. That should do very well. Let me know your plans in good time. You're happy at Janslum?'

'Yes, Grandmother. I've been at Groningen all day; tomorrow I shall be in Leeuwarden and plan to go back to Leiden at the end of the week.'

'When will you be over here again?'

'There's a seminar in a month's time—I shall see you then.'

She said goodnight and lay back on her pillows, her elderly mind busy. Somehow she didn't like the sound of Nicola's aunt, but there was nothing much she could do about that; perhaps she was misjudging Nicola, a young woman she didn't like and who, as far as she knew, had never put herself out to do anyone a kindness unless it was of benefit to herself.

Lady Merrill lay and thought about that until at last she went to sleep.

CHAPTER FOUR

OCTOBER HAD SLIPPED into November, bringing colder weather and dark evenings. Lady Merrill was content to sit indoors or walk, well wrapped up, in the grounds of the house. It was Cressida who took the dogs for their walk each morning and evening, bundled in her old mac and wearing a scarf over her mousy locks. She enjoyed these walks, her head full of plans, mostly about clothes and, rather worriedly, about her future. Lady Merrill hadn't told her how long she was to stay and when she mentioned the companion to anyone they were vague as to when she would return. Surely she would be given a week's notice at least? she thought. All the same, given the day off, she took herself to Yeovil, purchased a copy of the *Lady* magazine and studied the adverts. There was no lack of urgent requests for mother's helps and nannies and a fair sprinkling of appeals for kind persons to cope with old ladies, old gentlemen or the housework. It shouldn't be too difficult to find another job. She marked the most promising of these over a cup of coffee and a bun and took herself off to the shops. She had another week's wages in her purse, to be laid out with care; shoes—she couldn't afford boots—and undies. She still had the hundred pounds intact so that next week's wages could be spent on another sweater, gloves and a handbag. Thus equipped, she felt, she would pass muster for a start, gradually gathering together a suitable wardrobe. When her father had been alive, she had bought nice clothes, for he had been generous to her, but now they had seen their best days although her coat was well cut and of good quality and was good for another winter or so.

She went back to Lady Merrill, well pleased with her modest prudent purchases, ate dinner in the old lady's company and spent an hour allowing her to win a game of cribbage before Elsie came to help her to bed.

'I shall miss you,' declared the old lady as Cressida wished her goodnight.

'I shall miss you too, Lady Merrill, but you'll have your companion back again and I'm sure you will be glad to see her once more.'

Lady Merrill looked vague. 'Yes, yes, I suppose I shall.' She trotted off on the faithful Elsie's arm and Cressida, with nothing better to do, went to her room and tried on the new shoes.

Once in her bed, nicely propped up with pillows and the necessities for the night on the bedside table, Lady Merrill picked up the telephone. It was barely ten o'clock and high time that she had a chat with Audrey Sefton. A night-bird herself, the old lady had no compunction about rousing such of her friends with whom she wished to gossip; fortunately Mrs Sefton hadn't gone to bed and listened with growing interest to what Lady Merrill had to say.

'But my dear, I don't know this woman...'

'Well, of course you don't,' said Lady Merrill testily, 'But if Aldrik says she's all right then that's all that matters. The thing is to let Cressida think that it is a job that someone you know, however vaguely, happened to have heard about—mutual friends and so on. Go on, Audrey, Aldrik is anxious to get the girl settled.'

'Yes, but why in Holland?'

'He won't lose touch...' Lady Merrill chuckled and heard her friend draw a breath.

'You don't mean...?'

'I don't mean anything. Will you do it?'

'Very well, although I dislike subterfuge as you very well know.'

'There is a very good reason. I'll let you know what Aldrik says. Goodnight, Audrey, and thank you.'

The old lady settled back into her pillows, well pleased with herself.

It was the best part of a week before the doctor returned to Leiden and had the leisure to visit Nicola's aunt. It was a cold grey afternoon when he picked her up from her parents' house in den Haag and drove up the coast to Noordwijk-aan-Zee, and the house, when they reached it, looked as bleak as the day, wilting rapidly into an even colder evening. It was a fair-sized villa, built some fifty years previously; red-brick and a great deal of fancy stonework, and surrounded by a garden, meticulously neat, bordered by shrubs and empty flowerbeds. The doctor found it dispiriting.

Jonkvrouw van Germert received them graciously, offered weak milkless tea and minuscule biscuits and assured them that she was delighted to see them. 'I lead a secluded life,' she observed, 'and at times I am lonely.'

Nicola sipped her tea, with every appearance of enjoyment. 'Tante Clotilde,' she began hesitantly, 'you say you're lonely. I suppose you wouldn't consider having a companion?'

Her aunt looked surprised. She did it very well, having rehearsed the whole conversation with Nicola. 'A companion?' She tittered. 'Am I quite old enough for that, Nicola? I don't need anyone to pick up my dropped stitches or read aloud; my eyes are still good.'

Nicola laughed gently. 'I didn't mean that kind of companion, Tante, but someone to accompany you on walks and drive the car, an intelligent woman who can listen as well as talk—in fact, someone to be in this house with you.' She added lightly, 'You told me yourself that you were considering it.'

Jonkvrouw van Germert appeared to think. 'I must say that put like that it sounds attractive, especially during the winter months. But why do you ask, Nicola?'

The doctor hadn't spoken. Now he said, 'I know of an English girl who is anxious to find a pleasant situation. She is at present with my grandmother, who is very pleased with her. She doesn't speak Dutch, of course, but that might be of added interest to you. She is, for lack of a better word, that old-fashioned thing, a lady, intelligent, and, from what my grandmother tells me—and she usually knows—a very kind and considerate girl.'

'Surely she would prefer to stay in her own country?'

'She has few friends and no immediate family. Aldrik thinks that it might benefit her to have a change of scene. However, I won't bother you further, Tante; Aldrik has any number of friends, he can ask around...'

Her aunt appeared to consider. 'I must say that the idea appeals to me. Not permanently, of course, but for the winter months, and by then this girl may find employment which is more suitable or start to train for something. I'd like to think about it.' She gave the doctor a gracious smile. 'I'll let you know within the next day or so.'

'I'm sure Tante Clotilde will decide to employ this girl,' said Nicola as they drove back to den Haag, 'and if she doesn't you can still ask the van der Bronses to look around. I hear Charity is expecting a child.'

'In a couple of months. They're delighted.' They began to talk of other things until he dropped her off at her home, refusing to go in with her with the plea of work to be done and a late visit to an ill patient in the hospital.

Nicola pecked his cheek—she disliked what she called 'demonstrative behaviour'—and he got into his car again and drove back to Leiden, dismissing her from his thoughts. He felt uneasy; Jonkvrouw van Germert was the answer to his scheme, and yet he wasn't satisfied. He didn't like her, although there had been no reason for his dislike. Her home was hideous, he considered, over-furnished and yet uncomfortable; on the other hand the surroundings were pleasant and he would be near enough to make sure that Cressida was happy. If she wasn't it would be easy enough to find something else. Of course she might refuse to leave England, but he thought it unlikely; she had had no experience at finding work and she had little money. There was no need for him to worry; he parked the car at the hospital and went to see his patient.

Although he told himself time and again that his interest in Cressida was purely derived from a wish to see someone unfortunate made happy, he might have felt the need to worry if he had overheard the conversation Nicola had with her aunt over the phone.

It was a couple of days later when Lady Merrill said suddenly in the middle of lunch. 'My—er—my companion will be returning in a week, Cressida, and I have been giving the matter some thought. Have you any plans?'

Cressida put her fork carefully down on the plate. 'No—no, I haven't, Lady Merrill, but I have no doubt that I shall be able to find something.'

Cressida cast around in her head. There was an aunt of her mother's living somewhere in Cumbria whom she had never seen, two cousins in Canada and another cousin in the States, all much older than she. 'Well, I'm sure I can find a room,' she began, 'just for a little while, you know.'

'Mrs Sefton—you know her, of course—telephoned me yesterday and asked after you, and, when I mentioned that you would be leaving shortly, wanted to know if you were interested in a job in Holland as companion to a lady living on her own. Middle-aged, I believe and speaks fluent English. She lives very comfortably by the sea. Not a permanent position but for the winter months.'

'Does Mrs Sefton know this lady?'

'No, but she knows an acquaintance of hers who mentioned it in a letter.' Lady Merrill smiled encouragingly. 'It might be better to go to someone already known rather than to a complete stranger.'

That made sense, reflected Cressida; besides, it would be nice to go abroad—and Dr van der Linus lived there. She had her passport too.

Lady Merrill watched the tell-tale expressions drift across Cressida's face; she wasn't going to say any more, she had already been involved in Aldrik's plans and told far too many fibs as well as inventing a mythical companion, but she hoped that Cressida would go to Holland because that was what he wanted, although she was sure that he didn't know why he wanted it. She could be wrong about that. She wasn't quite happy about this woman being an aunt of Nicola's; on the other hand Aldrik would be able to see Cressida from time to time and for the present she was content with that; besides, he had seen this woman and approved of her.

Cressida had made up her mind. 'I think I'd like to take this job. It will be a change to see another country. Does this lady wish me to write to her?'

'That would be a good idea. I'll get the address from Mrs Sefton.'

So Cressida wrote a brief polite letter and received one by return of post, couched in pleasant terms and offering a wage which was ample for her needs. She was expected in a week's time and directions as to how she was to get there were added. Very satisfactory, thought Cressida, suppressing a feeling of uneasiness which she couldn't account for. It had all been so easy, but she brushed the doubt aside; she was in no position to look a gift horse in the mouth.

She went to Yeovil once more on a free afternoon and added to her wardrobe a plain jersey dress in grey which she hoped would pass muster for more formal occasions, a pair of court shoes, going cheap in a closing-down sale, and another sweater.

She had, she considered, an adequate wardrobe which she proceeded to pack in her two cases which Elsie had taken away and dusted and polished for her. The last day came and she got out of bed feeling sad and rather reluctant to go. She had been happy with Lady Merrill and the entire household had been kind and friendly. She hoped that Jonkvrouw van Germert would be as kind.

'I shall miss you, child,' observed Lady Merrill. 'I hope you will be happy in Holland—write to me, won't you?' She offered an elderly cheek for Cressida's kiss. Baxter and Elsie bade her a reluctant goodbye too as they saw her into the car which was to take her to Yeovil and the train to London. Her travelling expenses had been sent, although there had been no allowance made for taxis or meals on the way. She was to travel to Harwich and take the night ferry to the Hoek. It seemed to her a needlessly round-about journey, especially as she had to cross London, but she had her instructions and presumably was expected to keep to them. At the Hoek she was to catch a train to den Haag and change again to a local train to Noordwijk-aan-Zee where she was to take a taxi to Jonkvrouw van Germert's house. In the train speeding up to Waterloo, she read the instructions once again and then settled down to watch the scenery, wondering when she would see it again. Probably in the spring, she reminded herself, for it had been made clear that she was to be employed only for the winter months. She wondered briefly about her stepmother, who hadn't replied to her letters, but she had had long letters from Moggy, happily settled with her sister and reiterating her offer to Cressida of a place to stay if ever she should need one. It was a comforting thought.

Cressida had travelled in Europe with her father before he remarried; France, Italy and Greece, and always in comfort, so that she was unprepared for the inside cabin she was to share with three other women on the ferry, and since she had to be careful of her money she made do with coffee and a ham roll before she climbed into her bunk. The three other occupants were older women, one of whom snored. She had a wakeful night and got up as early as she dared, washed and dressed by the aid of one small light and went on deck. It had been a rough crossing and the wind was blowing but after the stuffiness of the cabin she was glad of the fresh air. They were very near the Hoek now; she went and got herself a cup of tea and a roll and collected her luggage.

There weren't a great many passengers, she was quickly through Customs and the train was waiting in the station. It was a short journey to den Haag but she wasted a good deal of time looking for the right platform, unable to hurry with her two cases, and it was with relief that she settled in the train for Noordwijk-aan-Zee. Much revived by a cup of coffee, she watched the scenery until the ticket collector came round, pointing out in good English that the train didn't go to the little town but to the larger Noordwijk inland. 'You can get a taxi from the station,' he told her cheerfully. 'It is two kilometres, no distance.'

Which she was glad to discover was true; what was more, the taxi driver understood English and knew where Jonkvrouw van Germert lived. He drove through the wide aged gate up to the front door, got out and put her cases on the step, accepted his fare and a tip, wished her a happy stay and drove away as she rang the bell.

The door was opened by a cross-looking woman who stared at her without speaking but when Cressida uttered her mistress's name she stood back while Cressida, lugging her suitcases, went into the hall, then she walked away to disappear through a door on one side of the hall.

A gloomy place, thought Cressida, but obviously a well-to-do household if the heavy side-table and side-chairs, the thick carpet and the elaborate chandelier were anything to go by.

The girl came back, said, '*Kom mee*,' and led the way back across the hall and opened a door for Cressida to go through. The room she entered was as gloomy as the hall, rich brown and terracotta with a great deal of dark furniture. There was a fire opposite the door and a woman sitting in the chair drawn up to it.

'Come in, then—Miss Preece, isn't it? How do you do?'

Cressida crossed to the chair and offered a hand. 'Jonkvrouw van Germert?'

'Yes.'

Her hand was shaken after a moment's hesitation. 'Well, Corrie had better show you your room—lunch is at half-past twelve and we can talk then.'

She frowned slightly. 'You are very slight—I hope you are strong?'

'Oh, yes.' Cressida eyed her companion, a stout florid lady, very fashionably dressed, and wondered why she needed to be strong.

'Well, find Corrie and get unpacked; you have almost an hour.'

So Cressida went back into the hall and found Corrie standing at the front of the stairs. They each took a case and climbed to the square landing, where Corrie opened a door at the end of a narrow passage. The room looked over the garden at the back of the house and that was the best part about it. It was a small room, adequately furnished and cold, and there was a bathroom next to it. Left to herself, Cressida poked her nose into cupboards and drawers, tried the bed and looked out of the window. Of course, she told herself, it was a grey day; when the sun shone the room would look much nicer and once she had settled in she would have a vase of flowers and perhaps a small table lamp by the bed. She had some photos of her mother and father and her home—the place would soon be more cheerful, it was only that after the comfort of her room at Lady Merrill's house this one seemed a little bare.

She unpacked quickly, did her face and hair, and, mindful of the time, went back downstairs.

Over lunch Jonkvrouw van Germert outlined Cressida's duties, which were rather different from those at Lady Merrill's. She was to keep her own room clean and of course make her bed, water the many plants and arrange the flowers, wash the porcelain in the display cabinets in the drawing-room, answer the phone if the maid was out or busy, make sure that the daily cleaning woman had done her work properly and make herself useful as and when necessary.

'And my free day?' asked Cressida.

'A free day? Oh, do you expect that? But you will be living here in comfort with me, and I have no free day.'

Jonkvrouw van Germert saw the look on Cressida's face and made haste to change her tactics. It would never do for the girl to leave after dear Nicola had planned everything so carefully. 'Well, let me see, I go to the Bridge club on Wednesdays; supposing you consider yourself free to go out from 10 o'clock in the morning until seven o'clock in the evening?'

It seemed there was to be no question of an hour or two off each day and perhaps it would be sensible to wait for a few days before suggesting it. Cressida agreed, and then asked in her sensible way, 'And my salary? Is that to be paid weekly or monthly?'

'Oh, monthly. Now that we have decided on these tiresome details will you be good enough to come upstairs with me? I rest for an hour after lunch and you may read to me. My English is good,' said Jonkvrouw van Germert with a lamentable lack of modesty, 'but you will read slowly; if I do not understand a passage you will explain it to me.'

It had been a long day, thought Cressida, getting ready for bed that night and jumping into her bed, thankful for the hot-water bottle which Corrie had surprisingly found and filled for her. She wasn't as cross as she looked—probably she was tired, for there was certainly enough for her to do. The house wasn't over large but it was full of furniture and knick-knacks and the floors were polished wood. There was a cook; Cressida had been sent to the kitchen to fetch a fresh pot of coffee and had seen her there. She had offered a hand and the surprised woman had shaken it, giving her an unfriendly glance and muttering something in Dutch. Not a cheerful household, reflected Cressida, curling her small person around the warmth of the bottle; probably they had thought her coming would make more work for them but judging from the list of tasks she was expected to get through each day she might turn out to be a help.

She was disappointed, but that, she told herself firmly, was because Lady Merrill had been exceptionally kind. She would doubtless have her ups and downs but she had a roof over her head, quite a good salary and a chance to save some of it. Just before she dropped off she thought that she might, by some miracle, meet Dr van der Linus again, then she slept.

Her days, she discovered, were fully occupied—making herself useful covered a multitude of odd jobs as well as being Jonkvrouw van Germert's companion and at her beck and call— but she had the odd half-hour to herself from time to time when visitors called. She had arrived on a Thursday so that she had to wait a week for her free day and when it came at last it brought cold rain and a bitter wind. Not that Cressida minded that; she tidied her room, ate her breakfast, went to Jonkvrouw van Germert's room to bid her good morning and was told in a chilly voice to be sure and be back by seven o'clock, and then she ran down to the kitchen. Her Dutch was fragmental but she managed, '*Boodschappen*?' which she had learned meant shopping, and pointed at Corrie and the cook in turn.

They stared at her for a moment and then smiled and nodded, and she waited while they wrote what they wanted on a bit of paper.

'*Geld*?' asked Corrie.

She smiled again at once when Cressida said, '*Straks*,' which was a useful word she had made haste to learn since it meant later, presently or even not now.

The bus service was good though not so frequent in the winter months; all the same it took her swiftly to Leiden, where,

Jonkvrouw van Germert had told her in one of the more expansive moments, there was a good deal to see and even some nice shops. She had added, 'And if you want the cheaper places, there is Hema, rather like your Woolworths, I believe...' A remark which had annoyed Cressida very much.

In Leiden she went straight to the tourist office to get a map of the town and all the information she could find, and, thus armed, set out to enjoy herself. She had had to admit to herself within the first few days of living at the villa that she wasn't very happy there; Jonkvrouw van Germert didn't like her. Not that she had ever said so but her indifference was plain to see and she treated Cressida with a kind of long-suffering politeness which was hard to bear. Almost as though she didn't want a companion and certainly not me, Cressida had thought. What she really needed was another maid in the house; Corrie was overworked and the woman who came in to clean had no time to do more than polish the floors and clean the kitchen, and she herself discovered that she was expected to make beds, dust and occasionally set the table for meals. It was a job, she told herself stoutly, and it enabled her to see something of another country, and having a day off to herself once a week was something to look forward to.

She followed one of the leaflet's instructions and spent an hour or more at the Lakenhal before going in search of coffee. From the café she found her way to Breestraat running through the heart of the oldest part of the city, bent on viewing the old fortification, the Burcht, and that done she made her way to the Korenbeursbrug to enjoy the views her leaflet urged her to see. She looked her fill, and then, bent on seeing the Sint Pieterskerk, walked back towards Breestraat. It was as she was waiting to cross the street that she saw Dr van der Linus on the opposite pavement. She stood quite still, jostled by impatient people wishing to cross the street and finding her in the way. She was unaware of them, wholly taken up with the delight of seeing him again. He had crossed the street before she had decided what to do. His, 'Cressida, what a delightful surprise,' was uttered with just the right air of unexpectedness; he had been in France for two weeks and had returned several days before he was expected, and although he had planned to call on Nicola's aunt in order to make sure that Cressida had settled down nicely he had not expected to see her in Leiden. He took her hand and smiled kindly at her. 'You look well...'

'I've a job here, companion to a lady who lives in Noordwijk-aan-Zee.'

'You're happy? You don't find it strange?' He gave her a sharp glance. 'This lady is kind to you?'

It would have been a relief to tell him that she wasn't happy and that everything was strange and the lady was rather less than kind, but that would never do. She said in her quiet way, 'It is a little strange but everyone, or almost everyone, speaks English. I've only been here for a week. Noordwijk-aan-Zee is very attractive; I dare say it's very busy in the summer.'

He frowned a little, watching her face, sure that she would have liked to have said more but wasn't going to. It was a pity that he was on his way to the hospital and already late. 'It would have been nice to have had lunch together,' he told her, 'but I am late already. Let me have your address...'

She gave it to him and added, 'But please don't come and see me, I'm not sure if Jonkvrouw van Germert would like that.'

'Oh, why is that?'

'You're going to be very late for your appointment,' said Cressida. 'I dare say we shall meet again when there's more time.'

He took her hand in his. 'Indeed we will, I don't intend to lose sight of you.'

She watched him stride away, going towards the Rapenburg Canal and the medical school and she went on her way to the church. It was vast and empty and she perched on a solitary chair the better to think. It had been wonderful seeing the doctor again and surprising too. She had thought that he lived in Friesland but apparently he came to Leiden, she presumed to the hospital, and it wasn't very likely that she would see him again for some time. Even if she came to Leiden each week on her day off the chances of meeting him there were remote, but all the same she was aware of a warm, comforting glow at the thought that he had remembered her and stopped to talk even though it had been obvious to her that he was in a tearing hurry.

The church was cold; she walked back to Breestraat and had a cheese roll and coffee in a little café and went to look at the shops. She wasn't to be paid until the end of the month so her purchases were small and necessary but with Christmas approaching the shops had plenty in their windows. She spent a happy hour wandering from one to the other, deciding what she would buy at the end of the month, then had tea and a mouth-watering mountain of a cream cake before catching the bus back. She had enjoyed her day and as she stood on the step waiting for Corrie to open the door she reflected that perhaps she had been over-hasty in her first impression of Jonkvrouw van Germert; after all, they had to get to know each other. She went straight to the kitchen and handed over the purchases she had made for Corrie and the cook and then hurried to her room to tidy herself for the evening. Her employer changed each evening; Cressida got into the grey dress which would have to be worn until she had her wages and she could buy a second one. Perhaps if she went to the Hague on one of her free days she would find something to suit her pocket.

Jonkvrouw van Germert was in the drawing-room, wearing an elaborate dress and a good deal of gold jewellery. 'Oh, you're back,' she observed as Cressida went in. 'I shall be out for dinner—the car will be here at any minute now. I have told Cook that you can have your supper in the kitchen with her and Corrie—it will save them work. I shall want you to drive me into den Haag in the morning. I am going to the hairdresser.'

'I only have my English licence with me,' said Cressida.

Jonkvrouw van Germert didn't bother to answer her. 'I shall want to leave at nine o'clock.' She got up. 'I hear the car.'

Cressida remembered her manners and wished her goodnight.

It was a pity that she didn't know more about being a companion—she wasn't sure if eating in the kitchen was one of the drawbacks but since she was hungry there wasn't much she could do about it. When her employer was in a better mood it might be possible to bring the subject up. Summoned by Corrie presently, she joined her and Cook at the kitchen table to find that they were as uneasy about the situation as she was. The food, though, was good and they both did their best to talk to her, indeed by the end of the meal the conversation, with the help of gestures and guesswork, was quite animated. Her offer to help clear the table was refused and Corrie pointed to the ceiling. 'Not good here,' she managed. 'You above.'

'Oh, Corrie, what a kind thing to say,' said Cressida warmly, and although they hadn't understood her words the meaning was clear. They both smiled widely and wished her, '*Wel te rusten.*'

She had two friends, she thought as she climbed into bed.

Dr van der Linus, his work finished at the hospital, let himself into his house in Leiden, to be greeted by Mies and the dogs and go to sit in his pleasant drawing-room. He had stayed longer at the hospital than he had expected and his plan to drive to den Haag and see Nicola no longer held any attraction for him, and in any case she wasn't expecting him back for another two days. Sitting by the fire, a drink in his hand and the dogs at his feet, he thought about Cressida. He had dissembled well enough; she plainly had no idea that he already knew where she was and had in fact arranged for her to be there in the first place. He would go and see her as soon as he had time to spare. She had looked not exactly sad when he had seen her across the street but certainly not happy, although when she had seen him her whole face had lit up. He would find out when next he saw her. He ate the delicious dinner Mies set before him and spent the rest of the evening in his study. He had a busy day ahead of him; Outpatients, a ward-round, private patients to see... He dismissed Cressida from his mind.

He had a few hours free on the afternoon following; just time enough to go and see Cressida. He supposed that he should take Nicola with him, and after lunch drove to den Haag. She greeted him with a surprise which concealed vexation. 'Aldrik—you weren't coming back until tomorrow.'

'I came back two days ago,' he told her, 'but I've been busier than usual. I'm free for a couple of hours, so I thought we might go to your aunt's and see how Miss Preece is getting on.'

Nicola answered too quickly. 'Oh, must we? Couldn't we go for a drive? She won't be expecting us...'

He gave her a thoughtful look. 'Well, it is a drive to Noordwijk-aan-Zee, albeit a short one, and there's no need to stand on ceremony.' He picked up a coat she had tossed down on a chair. 'Put this on and we'll go—I haven't all that much time to spare.'

He was a quiet man and calm but she knew that he had an inflexible will. There was no point in annoying him, besides she wasn't sure of him yet...

She hoped that Tante Clotilde would put on a show of treating the wretched English girl as though she were a treasured member of the household. A pity she hadn't had the time to telephone; if only her coat hadn't been lying there handy... It was no good worrying. She laid herself out to be charming, asking questions about his trip to France and pretending to be interested in the answers.

Corrie admitted them and showed them at once into the drawing-room where Jonkvrouw van Germert was lying on a sofa, leafing through a magazine. Taken unawares, she threw a look which boded no good to Corrie and got to her feet, her face wreathed in a hasty smile.

'Nicola, dear, how delightful, and Aldrik. Forgive me, but I was having a brief rest. This is quite a large house you know and there is more than enough for the servants to do—I help out when I can but I'm not strong and get quickly exhausted.'

A piece of nonsense which caused the doctor to lift his eyebrows a fraction. 'Surely Miss Preece is able to take the less important chores off your hands?' he asked mildly.

'Oh, of course,' gushed his hostess, 'such a good girl and so willing. Of course you would like to see her. Corrie shall fetch her for you.'

She tugged the bell rope by the fireplace and when Corrie came told her to fetch Miss Preece.

Corrie, who intended to stay in the house only until such time as she could find a better job, saw a chance to get some of her own back—she had broken a jug that morning and Jonkvrouw van Germert had told her its value would be taken out of her wages, which weren't generous to begin with.

'Certainly, *Mevrouw*, but you'll have to wait a while. Miss Preece is in the middle of turning out the pantry as you told her to.'

Jonkvrouw van Germert went puce and drew such a deep breath that her corsets creaked. 'Very well, but ask her to come as soon as she can.'

She turned to the doctor, standing by the window, looking out at the wintry garden. 'Such a dear girl, always suggesting ways to help. Quite invaluable in the house.'

He made a most non-committal reply and watched his companions' unease from under his lids, and, when Nicola began an animated conversation, joined in quite pleasantly.

It was ten minutes before Cressida joined them and Jonkvrouw van Germert said at once, 'Ah, there you are, my dear. I want you to meet my visitors—my niece, Nicola van Germert and Dr van der Linus.'

Cressida had gone faintly pink at the sight of the doctor and then pale but she shook Nicola's hand and murmured politely before offering a hand to him. He took it in his and said blandly. 'Oh, but Cressida and I know each other—we met several times in England and saw each other briefly in Leiden a couple of days ago.' He was aware of Nicola and her aunt exchanging glances and went on, 'I do hope you have settled down, Cressida, and are enjoying yourself.'

He was still holding her hand in his, aware that it was red and rough; the pantry was probably only one of the chores he suspected she was expected to undertake. 'You're happy?' he asked in a voice which expected an answer.

She said in a pleasant polite little voice, 'Yes, thank you, Doctor,' and withdrew her hand gently, giving him only the briefest of glances.

'Well, I'm sure she should be,' said Jonkvrouw van Germert in a rather too loud a voice. 'It isn't every girl who has a good job found for her. I hope you've thanked the doctor, Miss Preece, for it was he who asked me to employ you, you know; he knew that his grandmother could only have you for a few weeks—she took you in out of the kindness of her heart, isn't that so, Aldrik?'

The doctor remained perfectly calm; only his eyes gleamed under their lids. He said evenly, 'That is so, but one must also add that Cressida filled a much needed want with my Grandmother, just as I trust that she is doing here.'

Cressida's cheeks were a shade paler. 'I didn't know. I thought that Mrs Sefton... I'm very grateful to you, Doctor.'

Rage and humiliation sent the colour flying into her face, and her eyes flashed with temper. At that moment she hated everyone in the room, especially the doctor. She said clearly, 'And now, if you will excuse me, I'll go back and finish scrubbing out the pantry.'

Her exit, considering that she was a small, unassuming girl, was magnificently dignified.

CHAPTER FIVE

CRESSIDA CLOSED THE door with a deliberate quietness far more effective than a good slam, and the doctor's firm mouth twitched. He said suavely, 'I see that I have been at fault. Quite unwittingly I must have given you the impression that Cressida was a domestic worker, Jonkvrouw van Germert.' He glanced at Nicola. 'Did you think that, Nicola?'

'Oh, I really don't remember what you said. And anyway, why all the fuss? The girl's got a good home here and I'm sure Tante Clotilde is most considerate towards her. After all, she has to earn her living—one job must be as good as another.' She shrugged elegant shoulders. 'And there's no need to make a fuss about cleaning a pantry, surely...?'

'Have you ever cleaned a pantry?' enquired the doctor gently.

She made haste to change her tactics. 'No, you know I haven't, Aldrik, and I'm sorry if I'm being unkind. I'll come tomorrow and have a talk to her, shall I? And perhaps Tante Clotilde and I can rearrange her duties.' She added in a sympathetic voice, 'Of course the poor girl was upset, but I'm sure I can try to put things right. Will you leave it to me?' She smiled coaxingly. 'Women are so much better at that sort of thing than men.'

The doctor hesitated and then agreed. Nicola was right, of course; she would be able to smooth things over far better than he could, for one thing she could talk to her aunt with a good deal more frankness than he could, and, since Jonkvrouw van Germert expressed her concern and agreed that Cressida's duties should be considerably altered, he left with Nicola shortly afterwards. There was no sign of Cressida and on the whole he thought it best not to see her until things had been changed and she had settled down. All the same, he still neither liked nor completely trusted Jonkvrouw van Germert.

It was a matter he was forced to dismiss once he returned to the hospital, and, since he didn't get home until much later that evening, the remaining hours of which were taken up with walking the dogs, eating a delayed dinner and then dictating letters and notes into his Dictaphone until well after midnight, he shelved the problem until he had the leisure to solve it to his liking.

Nicola, on the other hand, had the leisure to review the situation thoroughly. It had been most unfortunate that Aldrik had returned home several days ahead of the expected date, and, worse, had met Cressida. The girl couldn't have complained to him, since he had said nothing, and he had been angry when her aunt had told Cressida that it was he who had arranged the job for her on the first instance. Nicola frowned; any other man would have lost his temper or at least demanded to know why the girl was being treated like a servant, but Aldrik had exhibited no sign of annoyance. She had known him for some time now and long since decided that she would marry him—he had a splendid home, more than enough money, and was already a name to be reckoned with in the medical profession. She didn't love him, but he was handsome, had beautiful manners and many friends. She had never known him to show anger but now she wasn't sure... Presently she reached for the phone and dialled her aunt's number.

The pantry had never been so clean; Cressida vented her temper upon its shelves and floor and emerged presently to tidy herself and present herself in the drawing-room for her daily task of writing out the shopping-list for her employer. She had missed the afternoon cup of tea served at half-past three o'clock although Corrie had brought her a cup of coffee, and, without speaking, helped her to put everything back in its place.

Jonkvrouw van Germert was still dangerously high-coloured and embarked on an involved excuse for her treatment of Cressida; she had never had a companion, she explained, and had no idea that Cressida expected to be treated as a guest in the house. 'And heaven knows that there is more than enough for you to do in the house and I cannot see why you should object to a little light housework—I felt quite ashamed before Dr van der Linus.'

Cressida, her good nature torn in shreds, said that she was glad to hear it. 'It is quite obvious that I took this job under a misapprehension. I thought at first that things would improve but each day you have treated me more like a servant and less like a companion. I think that we do not suit each other, *mevrouw*, and that it will be better if I leave.'

'No, no, there is no need for that, I'm sure that we can come to some amicable agreement, Miss Preece. At least let us wait until tomorrow when we shall both feel better able to discuss the matter.' She added with a touch of malice, 'It is a pity that you didn't know that it was Dr van der Linus who persuaded me to take you.'

To which Cressida made no reply and the rest of the evening was spent in an atmosphere of frigid politeness.

She was unpicking the muddle of her employer's knitting when Nicola arrived. She put it down at once and got up to leave the room but Nicola stopped her. 'No, sit down again, I've come to talk to both of you.' She exchanged a look with her aunt. 'We really must discuss things, mustn't we?'

Cressida didn't answer. She had no wish to discuss anything; she didn't like Nicola any more than she liked her aunt and Nicola had been very possessive towards the doctor. Surely he didn't intend to marry her? If so, he was both blind and bent on being unhappy for the rest of his life. Nicola, thought Cressida, was a young version of her own stepmother. He deserved better than that, although she hadn't forgiven him for deceiving her, however kindly his intentions had been.

Nicola made herself comfortable. 'Could we have some coffee?' she wanted to know. 'I missed lunch. Perhaps Miss Preece wouldn't mind going to the kitchen and asking Corrie to bring some here?'

Cressida put down the knitting. 'Yes, of course,' she kept her voice determinedly polite. She wanted to be out of the way while Nicola conferred with her aunt. She was right, of course; the moment she was out of the way, Nicola said urgently, 'Now, Tante Clotilde, leave the talking to me...'

Cressida came back and Corrie followed her presently with the coffee-tray and the three of them sat around drinking it and discussing the weather, the approach of Sint Nikolaas and Christmas, but soon Nicola put her coffee-cup down.

'Aldrik—Dr van der Linus—asked me to come and talk to you, Miss Preece. I'm afraid that you upset him yesterday. You see, he had gone to a great deal of trouble on your behalf, first persuading his grandmother—you didn't know that Lady Merrill was that?—to take you in under the guise of companion which she did while he sought for a permanent post for you. Of course he told me about you—we have no secrets—and I suggested that my aunt should employ you. He came here and discussed it with us both and was quite satisfied that it was just the kind of work you could do—you have no qualifications, have you? You can imagine how he feels at your show of ingratitude. He told me how much he pitied you and he has been to a good deal of trouble on your behalf. The least you can do is to show your real gratitude by doing your work without complaining.'

Cressida had listened without a sound to this speech. That she was boiling over with rage wasn't discernible; her ordinary face was composed even if it was pale, and when she spoke her voice was quiet and pleasant.

'Out of the frying-pan, into the fire,' she observed, and had the satisfaction of seeing the puzzlement on her companions' faces. 'I don't think there is anything we can say to each other, Juffrouw van Germert. You may have come with the best intentions, but I doubt it.' She put the knitting down, and set her cup and saucer on the tray. 'I'll leave you, if I may?' She looked at Jonkvrouw van Germert, whose formidable bosom was heaving quite alarmingly. 'I expect you would like to discuss me together.'

She went straight upstairs to her room, took her two cases from under the bed and packed her things, doing it neatly and unhurriedly, then changed into her warmest clothes, checked her handbag for money and passport, and, carrying her luggage, went downstairs. The drawing-room door was shut and she made no attempt to go there but went through the hall to the kitchen where she bade an astonished Corrie and Cook goodbye and then, via the back door, left the house.

It was bitterly cold and the cases were awkward, but, carried along on a right royal rage, she hardly noticed this. At the bus station she was lucky, for a bus was due to leave within a few minutes, and she got herself on board and sat, her head empty of thought, until it finally reached Leiden. It was no distance to the station, she bought a ticket to the Hoek and sat down on the platform to wait for the train. The enormity of what she had done was just beginning to penetrate her rage. There was no going back; indeed, wild horses wouldn't have persuaded her to do that. To go back to England was the obvious thing to do; luckily she had the best part of the hundred pounds in her purse and she knew that a ferry sailed from the Hoek at around midnight. It was a little after five o'clock, she had ample time to get there and at this time of year there should be no trouble getting a ticket. Beyond that she wasn't going to think. She couldn't go back to her home but surely she would find work of some kind in London; anything would do until she found her feet. She sat there, getting colder and colder, not allowing herself to think of

Dr van der Linus, but, try as she might, her thoughts returned to him time and again. She hadn't expected to meet him again but she never would have forgotten him, she had thought of him as a friend and she had confided in him. She could, at a pinch, forgive him for deceiving her about his grandmother, but to arrange for her to go to Holland and to someone who disliked her and didn't want her anyway was something she was unable to condone, and to crown the whole unhappy business he had allowed Nicola to take her to task for not being grateful. Worst of all, though, he pitied her, in much the same way as he had pitied the dog she had found. She would have liked to have a good cry but it was far too cold.

The train came presently and she found a seat, had a cup of the excellent coffee brought round, and, once they got to Rotterdam, found the train for the Hoek and got on board. She would have hours to wait there before she could go on board the ferry but she could sit in the café and have a bowl of soup in its noisy warmth.

The station at the Hoek was almost deserted; it was too early for the boat train and the local trains taking the workers home had dwindled to infrequency. The café was half full and she found a seat at a table by one of its windows and dawdled over a bowl of *Erwetensoep*, steaming hot pea soup, as thick as porridge and spiced with pork and sausage, and a roll, and then, leaving her cases in the care of the elderly couple who were sharing her table, she went to ask about a ticket. Its price made a serious hole in her money and a berth was out of the question, but she would be able to curl up on a bench somewhere, for the ship was half empty, she was told. She went back to the café and ordered a cup of coffee. The place was filling up now and in another half-hour or so the boat train would arrive and all the seats would be taken. The elderly couple were going on the ferry too, that much she had understood, but conversation was difficult, so they lapsed into a friendly silence and she was left to her thoughts.

She would have been missed by now, of course, and if Jonkvrouw van Germert had enquired, Corrie would have told her that Cressida had left with her luggage, but she didn't think anyone would try to fetch her back. Nicola would doubtless make up some story for the doctor's benefit and that would be the end of it. She fell to making plans—she would be in London early on the following morning, she could leave her luggage at the station, look up the nearest job centre in the phone book and get a job—any job—and then find a room, and if all else failed she would go to Castle Cary to Moggy. She was being optimistic, she knew, but domestic workers were in short supply and she would do anything while she looked around for the kind of work which she could do. The *Lady* magazine, she remembered, had been full of advertisements for help in the house and child-minders; she had only to buy a copy and find the nearest phone box... Carried away on a cloud of optimism, she ordered another cup of coffee.

A train came in, not the boat train, although quite a few passengers got out and made for the exit to the ferry, and she wondered if it might be a good idea to go on board. It was warm in the café and she felt a certain comfort from the company of the nice elderly couple still sitting opposite her. She stared out of the wide window and gazed at the people hurrying to and fro and then glanced round the café. It had filled up, customers coming in as fast as those leaving; perhaps it would be a good idea to get on board before the boat train got in. Too late—it slid into the station silently and the platform was alive with passengers. There was still plenty of time before the ferry sailed and a good many of them crowded into the café, looking for seats and calling the waiters. Someone sat down in the empty seat beside her and she turned away from the window.

The doctor said quietly, 'Hello, Cressida.'

She was aware of the most intense delight at seeing him; she suppressed it at once and asked coldly, 'Why are you here? How did you know?'

'Corrie told me.' He was sitting very much at his ease and the elderly couple, gathering together their bags and parcels, gave him an enquiring look and then smiled when he spoke to them, nodding in a satisfied way before bidding him and Cressida goodbye.

'How kind of Corrie,' said Cressida, 'and now if you will be good enough to move I'll go on board the ferry.'

'Well, no, I think not. We might have a little talk. Would you like a cup of coffee?'

'I don't want to talk,' said Cressida bitterly, 'and I've had three cups of coffee. Oh, go away, do.'

She might just as well have asked an oak tree to uproot itself; the doctor's massive person remained sitting comfortably in his chair, and he had every appearance of a man who intended to stay where he was until he saw fit to move. She said in a despairing voice, 'Oh, please let me go—I've got my ticket...'

'Have you any money?' he asked so casually that she answered him at once. 'Oh, yes, the rest of the hundred pounds...' She stopped and turned to look at him. 'Mr Tims said—but it was you, wasn't it? You arranged it too, didn't you? Not content with pitying me, you had to...to...'

The doctor realised that this was the crux of the matter. 'What is all this nonsense about pitying you? Why should I? A great girl like you, quite able to earn your living once you had a leg up. Pity is the last thing I feel for you, my girl, and the quicker you disabuse yourself of that silly idea the better.'

He lifted a finger to a passing waiter, ordered a pot of tea and sat back, saying nothing until after the tea had been brought. 'Pour the tea, dear girl,' he suggested. 'It will improve your temper and then you can tell me exactly what has happened.'

'I don't want—' began Cressida crossly.

'Tut-tut, you have no reason to be peevish; a cup of tea can solve almost any problem for the British.'

So she poured the tea and drank most of hers until she put down the cup because the tears were running down her cheeks.

She turned her head away, sniffed and put up a hand to wipe them away and had a large, very white handkerchief put into it. 'Wipe your face and have a good blow,' advised the doctor and when she had done so. 'Now start to talk, Cressida, and begin at the beginning when you first arrived at Jonkvrouw van Germert's house.'

'Yes, all right, but first why did you send me there?'

'It hadn't been my intention, I had planned to send you to friends of mine in Friesland, but when Nicola suggested that her aunt would be glad to have you as a companion it seemed a better idea. I am a good deal in Leiden and I could have kept an eye on you.'

'Yes, well, I'm sure that Jonkvrouw van Germert was being kind.'

'Possibly.' The doctor's voice was dry. 'Why didn't you tell me you weren't happy when I saw you in Leiden?'

'I didn't know that you already knew that I was there, did I? I'd only been there a week and I thought—I thought I'd been rather clever to get a job so quickly after leaving Lady Merrill. You didn't tell me about her, either.' She gave a gulping breath and so he said carelessly,

'Why should I have done? Go on.'

There wasn't more much to tell and beyond telling him that Nicola had talked to her that afternoon she said nothing.

The doctor asked casually, 'So it was Nicola who told you that I found you work out of pity? I dare say that she pointed out your ingratitude, and told you that Lady Merrill was my grandmother and hinted that I had discussed the whole matter with her, even suggested that I had sent her?'

'How did you know?'

'I didn't, but I know Nicola.' He added briskly, 'And now, having cleared up the matter, let us leave this place; the smell of food is horrendous and there are far too many people here.'

Cressida looked at the clock on the far wall. 'The ferry hasn't gone—they'll let me on if I hurry.'

'No, they won't, and don't think that they will let down the gangplank for a chit of a girl. You're coming back with me.'

'I'm not. I refuse. I'd rather die.'

'Don't be dramatic. You're coming back with me and my housekeeper will put you to bed and fuss over you and in the morning I shall drive you up to Friesland to some friends of mine and you'll stay with them until we find you the perfect job.'

'I bought my ticket.'

'We can get a refund. Come along now, I've had a long day.'

He picked up her cases and walked out of the station to the car, put the cases in the boot and stowed her in the front seat. 'Hungry?' he asked as he started the car.

'Yes.'

'We'll soon be home.' He didn't speak again and she was left with her thoughts and very muddled they were.

The Bentley made light of the journey. They were in Leiden while she was still sorting out her problems and presently the doctor stopped in a pleasant narrow street lined with old gabled houses and got out, opened her door and led her across the narrow cobbled pavement and up double steps to a handsome door with a fanlight over it. He unlocked it and pushed her gently before him just as Mies came from the kitchen.

Cressida stood in the hall, his arm around her shoulders, listening to him talking to his housekeeper, who presently clucked in a motherly fashion and led her away and up a charming little staircase to a pretty bedroom where she took Cressida's coat from her, still clucking, and opened the door to a small and exquisitely fitted bathroom and left her.

Cressida looked around her. The bed looked inviting; to fall into it and go to sleep at once was a tempting idea. Instead she went to look at herself in the triple mirror on the delicate little table under the window. She was horrified at what she saw; a tear-stained face, not over-clean, hair all over the place and a pink nose. She washed and combed her hair and wondered what to do next. Should she go downstairs or was she supposed to go to bed? She had no clothes until someone brought her cases. She opened the door cautiously and peered down the stairs.

The doctor was in the hall and both the dogs were with him. 'Come on down if you're ready,' he invited. 'Mies is putting supper on the table—you said you were hungry.' When she reached the bottom of the stairs he asked, 'What do you think of Caesar? This is Mabel, rather large but as mild as a lamb.'

His manner was brisk, like that, she supposed, of an elder brother taking dutiful care of a younger sister, and exactly what was needed to reassure her, as the doctor very well knew.

'In here,' he invited and opened a door. The room was of a good size with panelled walls and an ornate plaster ceiling from which hung a brass candelabrum. The furniture was old and beautifully cared for and the oval table had been laid with a damask cloth and shining silver and glass.

'But it's past midnight,' said Cressida. 'Who's going to clear away and wash up?'

'Mies has help in the mornings; the two girls who come will clear away and tidy things up.'

Mies came in then with a tureen of soup and said something, and he made a reply which made her smile broadly as she answered him. 'Mies says she will go to bed when you do and you are to enjoy your supper.'

The soup smelled delicious and tasted even better, Cressida was hungry, she polished off the soup, the cheese souffle which followed and the crème brulée which rounded off their meal, and then, mindful of the lateness of the hour, refused coffee and asked if she might go to bed.

The doctor bade her goodnight, handed her over to Mies and went to his study to finish the work he had been doing when Corrie had telephoned. The dogs went with him and he sat at his desk with them beside him, deep in thought. It was quite some time before he bestirred himself, and, with a sigh, picked up his pen.

As for Cressida, finding that someone had taken her cases to her room and unpacked what she might need for the night, she sank into a hot bath, only half awake, and then tumbled into bed. There was too much to think about all at once; sensibly she closed her eyes and went to sleep.

A stout girl with a rosy face and a broad smile wakened her with a small tea-tray, drew back the curtains, revealing a grey sky and a heavy frost, and then went away again. Cressida drank her tea, hopped out of bed and ran the bath. She had no idea what was to happen next but it seemed sense to get dressed and be ready for whatever transpired.

The doctor came out of his study with the dogs as she reached the hall. His good morning was friendly and decidedly brisk. 'Breakfast and then we'll be off. We are expected for lunch.'

Cressida found her voice. 'Yes, that's all very well, but where and what happens to me when we get there? It's really very kind of you to bother about me, but I've still got my ticket...'

He swept her into the dining-room and pulled out a chair. She sat down because it seemed the only thing to do; besides she was hungry and her eyes had caught a basket of delicious croissants on the table. Eggs too, and a sizeable dish of ham as well as elegant silver-topped glass jars filled with marmalade and jam. Mies came in with a silver coffee-pot, beaming and nodding. '*Smakelijk eten*,' she said.

Cressida, wrinkling her nose at the heavenly smell of coffee, said a polite, '*Dank U*,' reflecting that she was going to enjoy every crumb of her meal.

The doctor had seated himself at the head of the table, the dogs on either side. 'Perhaps you would rather have tea?' he said.

'Oh, no, thank you. Do you want me to pour?'

'Please. Try one of these croissants.' He passed the basket, the elaborate silver egg stand and the salt and pepper and then enquired as to whether she had slept well.

'Yes, it was a lovely comfy bed. I meant to stay awake and think but I was rather tired. Could we please talk, Dr van der

Linus? There really is no need to go all the way to Friesland. I'm sure I can get work if I go back to England.'

He helped himself to ham. 'What as?'

'Well, as a companion, I suppose...' The memory of Jonkvrouw van Germert was a bit daunting but surely not all employers were like her?

He passed his cup for more coffee. 'Let us strike a bargain. Come with me to Friesland this morning and if you don't like the idea of finding work there I will personally put you on the ferry for England.'

She bit into a croissant. If she went back to England she would never see him again, on the other hand since she had chosen to make her way in the world that was a matter of little importance. The wretched Nicola would get round him and he would forgive her and marry her and be unhappy ever after...

'You can have ten minutes,' said the doctor in a no-nonsense voice, 'and bring everything with you.'

She swallowed her coffee and started up the stairs and then dawdled when she heard him say, 'Ah, Nicola,' as he answered the ringing phone. It was a pity that her knowledge of Dutch was so sparse and there was nothing to tell from his voice.

Mies saw them on their way with a good hearty handshake and what Cressida took to be kindly advice. The dogs, on the rugs on the back seat, settled down, and the doctor drove off.

'Shouldn't you be at the hospital?' asked Cressida.

'Occasionally I take a day off.' He took the road through Alkmaar and over the Afsluitdijk and she found so much to see that conversation wasn't really necessary. They were nearing Leeuwarden when the doctor said, 'These friends of mine—the van der Bronses, Tyco and Charity—they've been married just over a year, she's expecting a baby in a couple of months, there are two little girls who are from his first marriage, Teile and Letizia—they're twins and they adore Charity.'

'They don't mind having me like this at a moment's notice?'

'They're pleased. They haven't been living in Friesland very long; Tyco's father decided to sell his business and move into a villa he owns just outside Sneek, not too far away, and Tyco took over his big house. He's consultant at Leeuwarden and goes to Amsterdam fairly regularly. He's a very good surgeon. We were at medical school together.'

'Do you live near here?'

'Yes. North of Dokkum, a few miles from the Waddenzee.' He offered no more information and she didn't like to ask questions; there was, she reflected briefly, no future in their acquaintance.

Half an hour later he was stopping before the van der Brons home, a large country house set in a pleasant small park with open country all around. Nothing could have been warmer than the welcome Cressida received. She had been feeling incredibly nervous of meeting the doctor's friends but at the first sight of them she knew that she had been needlessly so. Mr van der Brons, as large a man as the doctor, had a kind face and twinkling eyes, he was handsome too which made it all the more surprising that his wife was as ordinary to look at as Cressida herself. True, she was wearing the kind of clothes Cressida envied at first look, and she was beautifully made-up, but she was still plain. Cressida took instant comfort from that fact.

The doctor kissed his hostess soundly, shook his friend by the hand and introduced Cressida.

'Come in,' said Charity, 'the girls are longing to see you. Bring the dogs, Aldrik. Samson will be pleased; they can have a good run after lunch.'

They all went indoors and the doctor said, 'I must go back this afternoon—a clinic at four o'clock and I must call in at home on the way.'

'Come upstairs and see your room?' invited Charity, 'I'm so glad you could come, I don't get out a great deal.' She patted the elegant drapery over her tummy. 'We can have a good gossip.'

'You're very kind to have me. I wanted to go back to England but Dr van der Linus wouldn't let me.'

'Quite right, too.' Charity opened a door in the gallery at the top of the staircase. 'Here we are, someone will unpack for you while we're having lunch and while the men take the children and dogs for a walk we'll get to know each other.' She opened the door again. 'Come down when you're ready—we'll look out for you.'

Cressida, left to herself, explored the bedroom and the bathroom beyond, looked out of the window and then did her face and hair. It was rather like being in a dream, she reflected, and she supposed that sooner or later someone would tell her what was to happen next. Was she to stay here for one night? Was there a suitable job waiting for her? Or was she to stay longer and rely on local advertisements or agencies, and why had the doctor brought her all this way, as far away from the ferry as possible, or almost?

No way was she going to get the answers to her problems, not for the moment at any rate; they were waiting for her in the drawing-room and the two little girls were there too, and over drinks and lunch the talk never once touched on herself, but after the meal, when the children went to get their outdoor things and Charity went with them, Cressida found herself beside the doctor while Mr van der Brons was telephoning.

'I really must know what's going to happen to me,' she hissed at him. 'I can't stay here, I simply can't, you must tell me.'

He smiled down at her, very large and very calm. 'Charity will explain while we're out, and if when we get back you still want to go back to England I'll run you back to Leiden and put you on the train.'

He patted her shoulder and wandered away to where the others were waiting in the hall. She watched him go, feeling frustrated; she hadn't had the chance to say half the things which were on her mind.

Charity came back into the room. 'I'm going to put my feet up,' she said cheerfully, 'curl up in a chair and we can have a good gossip.'

Cressida curled up. 'Look,' she began, 'I'm most grateful to you and your husband for having me but I can't get Dr van der Linus to tell me anything...'

'Men can be tiresome,' observed Charity. 'They arrange things and expect everyone else, especially wives, to know all about it. Did he mention the ter Beemstras? No? Well, they live a few miles from here, youngish, six children and desperate for someone to help with them. You see, the idea of six is a bit daunting, isn't it? But it's not like that at all. The three eldest are at school all day—boys, the twins are five years old and the littlest one is three. I rather think that Aldrik thought you might like to take them on. Actually, he had them in mind when he came back to Holland, but Nicola persuaded him that you would be happier with her aunt.'

She rearranged a cushion to her satisfaction. 'If I had known I would have warned him—I've met Jonkvrouw van Germert once and that was once too often, and I can't stand Nicola, she's got her claws into Aldrik. You can't think how pleased I was when he phoned to say he was bringing you to us.' She beamed at Cressida. 'If you like the idea I'll get Beatrix ter Beemstra to come over and talk to you. They're a happy family and the house is nice and they'll be generous with a salary.' She added in her friendly way, 'It would be lovely to have you not too far away; you could pop over for coffee or lunch or something. The twins get on well with ours and the baby's a darling. Now I'm going to take a nap while you think about it.'

She closed her eyes and Cressida, with no chance to say a word, set about considering her situation. The idea of six children didn't daunt her; she liked them and she thought that she would like Friesland with its wide horizons and endless fields, and, although she told herself that it would make no difference, she might see the doctor from time to time. She liked Charity and Tyco and the twins and perhaps the ter Beemstras would like her too and she could settle down with them. If she went back to England she would be going to unknown people, even if she were lucky enough to find a job quickly.

Charity's soft voice broke into her thoughts. 'Would you like to meet Beatrix ter Beemstra? Just to talk about it...'

Cressida took a deep breath. 'Yes, please, if you think I'd do.'

Charity went over to the side-table by one of the windows and lifted the receiver as the door opened and the men, children and dogs came in. The doctor went straight to Cressida. 'I'm leaving in a few minutes.' He glanced across at Charity. 'Are you getting fixed up with the ter Beemstras?' And when she nodded he said, 'Good, I think you'll be happy with them. I'm sorry that you had such an unpleasant time with Jonkvrouw van Germert; it is a relief to me to know that you will be comfortably settled.'

Rather like finding a home for a stray kitten, thought Cressida. Now he was free to wash his hands of her. She swallowed the bitter thought.

She held out a hand. 'Goodbye, Dr van der Linus and thank you for your kindness.' She saw the surprise on his face and wondered what he had expected her to say.

CHAPTER SIX

STANDING IN THE porch with her new-found friends around her, Cressida wondered if she would ever see the doctor again. The Bentley disappeared into the gathering dusk and they went back to the drawing-room to have tea and then play Monopoly with the twins until it was their bedtime.

Charity went upstairs presently to tuck them up for the night and Tyco, sitting opposite Cressida, said in his kind way, 'I think you'll like the ter Beemstras, they're good friends of ours, but if anything bothers you don't hesitate to let us know. I promised Aldrik that I would keep an eye on you.'

'Thank you very much. I'm sure I'll be happy with your friends.' She hesitated. 'I didn't like to ask Dr van der Linus but I do hope that I haven't been the cause of any—any difference between him and Juffrouw van Germert.'

'I can safely reassure you about that.' He smiled at her and got up as Charity came back into the room. 'I believe he intends to see her this evening.'

'Oh, good, I'm glad,' said Cressida, who didn't feel glad at all.

Sitting between them presently, eating delicious food with Jolly, the butler, hovering benignly in the background, Cressida felt happy for the first time in days—well, almost happy; the thought that she had seen the doctor for the last time was ever present in the back of her mind. Even if he came to see the van der Bronses, he was hardly likely to see her. She wondered just where he lived and asked Charity.

'Oh, not far away—the other side of Dokkum, about ten miles from here. It's rather out of the way, though. He loves it, but Nicola hates it. He has a house in Leiden though—you've been there—handy for him, for he goes to and fro a good deal. I suppose he'll be there for Christmas; his father died a few years ago and his mother is on a long visit to one of his sisters. He has another sister with children, I dare say they'll be with him as well as aunts and cousins. Oh, and Nicola, wrapped in furs and looking gorgeous.'

Her husband laughed gently. 'I hate to disagree with you, my love, but I believe Aldrik will be in England for Christmas—with Lady Merrill. He'll be back here for New Year.'

That, thought Cressida vulgarly, will be one in the eye for Nicola, but she was instantly sobered by the thought that probably Nicola would go with him.

She went to bed presently, convinced that she would lie awake most of the night, there was so much on her mind, but of course she was asleep as soon as her head was on the pillow.

The little girls were driven to school by their father on his way to his consulting rooms in Leeuwarden and Mevrouw ter Beemstra wouldn't arrive until just after ten o'clock for coffee; Charity took Cressida round the house and never mentioned Aldrik once. Cressida didn't know whether to be pleased about this or not. On the one hand the sooner she thought less about him the better, but, on the other, it would be nice to know more about him.

Beatrix ter Beemstra was a tall good-looking young woman of five and thirty with corn-coloured hair and very blue eyes. She spoke good English and she had a happy face. She shook hands with Cressida and gave her a frank look. 'Six,' she said and laughed, 'six children—we think they're wonderful, but that's because they're ours. Will you come and give us a try?

The eldest boys are at school all day, there are three—my husband takes them into Leeuwarden each morning, then there are two little girls, five years old, twins, and Lucia, she's just three years old—we call her Baby.'

Jolly brought in the coffee and the three of them sat for an hour while she explained just what Cressida would have to do. 'If you find it too much just say so. We still have Nanny with us, she looks after Lucia to a large extent and of course you won't be expected to do anything but look after the children, speak English to them and be prepared to play with them and go for walks and so on.' She smiled at Cressida. 'Would you like to try?'

Cressida liked her and she would be kept busy enough not to have time to repine. Besides, the wages were really very generous; she would be able to save a good deal, gain experience, learn to speak Dutch, and when she was ready she could return to England. She wasn't sure what she would do when she got there but it was something to aim for.

She said now, 'Yes, please, if you're sure I'll do. When would you like me to start?'

Charity said quickly, 'Oh, please let us have her here for a day or two, just until after Sint Nikolaas—it's only two days away.'

Beatrix ter Beemstra agreed readily enough. 'That will give you a couple of weeks before the boys start their holidays. The twins start school in the New Year, though we shan't send them until half-term, but of course they'll all be home for Christmas.' She added a little anxiously, 'You like walking and cycling? Good—there's a bike for you—the children go for miles.'

She got up to go. 'I hope you'll be very happy with us. We shall do our best to make you feel at home.'

She shook Cressida's hand, kissed Charity and drove off in her Mini.

'Tomorrow,' said Charity comfortably, 'we shall go into Leeuwarden and shop for Sint Nikolaas—he comes to the village and we all go to meet him. The children love it; he hands out oranges and sweets and they put their shoes in the hearth and he leaves something in them. Come to the kitchen with me, I must talk to Mrs Jolly about dinner this evening. Tyco will be home for lunch and so will the children.'

If it hadn't been for the persistent niggling thought at the back of her mind about Aldrik, Cressida would have been completely happy. She felt at home—and not only with the van der Bronses, but with the countryside and the quiet. Leeuwarden wasn't all that far away but here at the nice old house there were only fields, empty of cows now that it was winter, and half-frozen canals, and not far away, shielded by bare trees, the tiled roofs of the village, dominated by its church. She was going to be happy here, she told herself resolutely, and, indeed, for the rest of that day, in the friendly company of the two little girls and Charity and Tyco, she was.

Charity had a little car of her own, another Mini, and Cressida drove them both into Leeuwarden the following morning. It was a pleasant city with some charming old buildings; she promised herself that she would explore it on one of her free days later on and following Charity she went to the shops.

She had the rest of the hundred pounds in her purse and since she would be earning quite handsomely in the near future she bought chocolate letters for Teile and Letizia, and, at Charity's insistence, some thick woollen tights for herself. 'If you're to go cycling with the children you'll need them,' said Charity. 'Did that woman pay you?'

'Well, no, but I was there less than a fortnight. I'd rather not bother about it. I've enough money until I get paid.'

They went back presently, laden with their parcels: bracelets for the twins, a scarf for Mrs Jolly, a box of cigars for Jolly and a rich silk tie for Tyco, and added to these boxes of sweets and crystallised fruit, and a magnificent chocolate cake, to be met by the children and Tyco and presently eat lunch. Listening to the happy chatter all around her, Cressida reflected that it was a good thing that she would soon be gone; she wasn't serious but she was filled with a wistful longing to be happy as the van der Bronses were happy, and, since that seemed highly unlikely, the sooner she got herself settled with plenty to fill her days and her thoughts the better it would be.

Tyco came home early on the following day and drove them all to the village to watch Sint Nikolaas, on his splendid white horse with Zwarte Piet beside him, enter the village and gravely acknowledge the greetings of everyone there, and then proceed to the village hall where he delivered a homily to the children and then read each child's name from the list in his hand. One by one they went to him to be asked if they had been good, and, since legend had it that Zwarte Piet would pop any naughty child into the sack he carried on his shoulder, they were all good, running back triumphantly to their mothers and fathers clutching their orange and bag of sweets. Teile and Letizia went in their turn and then joined in the singing as the *sint* departed, mounted his horse and rode away. Cressida had enjoyed the simple ceremony but there were still treats in store, she was assured by the children as they drove back to the house, and sure enough they had barely finished tea when there was a thunderous knock on the house door and Jolly came in with a small sack. Sint Nikolaas, he informed them, had called only a few moments ago and left it, at the same time reminding the children that they must put their shoes out when they went to bed with a wisp of hay in them for his horse.

Mr van der Brons opened the sack. The twins first, of course; several gaily wrapped boxes for each of them and then gifts for Jolly and Mrs Jolly, and a package for Cressida which she was made to open at once. Gloves, soft leather, lined with silk and elegant as well as warm. 'Thank the *sint*,' said Charity, 'we all have to.'

Charity was next, and under the wrappings a small velvet box containing a pair of diamond earrings. She thanked the *sint* and smiled at Tyco, looking so happy that Cressida felt a lump in her throat. Tyco was last. He admired the tie, praised the *sint*'s good taste and vowed that he would wear it that very evening, which was the signal for Charity to mention that a few friends would be coming in to dinner. 'I shall wear my earrings,' she said happily. 'We had better go and tidy ourselves before they get here.' She glanced at her husband. 'Do you suppose Sint Nikolaas would agree to the girls staying up for dinner?'

'There will be so many of us that two more won't be noticed, darling. Best behaviour, of course; Oma and Opa will be here.'

They went their separate ways and Cressida got into the grey dress which was hardly festive but would do at a pinch, she supposed. She did her face with care and took pains with her hair, all the while wondering what the doctor was doing.

Dr van der Linus was at the hospital in Leiden, using all his skill to keep alive an elderly man who had collapsed in the street that afternoon. He should by rights have been in den Haag at Nicola's home, where her parents were giving a dinner party, but he had asked that someone should telephone them and explain that he would be very late or possibly not get there at all. After that he hadn't thought about it at all; he was wholly engrossed in his patient. The young houseman who had sent his message had been shocked by the petulance of the voice which answered him. He was to tell Dr van der Linus that his absence was most inconvenient and that he had been very inconsiderate. The receiver had been slammed down before the young man could say anything more. He went back and said merely that he had given the doctor's message; if the owner of the voice was the young lady the hospital grapevine alleged he would eventually marry then he for one was convinced that she wouldn't do at all; the chief was liked and respected and unfailingly patient and courteous with the most trying of medical students. He deserved better.

The doctor, going home at last, ate his solitary supper, sent Mies to her bed and took the dogs walking. It was very cold with a moon doing its best to escape the clouds and he walked briskly. He was tired but satisfied that the man had a good chance of recovery. He didn't think about Nicola at all, only as he let himself and the dogs into his house he wondered what Cressida was doing. 'But of course she will be in bed and asleep,' he muttered to himself and Caesar as they followed Mabel into the kitchen.

She was certainly in bed, but she wasn't sleeping, she was thinking about him.

She had had a happy evening. Tyco had a large family, parents and brothers and sisters, and there had been children too. Dinner had been on a grand scale; Cressida reflected with pleasure upon the delights of lobster bisque, roast pheasant, champagne sorbets and a magnificent ice pudding. They had drunk champagne too and afterwards there had been friends calling in for drinks. It was a pity that the doctor couldn't have been there too but she supposed that he would spend his spare time with Nicola. As long as he was happy, she thought sleepily, and nodded off. She woke in the night, sad and lonely, feeling as though she had lost something dear to her. That was nonsense, she told herself; perhaps it was a forgotten dream which had given her that bereft feeling and the small hours of the morning were notorious for their gloom. She slept again uneasily and got up to finish her packing. The ter Beemstras would be coming for her soon after ten.

She said goodbye to Tyco at breakfast, kissed the twins and promised that she would come and see them as soon as she could, then sat down again to have another cup of coffee with Charity.

'We shall see you at Christmas, if not before. We may be a little out of the way here but we are quite social. I do hope Aldrik comes up to Janslum—Tyco says he'll be in England with his grandmother but he's sure to be back for New Year. He goes to and fro the way anyone else would catch a bus, if you see what I mean.'

Mevrouw ter Beemstra was punctual; Cressida, her goodbyes said with hidden reluctance, got into the car beside her new employer, and was immediately much heartened by that lady's profound relief. 'I've been so afraid you might have second thoughts,' she said. 'It's the six children—they put people off, you know...'

Cressida reassured her. 'I don't know much about it,' she said, 'but I should have thought that several children must be a lot easier to amuse than one, and they're never lonely...'

Their drive was a short one and the house when they reached it looked pleasant. Smaller than the van der Bronses', but with a good deal of ground around it. The door was flung open as they got out and children and dogs came tumbling out to greet them.

'The boys have stayed at home especially to greet you,' said Mevrouw ter Beemstra, 'and my husband also will come for lunch and take them back with him for afternoon school. Now I will tell you their names; Willum, our eldest son, Jacobus, Friso, and the twins Sepke and Galske and the baby Lucia. They speak a little English and I hope you will speak English to them at all times, Miss Preece—must I call you that?'

'I'd like it if you would call me Cressida and I'd like the children to call me that too. Miss Preece makes me sound like an elderly governess.'

She shook hands with the children in turn, first Willum, twelve years old, rather a solemn boy, and, she suspected, very conscious that he was the eldest. Jacobus, two years younger, had a round jolly face and a thatch of unruly gold hair and Friso, eight years old, was very like him. The twins were sturdy with bright blue eyes and blonde pigtails and looked older than their five years, they each held a hand of Lucia, a cherub with golden curls who, when it came to her turn, put up her face to be kissed and shouted, '*Dag, Cressy*!' and burst into giggles.

'We call you Cressy,' said Willum, and they all nodded, and when their mother remonstrated Cressida said, 'Oh, I think that's a splendid idea, so much easier than Cressida, isn't it?'

They all went into the house then, through the tiled hall and into a lofty room with windows at each end, very comfortably furnished and cluttered with books and toys. *Mevrouw* swept a pile of magazines off a roomy sofa and bade Cressida sit down. 'The room is not tidy, but the playroom and nursery are at the top of the house and it is too far, you understand? But now that you are here there will be someone to be with them. The boys are old enough to go cycling together and Willum has his own room now, but the little girls may not go out alone.'

She sat down beside Cressida. 'Let us have coffee and then you shall see your room and the house and meet everyone.'

A tall bony woman brought the coffee and Mevrouw ter Beemstra said, 'This is Leike, she speaks no English but she will help you all she can.'

Cressida shook hands and Leike smiled from a fairly stern face. Looking around her, Cressida had that nice warm feeling that she was going to be happy.

Mijnheer ter Beemstra came home for lunch. A large man, thick-set, and a good deal older than his wife with a rugged good-humoured face. His children fell upon him, all talking at once, as his wife introduced Cressida. He shook hands, smiling broadly. 'We are glad to welcome you, Miss Preece, and we hope that you will be happy with us; you will also be busy...'

Sitting up in bed, much later, Cressida paused in writing a letter to Moggy to review her day. It had been full, not a minute wasted from the moment when she had been led upstairs to her room, a small cosy place comfortably furnished and with a view out over the wide fields beyond the grounds, then, accompanied by all six children, she had been taken on a tour of the house. The children had come to show her everything and they had rooms close to hers, and at the end of a long passage there was a big playroom and beside it a smaller room, used as a nursery for Baby. Here she had met Lucia's nurse, elderly, her beady eyes studying Cressida with guarded politeness. Of course, Cressida had thought, she was afraid that Cressida was going to usurp her position, something she had no intention of doing. She had contrived to let the nurse understand this with the help of Willum, who'd laboured away doing his best to translate for her. It had been a relief to see the nurse relax presently.

English was to be spoken at meals; lunch had been a hilarious affair with her encouraging and correcting and offering, rather diffidently, to improve upon an accent. Afterwards, walking down to the village to buy stamps at the little post office, accompanied by everyone except Lucia, she had been teased into trying her Dutch. Which, Willum solemnly told her, was very bad.

At the end of the day, getting them to bed had been a major operation, so that when she went downstairs finally and Mevrouw ter Beemstra suggested that she might like to go to bed herself she was glad to go. Perhaps, she reflected, it would be a good idea if she did that every evening, she could always plead letters to write and probably once she had got settled in there would be odd jobs of mending and so on which she could do in the playroom.

She punched her pillows into greater comfort and thought about her free day. It was to be Thursday because the girls went to dancing class in the afternoon and the boys had fencing lessons; she could, if she wished, go in to Leeuwarden with Mijnheer ter Beemstra after breakfast and return when she liked; there was a bus which went through the village in the evening, but if she missed it, she only had to telephone and she would be fetched. The last weekend of each month was to be hers too. She could stay in the house if she wished and go somewhere each day or she could go away for the weekend. 'I believe that Charity will love to have you,' said Mevrouw ter Beemstra kindly.

She would go to Leeuwarden, she decided, and have a good look round, and since Christmas was only a couple of weeks away she would buy small gifts and one or two cards—for Moggy and her sister and Mr Tims, Charity and Tyco and Cook and Dr van der Linus. She wondered what he was doing, picturing him in Nicola's company. She allowed her imagination to run away with her; Nicola would be quite exquisitely dressed and looking prettier than ever, trilling her tinkling laugh, asking him sympathetically something about his day's work, making him smile. Cressida was suddenly consumed with a profound dislike of the girl; she was all wrong for the doctor and he was extremely silly not to see that for himself. Well, let him cook his own goose, she muttered, and picked up her pen once more and wrote several pages of cheerful news to Moggy.

She slipped into the life of the household quickly, helped by Mevrouw ter Beemstra's kindly hints and the enthusiastic encouragement of the children. Her days were busy, for there were always children around, with the constant need to speak English and whenever possible have it read to them. She set herself, within the first day or so, to learn as many Dutch words as possible, and it was surprising how easy it was to understand the children; committed to speak English with all of them, she didn't venture to try them out, but she listened while she was with them and boldly tried out the few words she had understood on the maid and the elderly cook in the kitchen, quite undeterred when one of them failed to understand her.

Her duties, away from the children, were light—she made her bed but no one expected her to do any household chores although there was plenty of mending and occasional ironing to do for the children—but her days were full enough, keeping six children occupied while they were not at school. She made sure that they bathed, washing their flaxen hair, putting plasters on grazed knees, helping them with their English lessons. The two elder boys brought home a good deal of homework and since she had a smattering of Latin grammar and knew something of geometry and algebra she rose in their regard. It was with Friso and the two girls that she had most contact; their English was sketchy and they were at an age when learning was a bore anyway. All the same, by the end of the first week she had devised several ways of making it more attractive to them, taking them for walks or cycle rides, getting them to tell her names of the trees and flowers and everything else in sight and then repeating everything in English. Baby, of course, was no trouble at all; her nurse relinquished her from time to time and Cressida soon had her prattling away, quite happy to speak any language anyone should choose to teach her.

The week flew by and on the Wednesday evening Charity telephoned to invite her over for her free day. 'I'll come and fetch you,' she offered, 'and Tyco shall take you back after dinner. I'll be there about half-past nine so mind you're ready.'

The weather had turned fine with a pale blue sky, a searing cold wind and thin ice on the canals. Cressida, wrapped in her winter coat and wearing the woolly hat and scarf she had bought in Leiden, bade the ter Beemstras goodbye and got into Charity's car.

'Ought you to be driving?' she asked as they started off.

'I promised Tyco this morning that I won't take the car out again until after I've had the baby. He's fussy...' Somehow it sounded high praise.

'I can drive you,' said Cressida.

'Oh, thanks—we'll go shopping together. I love Christmas, don't you?' Charity overtook a farm tractor with caution. 'Well, how do you like the job? The ter Beemstras are delighted with you—Beatrix told me when I phoned yesterday.'

'It's marvellous. They're so kind and I don't have to do any housework.'

'I should hope not. I can't think what came over Aldrik, letting you go to that horrible woman.'

'Well, if he's in love with Nicola and she suggested it I suppose he thought it would be all right.'

'He's not in love with her, though. She's fastened on to him and he's too busy and wrapped up in his work to do anything about it.'

Somehow this piece of news cheered Cressida up. 'Oh, do you think so?' She would have liked to have pursued the matter but they had arrived at Charity's home and Jolly came out to drive the car round to the garage for her and beg them to hurry inside. 'Mrs Jolly's got the coffee ready, *Mevrouw*, and there's a good fire in the small sitting-room.'

There was a great deal to talk about; Christmas—and things to do with the children during the school holidays. 'Tyco's family come over for Christmas and of course we'll have a party. You'll come...?'

'Will I? Supposing the ter Beemstras want to go out? There'll be the children to mind.'

'They'll come too. Baby's nurse will come and our housemaid is marvellous with children and we can pop in and out. They have a room to play in and their own food. Tyco says they've always done it, and they come and join the grown-ups when the presents are handed out.'

'Won't it be a bit much for you?'

Charity poured more coffee. 'Me? No, no. Besides, there's you and Tyco's sisters and Mrs Jolly and the ter Beemstras. It'll be great fun.'

She glanced at Cressida. 'I'm sorry Aldrik won't be here. He's splendid with children.' She sighed. 'I suppose if Nicola succeeds in getting him to marry her she'll have lots of nasty little Nicolas...'

'She doesn't look as if she would like even one.'

'That won't suit Aldrik; he told me once that he would like a large family when he married.'

She got up. 'Come and see the nursery, it's all ready—the girls helped me and we've had such fun. Tyco keeps bringing home teddy bears and rattles...'

They spent a pleasant hour while Cressida admired everything before going to Charity's bedroom to go through her wardrobe and try on her hats. They went downstairs for lunch presently and just as they reached the hall the front door opened and Tyco and Aldrik came in.

'Hello, darling—Cressida too.' Tyco kissed his wife, 'Aldrik's on the way to Janslum; I've brought him home for lunch.'

Charity lifted her face for Aldrik's kiss. 'How very nice, and here's Cressida, spending her day off with us.'

Cressida offered a hand and smiled up at him, aware of a deep delight at seeing him again. He took it in his own large one and bent and kissed her cheek. 'This is an unexpected pleasure,' he told her, and Tyco, his arm around his wife, winked at her. 'I have been wondering how you have been getting on.'

Cressida had gone rather pink. She had enjoyed the kiss but it mustn't be allowed to go to her head, she reflected. 'I'm very happy,' she told him. 'Everyone is kind and the children are dears.'

She came to a halt, wishing very much to tell him every detail of her days. That would bore him, she thought, so instead she asked politely, 'I hope you haven't been too busy?'

The doctor, who had been out of his bed for most of the night after a long day at Amsterdam Hospital, assured her that he hadn't been at all busy, and Tyco suggested that they might all go to the drawing-room and have a drink before lunch.

'Teile and Letizia will be here in a few minutes,' said Charity. 'Mrs Jolly's gone to fetch them.'

Lunch was a very cheerful meal; Christmas was near enough for it to be the main topic of conversation and the twins could talk of nothing else, but presently Tyco said, 'Well, I've a couple of patients to see and I said I'd look in at the hospital. I'll drop these two off as I go. Tell Jolly to fetch them after school, my love, will you? I'll be back about five o'clock.' The children went to get their outdoor things and as Charity got up too he said, 'And you'll put your feet up, darling.'

'While you're doing that,' said Aldrik casually, 'I'll take Cressida over to Janslum. It will give her the chance to see something of the country.'

Charity was buttoning the twins into their coats and Cressida got up to help her. She said over her shoulder, 'It's most kind of you, Doctor, but I shall be very happy to stay here and read—or something—while Charity rests.'

'Oh, I'm not being kind.' He spoke carelessly. 'Tyske—my housekeeper—has made *speculaas* and I won't be able to eat all of them; besides, the dogs are there—I brought them up with me last night.'

He added briskly, 'Caesar is very fit, I thought you might like to see him—and Mabel, of course.'

'Well, yes, I would—thank you. I'll come...'

'You'll enjoy the drive,' said Charity, 'and you'll both come back here for dinner—seven o'clock, because Cressida wants to be back by ten o'clock.' She added, 'And bring the dogs, Aldrik; Samson hasn't seen them for a time, and they can have a romp together.'

Her husband gazed at her fondly. 'Darling, we will all do exactly as you ask, but if I find you haven't curled up for at least two hours I shall beat you when I get home.'

They all laughed and then Aldrik said, 'Get your coat, Cressida, and we'll be off.' He gave Charity a quick kiss. 'Thanks for the lunch, my dear,' and he bent to kiss the little girls' cheeks. Whatever it was he said to them sent them running into the hall to search the pockets of his heavy jacket and find the chocolates he had brought with him. Cressida, tying a scarf over her tidy head, thought how happy everyone was. I'm happy too, she reflected, I suppose it's because I'm settled and everyone is so nice.

Sitting beside the doctor presently, driving along a narrow brick road between polder land, she said, 'Charity told me that you're going to England for Christmas. Do you go every year?'

He slid the car into an even narrower road. 'Usually; my grandmother is too old to travel over here. My mother spends Christmas with her but she is visiting one of my sisters. I don't like to think of the old lady being on her own.'

'You come back for New Year?'

'Oh, yes.'

'Then I expect you'll be getting married?'

He said drily, 'The idea had occurred to me. Should I be flattered at your interest, Cressida?'

She looked away from him out of the car window. 'Have I been nosy? I'm sorry. I—I was just making conversation.'

'Surely there is no need for us to have to do that? Let's talk instead.' He turned and smiled at her. 'I wonder if you will like my home—we're almost there, another mile or so. We're quite close to the sea now. As we go back we'll take the other road through Dokkum. Are you to be free on every Thursday?'

'I think so, and once a month I'm...' She stopped just in time from telling him that she would have a weekend to herself.

'Once a month?' he prompted.

'Oh, nothing,' she mumbled, 'nothing important.' She had gone pink; the very idea of telling him about her weekend...he might have thought that she was fishing for an invitation to go out with him. He was nice enough to have responded too even if he hadn't wanted to. She remembered how he had put himself out on her behalf and said hastily, 'Charity and I are going shopping together. It's lovely having her so close, I've—I've planned to do such a lot.'

He didn't reply and she was searching her head for a suitable topic of conversation when the road widened into a very small village square encircled by cottages, an austere church, two shops and a village school.

'Janslum,' said the doctor. 'I'm just up the lane.'

Cressida, with the vague idea of a smallish country house with a nice garden, was taken aback as he swept the car through an open gateway between high pillars and along a straight drive between small wintry blown trees. It curved presently and the house came into view.

'You live here?' gasped Cressida. 'All by yourself?'

'Not quite by myself,' he conceded, 'and later of course...'

'When you are married.' He had got out to open her door and help her and she stood beside him, looking at the house, white-walled and gabled with tall windows on either side of the porch, the windows above getting smaller and smaller until they reached the roof. There were lights shining from the downstairs rooms and as she looked the door was opened and she could see the hall beyond, aglow with soft lamp-light.

'It's perfect,' she said to no one in particular. 'Just right.'

CHAPTER SEVEN

THE DOCTOR DIDN'T say anything, but he smiled a little as he swept her indoors. 'This is Wester, who looks after the house for me. His wife Tyske does the cooking. I should sink without trace without them.'

Wester smiled discreetly and shook the hand Cressida held out.

'I've brought Miss Preece for tea,' explained the doctor. He glanced at his watch. 'There's plenty of time; would you like to look round the grounds, Cressida?'

'Oh, yes, please.'

'It's very nearly dark but there is a moon. Come this way...'

He led her round to the side of the house, down a few shallow steps and through a shrubbery. There was a gate at the end and as they reached it he asked, 'Do you like horses?'

'Horses? Me? Yes, I do. When Father was alive I used to ride with him. My stepmother sold Father's horse and my pony.' She bent down to fondle Caesar's ears and pat Mabel, pacing along beside her. The memory still hurt.

'Take a look at these,' invited the doctor cheerfully, and whistled. The two enormous beasts who loomed up at a gallop by the gate were followed by an old pony and a donkey.

'Heavens above—the size of them! They're percherons, aren't they? Do you work them?'

'Just when we make hay and plough. They're elderly—I got them from the knackers—there's room enough for them here and they deserve a year or two of peace and quiet.'

She stroked the enormous noses breathing gently over them. 'And the pony and donkey?'

'They happened to be there. The pony's very old, and he and the donkey are fast friends.' He nodded towards the end of the field beyond the gate. 'The stables are over there. I've a mare I ride when I'm here—she's already in for the night. The boy will be along soon to bed these four down.'

He handed out lumps of sugar and Cressida said, 'Oh, may I…?'

He gave her the rest of the sugar and she took off her glove and offered it in turn. 'Oh, how can you bear not to live here?' she wanted to know.

'Well, I have my work.' He smiled down at her. 'Holland is a small country and I have my car. I spend as much time here as I can manage.' He broke off as a strong-looking lad came plodding towards them. 'There's Wigbald.' He called out to the boy who as he joined them said something in Fries and the doctor replied in the same tongue before saying, 'Cressida, this is Wigbald who runs the stables for me and does the ploughing and a good deal of the heavy work. He will be a good farmer when he is grown.'

He spoke to Wigbald again, the boy came forward and she held out a hand and had it wrung remorselessly. 'Nice to meet you,' said Cressida and smiled widely at him, hoping he would at least see that she was pleased to meet him. It seemed he was for he made quite a long speech, not a word of which could she understand. He then thumped the beasts gently on their enormous rumps and turned to the stables, followed by the pony and the donkey.

Cressida watched their stately plodding until they had reached the stables. 'That's a very funny name,' she said. 'Wigbald—how do you spell it?'

The doctor obliged. 'Fries names are a little out of the ordinary and we like to keep them in the family, as it were.' He took her arm. 'You'll get cold standing there—my fault. We can walk round the shrubbery and cross the lawn and go in through the kitchen.'

It was almost dark now but the sky was clear and full of stars and coming out of the shrubbery on to the grass she saw the house again, the back this time, with lighted windows casting brightness on to the velvety lawn. Without stopping to think she said, 'But Nicola must be mad to dislike this—it's the most wonderful house I've ever seen.' She stopped abruptly. 'I'm sorry, I had no business to say that. I—I expect den Haag is a very nice place; some people prefer the town, don't they? I mean, it's really a long way from anywhere here, isn't it?' She went on a little desperately, for he had remained silent, 'Although I suppose Leeuwarden isn't too far away.'

'Don't babble, Cressy, there is no need.' He sounded kind and a little amused. They had reached a stout door at the bottom of a pair of steps and he led her down and opened it on to a flagged passage with plastered walls at the end of which there was another door. The kitchen was beyond, a large square room, its flagstones covered in matting, a row of windows at semi-basement level. A vast dresser loaded with china took up almost all of one wall and facing the door was a large Aga before which sat a tabby cat who ignored the dogs. Tyske was at the table, stuffing a chicken; she looked up as they went in and said something to the doctor which made him laugh. 'Tyske says that we must be cold and she will bring tea at once.'

What was there to laugh about in that? reflected Cressida as she was led out of the kitchen, up a few steps and through a small door which took them into the hall. The door was beside a wide staircase which ascended to a half-landing before turning at right angles to a gallery above. The house door was ahead of them and a wide sweep of black and white tiles, partly covered by thin silk rugs. Along one wall was a walnut sidetable with a panelled frieze elaborately carved, upon which was a bowl of chrysanthemums, and on either side of it Dutch burgomaster chairs each with an intricately carved crest. On the opposite wall there was a marble fireplace in which a log fire burned briskly, flanked by winged armchairs, their walnut cabriole legs gleaming in the firelight, upholstered in dark red brocade. The walls were white and almost covered by portraits and landscapes in heavy gilt frames. A brass chandelier hung from the high plastered ceiling and there were ormolu wall lights spaced around the walls. A long case clock stood in one corner, chiming the hour.

She stood still, taking it all in unhurriedly. 'It's beautiful,' she said presently, and the doctor nodded.

'Most of the furniture is original and was brought here when the house was built.'

'It's old, the house...'

'Parts of it are sixteenth-century; it got added to from time to time but except for the plumbing and heating and electricity it hasn't been altered for almost two hundred years.'

They crossed to arched double doors and he ushered her through them into the drawing-room. There was a bright fire here too, under a massive stone hood with a coat of arms carved upon it. It was a very large room and yet it contrived to be lived-in and comfortable. The furniture was a nice mixture of satinwood and rosewood although the two walnut and marquetry display cabinets on either side of the fireplace were of an earlier date and filled with massive silver and a Meissen tea set, a collection of small bowls and dishes and a massive centrepiece.

There were sofas on either side of the fire and a number of easy-chairs and the room was lighted by the lamps standing on the various small tables. The enormous cut-glass chandelier hanging from the ceiling, although unlighted, reflected the lamp-light and the flames from the fire, giving the room a warm glow.

The doctor gave her time to look around before inviting her to sit by the fire. 'We'll have our tea here,' he said, sitting down opposite her, 'then we must go back; it wouldn't do to keep Charity waiting.'

Cressida said, 'You have a beautiful home and so peaceful and far away—well, I know you can't be far away from anywhere in Holland but it seems like that.'

'You like the country?'

'Oh, yes, although I liked Leiden. I'm going to explore this part of Holland...'

'Friesland.' He was laughing.

'Yes, well, Friesland.' She smiled at him a little shyly as the door opened and Wester came in with the tea-tray. The dogs, who had stayed in the kitchen to have their meal, came in with him, followed by the cat. The three of them sat down before the fire, the cat in the middle.

'What is his name?' asked Cressida.

'Smith! He adopted us a year or so ago; the dogs are devoted to him.'

Wester had set out the tea things, a plate of sandwiches, another of little cakes and *speculaas* on a table between them and gone again.

'Be mother,' said the doctor. 'I have two lumps of sugar.'

He was friendly in a casual fashion and she felt at ease with him. She had been rather taken aback with the grandeur of his home but he was so very much at ease himself that she forgot to be shy. Besides, the conversation he carried on was calculated to set her mind at rest: gardens and gardening, music and books, Friesland's past history... They ate their tea in complete harmony. Cressida had quite forgotten Nicola, and, as for the doctor, although he hadn't forgotten her, he had certainly dismissed her from his mind as a problem to be dealt with at some not too distant date.

Cressida was disappointed that she hadn't seen more of the house, but Aldrik hadn't suggested it and she hadn't liked to ask; besides it was time for them to return. She asked if she might go to the kitchen and say goodbye to Tyske, 'For she gave us such a lovely tea,' she pointed out, and then shook hands with Wester, who bowed over her hand—just as though I were someone important, she thought, not noticing the doctor's smile. Nicola, when she had been to Janslum, had ignored Wester and eaten the delicious lunch Tyske had prepared for them without comment.

They didn't talk much as they drove back to the van der Bronses' house, Cressida sat quietly, feeling the warmth of the breath of the dogs on the back of her neck whenever they leaned forward. She was happy; she was having a lovely day off and she was going back to a job that she was enjoying. She'd had no idea that half a dozen children could be such fun even if they were hard work and took up every moment of her day.

At the house, as the doctor helped her out she did her best to thank him. 'I can't remember when I've had such a splendid time,' she told him. 'Thank you very much. There must have been so many other things you would have liked to have done—I'm sure you don't get much free time.'

She was thinking of Nicola now and wondered if she had minded the doctor spending a whole day away from her.

'It is I who thank you,' he told her. 'I'm always happy to come to my home here and it is an added pleasure to show it to someone. I'm glad you liked to see it.'

'Oh, I did like it, the horses and that lovely kitchen and the dogs.' She stopped, aware that she was probably boring him. 'Anyway,' she went on briskly, 'thank you.'

They were standing on the sweep before the door and although it was really very cold she felt nothing but a warm glow. She lifted a happy face to his and he bent and kissed her.

* * *

Charity, who had gone to the window and seen the car's headlights sweep up to the door said, 'Tyco, he's kissing her...'

Her husband lowered his newspaper. 'A quite normal thing to do, my love.'

'Yes—no, it isn't. He's supposed to be going to marry that Nicola...'

'I hardly think that Aldrik is likely to be firmly influenced by what he is supposed to be doing. I have known him for years—he does what he wants to do.'

Charity came away from the window. 'Oh, do you suppose...?'

Tyco abandoned his reading. 'My darling, let us suppose nothing but wait and see.'

'Men,' said Charity. 'You're so different from us.'

'What a good thing that is, my love.' He pulled her towards him and kissed her soundly.

Dinner was a pleasant meal. Teile and Letizia had been allowed to stay up and the talk was a mixture of childish chatter and light-hearted talk. No one mentioned Nicola, nor did they comment on Cressida's unfortunate stay at Noordwijk-aan-Zee, and when they had had their coffee and she reminded Charity that she would have to go back to the ter Beemstras' the doctor got up as well.

'I'll drop you off,' he observed, 'it's on my way.' Which it wasn't, but Cressida, still a little muddled as to the geography of her surroundings, didn't know that. She made her farewells, promising to go shopping with Charity on the following week, and got into the Bentley again. Aldrik hadn't spoken and the drive to the ter Beemstras' was short. She wished very much that he would kiss her again but he didn't, only went into the house with her, exchanged a few courteous remarks with the ter Beemstras, shook her hand and went away again, without expressing a wish to see her again.

'Oh, well,' reflected Cressida, getting ready for bed, 'why should he? I dare say it was his good deed for the day.'

However there had been no need to kiss her, and certainly not with such—she sought for a word—satisfaction. She had enjoyed it, although she reminded herself prudently that she had been kissed so seldom that it had stirred her rather more than it might have stirred any other girl—Nicola, for instance. Horrible girl, thought Cressida, as she closed her eyes, and I wonder what he's doing? Ringing her up, most likely, telling her what a boring afternoon he had. She drifted off to sleep.

The doctor was in his study with Mabel and Caesar, making notes for the lecture he was to give in Leiden in a few days' time. Telephoning Nicola hadn't entered his head and when he was interrupted by a phone call from her he frowned impatiently.

'Darling,' trilled Nicola, 'are you very lonely up there? Are you coming back tomorrow? There's the van Douws' dinner party—you haven't forgotten? I'm just off to have dinner with one or two friends, I'm so lonely without you.' And when he didn't answer, 'Aldrik?'

'Enjoy yourself,' he told her. 'I'll pick you up tomorrow evening about seven o'clock. I'm not lonely, I'm getting a good deal of work done.'

'Oh, work,' said Nicola. 'What have you done all day?'

He told her briefly.

'I'm so glad the poor girl has settled down at last,' said Nicola softly. 'I feel very badly about her unhappy stay at Tante Clotilde's. It was all my fault. I thought she was a working-class girl, used to household chores. I'm so relieved that she has a more suitable job now. I dare say she'll meet someone of her own sort—a farmer or a bank clerk—someone like that.'

The doctor thought of several replies but he uttered none of them. He said again, 'Enjoy your evening, Nicola. I'll see you tomorrow.'

He wrote without interruption for a time then he went into the drawing-room. The room looked beautiful in the light of the lamps and the fire welcomed him. He looked at the chair where Cressida had been sitting and wished that she was still there.

He went to sit by the fire, one arm round Mabel's vast shoulders, Caesar sprawled over his feet, and when Wester came in presently he told him to lock up and go to bed. The old house was quiet, he could hear the wind whistling in from the Waddenzee but it was a sound he loved. Cressida would like it too, he reflected; he would bring her here again and drive her to the flat coast to watch the wild sea breaking against the dykes. He thought that it would be some time before she trusted him completely and it would be necessary to disabuse her of the idea that he and Nicola were to marry. He had never mentioned marriage to Nicola although he had to admit that he had considered her for a wife. She was pretty, amusing, knew how to dress and would run his homes efficiently, although he was aware that no one who worked for him liked her, but he had known for some days now—weeks, he amended—that he wanted Cressida for his wife. What had begun as an act of kindness on his part had become the most important thing in life. He would need patience and time, but he was a patient man. That she liked him he was sure, but she was wary of him too, and not surprisingly after her miserable time with Jonkvrouw van Germert.

He would have to talk to Nicola. He had known that she wanted to marry him but he was certain that she had no love for him. She enjoyed his company—besides, he was a wealthy man and able to give her everything she wanted—but he was aware too that she could be just as fond of any man who could give her a secure future. She would have been a very suitable wife, of course, but he marvelled that he had ever considered her as his. With hindsight he saw now that she had been clever enough to adapt to his life and ideals so that he, wrapped up in his profession and heart-whole, had allowed the idea of marrying her to enter his head. 'Something which must be remedied,' he observed to the dogs, who cocked friendly ears but made no move.

***

With Christmas barely two weeks away the ter Beemstra household was a hive of activity. The house would be full, Mevrouw ter Beemstra told Cressida: aunts and uncles, grandparents, brothers and sisters would be coming. 'There will be four more children.' She sounded apologetic. 'Ten all told! You will manage? Baby's nurse will help out, of course, and we will all assist you.'

Cressida assured her that she would manage in a voice which disguised her uncertainty of this. True, it would be for a few days only, and the children would probably amuse themselves for a good deal of the time. She shut her mind to the problem of getting ten children out of bed and washed and dressed and returning the same number to their beds each evening, but bridges should never be crossed until one reached them.

The following week was largely taken up with the making of paper chains, addressing of Christmas cards and the secret tying up of presents, and her days were filled. She was to go to Charity's again for her day off and drive to Leeuwarden to shop, and if, at the back of her mind, she had hoped to see Aldrik van der Linus or even have news of him, she was to be disappointed.

Tyco came to fetch her after breakfast before going to Leiden for the day, and at his house she got into the Mini, settled Charity beside her and took them to Leeuwarden at a careful pace, still not very happy about driving on the other side of the road. Directed by Charity, she parked the car at a hotel in the centre of the city while Charity reserved a table for lunch before the pair of them made for the shops.

It had been a splendid day, reflected Cressida in her bed that night; Charity was a dear and they had talked about everything under the sun—excepting Aldrik—and they had done their shopping to their entire satisfaction although Cressida's purse was woefully empty. Back at the house Tyco had been waiting for them, ready to entertain them with an account of his day at Leiden and then admire the presents Charity had bought. Teile and Letizia had come back then and everything had been bundled away out of sight before tea. Tyco had driven her back to the ter Beemstras' after dinner that evening and gone indoors with her to spend a few minutes with them, and when he left he told her in his kind voice that they looked forward to seeing her again as soon as Christmas was over. No one had mentioned Aldrik; she supposed that he was already in England.

There were flurries of snow from a leaden sky the next day and by the day before Christmas Eve the countryside looked like a Christmas card. The school holidays had started and Cressida spent a good deal of the time making snowmen in the grounds with the children, going for brisk walks whenever the snow stopped and overseeing the changing of shoes, the drying of parkas and the drinking of hot cocoa the moment they got indoors. It was an energetic life with no time to spare but she enjoyed it and the exercise and the children's cheerful company had put colour into her cheeks and a sparkle in her eyes. She had taught them a carol too—'Good King Wenceslas'—badgering them to get the words right while she thumped the piano in the playroom. Even little Lucia joined in and Cressida hoped that it would be proof of her efforts to teach the children English.

They had had a final rehearsal, Lucia had been whisked off to her bed by her nurse and Cressida was helping the children to tidy the room when the door opened and the doctor walked in.

His, 'Hello,' was addressed to everyone in the room. 'I was sent up on my own; everyone's bustling about downstairs.'

The children surged round him, for he had known the whole family for some years, all talking at once.

'English,' warned Cressida, raising her voice to be heard.

'Just for a minute we speak Fries, dear Cressy,' said Willum. 'It is Christmas.' He gave her a wide smile. 'And we have not seen Oom Aldrik for some time.'

'All right. Ten minutes, then. I'm going to see Nurse about something.'

She whisked herself out of the room without looking at the

doctor. She had been so delighted to see him; she supposed it was the unexpectedness of his arrival which had made her feel so excited. She had imagined him to be in England by now—perhaps he wasn't going after all. Nicola, she felt sure, had very persuasive powers.

She found Anna, Baby's nurse, in the night nursery. Her small charge already asleep, she was tidying the chest of drawers, but she looked up as Cressida put her head round the door and gave a reluctant smile. They got on well now, but for the first few days Cressida had been hard put to it to convince the nurse that she had no intention of interfering with little Lucia's routine. For half an hour each day she came to the nursery and taught the moppet simple English but always with Anna there too.

Cressida marshalled her scanty knowledge of Dutch, seeking permission for Lucia to stay up a little later on Christmas Eve so that she might sing the carol with her brothers and sisters. It took a few minutes to make herself understood and another few minutes while they exchanged remarks about the weather, and, having shown willing, as it were, Cressida went back to the playroom.

The doctor was still there. 'Ah, good, Cressy, will you come downstairs with me? There's something I want to give you...'

'It may be for us; is it?' asked Friso.

'That's something you'll know on Christmas morning, and don't tease Cressy to find out what it is, for she won't tell.'

The little girls kissed him and the boys shook his hand and screamed, 'Happy Christmas!' as he opened the door and ushered Cressida through.

He made no effort to go downstairs but stood looking down at her.

'Do you not wish that you were coming with me to England?' he asked.

She didn't answer at once while she thought about it. 'Well, I'd love to go home, but only if my stepmother wasn't there, if you see what I mean, and I'd like to see Moggy, but I'm really happy here. I felt, well, a stranger in Leiden, but here I feel quite at home, which is funny because half the time I don't understand a word of what anyone says.'

He laughed, 'I'm not surprised, Fries is a strange language, and the Hollanders don't understand it either. Will you be free at Christmas?'

'Heavens, no. The house will be full of family and there are four more children coming.'

'I must make it up to you when I get back...'

'Thank you, you're very kind, but there's no need. I mean, you've done such a lot for me already and you don't have much time and when you do you must have friends—and things to do...'

'Am I being snubbed, Cressy?' he asked blandly.

"Snubbed?' She was so shocked at the idea that she put a hand on his arm. 'How could I ever snub you? I don't know what I should have done without you.'

She stared up into his face, suddenly and blindingly aware that she didn't know what she *would* do without him; moreover the prospect of it didn't bear thinking about. She said slowly, 'I think you don't need to be concerned about me any longer, I mean you can forget me without feeling you need to bother. I don't think I am explaining myself very well but you've your own life and it's quite different from mine... Oh, dear, I really can't explain...'

'Then don't try,' he advised her briskly. 'Enjoy life here and have a happy Christmas.' He patted her hand in a big-brotherly way and added, 'Come down to the hall and get the parcel I've got for the children. I still have to call on the van der Bronses and then go to Janslum before I drive down to the ferry.'

She longed to ask him if Nicola was going with him but all she said was, 'I hope you have a lovely Christmas and please remember me to Lady Merrill.'

She went downstairs and he gave her a brightly wrapped box. 'I'd be grateful if you'd hide it away for them.' She wished very much that he would kiss her but he didn't, he wished her goodbye and went in search of Beatrix ter Beemstra, and within a few minutes he had driven himself away.

Cressida went slowly back upstairs, hid the box under the bed in her room and went back to the children. They were all excited and noisy and she had her hands full for the next twenty minutes or so, calming them down and making sure that they were clean and neat for their supper, a meal everyone was to share for once seeing that the household was involved in getting ready for the guests who were coming in the morning. The meal over, she got them to their beds and then went to Mevrouw ter Beemstra's room to pin up a dress that she had discovered at the last minute was too long.

Mevrouw ter Beemstra stood patiently while Cressida pinned, a little puzzled because Cressida was so quiet and pale. 'You feel well?' she asked anxiously. 'You are to tell me if there is anything? You are not unhappy?'

Cressida assured her that she had never felt better and there was nothing the matter. She made her voice cheerful, adding, 'I'm looking forward to Christmas very much; it's such fun with children, isn't it?'

Mevrouw ter Beemstra had been pursuing her own train of thought. 'Of course, Aldrik came to see you and I think that you wish that you could have gone to England with him? Is that not so? Such a kind man, he brought the children a present—he never forgets.'

Cressida, her mouth full of pins, was unable to answer. He'd forgotten her, hadn't he? Telling her to enjoy life in that brisk manner. At the moment she felt as though she would never enjoy life again as long as she lived and if this was how one felt when one found oneself in love then the quicker one fell out of love again the better.

She sat back on her heels to see the effect of her work and began a bright conversation with her employer which put that kind lady's mind at rest, and then she took the dress along to

Anna, who sewed beautifully and was waiting with a needle and thread. Since it was quite late by now Cressida took herself off to bed and had a nice comfortable cry before she went to sleep. She woke up quite early in the morning feeling sensible and clear-headed about the whole thing. It was most unfortunate that she should have fallen in love with the doctor but that wouldn't and mustn't alter the mild friendship he had shown towards her, and now that she had made it clear that she was nicely settled in a job and perfectly happy he could forget her, and, no doubt, in the course of time, marry Nicola. It was a fate she didn't want for him, but if he loved the woman there was nothing she could do about it. If, on the other hand, he didn't love her, then, Cressida decided, she would do her best to stop him getting married. She had no idea how she was going to do this but it was an uplifting thought and carried her through an extremely busy morning. The four children arrived before lunch and since there were now so many they were to have their meal in the playroom with Cressida presiding. Quite a tableful, she conceded, handing out plates of soup and acting as mediator between the two older boys and their cousins. The little girls were over-excited too and she was relieved when the meal was finished and she could get them into hats and coats and allow them to stream into the garden to fight each other with snowballs, and, with her help, make a series of snowmen.

It was too cold to stay out for long, so she shepherded them indoors again, saw to their tea and then sent them all to collect the presents they had parcelled up so laboriously. They were to be put under the Christmas tree that evening and handed out in the morning and there was a good deal of stealthy coming and going until all the presents were arranged on a table in the hall ready for Mijnheer ter Beemstra to put under the tree later that evening. Since it was such a special day all the children were to stay up for supper which meant scrambling into best clothes, and, for the girls, having their hair arranged just so. Cressida barely had time to get into the grey jersey dress, of which she was heartily sick, and do her own face and hair before the gong sounded and she lined up the children and set them in a tidy queue to go down to the drawing-room, bringing up the rear with Anna and little Lucia.

The drawing-room was a large room very full of people. Cressida had been introduced to everyone who had arrived but now they all looked alike to her; moreover, the women were wearing smart, expensive dresses. She stuck out like a sore thumb, and she wished that she had a uniform like Anna. She was a sensible girl, though; she had no intention of spoiling her evening by moaning over her unsuitable clothes. She made the rounds with the children, shaking hands with everyone and exchanging small talk, and found herself presently with a glass in her hand, talking to a rather fierce old gentleman who reminded her that he was Mevrouw ter Beemstra's father. He spoke English but insisted that she tried out her few words of Dutch. 'If you are going to stay here,' he rumbled, 'you'll have to speak the language.' He studied her face. 'I hear the children are doing well. You like teaching?'

'Well, I don't teach much, you know, just speak English all the time and they learn bits of poetry and that sort of thing. They're nice children and very quick.'

They were joined by an elderly lady, one of the aunts, Cressida supposed, who asked her how she liked Friesland, and since her English was only a little better than Cressida's Dutch the old gentleman amused himself helping them out until the gong went again and they trooped into the dining-room.

It looked very festive with tinsel decorations and a lovely centrepiece of holly and Christmas roses, and as well as the large dining table a smaller one had been set at right angles to it and here the children sat with Cressida at one end and Anna at the other.

The meal was a leisurely one, and, since the children were there, not elaborate: soup, little pastry parcels which were filled with smoked salmon, roast pheasant with straw potatoes and braised celery and finally ices topped with whipped cream and nuts. Lucia was half asleep by the time they had finished but she woke at once when Willum reminded her in a loud voice that they were going to sing their carol. Carefully coached by Cressida, he got to his feet and announced that if everyone would go to the drawing-room they would be entertained with a Christmas carol, whereupon everyone clapped and made haste to do as he asked, followed, when everyone was settled, by the children. There was a grand piano in the drawing-room, Cressida sat down at it as the children filed into their places and she began on the well-known tune. The children sang beautifully. One of them, she wasn't sure which one, was tone deaf, but it hardly showed and they had learnt the words carefully. The applause was deafening and they sang it all over again before doing the rounds once more, bidding everyone goodnight. As they were going out of the room Mevrouw ter Beemstra said, 'Do come down again if you like, Cressida.' She glanced at the clock. 'It is already late but if you wish...'

Cressida thanked her, but agreed that it was late, she didn't add that there were ten children to see into their beds, which, even with Anna's help, would take quite some time. She wished the room in general goodnight and went upstairs, where the more rebellious of the children had to be rounded up, stood over while they cleaned their teeth and then tucked up in bed.

She went to bed herself almost at once, too tired to do more than wonder if Aldrik had reached his grandmother's house safely. Also she wondered if and when she would see him again.

CHAPTER EIGHT

CRESSIDA WAS SO tired at the end of Christmas Day that she could have fallen on to her bed and gone to sleep without even bothering to undress, but she resisted the urge to do this, undressed, had a bath and got into bed, where she lay sleepily reviewing her day. It had been an exceedingly busy one but she had enjoyed every minute of it. The children had been a handful, of course; keeping the peace between ten children all tearing open their presents at the same time when they should have been having their breakfast had been a Herculean task, but, as Mevrouw ter Beemstra had pointed out, they would never have sat through morning church otherwise and going to church in the village on Christmas morning was a tradition which had to be maintained. There had been no turkey or Christmas pudding at lunch, but vegetable soup followed by goose with red cabbage and then a spectacular dessert of ice-cream, whipped cream and fresh pineapple had proved excellent substitutes, and there had been champagne for the grown-ups and fruit drinks for the children. There was no question of a respite after the meal; the children had been buttoned into their outdoor clothes again and left loose in the garden with Cressida in charge. What afternoon there was left had been more than filled by the need to assist the smaller ones to learn to ride their tricycles and bicycles, set up a target so that the older boys could try out their air pistols and keep the peace between the little girls, casting eyes on each other's dolls and wanting them. They had had tea in the playroom and then played grandmother's footsteps and hunt the slipper, games they had never heard of but which Cressida remembered very well from her own childhood and which tired them out nicely. They had had their supper in the small sitting-room leading from the drawing-room and the next hour or so was entirely taken up with marshalling them tidily so that they could say goodnight to the grown-ups in the drawing-room and then be coaxed to their beds after their baths. Cressida reflected that she could have gone to bed herself then quite happily but the ter Beemstras had insisted that she should join everyone else for a buffet supper, so she had changed into the grey jersey and gone back downstairs, where she had been instantly made at home by Mevrouw ter Beemstra, handed from countless cousins and aunts and uncles once again and thanked for the care she had had for the children.

She was plied with drink too and delicious bits and pieces, and presently found herself sitting by the *domine*, a youngish man with a rather stern face. His English was good and he was interested in her; she found herself talking freely to him although she said nothing about her unfortunate stay with Jonkvrouw van Germert, but she did talk about the doctor because he was always at the back of her mind and thinking about him wasn't enough. The *domine* listened gravely. 'You have been lucky to have found such a good and kind friend,' he had told her. 'You will be grateful to him for the rest of your life.'

'Yes, I expect I shall,' Cressida had said quietly. Her companion had made it seem as though the doctor had been an episode in her life to be remembered with gratitude but never to be revived.

She had wished everyone goodnight presently and gone up to her room and to her bed. It had really been a very happy day, she muttered sleepily; she had had presents too, handkerchiefs and notepaper and a charming silver bracelet. She should have been feeling happy. It was strange therefore that she should cry herself to sleep.

She woke during the night. 'He could have sent me a Christmas card,' she said sadly, and presently she went to sleep again.

She was up early and soon was urging the children out of their beds and into their clothes and all the while the doctor loomed at the back of her mind, and that despite the fact that she had wakened with the intention of thinking no more about him.

An intention not upheld by Aldrik van der Linus, however. He had thought of her constantly and in answer to his grandmother's discreet probings had made no bones about telling her that it was his intention to marry Cressida.

His grandmother received the news without surprise. 'A sweet girl,' she had told him, 'and very sensible too. Has she any idea...?'

'No. I had hoped that we would become friends and in a sense we are, but although she doesn't blame me for her unfortunate stay with Jonkvrouw van Germert she is under the impression that I intend to marry Nicola. I shall need to go carefully.'

'You have made things clear to Nicola?'

'Yes, if by that you mean that she doesn't expect to marry me; indeed she assured me that she had never considered me as a prospective husband and was only too delighted that I had fallen in love at last.'

To which his grandmother made no reply. Men, reflected that lady silently, could be so blind, and the cleverer they were the blinder they seemed to be. Nicola, she had no doubt, had every intention of marrying him; he was too good a prize to give up. She said merely, 'You must be relieved that Cressida is so happy.'

'Indeed I am. I shall go and see her as soon as possible after I get back to Janslum. I have some patients to see in Leiden and a short list at the hospital but I should be able to manage a day or two after that.'

* * *

Cressida, unaware of this, busied herself with the children, thankful when the four young visitors departed for their homes once more. Six, she reflected, were manageable, but ten were a bit too much.

The weather was still wintry with flurries of snow and biting winds, but the children seemed impervious to this; wrapped in her elderly winter coat and a pair of borrowed wellies, a woolly cap pulled down over her ears and a scarf tied round her neck, she accompanied them on expeditions to many nearby canals and a small lake, where they donned their skates and spent hours racing to and fro, and after the first day, realising that she would freeze to death if she didn't do something about it, she prevailed upon Willum to lend her a pair of old skates—Friesian skates, he told her in his careful English, just right for learners—and with his help and a good deal of encouragement from the other children she ventured upon the ice. Of course she fell over a great deal, to be hauled to her feet with commendable patience by Willum or Jacobus, but the by the end of the second day she was able to stagger a few steps on her own and even manage a short distance with the boys, once they were on either side of her, clasping her hands, before she lost her nerve and fell, spiralling slowly on to the ice.

By the end of the week though she was striking out boldly on her own, still falling a good deal of course, amid peals of laughter from the children, but smugly pleased with herself.

She told Charity about it when she went to spend her free day with her. 'I'm black and blue,' she confided, 'but it's such fun and it keeps the children amused.'

'You're still happy? The ter Beemstras are kind to you?'

'Oh, yes, and once the children go back to school I shall have more time... Everyone seems to be getting excited about New Year...'

'Oh, yes, *Olie Ballen* and champagne. Great fun. Are the ter Beemstras having a house party? We've got Tyco's family coming again. Usually we go there but he doesn't want me to go too far from home...'

Cressida nodded. 'Quite right too. Yes, there is to be a houseful again. Willum is to be allowed to stay up this year; Jacobus and Friso are furious about it. The other four children won't be coming though so once I get them to bed the others should be manageable.' She smiled widely. 'They are sweet, you know, even when they're naughty.'

Charity looked at her anxiously. 'You don't regret being there? You might have got a much cushier job in England.'

'What as? I can't do anything, you know—only housework and the flowers and fetching and carrying. Children are much more fun. Besides, they keep me very busy.'

The next day the guests arrived; aunts and uncles, cousins, old friends—Cressida had met most of them at Christmas. They greeted her kindly, observed in their excellent English how well she coped with the children, and looked forward to seeing her that evening at dinner.

Cressida, getting into the grey dress—which she never wished to see again—reflected that so far everything was going well. The children had gone to bed like lambs and she actually had time on her hands before going down to the drawing-room. She went along to the playroom and sat down in a window-seat, looking out into the dark night. It had stopped snowing and presently there would be a moon but now there was the merest glimmer of stars. She stared up at them and wondered where the doctor was. Back in his lovely home, no doubt, with Nicola and a houseful of guests.

His, 'Hello, Cressy', was so part and parcel of her thoughts that she took a moment to realise that he was actually there, in the room, leaning against the door, still in his heavy car coat, bringing a blast of icy air from the cold night into the room.

'Well,' said Cressida, 'well, what a surprise.' She was aware that this didn't sound very welcoming or friendly and added hastily, 'I mean, how nice to see you, Doctor.'

He came to stand before her, looming over her, blotting out the room with his vast size, and since he said nothing she plunged into speech.

'You're not staying here of course—you're on your way to Janslum. I expect you have a houseful of guests; I had no idea that New Year was so important in Holland...'

'Friesland,' he corrected her smilingly. 'Oh, but it is. We come miles in order to celebrate it and wish each other well. My sisters and their husbands and children will be at home waiting for me...'

'And Mabel and Caesar and the horses, pony and donkey,' said Cressida in a far-away voice, 'and that nice Wester and his wife.' She sat up—this would never do; on no account must he feel sorry for her. She went on briskly, 'I expect you had a happy Christmas? I hope Lady Merrill is well?'

'In excellent health. She sends you her love. Are you happy, Cressida?'

She hadn't expected that so that she answered too quickly. 'Oh, yes. The children are such fun and Mevrouw and Mijnheer ter Beemstra are so kind. We had a lovely time at Christmas.' She went pink, for it had sounded as though she was reminding him that he had ignored her completely, although he had no reason to have done otherwise. She hurried on, anxious to let him see just how happy she was. 'The children have taught me to skate, I'm not good at it yet, but I can stay on my feet for a little while. It's been very cold here and there's been a lot of snow.'

She looked up and caught his eyes. There was a gleam in them which she thought was amusement and indeed she was making a fine hash of a casual conversation.

He bent down and drew her to her feet and laid his hands on her shoulders. 'I came to wish you a happy New Year, Cressy,' he told her, 'and it will be, you know.' He kissed her gently on her cheek, looking down at her gravely. 'I thought of you while I was in England.'

She was suddenly very cross. 'Oh, did you?' she asked,

peeved. 'Then why didn't you send me a Christmas card? Lady Merrill sent me one and so did Moggy and her sister and Mr Tims.' She drew in her breath like a child. 'I'm sorry, I didn't mean any of that, truly I didn't. You've been so kind to me and I shall always be grateful. Perhaps I'm tired.' She smiled shakily. 'I hope you have a marvellous New Year with lots of patients and everything you could possibly wish for.'

'Well, not too many patients,' he was laughing a little, 'and I intend to have everything I wish for. Do you know what I wish for, Cressy?'

The door opened and Willum came in and the doctor took his hands from Cressida's shoulders and said easily, 'Hello, Willum, do you want Cressy?'

'Yes, I can't find the tie I had for Christmas—the green one—I want to wear it.' He added importantly, 'I'm staying up for dinner.'

'Splendid.' The doctor didn't sound in the least put out at the interruption. It couldn't have been anything important, thought Cressida; perhaps he had been going to tell her that he was going to marry Nicola, and that they had made up their differences. She was a clever enough young woman to convince him that she had been acting for the best when she had arranged for Cressida to go to her aunt and he would have forgiven her.

The doctor said softly, 'No, Cressida, don't try and guess. Wait until I tell you.' He went to the door. 'I must be off or it will be after midnight before I get home and that wouldn't do at all. I'll wish you both a happy New Year and leave you to find that tie.'

He went away and Cressida heard a good deal of laughter in the hall downstairs and then the solid sound of the front door shutting.

'Let's go and look for it,' she told Willum.

Dinner was elaborate and festive and afterwards everyone went to the drawing-room and drank champagne and ate the *Olie Ballen*. They were nice, Cressida decided, like small doughnuts, each encased in a paper napkin to keep the grease and sugar off the guests' clothes, and presently their glasses were filled once again and as the great *stoelklok* in the corner of the room chimed midnight, a toast was drunk to the New Year and everyone went around kissing each other and shaking hands. Someone turned on the record player and several people started to dance, the signal for Cressida to capture a reluctant Willum, bid everyone goodnight and see him safely into his bed. She didn't go downstairs again; it had been a lovely evening and the very best bit of it had been Aldrik's visit. Although, she thought sleepily, it had been a pity that Willum had had to come into the room when he had. Of course she knew that sooner or later the doctor would marry Nicola, she was so exactly right for a well-known doctor, but it would have clinched the matter, so to speak, if he had told her himself; she was finding it hard to plan her future but she thought in a muddled way that it might be easier once he was married.

After the excitement of the New Year the days were rather dull but very soon the boys went back to school so that the pattern of her days was changed again. She was still fully occupied but now she had an hour or two free during the day, which she occupied by exploring the village and the surrounding countryside. It was on the second day that she went for an expedition that she met the *domine* again and was invited to look round the church with him. She liked him and she was eager to learn all that she could about Friesland and the people who lived there, and he for his part seemed pleased to tell her all that he knew. The church disappointed her; it was white-washed and rather bare although the pulpit with its sounding-board was very handsome, but it had a long and interesting history and she was a willing listener. Before she left him he invited her to go again so that she might look at the church registers. She accepted willingly; it was nice to have a friend and very soon now Charity would have her baby and there would be an end to their shopping expeditions at least for the time being. She told Mevrouw ter Beemstra about it when she got back and that lady nodded approvingly; Domine Stilstra was a serious man, no longer young but well liked by everybody. It crossed her mind that it wouldn't be a bad thing if he were to marry; Cressida would make him a most suitable wife... She observed kindly, 'Domine Stilstra is a most interesting man; he knows so much of our history and spends a great deal of his time studying old customs.'

It had stayed cold and the canals and ponds were frozen solid although the sun had shone from time to time, but two days after Cressida's tour of the church the sky became overcast and the wind, always cold, became bitter. None the less Anna wrapped herself and Lucia warmly and declared her intention of going to see her sister who lived on the other side of the village. Mevrouw ter Beemstra had gone to Leeuwarden to the hairdressers and Cressida, struggling for the right words to persuade her not to go, found her vocabulary quite inadequate. To her anxious arm waving in the direction of the darkening cloudy sky, Anna merely smiled and patted her shoulder with a reassuring, 'OK.'

Cressida dredged up what she hoped were the right words and asked if Anna would be back for playroom tea, whereupon Anna broke into a long reply, which, since she couldn't make head or tail of it, did little to reassure Cressida. She watched the two of them go with the unhappy feeling that she should have stopped them; on the other hand probably she was being fussy. After all, Anna had lived in Friesland all her life and would know the weather like the back of her hand.

She didn't go out herself. Both Sepke and Galske were at home, sharing, as they shared everything, a nasty cold. She settled them by the playroom stove, with a packet of tissues and their favourite toys, and then got out the mending basket and began on the task of repairing a rent in one of Friso's shirts. The afternoon darkened rapidly and she drew the curtains and turned on the lights, listening worriedly to the wind howling across the empty fields. Presently she went downstairs to see if Anna and Lucia were back but there was no sign of them and although she was partly reassured by the cook's unworried face she wished that Mevrouw ter Beemstra were at home.

They had their tea and there was still no sign of any one of them and when she heard the car stopping outside the house she ran downstairs intent on telling Mijnheer ter Beemstra. As she reached the front door she saw its tail lights disappearing again and Willum told her that his father had to return at once to his office. 'What do you want him for?' he asked.

'Oh, well, I dare say it's all right but Anna and Lucia are still out—I expected them back for tea. Your mother will be back presently and she'll know what to do. Come along upstairs, you're all three cold and wet…is the weather very bad outside?'

'Very bad, and there is warning of a storm,' said Willum. 'I hope that our mother takes care.'

'She's a very good driver,' said Cressida cheerfully, and tried to ignore a particularly violent gust of wind howling round the house.

She had the boys settled at the table eating their tea when Mevrouw ter Beemstra returned. She heard her voice in the hall and went down to meet her.

'The weather is very bad,' said Mevrouw ter Beemstra. 'It is difficult to drive. The children are safe home?'

'Anna and Lucia went out after lunch and they are not back. I came down to tell *Mijnheer* when he brought the boys back but he didn't stop only drove away at once. Anna said she was going to her sister's; perhaps she is still there?'

Mevrouw ter Beemstra looked worried. 'She would never stay if she saw that the weather was worsening. I am so afraid that she has taken the short-cut across the fields—it is only a short distance that way and she may have thought she could get back here before the storm broke… We have had a warning of severe wind, I must go and see…'

'I'll go,' said Cressida. 'It's the path leading from the end of the garden at the back of the house, isn't it? Willum pointed out the cottage to me one day, I'm sure that I can find it. If I have a torch it won't be difficult.'

Brave words. She was scared of going out into the dark evening but perhaps Anna and Lucia were sheltering somewhere along the path, not too far away, afraid to go on without a light.

'I'll get my boots—if I could have a powerful torch.'

She was ready to go within five minutes, seen out of the kitchen door by Mevrouw ter Beemstra. 'Don't worry if we don't get back quickly; if Anna is near enough to her sister's cottage, I'll take them back there until the worst of the storm is over. Can it be reached from the village?'

'By car, no. At least a Range Rover could get to within a short distance but there's a canal...'

Mevrouw ter Beemstra looked as though she was going to cry and Cressida said quickly, 'Don't worry, they can't be far away. They may still be with Anna's sister. If they are, I'll come back and tell you.'

She turned on the torch, reassured by its powerful beam, and started with haste down the path which led to the end of the grounds at the back of the house.

The wind was terrific, tearing at her clothes and the scarf she had tied round her head. The rain was ice-cold and the ground beneath her feet treacherous with ice too. She shone the torch before her until she reached the path and then went even more slowly, for she was walking into the teeth of the wind now and could hardly keep on her feet. Every few yards she stopped and shone the torch round her in the hope that she might see Anna and Lucia. It seemed unlikely, there was no shelter and no hedges, only frozen canals between the fields, narrow enough to jump over. There was a much wider canal further on, she knew, with a rickety bridge over it. The thought of having to cross it made her feel sick but the cottage was only a few hundred yards from it and there was no other way. Reaching it, she eyed it fearfully and actually had one hand on the flimsy wooden rail when she heard a sound, and when the wind paused in its bellowing she heard it again. She turned the torch in all directions, lighting up the fields around her and then shone it on to the canal. Anna was crouched on the bank, shielding Lucia with her body.

Cressida gave a wobbly shout and started towards her at the same time as the rain turned to blinding snow. It blotted out everything, whirling round her, driven by the wind and for a moment she stood still, making quite sure that she hadn't moved since she spotted Anna, then she moved carefully forward, praying that she wasn't going round in a circle, and to her relief saw them only a yard or two away.

Crouched down beside them, she could see that Anna's face was very white. Her Dutch deserted her, all she could think of to say was, 'OK?' At least it was a start. Anna shook her head and pointed to one leg.

'*Gebroken*', she muttered, and then urgently, 'Lucia?'

The child was almost asleep with the cold and the pulse in the small wrist was faint, as far as Cressida could tell, though, she wasn't hurt. It was poor Anna who needed urgent help; she must be in pain, thought Cressida and she was lying awkwardly, shielding the little girl's body with her own.

'I'm going to get help,' said Cressida, and added, '*hulp*' and held up five fingers, hoping that Anna would understand that she would be gone for five minutes. That was nonsense, of course, she would never get back in five minutes, but it helped to look on the bright side.

She got to her feet, numb with the cold, patted Anna on the shoulder and started back the way she had come. Hopefully anyone watching from the house would see her torch and come to meet her. She didn't know how long Anna and Lucia had been lying there but Lucia had seemed half asleep despite her whimpers and Anna must surely be half frozen to death. The thought sent her scurrying along the slippery path and she fell down almost at once. The ground was iron-hard and she had to scramble painfully to her feet as best she could before going on more cautiously.

'More haste, less speed,' said Cressida, in a rage with herself, the wind and snow and the terrifying feeling that she was alone in a strange world. She had dropped the torch too, but luckily it was not broken. She picked it up and shone it ahead of her and was almost blinded by the beam from another torch. It was too much; she screamed and was instantly engulfed in the doctor's great arms.

'Silly girl, it is I!' he bellowed into her ear.

Even in a trying situation such as this, she thought, he gets his grammar right, and she promptly burst into tears.

'Where are they?' he asked her, shouting into the wind.

She waved behind her. 'Anna's hurt her leg—I was coming to get help. I think Lucia is all right.'

'Stop crying.' He spoke close to her ear. 'Just where?'

Unfeeling brute, she reflected and then pulled herself together. 'By the canal on the left...'

'Stay here, on no account move.' He kissed her quite roughly and was gone, leaving her almost frozen solid but with a warm glow under her ribs on account of the kiss.

He was a great deal quicker than she had been—in no time at all he was back with Lucia in his arms. He dumped the child on to Cressida, stayed only long enough to warn her to stay where she was and disappeared into the snowy darkness once again.

He was a little longer this time. Not surprisingly, for Anna was a well-built woman and unconscious now—a dead weight.

'Follow me and don't lag behind,' he ordered Cressida, something she had no intention of doing anyway, and she stumbled along as close as she could manage with Lucia hugged close to her, crying now and wanting her mama.

It seemed a long time before they reached the end of the path and saw the lights of the house shining and then a sudden surge of people coming towards them through the snow. Someone—she thought it was Mijnheer ter Beemstra—took Lucia from her, and she straightened her cramped arms and plodded on. She was very tired now and the doctor was somewhere ahead of her, lost in the whirling snowflakes. The house was quite close now, she heaved a sigh of relief and tripped over her own numb feet and once more fell down.

It was really too much trouble to get up. She stayed where she was, aware that it was a foolish thing to do, but she couldn't be bothered to make the effort. She was so cold that it didn't matter any more. She closed her eyes—a nap would be pleasant.

In the house there was ordered chaos with the doctor issuing instructions with unhurried calm. Lucia to her mother, to be undressed and put into a warm—not hot—bath and then into bed, given hot milk and not left until he had had time to look at her. Anna was laid on the kitchen table, divested of as much clothing as possible, wrapped in blankets and then examined.

Her leg was broken, he knew that already—a Pott's fracture just above the ankle. She was still unconscious and he was able to pull the bones into alignment with the help of Mijnheer ter Beemstra, who had just arrived, apply temporary splints and bandage the limb. He had just finished this when he said, 'Where is Cressida? I'd better take a look at her—she'll need bed and warmth...'

She wasn't to be found. Leaving a slowly recovering Anna to the care of the cook, Aldrik got into his coat again, his face grim, and, armed with a torch once more, went back out into the night. He found her quite quickly, for she had been within shouting distance when she fell. He dropped on a knee beside her and shone the torch in her face and let out a great gusty sigh. She was already asleep, she was also ice-cold and her pulse was slow and faint. He lifted her carefully and carried her back to the house and into the warm kitchen, where he found Cook and Mijnheer ter Beemstra hovering over Anna.

'Dirk, get on to the hospital in Leeuwarden, will you? As soon as possible Lucia and Anna must get there for a check-up and so must Cressida.'

He put her down comfortably into Cook's large chair and took off the wellies and her gloves and then, helped by the housemaid, her coat and sodden headscarf. 'Fetch some blankets, will you?' he asked the girl, and went to look at Anna, conscious once more, and then upstairs to see Lucia, who was already, with the resilience of the young, almost her small self again.

Back in the kitchen he found Cressida rousing.

'However did you get here?' she wanted to know, and then peevishly, 'You should know better than to travel in this weather.'

He was taking her pulse, now satisfactorily normal. 'I was on my way to Janslum—I called to see how you were getting on.'

He took the warm milk Cook had fetched and held it for her while she sipped. 'You will go to Leeuwarden for a check-up,' he told her with impersonal kindness. 'I think you are perfectly all right but all the same you must be examined. Lucia and Anna will go too.'

'Now?'

'Yes, in my car. Anna and Lucia will go with Dirk ter Beemstra, but we shall have to wait until the blizzard has blown out.'

He made her drink the rest of the milk and spoke to the housemaid.

'You will go upstairs and get into a warm bath and put on dry clothing; Sierou will go with you.' He nodded to the maid and Cressida got to her feet. She peered out at him from her cocoon of blankets.

'Why did you kiss me like that?' she wanted to know.

He showed no surprise at her question. 'Shall we say that it was a happy meeting?' He smiled a little. 'Run along now and do as I say.'

Half an hour later she was downstairs again wearing one of Mevrouw ter Beemstra's winter coats. It had a hood and was a great deal too large but it was beautifully warm. That lady had wept over her when she had gone to see how Lucia was. 'I'll never be able to thank you enough, Cressida. You have been so brave.' She shuddered. 'And if Aldrik hadn't come along when he did, what would have happened?'

'Well, he did come,' said Cressida bracingly, 'and everything is all right. Poor Anna—she was so brave, crouching over Baby although her leg must have hurt dreadfully.'

They went downstairs together and found Aldrik and Dirk ter Beemstra carrying Anna to Dirk's car. The children, forbidden to come downstairs from the playroom until everything was normal again, had taken up position on the landing and were watching through the banisters.

'Come back, Cressida,' Willum called, 'we shall miss you.'

Cressida waved to them. '*Tot ziens,*' she replied, airing her Dutch.

Leeuwarden wasn't far away but the journey, even undertaken by the two men who knew the road like the backs of their hands and were skilled drivers, took on the aspect of a nightmare. Cressida, bundled in rugs beside Aldrik with the dogs' warm breath on her neck, cowered in her seat each time the car skidded. The snow had eased a little and so had the wind but it wasn't the night for a drive.

The doctor drove steadily and apparently without any fears for their safety and while he drove he kept up a steady flow of small talk so that she was forced to answer him and take her mind off the possibility of them skidding into a canal or going full tilt into a snowdrift; all the same she couldn't help asking just once if they were nearly there.

'Yes. Don't be frightened, Cressy, I won't let anything harm you.'

He was reassuringly calm and she felt ashamed of her fears and mumbled, 'Oh, I know, I know. I'm quite sure-I don't feel quite me or I wouldn't be such a coward.'

'Cressy, cowards don't walk out into a blizzard with only a torch and a guardian angel.' He actually laughed then, righted the Bentley out of a skid and drove on.

He got them to the hospital and they kept her in that night.

They kept Lucia in too, and Anna was to stay for a day or two while her leg was put in plaster and she learned how to manage the crutches. That she hadn't got pneumonia was a miracle. Cressida, who had been whisked away to be examined and put to bed, had no chance to do more than bid Aldrik a hasty goodbye; she could only hope that he reached his home fairly safely through the appalling weather.

Dirk ter Beemstra came the next day and fetched her and Lucia home; the blizzard had blown itself out, the sun shone and the snow ploughs had cleared the main roads. Everything was back to normal in a surprisingly short time—excepting for Cressida's heart, which she was sure would never be normal again. Beyond Dirk ter Beemstra's casual remark that Aldrik had got home safely she heard nothing of the doctor and she had been too shy to ask for news of him. Besides, the household was entirely disrupted for several days; she had stepped into Anna's shoes temporarily and she had more than enough to do to fill her days and thoughts.

A week went by, Anna came back and spurned the cosseting Mevrouw ter Beemstra would have given her. She stumped around on her crutches, only relinquishing Lucia to Cressida's care for her daily walk, but she had taken Cressida's hand one day and made a long speech which Cressida couldn't understand, and then shaken it vigorously. Friends for life, thought Cressida happily. She did her best not to think about Aldrik and as the days went by she decided sadly that she wouldn't see him again. He had come into her life and gone again and there was nothing to do about it.

She went to see Charity on her first free day; the baby was expected any day now and that was all they talked about. There was a nurse already in the house and the children were wildly excited. Tyco came home while she was there and Cressida felt a pang of envy at the tender care he gave his wife. To be loved like that...

Aldrik hadn't been mentioned and when she could bear it

no longer she asked how he was in what she hoped was a casual manner.

'Aldrik?' said Charity, 'Oh, he's in Brazil—or do I mean Argentina?—on a lecture tour. He won't be back for a bit. He said he's going to be back in time for the christening, though.' Charity sneaked a quick look at Cressida. 'That was lucky that he went to the ter Beemstras' and found you. Were you scared?'

'Terrified, but it was Anna who had the worst of it, and Baby...'

'Anna shouldn't have taken her out,' said Charity in such a severe and matronly voice that Cressida laughed and Charity laughed with her.

It was at dinner that evening, sitting between the Beemstras, that Cressida found herself listening to their talk. From time to time they excused themselves and spoke their own language and she hadn't minded this, but now she understood some of what they were saying.

'She is not good enough for him,' declared the lady of the house, and, since Dutch, when correctly and not too quickly spoken, was at times understandable, Cressida understood that. 'But of course he is a rich man and well thought of and she can be charming. They are to marry soon, I hear.'

She smiled across the table at Cressida. 'Forgive us, we gossip, Cressida. We talk of Nicola van Germert, who is to marry very soon. I for one am sorry for her husband,' she added maddeningly, 'but let us talk of something else—how is Charity? They hope for a boy, I expect?'

Cressida said that yes, she thought they did, but since Charity had declared her intention of having at least four children it didn't matter much either way. A remark which was approved by Mevrouw ter Beemstra, being the proud mother of six.

Cressida lay awake for a good deal of the night. She wished that she understood the Dutch language so that she could find out about Nicola, she wished that she had the courage to ask whom she was to marry and above all she wished very much that Aldrik would come home again. If he was going to marry Nicola then she wanted to see him just once more. She went to sleep eventually and woke with a terrible headache. Love, she reflected, was by no means all it was cracked up to be.

CHAPTER NINE

DURING THE NEXT few days Cressida pondered the problem of finding out about Nicola and Aldrik—for of course it would be he—hadn't Mevrouw ter Beemstra described him even if she hadn't given him a name? Too good for Nicola, she had said, and rich. She supposed that to live in a house like his at Janslum as well as having another house at Leiden one would need to be rich... To ask outright was impossible, inviting a polite snub or at best arousing curiosity. She decided finally to wait until she saw Charity again.

On the evening before her day off Tyco phoned; Charity had had a son that morning. She could hear the pride and happiness in his voice as he told her. 'And I'm coming for you as we arranged in the morning,' he went on. 'Charity is splendidly fit and wants to see you. She can't wait to let you see little Tyco. Stay for lunch and help me keep the girls in order, they are so excited. Now could you get hold of Beatrix? I had better tell her the news.'

So Cressida spent her day admiring the baby and listening to a blissfully happy Charity, lying back on the day bed in the bedroom, wrapped in the prettiest gown Cressida had ever seen, and then going downstairs to keep the girls entertained while Tyco sat with his wife. The rooms were awash with flowers too and the phone rang all day so that by the evening Cressida was tired but awash too with the contented happiness all around her.

'I don't know what we should have done without you,' said Tyco, driving her back after tea. 'It hasn't been much of a day off for you.'

'I've loved it,' said Cressida, and she meant it. 'And Charity looks lovely—it must be so nice to have a baby in your home and not in a hospital ward.'

Tyco chuckled. 'Ah, that is one of the advantages of marrying into the medical profession.'

It was long afterwards as she got ready for bed that she wished that she had been quick enough to ask about Aldrik and Nicola; it would have been easy to say, 'Oh, by the way, talking about doctors, how is Aldrik?'

'I'll never know,' she muttered unhappily, 'for there is no one to tell me.'

Someone did tell her, however, the very next day.

She had come indoors with the three girls after a brisk walk and was on her way upstairs to the playroom where Anna would be waiting in her chair to keep an eye on them for an hour while Cressida had some time to herself, when Mevrouw ter Beemstra came out of the drawing-room.

'Cressida, you have a caller, will you come down as soon as you have seen to the children?'

She had smiled but she had looked put out too and Cressida wondered why. Who on earth would want to see her? If it had been Tyco she would have been told at once and surely it wasn't Aldrik? Her heart leapt at the thought. It seemed to her that it took longer than usual to get the children's outdoor things off and tidied away and to make sure that they had all they needed to amuse them for an hour, and Anna wanted to talk—Cressida was too kind-hearted to cut her short. By the time she had tidied her hair and done something to her face fifteen minutes had gone by. She hoped the caller, whoever he or she was, wasn't impatient. It was on the way downstairs that she remembered the *domine*. She was smiling as she opened the drawing-room door.

Nicola was sitting, very much at her ease, in one of the armchairs by the fire, and Mevrouw ter Beemstra, sitting opposite her, turned round as Cressida paused in the doorway.

'There you are, Cressida. Nicola has been staying up here and thought she would call and see how you are getting on. I'll leave you to have a talk—you'll stay for a cup of tea?' she asked Nicola.

'No, no—I must get back—there is so much to do. I know you will forgive me.'

Mevrouw ter Beemstra looked relieved as she went away.

Nicola glanced around the room. 'How fortunate that you are so well settled here. The children are still young too, so you can depend on staying for a long time yet. It is such a relief to us.'

'Us?' Cressida asked quietly.

'Well, Aldrik and myself, of course. Who else? We have been concerned about you…'

'How kind. When are you getting married?'

Nicola looked down at her lap, hiding the gleam of triumph in her eyes; someone must have misled Cressida into thinking that she was marrying Aldrik. Well, she for one wasn't going to enlighten her; she had come to make mischief but there was no need. Let the silly girl go on believing that Aldrik and she were to marry—serve her right. She didn't want Aldrik herself now; she had been furious when he had made it plain to her that any idea of marrying her had been something she had thought up for herself without encouragement from him, as indeed it had been. Her pride not her heart had been hurt, for she had every intention of marrying a man she had known for some time, a man with a great deal of money and the lifestyle she enjoyed. It had rankled though that Aldrik had refused to dance to her tune and she at once saw a chance to get even with him and mislead the plain creature sitting opposite to her.

She said sweetly, 'Very soon.' She smiled and twisted the diamond ring on her finger and Cressida said,

'When he comes back from his lecture tour?'

'The very next day,' agreed Nicola, busy thinking up plausible lies. 'He asked me to come and see you—he had some silly idea that you had begun to like him a little too much.'

She watched the colour come into Cressida's cheeks and hid a smile. 'Of course I told him that was nonsense, I mean you haven't anything in common, have you?'

Cressida didn't answer that. Instead she said steadily, 'I hope you will be very happy. Janslum is such a lovely home...'

'Janslum? I hate the place.' Nicola saw Cressida's surprised look and hastily amended that. 'I love his home in Leiden and after all he works there for most of the time. He travels too from time to time and of course I shall go with him.'

Cressida asked politely, 'I expect you know Lady Merrill?'

Nicola knew her; on the one occasion when Lady Merrill had gone over to Janslum they had met and felt a mutual antipathy for each other. 'Such a charming old lady, we got on splendidly,' she said smugly.

She was clever enough to leave it at that. 'Well I must be on my way. Aldrik will wonder where I've got to—he phones each evening, luckily Janslum isn't all that distance and the roads are almost clear again.'

Cressida got up. 'I'll fetch Mevrouw ter Beemstra, you will want to say goodbye...'

'No, no, don't disturb her. She knew that I had come to see you.'

Cressida accompanied her to the door, her feelings at boiling-point behind the polite emptiness of her unassuming features. She wished Nicola goodbye, waited until she had got into her car and driven away and then relieved her feelings by putting out a tongue in a childish gesture.

'I did not know that you were a friend of Nicola's,' observed Mevrouw ter Beemstra later that day.

'I'm not, *Mevrouw*. She only came to see me because someone had asked her to.'

'I do not care for her. She does not like children,' said Mevrouw ter Beemstra darkly.

'I don't like her either,' agreed Cressida, and went to the playroom to help the boys with their English lesson.

It wasn't until she was in her room getting ready for bed that she had the time to think about her own affairs. She went over Nicola's news, trying to remember every word that she had said. She hadn't said exactly when Aldrik was returning but she had given the strong impression that it was soon. Her cheeks grew hot, remembering what Nicola had said—that he was afraid that she had grown to like him too much. She couldn't and she wouldn't see him again, she had mistaken pity for friendship and liking and that tasted bitter in her mouth. Somehow she would have to go back to England. That was easier said than done; in fact, she couldn't think how it would be possible. The ter Beemstras had been so kind to her, paid her well and treated her as one of themselves, and she was very grateful. To leave them was unthinkable—more than that, impossible.

She was sitting with the twins on the following morning, patiently showing them a large map of the world and reciting the countries in English, when their mother came into the room.

'Cressida, I would like to talk—if Sepke and Galske could amuse themselves for a while?'

'I'll get their painting books. Would you like me to come downstairs?'

'Please.' She went away, leaving Cressida wondering what they would have to talk about—the little girls going to school, she supposed, or perhaps the boys weren't doing as well with their English at school as their father expected. She fetched paints and water and painting books, told them to be good children and ran downstairs.

Mevrouw ter Beemstra was in the drawing-room, a half-knitted pullover for one of the boys in her lap. 'Come and sit down, Cressida,' she said kindly. 'While you were out with the children there was a telephone call for you—a Miss Mogford. She wished to speak to you urgently. I told her that you would be back shortly and she asked that you should ring her after half-past eleven...'

'Moggy,' exclaimed Cressida, 'but she's not on the phone—she was our housekeeper before my father died—she's retired now.'

'She was telephoning from a—a box. Is that right? Therefore she tells me the time that you should ring her. It is a quarter past eleven now. When it is time, go to the library, it is quiet there, and see what is the matter. I hope it is not bad news...'

'Was she—did she sound upset?'

'Crying, I believe. I had a little difficulty understanding her...'

'Well, she's a Dorset woman, and she doesn't speak in the same way as someone from London or one of the big cities.'

'I understand. Like our Anna. You are fond of her, Cressida?'

'She came to my mother and father when they married, so I've known her all my life.' The remembrance of Moggy's elderly face brought a lump into Cressida's throat. 'I'm very fond of her.'

'We will have a cup of coffee together and then it will be time to telephone,' said Mevrouw ter Beemstra, 'and if it is necessary then you must go to your home and give her what help is needed. I hope that will not be so, but if it is then we will help you.'

Cressida thanked her, put down her coffee-cup and went to the library, the one room in the house where the children were not allowed to enter unless they were invited by their father. She dialled the number Mevrouw ter Beemstra had taken down. A moment later she heard Moggy's soft Dorset voice.

'Miss Cressy? I'm that sorry to bother you but I don't know what to do. I'm at my wits' end and no one to ask. It's all so sudden like and I'm sure my sister never meant it...'

'Moggy, dear, it's all right,' Cressida spoke encouragingly. 'Just tell me what has happened and I'll help. Is your sister ill?'

'She's dead. Oh, Miss Cressy, whatever shall I do? She meant to alter her will, see, and leave the cottage to me, but she died sudden like and it's to go to her husband's nephew and 'e says as I must be out by the end of the month, and there's 'er two cats and he don't want 'em, and who's to take in two cats? For I'll not leave them...'

'The end of the month. That's two weeks away. Moggy, I'm coming back—I'll see the solicitors for you and see what can be done. Now don't worry, Mevrouw ter Beemstra has said that I can go to England if I'm needed. I'll be with you in a few days. Just stay where you are, Moggy. Don't sign anything and if anyone bothers you just say that I'll deal with them when I get there.'

'But your job, Miss Cressy—'

'I'm sure that I can come back, Moggy.' As she spoke Cressida realised that here was the chance she had wanted to leave Friesland, to go as far away from Aldrik as she could. It was strange that now that she had it she was loath to take it. All her good resolutions dissolved before her longing to see Aldrik just once more. Only for a moment; then Moggy's voice interrupted her thoughts.

'You will come, Miss Cressy?'

'Yes, Moggy. Just as soon as I can—two or three days...'

She said goodbye and went to tell Mevrouw ter Beemstra about it.

'Of course you must go, Cressida. A seat will be booked on a plane for you and we will drive to Schiphol with you and you are to stay as long as it is necessary. We will miss you very much, but it is your duty. You wish to go at once?'

'I explained to Miss Mogford that I would try and get to her in two or three days' time and she is content with that. Could I go the day after tomorrow? I can talk to Anna and explain to the children and pack, and please may I phone Charity?'

'Better than that, you shall definitely go and see her. Tomorrow morning Sepke and Galske are to spend an hour or two at the school they will go to next term. Anna can look after Baby, the boys will not be here, so you will be free. Take the little car and go over to the van der Bronses'.'

'You're so kind,' said Cressida soberly, 'and I'm leaving you in the lurch.'

'Lurch? What is this lurch?' and when Cressida explained she said, 'Think not of lurches,' and she added magnanimously 'We are in your debt. All shall be arranged.'

Charity was in the nursery, where Cressida had expected her to be. She had driven herself over in the little Mini and Jolly admitted her and ushered her without ceremony upstairs.

Charity was on a low stool dressing her infant son, but she looked up with real pleasure when she saw Cressida.

'How nice—you're just in time for coffee.' She did up poppers with brisk efficiency, kissed the feathery hair on the small head and popped her son into his cot. 'Nanny is in the next room...' She stood for a moment while a cosily plump person in a white apron came into the room and settled by the window with her knitting and then she took Cressida's arm.

Downstairs in the small sitting-room at the back of the house she said, 'You never come like this—suddenly—what's happened, Cressy?'

Over coffee Cressida told her. 'So I'll have to go back to Templecombe,' she finished, 'but I'm not sure if I shall be able to come back.'

'Do you want to?' asked Charity. 'There's some other reason, isn't there? I won't pry.' She busied herself filling up their cups. 'Did you see Nicola when she came? Heaven knows why she needed to call and congratulate us; she couldn't care less. I was surprised that she was going to see the ter Beemstras—they hardly know each other.'

'She came to see me.'

Charity handed the biscuits and waited.

'She's going to be married. She came to tell me, she said that—that Aldrik had asked her to see me.'

'He's not even in Holland.'

'No, but he's coming back quite soon, they're going to be married as soon as he's home. I—I want to go before he gets here.' Cressida lifted her unhappy gaze to her friend's face. 'She said that he had sent her because he was afraid that I was getting too fond of him.'

'Are you, Cressy?'

'Oh, yes, only I didn't think that it showed. I've been so careful—only I thought that we were friends. I feel so silly, I can't possibly meet him again. I was wondering what I should do and then Moggy phoned.'

'I don't believe that they are going to be married,' said Charity. 'In fact...' She didn't go on; she could be wrong, for she hadn't had much interest in any world but her own happy one for the last few days. Tyco might know and if he didn't he would find out and tell her what to do. 'Ah,' she asked instead, 'and when do you plan to go?'

'Tomorrow. Mijnheer ter Beemstra is driving me to Schiphol. They've been very kind. I shall be in Templecombe by the evening.'

'Have you enough money?'

'Yes, thank you. They're paying my fare. If I don't come back I must return it.'

'Don't do that, Cressy; they want to repay you for all you've done and for going out to look for Anna and Baby.' She hesitated. 'Is there anything I can do for you—messages or the like?'

Cressida got to her feet. 'No, Charity, dear, I'll say my goodbyes tomorrow but please say goodbye to Tyco for me and thank you both for being so kind to me. I've been very happy here. I'm glad I was here when little Tyco was born. Oh, and I do love the little girls.'

Charity went to the door with her and watched her get into the Mini. Tyco was in Leeuwarden at the hospital, it would be easy enough to ring him up, but he would be home at teatime and he would know what to do. She waved goodbye and went indoors, longing for the day to be over and for Tyco's reassuring calm.

There was one other person Cressida wanted to say goodbye to—the *domine*. He was in his study at the severe little house by the church, writing what she supposed was his sermon. He was pleased to see her but his face fell when she told him why she had come.

'I had hoped that you would be staying with us,' he told her. 'I believe that we might have become good friends.'

'Well, I hope we're friends already,' said Cressida, 'I've been very happy here, you know, and I'll not forget any of you. Perhaps we shall meet again one day.'

'You do not intend to come back?'

'I don't know. It very much depends on Miss Mogford. I can't just leave her, you see—she was with my family for years and years and she has no family now that her sister has died, and no money.'

'That is sad. You will miss us, then?'

'Indeed I shall.'

'But I think that there is some reason why you wish to go away from Friesland and not return.' His eyes searched her face. 'You do not wish to talk about it but I would respect your confidence.'

'Oh, I know you would, and you're quite right, there is a reason I want to go away from here. If Miss Mogford hadn't telephoned me I think that I would have gone anyway; the only thing that would have stopped me was the inconvenience to Mevrouw ter Beemstra.'

Presently she said goodbye and drove back to the house, packed her case and went to talk to Anna in the queer mixture of Dutch and English which they used together, and then when Mevrouw ter Beemstra came back with the twins there were the careful explanations to make the little girls understand and the last-minute arrangements to make with their mother.

Leave-taking was hard; she hadn't realised quite how much she had absorbed of the life in Friesland and now that she was going away she felt that she was leaving part of herself behind. She had been happy there and she had grown to love Aldrik there too; it wasn't just part of herself, she reflected sadly, it was her whole heart. Since there was nothing else to be done, however, she would do her best to forget him and make a new life in England. She would have to help Moggy first, of course, although she had no idea at the moment how she could. She would at least go and see Mr Tims or write to him and get his advice. If the nephew who was to have the house didn't want to live in it he might even agree to rent it to her at a rent she could afford; he might even be generous enough to add a little to her pension and if she could herself find a job locally she could get settled in the house with Moggy and share the expenses. It would be like old times...

She watched the flat coast of Holland disappear under the plane's wing, fighting her tears. Everyone had been so kind; the children had been upset and so had the ter Beemstras and she was really going to miss Charity and Tyco.

She swallowed her tears with the coffee and then concentrated on the problem of settling poor Moggy.

She was in Templecombe by teatime. The cottage was close to the station and she walked to it, burdened by her heavy case and a plastic bag filled with presents from the children and several packages from Charity and Mevrouw ter Beemstra, as well as the rather wilted bunch of flowers she had bought at Schiphol for Moggy; she had bought a bottle of wine too. It might help them to make sensible plans together.

Moggy, she saw with a shock, had aged in the few months since they had last seen each other, but her welcome was very warm.

Moggy, who never cried, cried now. 'I'm a selfish old woman,' she mumbled into Cressida's sympathetic shoulder, 'but I'm at my wits' end. A couple of weeks, that's all I've got to find somewhere to go. I went along to the job centre in Yeovil but the lady there said I'd find it difficult to get anything—I'm too old.'

'Hush, Moggy, dear,' said Cressida, 'I'm going to write to Mr Tims and see if he can help and if he can't I'll go and see Stepmother and ask her to help. Then I'll get a job and we can pay her back. I'd better see whoever is advising the nephew...'

'It's Snide and Snide in Yeovil—my sister's nephew lives in Leeds.'

They had dropped everything in the little hall and gone to sit in the kitchen and Moggy had made tea.

'You mean to say that he is coming here to live?'

Moggy shook her head. 'That's just it—he's going to sell the place lock, stock and barrel—there's been one or two enquiries already.'

'Is he a poor man?'

Moggy snorted. 'Got a tidy little business, 'e 'as, no children and a wife who goes out to work.'

Cressida finished her tea. 'Well, you're not to worry any more, Moggy. I'm sure something can be done about it.'

She spoke reassuringly, but she had her doubts, and Moggy was too upset to share them.

She went first to Snide and Snide where, after being kept waiting for all of half an hour, she was seen by the junior partner in the firm, a young man who took one look at her and decided that this rather plain girl with the quiet voice hardly merited his full attention. No, he told her, their client was adamant about Miss Mogford leaving the cottage; he intended to sell it.

'How much does he want for it?' asked Cressida.

He named a sum which she thought excessive, and in any case there was no hope in raising such a sum unless her stepmother would help.

She went away presently and was glad to go. She didn't like the younger Mr Snide and she was aware that he felt the same about her. She tried Mr Tims next, this time with a carefully worded letter, and she received a reply by return of post telling her that really there was little he could do unless she was in a position to buy the cottage. However, he did promise to look into the matter in case there was some loophole.

Cressida was discouraged but she had no intention of giving up. Despite protests from Moggy she took herself off to her home.

The girl who answered the door knew Cressida. 'Miss Cressida—have you come back home? How nice to see you...'

'I've only come to see my stepmother, Mary. If you would tell her I'm here, please?'

Her stepmother looked up from her chair as she went in.

'Cressida—the last person I expected to see. Why have you come? You didn't expect to be welcome, did you?'

'No. I wouldn't have come on my own account. I want to talk to you about Miss Mogford.' Cressida sat down unbidden. 'If you would listen,' she began, and explained briefly. 'I wondered if you would lend us the money to buy the cottage? I'll pay you back as soon as I've got a job; something each month.'

Her stepmother gave an angry laugh. 'What a silly little fool you are, Cressida. Do you really suppose that I would lift a finger to help either you or Miss Mogford? You've wasted money on a bus, my girl. Now go away and don't come back; next time you won't be admitted.'

There was nothing for it but to go back to Moggy, to make light of her visit to her stepmother and tell her that there was almost a fortnight still, 'And anything could happen,' said Cressida hearteningly. A statement which seemed to cheer Moggy but which did nothing to improve her own low spirits.

Three days after Cressida had gone back to England the doctor returned to Holland. His lecture tour had been successful, even if gruelling, and he had carried out his role as examiner of medical students in several of the medical schools he had visited with such proficiency that he had earned high praise. He had no thought for that. On the long flight back he bent his powerful brain to the ways and means of seeing Cressida as soon as possible. She had got under his skin and taken possession of his heart as well and he supposed with hindsight that he had fallen in love with her the moment he had set eyes on her, sitting forlornly on the grass with Caesar. She was, he reflected, the only woman in the world for him; he would tell her so the moment he saw her. Before then he had commitments which couldn't be ignored; by the time the plane landed at Schiphol he had a tightly scheduled programme planned which he had whittled down to three days' hard work in Leiden. Far too long but she would still be there...

Wester was waiting for him with the Bentley, the two dogs in the back, panting with delight at the sight of him, and they drove at once to Leiden. It was still early morning and the doctor, stopping only to shower and eat his breakfast, went to the hospital to confer with his registrar, see his patients and in the afternoon take an out-patients clinic.

'You're doing too much, Doctor,' said Wester severely when he got back to his house, and Mies chimed in,

'All that way in one of those dreadful aeroplanes, too, you're tired to the bone and don't deny it.'

The doctor looked from one to the other of his faithful old friends. 'Yes, I'm tired, but I want to get to Janslum as soon as I can and that means doing some work.'

He didn't say why he needed to go but they both nodded and when he had gone to his study Mies said, 'It'll be that nice English miss he brought here...'

Wester nodded. 'He brought her to Janslum, a *deftig* young lady.'

It was midnight of the third day when the doctor opened his house door content that he had done everything he had planned to do. Now he was free to go to Friesland. Too late tonight, he reflected, but first thing in the morning...

He and Wester and the dogs set off before it was light, sent on their way by a cosily wrapped Mies. Halfway there, he said,

'Phone Tyske, will you, Wester, and ask her to have breakfast for us—in about an hour's time?'

It was a cold morning, inclined to drizzle from a lowering sky, and it was no better by the time they had breakfasted. The doctor took the dogs for a brisk walk and then got into his car and drove rather too fast to the ter Beemstras' house. It was mid morning now and he judged that Cressida would be available.

It was Beatrix ter Beemstra who came to greet him when he was admitted. 'How nice to see you, have you had a good trip? You have been away for too long—were the lectures successful?'

Aldrik was a man of monumental patience; he even spent several minutes discussing the weather, enquiring after the children and Anna's leg before asking to see Cressida.

'She's not here—you didn't know? No, of course you didn't. She went back to England six days ago. Her old housekeeper telephoned—she was in some kind of trouble and Cressida said that she would have to go and help her.' Beatrix glanced at the deceptively calm face before her. 'I think she was glad to go—indeed, she said that she needed to get away. She didn't say why and I didn't ask her. She is a dear girl and she would not have wished that unless her reasons were very real.'

'You have her address?'

'Well, I'm afraid not—when she went she went within a day, you know, and there was so much to arrange. Charity will know, however. We miss her very much—such a gentle girl.'

The doctor stayed for a few minutes longer, making polite small talk, and then he got into the Bentley again and drove to Charity's house.

Here he had no need to stand on ceremony. He gave her a friendly hug and she kissed his cheek and then stood back to look at him.

'Before I take you to see your godson, Aldrik, Cressy's either with this Miss Mogford or at her stepmother's. I'll tell you about it and you'll know what to do. Please come and see the infant Tyco first, then we'll have coffee and I'll tell you as much as I know.'

The baby was asleep. Charity hung over the cot. 'The spitting image of his dad,' she said proudly. 'Next time when you come perhaps he'll be awake.'

'He's a splendid fellow and you are right, he is just like Tyco. Do the girls like him?'

'When they are at home I have to fight my way to get at him—we're all so happy...' She stopped and went pink. 'And you're not, are you? But you will be. Come downstairs and we'll talk.'

Over coffee she explained about Nicola's visit. 'I knew it wasn't true but she had made it all seem as though it were and it was unforgivable of her to tell Cressy those lies about you being afraid that she was getting fond of you. No wonder she couldn't wait to get back to England. Poor old Miss Mogford's troubles came at just the right time.'

She peeped at Aldrik's face. It looked quite frighteningly grim.

'I can catch the night ferry,' he said at once, 'and be there during the morning. Have you Miss Mogford's address?'

'Yes, I've written it down for you, but she may be at her stepmother's house. I'd go there first. Will you go to Lady Merrill's?'

He nodded. 'I can call in at Cressy's home on the way.' He got to his feet, 'My dear, you've been a real friend.' He bent to kiss her. 'Tell Tyco I'll see him when we get back and be sure and take care of that son of yours.'

When he got back home he told Wester to pack a bag and book a berth on the night ferry from the Hoek and then he took the dogs for a long walk. The time had to be filled in before he could leave for England.

He drove away from Harwich on a dismal grey morning, he had had breakfast on board and he didn't intend to stop until he reached Cressy's home, he had studied the map and took the road through Hatfield, Watford and Slough, cutting out London entirely, to join the M3 and later on the A303. He drove steadily, keeping to the maximum speed, and the further west he went, the better the weather. When at last he stopped in the drive before Cressida's home the sun was shining.

Mrs Preece was coming downstairs as the maid admitted him. She recognised him at once and came forward, smiling archly. 'Doctor—how delightful to see you again. You are on your way to see Lady Merrill? Too late for coffee, but do have a drink and tell me all your news.'

'You are very kind, but I can't stop. I came to see if Cressida is here?'

The smile became fixed. 'Certainly not. She walked out of this house and she can stay out of it.'

'But has she been here recently?'

'Why do you want to know?' and when he didn't answer, and just stood there looking at her, she said, 'She came here two days ago, if you must know.' She added sulkily, 'She wanted to borrow money to buy Miss Mogford's sister's cottage, if you please. I sent her packing.'

'Back to Miss Mogford's?' The doctor's voice was very quiet.

'How should I know? The old woman's got all she deserves anyway, leaving me in the lurch—it's impossible to get servants nowadays.'

'I'm sorry to have disturbed your morning,' said Aldrik smoothly and bade her goodbye. His poor little Cressida, he thought, getting into his car and taking the road to his grandmother's house. While he had been with Mrs Preece he had been thinking; contacting Mr Tims might be the best thing to do. It wasn't much use seeing Cressida unless he knew exactly how matters stood.

Lady Merrill was delighted to see him. 'Lunch,' she told him briskly, 'you're worn out. Why are you here? Something to do with Cressida, I'll be bound.'

He told her over lunch. 'I think I'd better get hold of Tims,' he finished, 'now.'

Mr Tims made everything plain in a few dry-as-dust sentences.

'Can I buy the place?' asked the doctor. 'Will this man sell?'

'If the price is attractive, yes.'

'Will you phone him, ask him what price he wants, and buy it?'

Mr Tims was shocked. 'My dear Aldrik, aren't you being a bit hasty? A little bargaining...'

'Will you hasten and phone him now and ring me back?—I'll be here for the next hour or so.'

'Very well. You're throwing money away...'

Mr Tims hung up and began to dial another number. He had always been impressed by Aldrik's calm manner and good sense but he had sounded very unlike himself. Half an hour later he phoned Lady Merrill's house.

'Well, you have your cottage,' he told the doctor, 'and you've paid double its worth.' He sounded faintly disapproving but Aldrik took no notice. 'Splendid, and thank you—now there's one thing more...' He began to speak and Mr Tims, listening, permitted himself a smile.

Cressida was putting on the kettle for a cup of tea—Moggy liked her tea sharp at four o'clock—when the knocker was thumped and a small boy handed her an envelope. It was addressed to her and she turned it over in a useless sort of way while he waited. His fidgeting roused her, though; she found her purse and gave him twenty pence and went back to the kitchen where she opened it. It was from Mr Tims asking her to go to the office; if she would go to Brown's Garage a car would take her. He would expect her within the next half hour.

Cressida read it twice, roused Moggy from her nap and read it to her and then went to get her outdoor things. 'That nephew of your sister's has changed his mind,' she declared. 'I dare say he's at Mr Tims's office now. But I wonder why it's just me he wants?'

'I dare say you'll understand what's being said better than

me,' said Moggy. 'Don't you waste a moment, Miss Cressy; 'e'd never 'ave a taxi for you if it weren't important.'

Mr Tims's office was in a side-street, its windows discreetly curtained and the doorknocker splendidly polished. Cressida beat a tattoo on it and was admitted by a clerk and told to go upstairs to Mr Tims's room. Outside the door she took a deep breath and knocked, and, requested to enter, did so.

Mr Tims was sitting behind his desk and the doctor was lounging against the window, his large person obscuring most of the light of a fading day.

'Oh,' said Cressida inadequately, but since she had lost her breath for a moment it would have to do.

'Hello, Cressy,' said the doctor in a voice of such tenderness that she lost her breath again, which gave Mr Tims the chance to speak.

'I have asked you to come here at Dr van der Linus's request. He has purchased the cottage in which Miss Mogford is at present living so that she may stay there for the rest of her life.'

He glanced up. Neither of the two people with him were listening, or so it seemed to him, they were looking at each other in a manner which suggested that they were unaware of him, or anything else for that matter.

'The doctor will explain,' he said in his dry voice, and went out of the room.

'I'll explain later,' said Aldrik and crossed the room in two strides to wrap Cressy in his great arms, 'and we'll have no more of this, you'll marry me so that I know where you are and what you are doing. You've been disrupting my whole life—I have never met such a girl.'

He kissed her very hard and then again, gently this time. 'My darling tiresome girl, I love you.' He smiled down at her. 'Will you marry me?'

She smiled, her ordinary face suddenly beautiful. 'Well, yes, I should like that very much, but first shouldn't you explain?'

'A waste of time,' said the doctor testily, 'there are other things more important.'

'If you say so, dear Aldrik.' She sounded meek but her eyes sparkled.

The doctor studied her face with great satisfaction. 'My beautiful girl,' he said, and fell to kissing her once more.

It was nice to be called beautiful, reflected Cressida, kissing him back with goodwill, even though it wasn't true, and, anyway, she felt beautiful. With what breath she had left she said, 'Aldrik...'

'"For God's sake hold your tongue, and let me love",' growled the doctor, and meant every word; John Donne's age-old plea seemed exactly right for the occasion.

* * * * *

Always And Forever

CHAPTER ONE

THERE WAS GOING to be a storm; the blue sky of a summer evening was slowly being swallowed by black clouds, heavy with rain and thunder, flashing warning signals of flickering lightning over the peaceful Dorset countryside, casting gloom over the village. The girl gathering a line of washing from the small orchard behind the house standing on the village outskirts paused to study the sky before lugging the washing basket through the open door at the back of the house.

She was a small girl, nicely plump, with a face which, while not pretty, was redeemed by fine brown eyes. Her pale brown hair was gathered in an untidy bunch on the top of her head and she was wearing a cotton dress which had seen better days.

She put the basket down, closed the door and went in search of candles and matches, then put two old-fashioned oil lamps on the wooden table. If the storm was bad there would be a power cut before the evening was far advanced.

This done to her satisfaction, she poked up the elderly Aga, set a kettle to boil and turned her attention to the elderly dog and battle-scarred old tomcat, waiting patiently for their suppers.

She got their food, talking while she did so because the eerie quiet before the storm broke was a little unnerving, and then made tea and sat down to drink it as the first heavy drops of rain began to fall.

With the rain came a sudden wind which sent her round the house shutting windows against the deluge. Back in the kitchen, she addressed the dog.

'Well, there won't be anyone coming now,' she told him, and gave a small shriek as lightning flashed and thunder drowned out any other sound. She sat down at the table and he came and sat beside her, and, after a moment, the cat got onto her lap.

The wind died down as suddenly as it had arisen but the storm was almost overhead. It had become very dark and the almost continuous flashes made it seem even darker. Presently the light over the table began to flicker; she prudently lit a candle before it went out.

She got up then, lighted the lamps and took one into the hall before sitting down again. There was nothing to do but to wait until the storm had passed.

The lull was shattered by a peal on the doorbell, so unexpected that she sat for a moment, not quite believing it. But a second prolonged peal sent her to the door, lamp in hand.

A man stood in the porch. She held the lamp high in order to get a good look at him; he was a very large man, towering over her.

'I saw your sign. Can you put us up for the night? I don't care to drive further in this weather.'

He had a quiet voice and he looked genuine. 'Who's we?' she asked.

'My mother and myself.'

She slipped the chain off the door. 'Come in.' She peered round him. 'Is that your car?'

'Yes—is there a garage?'

'Go round the side of the house; there's a barn—the door's open. There's plenty of room there.'

He nodded and turned back to the car to open its door and help his mother out. Ushering them into the hall, the girl said,

'Come back in through the kitchen door; I'll leave it unlocked. It's across the yard from the barn.'

He nodded again, a man of few words, she supposed, and he went outside. She turned to look at her second guest. The woman was tall, good-looking, in her late fifties, she supposed, and dressed with understated elegance.

'Would you like to see your room? And would you like a meal? It's a bit late to cook dinner but you could have an omelette or scrambled eggs and bacon with tea or coffee?'

The older woman put out a hand. 'Mrs Fforde—spelt with two ffs, I'm afraid. My son's a doctor; he was driving me to the other side of Glastonbury, taking a shortcut, but driving had become impossible. Your sign was like something from heaven.' She had to raise her voice against the heavenly din.

The girl offered a hand. 'Amabel Parsons. I'm sorry you had such a horrid journey.'

'I hate storms, don't you? You're not alone in the house?'

'Well, yes, I am, but I have Cyril—that's my dog—and Oscar the cat.' Amabel hesitated. 'Would you like to come into the sitting room until Dr Fforde comes? Then you can decide if you would like something to eat. I'm afraid you will have to go to bed by candlelight...'

She led the way down the hall and into a small room, comfortably furnished with easy chairs and a small round table. There were shelves of books on either side of the fireplace and a large window across which Amabel drew the curtains before setting the lamp on the table.

'I'll unlock the kitchen door,' she said and hurried back to the kitchen just in time to admit the doctor.

He was carrying two cases. 'Shall I take these up?'

'Yes, please. I'll ask Mrs Fforde if she would like to go to her room now. I asked if you would like anything to eat...'

'Most emphatically yes. That's if it's not putting you to too much trouble. Anything will do—sandwiches...'

'Omelettes, scrambled eggs, bacon and eggs? I did explain to Mrs Fforde that it's too late to cook a full meal.'

He smiled down at her. 'I'm sure Mother is longing for a cup of tea, and omelettes sound fine.' He glanced round him. 'You're not alone?'

'Yes,' said Amabel. 'I'll take you upstairs.'

She gave them the two rooms at the front of the house and pointed out the bathroom. 'Plenty of hot water,' she added, before going back to the kitchen.

When they came downstairs presently she had the table laid in the small room and offered them omelettes, cooked to perfection, toast and butter and a large pot of tea. This had kept her busy, but it had also kept her mind off the storm, still raging above their heads. It rumbled away finally in the small hours, but by the time she had cleared up the supper things and prepared the breakfast table, she was too tired to notice.

She was up early, but so was Dr Fforde. He accepted the tea she offered him before he wandered out of the door into the yard and the orchard beyond, accompanied by Cyril. He presently strolled back to stand in the doorway and watch her getting their breakfast.

Amabel, conscious of his steady gaze, said briskly, 'Would Mrs Fforde like breakfast in bed? It's no extra trouble.'

'I believe she would like that very much. I'll have mine with you here.'

'Oh, you can't do that.' She was taken aback. 'I mean, your breakfast is laid in the sitting room. I'll bring it to you whenever you're ready.'

'I dislike eating alone. If you put everything for Mother on a tray I'll carry it up.'

He was friendly in a casual way, but she guessed that he was a man who disliked arguing. She got a tray ready, and when he came downstairs again and sat down at the kitchen table she put a plate of bacon, eggs and mushrooms in front of him, adding toast and marmalade before pouring the tea.

'Come and sit down and eat your breakfast and tell me why you live here alone,' he invited. He sounded so like an elder brother or a kind uncle that she did so, watching him demolish his breakfast with evident enjoyment before loading a slice of toast with butter and marmalade.

She had poured herself a cup of tea, but whatever he said she wasn't going to eat her breakfast with him...

He passed her the slice of toast. 'Eat that up and tell me why you live alone.'

'Well, really!' began Amabel and then, meeting his kindly look, added, 'It's only for a month or so. My mother's gone to Canada,' she told him. 'My married sister lives there and she's just had a baby. It was such a good opportunity for her to go. You see, in the summer we get quite a lot of people coming just for bed and breakfast, like you, so I'm not really alone. It's different in the winter, of course.'

He asked, 'You don't mind being here by yourself? What of the days—and nights—when no one wants bed and breakfast?'

She said defiantly, 'I have Cyril, and Oscar's splendid company. Besides, there's the phone.'

'And your nearest neighbour?' he asked idly.

'Old Mrs Drew, round the bend in the lane going to the village. Also, it's only half a mile to the village.' She still sounded defiant.

He passed his cup for more tea. Despite her brave words he suspected that she wasn't as self-assured as she would have him believe. A plain girl, he considered, but nice eyes, nice voice and apparently not much interest in clothes; the denim skirt and cotton blouse were crisp and spotless, but could hardly be called fashionable. He glanced at her hands, which were small and well shaped, bearing signs of housework.

He said, 'A lovely morning after the storm. That's a pleasant orchard you have beyond the yard. And a splendid view...'

'Yes, it's splendid all the year round.'

'Do you get cut off in the winter?'

'Yes, sometimes. Would you like more tea?'

'No, thank you. I'll see if my mother is getting ready to leave.' He smiled at her. 'That was a delicious meal.' But not, he reflected, a very friendly one. Amabel Parsons had given him the strong impression that she wished him out of the house.

Within the hour he and his mother had gone, driving away in the dark blue Rolls-Royce. Amabel stood in the open doorway, watching it disappear round the bend in the lane. It had been providential, she told herself, that they should have stopped at the house at the height of the storm; they had kept her busy and she hadn't had the time to be frightened. They had been no trouble—and she needed the money.

It would be nice, she thought wistfully, to have someone like Dr Fforde as a friend. Sitting at breakfast with him, she'd had an urgent desire to talk to him, tell him how lonely she was, and sometimes a bit scared, how tired she was of making up beds and getting breakfast for a succession of strangers, keeping the place going until her mother returned, and all the while keeping up the façade of an independent and competent young woman perfectly able to manage on her own.

That was necessary, otherwise well-meaning people in the village would have made it their business to dissuade her mother from her trip and even suggest that Amabel should shut up the house and go and stay with a great-aunt she hardly knew, who lived in Yorkshire and who certainly wouldn't want her.

Amabel went back into the house, collected up the bedlinen and made up the beds again; hopefully there would be more guests later in the day...

She readied the rooms, inspected the contents of the fridge and the deep freeze, hung out the washing and made herself a sandwich before going into the orchard with Cyril and Oscar. They sat, the three of them, on an old wooden bench, nicely secluded from the lane but near enough to hear if anyone called.

Which they did, just as she was on the point of going indoors for her tea.

The man on the doorstep turned round impatiently as she reached him.

'I rang twice. I want bed and breakfast for my wife, son and daughter.'

Amabel turned to look at the car. There was a young man in the driver's seat, and a middle-aged woman and a girl sitting in the back.

'Three rooms? Certainly. But I must tell you that there is only one bathroom, although there are handbasins in the rooms.'

He said rudely, 'I suppose that's all we can expect in this part of the world. We took a wrong turning and landed ourselves here, at the back of beyond. What do you charge? And we do get a decent breakfast?'

Amabel told him, 'Yes.' As her mother frequently reminded her, it took all sorts to make the world.

The three people in the car got out: a bossy woman, the girl pretty but sulky, and the young man looking at her in a way she didn't like...

They inspected their rooms with loud-voiced comments about old-fashioned furniture and no more than one bathroom—and that laughably old-fashioned. And they wanted tea: sandwiches and scones and cake. 'And plenty of jam,' the young man shouted after her as she left the room.

After tea they wanted to know where the TV was.

'I haven't got a television.'

They didn't believe her. 'Everyone has a TV set,' complained the girl. 'Whatever are we going to do this evening?'

'The village is half a mile down the lane,' said Amabel. 'There's a pub there, and you can get a meal, if you wish.'

'Better than hanging around here.'

It was a relief to see them climb back into the car and drive off presently. She laid the table for their breakfast and put everything ready in the kitchen before getting herself some supper. It was a fine light evening, so she strolled into the orchard and sat down on the bench. Dr Fforde and his mother would be at Glastonbury, she supposed, staying with family or friends. He would be married, of course, to a pretty girl with lovely clothes—there would be a small boy and a smaller girl, and they would live in a large and comfortable house; he was successful, for he drove a Rolls-Royce...

Conscious that she was feeling sad, as well as wasting her time, she went back indoors and made out the bill; there might not be time in the morning.

She was up early the next morning; breakfast was to be ready by eight o'clock, she had been told on the previous evening—a decision she'd welcomed with relief. Breakfast was eaten, the bill paid—but only after double-checking everything on it and some scathing comments about the lack of modern amenities.

Amabel waited politely at the door until they had driven away then went to put the money in the old tea caddy on the kitchen dresser. It added substantially to the contents but it had been hard earned!

The rooms, as she'd expected, had been left in a disgraceful state. She flung open the window, stripped beds and set about turning them back to their usual pristine appearance. It was still early, and it was a splendid morning, so she filled the washing machine and started on the breakfast dishes.

By midday everything was just as it should be. She made sandwiches and took them and a mug of coffee out to the orchard with Cyril and Oscar for company, and sat down to read the letter from her mother the postman had brought. Everything was splendid, she wrote. The baby was thriving and she had decided to stay another few weeks, if Amabel could manage for a little longer—*For I don't suppose I'll be able to visit here for a year or two, unless something turns up.*

Which was true enough, and it made sense too. Her mother had taken out a loan so that she could go to Canada, and even though it was a small one it would have to be paid off before she went again.

Amabel put the letter in her pocket, divided the rest of her sandwich between Cyril and Oscar and went back into the house. There was always the chance that someone would come around teatime and ask for a meal, so she would make a cake and a batch of scones.

It was as well that she did; she had just taken them out of the Aga when the doorbell rang and two elderly ladies enquired if she would give them bed and breakfast.

They had come in an old Morris, and, while well-spoken and tidily dressed, she judged them to be not too free with their money. But they looked nice and she had a kind heart.

'If you would share a twin-bedded room?' she suggested. 'The charge is the same for two people as one.' She told them how much and added, 'Two breakfasts, of course, and if you would like tea?'

They glanced at each other. 'Thank you. Would you serve us a light supper later?'

'Certainly. If you would fetch your cases? The car can go into the barn at the side of the house.'

Amabel gave them a good tea, and while they went for a short walk, she got supper—salmon fish cakes, of tinned salmon, of course, potatoes whipped to a satiny smoothness, and peas from the garden. She popped an egg custard into the oven by way of afters and was rewarded by their genteel thanks.

She ate her own supper in the kitchen, took them a pot of tea and wished them goodnight. In the morning she gave them boiled eggs, toast and marmalade and a pot of coffee, and all with a generous hand.

She hadn't made much money, but it had been nice to see their elderly faces light up. And they had left her a tip, discreetly put on one of the bedside tables. As for the bedroom, they had left it so neat it was hard to see that anyone had been in it.

She added the money to the tea caddy and decided that tomorrow she would go to the village and pay it into the post office account, stock up on groceries and get meat from the butcher's van which called twice a week at the village.

It was a lovely morning again, and her spirits rose despite her disappointment at her mother's delayed return home. She wasn't doing too badly with bed and breakfast, and she was adding steadily to their savings. There were the winter months to think of, of course, but she might be able to get a part-time job once her mother was home.

She went into the garden to pick peas, singing cheerfully and slightly off key.

Nobody came that day, and the following day only a solitary woman on a walking holiday came in the early evening; she went straight to bed after a pot of tea and left the next morning after an early breakfast.

After she had gone, Amabel discovered that she had taken the towels with her.

Two disappointing days, reflected Amabel. I wonder what will happen tomorrow?

She was up early again, for there was no point in lying in bed when it was daylight soon after five o'clock. She breakfasted, tidied the house, did a pile of ironing before the day got too hot, and then wandered out to the bench in the orchard. It was far too early for any likely person to want a room, and she would hear if a car stopped in the lane.

But of course one didn't hear a Rolls-Royce, for it made almost no sound.

Dr Fforde got out and stood looking at the house. It was a pleasant place, somewhat in need of small repairs and a lick of paint, but its small windows shone and the brass knocker on its solid front door was burnished to a dazzling brightness. He trod round the side of the house, past the barn, and saw Amabel sitting between Cyril and Oscar. Since she was a girl who couldn't abide being idle, she was shelling peas.

He stood watching her for a moment, wondering why he had wanted to see her again. True, she had interested him, so small, plain and pot valiant, and so obviously terrified of the storm—and very much at the mercy of undesirable characters who might choose to call. Surely she had an aunt or cousin who could come and stay with her?

It was none of his business, of course, but it had seemed a good idea to call and see her since he was on his way to Glastonbury.

He stepped onto the rough gravel of the yard so that she looked up.

She got to her feet, and her smile left him in no doubt that she was glad to see him.

He said easily, 'Good morning. I'm on my way to Glastonbury. Have you quite recovered from the storm?'

'Oh, yes.' She added honestly, 'But I was frightened, you know. I was so very glad when you and your mother came.'

She collected up the colander of peas and came towards him. 'Would you like a cup of coffee?'

'Yes, please.' He followed her into the kitchen and sat down at the table and thought how restful she was; she had seemed glad to see him, but she had probably learned to give a welcoming smile to anyone who knocked on the door. Certainly she had displayed no fuss at seeing him.

He said on an impulse, 'Will you have lunch with me? There's a pub—the Old Boot in Underthorn—fifteen minutes' drive from here. I don't suppose you get any callers before the middle of the afternoon?'

She poured the coffee and fetched a tin of biscuits.

'But you're on your way to Glastonbury...'

'Yes, but not expected until teatime. And it's such a splendid day.' When she hesitated he said, 'We could take Cyril with us.'

She said then, 'Thank you; I should like that. But I must be back soon after two o'clock; it's Saturday...'

They went back to the orchard presently, and sat on the bench while Amabel finished shelling the peas. Oscar had got onto the doctor's knee and Cyril had sprawled under his feet. They talked idly about nothing much and Amabel, quite at her ease, now answered his carefully put questions without realising just how much she was telling him until she stopped in mid-sentence, aware that her tongue was running away with her. He saw that at once and began to talk about something else.

They drove to the Old Boot Inn just before noon and found a table on the rough grass at its back. There was a small river, overshadowed by trees, and since it was early there was no one else there. They ate home-made pork pies with salad, and drank iced lemonade which the landlord's wife made herself. Cyril sat at their feet with a bowl of water and a biscuit.

The landlord, looking at them from the bar window, observed to his wife, 'Look happy, don't they?'

And they were, all three of them, although the doctor hadn't identified his feeling as happiness, merely pleasant content at the glorious morning and the undemanding company.

He drove Amabel back presently and, rather to her surprise, parked the car in the yard behind the house, got out, took the door key from her and unlocked the back door.

Oscar came to meet them and he stooped to stroke him. 'May I sit in the orchard for a little while?' he asked. 'I seldom get the chance to sit quietly in such peaceful surroundings.'

Amabel stopped herself just in time from saying, 'You poor man,' and said instead, 'Of course you may, for as long as you like. Would you like a cup of tea, or an apple?'

So he sat on the bench chewing an apple, with Oscar on his knee, aware that his reason for sitting there was to cast an eye over any likely guests in the hope that before he went a respectable middle-aged pair would have decided to stay.

He was to have his wish. Before very long a middleaged pair did turn up, with mother-in-law, wishing to stay for two nights. It was absurd, he told himself, that he should feel concern. Amabel was a perfectly capable young woman, and able to look after herself; besides, she had a telephone.

He went to the open kitchen door and found her there, getting tea.

'I must be off,' he told her. 'Don't stop what you're doing. I enjoyed my morning.'

She was cutting a large cake into neat slices. 'So did I. Thank you for my lunch.' She smiled at him. 'Go carefully, Dr Fforde.'

She carried the tea tray into the drawing room and went back to the kitchen. They were three nice people—polite, and anxious not to be too much trouble. 'An evening meal?' they had asked diffidently, and had accepted her offer of jacket potatoes and salad, fruit tart and coffee with pleased smiles. They would go for a short walk presently, the man told her, and when would she like to serve their supper?

When they had gone she made the tart, put the potatoes in the oven and went to the vegetable patch by the orchard to get a lettuce and radishes. There was no hurry, so she sat down on the bench and thought about the day.

She had been surprised to see the doctor again. She had been pleased too. She had thought about him, but she hadn't expected to see him again; when she had looked up and seen him standing there it had been like seeing an old friend.

'Nonsense,' said Amabel loudly. 'He came this morning because he wanted a cup of coffee.' What about taking you out to lunch? asked a persistent voice at the back of her mind.

'He's probably a man who doesn't like to eat alone.'

And, having settled the matter, she went back to the kitchen.

The three guests intended to spend Sunday touring around the countryside. They would return at tea time and could they have supper? They added that they would want to leave early the next morning, which left Amabel with almost all day free to do as she wanted.

There was no need for her to stay at the house; she didn't intend to let the third room if anyone called. She would go to church and then spend a quiet afternoon with the Sunday paper.

She liked going to church, for she met friends and acquaintances and could have a chat, and at the same time assure anyone who asked that her mother would be coming home soon and that she herself was perfectly content on her own. She was aware that some of the older members of the congregation didn't approve of her mother's trip and thought that at the very least some friend or cousin should have moved in with Amabel.

It was something she and her mother had discussed at some length, until her mother had burst into tears, declaring that she wouldn't be able to go to Canada. Amabel had said at once that she would much rather be on her own, so her mother had gone, and Amabel had written her a letter each week, giving light-hearted and slightly optimistic accounts of the bed and breakfast business.

Her mother had been gone for a month now; she had phoned when she had arrived and since then had written regularly, although she still hadn't said when she would be returning.

Amabel, considering the matter while Mr Huggett, the church warden, read the first lesson, thought that her mother's next letter would certainly contain news of her return. Not for the world would she admit, even to herself, that she didn't much care for living on her own. She was, in fact, uneasy at night, even though the house was locked and securely bolted.

She kept a stout walking stick which had belonged to her father by the front door, and a rolling pin handy in the kitchen, and there was always the phone; she had only to lift it and dial 999!

Leaving the church presently, and shaking hands with the vicar, she told him cheerfully that her mother would be home very soon.

'You are quite happy living there alone, Amabel? You have friends to visit you, I expect?'

'Oh, yes,' she assured him. 'And there's so much to keep me busy. The garden and the bed and breakfast people keep me occupied.'

He said with vague kindness, 'Nice people, I hope, my dear?'

'I'm careful who I take,' she assured him.

It was seldom that any guests came on a Monday; Amabel cleaned the house, made up beds and checked the fridge, made herself a sandwich and went to the orchard to eat it. It was a pleasant day, cool and breezy, just right for gardening.

She went to bed quite early, tired with the digging, watering and weeding. Before she went to sleep she allowed her thoughts to dwell on Dr Fforde. He seemed like an old friend, but she knew nothing about him. Was he married? Where did he live? Was he a GP, or working at a hospital? He dressed well and drove a Rolls-Royce, and he had family or friends somewhere on the other side of Glastonbury. She rolled over in bed and closed her eyes. It was none of her business anyway...

The fine weather held and a steady trickle of tourists knocked on the door. The tea caddy was filling up nicely again; her mother would be delighted. The week slid imperceptibly into the next one, and at the end of it there was a letter from her mother. The postman arrived with it at the same time as a party of four—two couples sharing a car on a brief tour—so that Amabel had to put it in her pocket until they had been shown their rooms and had sat down to tea.

She went into the kitchen, got her own tea and sat down to read it.

It was a long letter, and she read it through to the end—and then read it again. She had gone pale, and drank her cooling tea with the air of someone unaware of what they were doing, but presently she picked up the letter and read it for the third time.

Her mother wasn't coming home. At least not for several months. She had met someone and they were to be married shortly.

I know you will understand. And you'll like him. He's a market gardener, and we plan to set up a garden centre from the house. There's plenty of room and he will build a large glasshouse at the bottom of the orchard. Only he must sell his own market garden first, which may take some months.

It will mean that we shan't need to do bed and break-

fast any more, although I hope you'll keep on with it until we get back. You're doing so well. I know that the tourist season is quickly over but we hope to be back before Christmas.

The rest of the letter was a detailed description of her husband-to-be and news too, of her sister and the baby.

You're such a sensible girl, her mother concluded, *and I'm sure you're enjoying your independence. Probably when we get back you will want to start a career on your own.*

Amabel was surprised, she told herself, but there was no reason for her to feel as though the bottom had dropped out of her world; she was perfectly content to stay at home until her mother and stepfather should return, and it was perfectly natural for her mother to suppose that she would like to make a career for herself.

Amabel drank the rest of the tea, now stewed and cold. She would have plenty of time to decide what kind of career she would like to have.

That evening, her guests in their rooms, she sat down with pen and paper and assessed her accomplishments. She could cook—not quite cordon bleu, perhaps, but to a high standard—she could housekeep, change plugs, cope with basic plumbing. She could tend a garden... Her pen faltered. There was nothing else.

She had her A levels, but circumstances had never allowed her to make use of them. She would have to train for something and she would have to make up her mind what that should be before her mother came home. But training cost money, and she wasn't sure if there would be any. She could get a job and save enough to train...

She sat up suddenly, struck by a sudden thought. Waitresses needed no training, and there would be tips. In one of the larger towns, of course. Taunton or Yeovil? Or what about one of the great estates run by the National Trust? They had shops and tearooms and house guides. The more she thought about it, the better she liked it.

She went to bed with her decision made. Now it was just a question of waiting until her mother and her stepfather came home.

CHAPTER TWO

IT WAS ALMOST a week later when she had the next letter, but before that her mother had phoned. She was so happy, she'd said excitedly; they planned to marry in October—Amabel didn't mind staying at home until they returned? Probably in November?

'It's only a few months, Amabel, and just as soon as we're home Keith says you must tell us what you want to do and we'll help you do it. He's so kind and generous. Of course if he sells his business quickly we shall come home as soon as we can arrange it.'

Amabel had heard her mother's happy little laugh. 'I've written you a long letter about the wedding. Joyce and Tom are giving a small reception for us, and I've planned such a pretty outfit—it's all in the letter...'

The long letter when it arrived was bursting with excitement and happiness.

You have no idea how delightful it is not to have to worry about the future, to have someone to look after me—you too, of course. Have you decided what you want to do when we get home? You must be so excited at the idea of being independent; you have had such a dull life since you left school...

But a contented one, reflected Amabel. Helping to turn their bed and breakfast business into a success, knowing that she was wanted, feeling that she and her mother were making something of their lives. And now she must start all over again.

It would be nice to wallow in self-pity, but there were two people at the door asking if she could put them up for the night...

Because she was tired she slept all night, although the moment she woke thoughts came tumbling into her head which were better ignored, so she got up earlier than usual and went outside in her dressing gown with a mug of tea and Cyril and Oscar for company.

It was pleasant sitting on the bench in the orchard in the early-morning sun, and in its cheerful light it was impossible to be gloomy. It would be nice, though, to be able to talk to someone about her future...

Dr Fforde's large, calm person came into her mind's eye; he would have listened and told her what she should do. She wondered what he was doing...

Dr Fforde was sitting on the table in the kitchen of his house, the end one in a short terrace of Regency houses in a narrow street tucked away behind Wimpole Street in London. He was wearing a tee shirt and elderly trousers and badly needed a shave; he had the appearance of a ruffian—a handsome ruffian. There was a half-eaten apple on the table beside him and he was taking great bites from a thick slice of bread and butter. He had been called out just after two o'clock that morning to operate on a patient with a perforated duodenal ulcer; there had been complications which had kept him from his bed and now he was on his way to shower and get ready for his day.

He finished his bread and butter, bent to fondle the sleek head of the black Labrador sitting beside him, and went to the door. It opened as he reached it. The youngish man who came in was already dressed, immaculate in a black alpaca jacket and striped trousers. He had a sharp-nosed foxy face, and dark hair brushed to a satin smoothness.

He stood aside for the doctor and wished him a severe good morning.

'Out again, sir?' His eye fell on the apple core. 'You had only to call me. I'd have got you a nice hot drink and a sandwich...'

The doctor clapped him on the shoulder. 'I know you would, Bates. I'll be down in half an hour for one of your special breakfasts. I disturbed Tiger; would you let him out into the garden?'

He went up the graceful little staircase to his room, his head already filled with thoughts of the day ahead of him. Amabel certainly had no place in them.

Half an hour later he was eating the splendid breakfast Bates had carried through to the small sitting room at the back of the house. Its French windows opened onto a small patio and a garden beyond where Tiger was meandering round. Presently he came to sit by his master, to crunch bacon rinds and then accompany him on a brisk walk through the still quiet streets before the doctor got into his car and drove the short distance to the hospital.

Amabel saw her two guests on their way, got the room ready for the next occupants and then on a sudden impulse went to the village and bought the regional weekly paper at the post office. Old Mr Truscott, who ran it and knew everyone's business, took his time giving her her change.

'Didn't know you were interested in the *Gazette*, nothing much in it but births, marriages and deaths.' He fixed her with a beady eye. 'And adverts, of course. Now if anyone was looking for a job it's a paper I'd recommend.'

Amabel said brightly, 'I dare say it's widely read, Mr Truscott. While I'm here I'd better have some more air mail letters.'

'Your ma's not coming home yet, then? Been gone a long time, I reckon.'

'She's staying a week or two longer; she might not get the chance to visit my sister again for a year or two. It's a long way to go for just a couple of weeks.'

Over her lunch she studied the jobs page. There were heartening columns of vacancies for waitresses: the basic wage was fairly low, but if she worked full-time she could manage very well... And Stourhead, the famous National Trust estate, wanted shop assistants, help in the tearooms and suitable applicants for full-time work in the ticket office. And none of them were wanted until the end of September.

It seemed too good to be true, but all the same she cut the ad out and put it with the bed and breakfast money in the tea caddy.

A week went by, and then another. Summer was almost over. The evenings were getting shorter, and, while the mornings were light still, there was the ghost of a nip in the air. There had been more letters from Canada from her mother and future stepfather, and her sister, and during the third week her mother had telephoned; they were married already—now it was just a question of selling Keith's business.

'We hadn't intended to marry so soon but there was no reason why we shouldn't, and of course I've moved in with him,' she said. 'So if he can sell his business soon we shall be home before long. We have such plans...!'

There weren't as many people knocking on the door now; Amabel cleaned and polished the house, picked the last of the soft fruit to put in the freezer and cast an eye over the contents of the cupboards.

With a prudent eye to her future she inspected her wardrobe—a meagre collection of garments, bought with an eye to their long-lasting qualities, in good taste but which did nothing to enhance her appearance.

Only a handful of people came during the week, and no one at all on Saturday. She felt low-spirited—owing to the damp and gloomy weather, she told herself—and even a brisk walk with Cyril didn't make her feel any better. It was still only early afternoon and she sat down in the kitchen, with Oscar on her lap, disinclined to do anything.

She would make herself a pot of tea, write to her mother, have an early supper and go to bed. Soon it would be the beginning of another week; if the weather was better there might be a satisfying number of tourists—and besides, there were plenty of jobs to do in the garden. So she wrote her letter, very bright and cheerful, skimming over the lack of guests, making much of the splendid apple crop and how successful the soft fruit had been. That done, she went on sitting at the kitchen table, telling herself that she would make the tea.

Instead of that she sat, a small sad figure, contemplating a future which held problems. Amabel wasn't a girl given to self-pity, and she couldn't remember the last time she had cried, but she cried now, quietly and without fuss, a damp Oscar on her lap, Cyril's head pressed against her legs. She made no attempt to stop; there was no one there to see, and now that the rain was coming down in earnest no one would want to stop for the night.

Dr Fforde had a free weekend, but he wasn't particularly enjoying it. He had lunched on Saturday with friends, amongst whom had been Miriam Potter-Stokes, an elegant young widow who was appearing more and more frequently in his circle of friends. He felt vaguely sorry for her, admired her for the apparently brave face she was showing to the world, and what had been a casual friendship now bid fair to become something more serious—on her part at least.

He had found himself agreeing to drive her down to Henley after lunch, and once there had been forced by good manners to stay at her friend's home for tea. On the way back to London she had suggested that they might have dinner together.

He had pleaded a prior engagement and gone back to his home feeling that his day had been wasted. She was an amusing companion, pretty and well dressed, but he had wondered once or twice what she was really like. Certainly he enjoyed her company from time to time, but that was all...

He took Tiger for a long walk on Sunday morning and after lunch got into his car. It was no day for a drive into the country, and Bates looked his disapproval.

'Not going to Glastonbury in this weather, I hope, sir?' he observed.

'No, no. Just a drive. Leave something cold for my supper, will you?'

Bates looked offended. When had he ever forgotten to leave everything ready before he left the house?

'As always, sir,' he said reprovingly.

It wasn't until he was driving west through the quiet city streets that Dr Fforde admitted to himself that he knew where he was going. Watching the carefully nurtured beauty of Miriam Potter-Stokes had reminded him of Amabel. He had supposed, in some amusement, because the difference in the two of them was so marked. It would be interesting to see her again. Her mother would be back home by now, and he doubted if there were many people wanting bed and breakfast now that summer had slipped into a wet autumn.

He enjoyed driving, and the roads, once he was clear of the suburbs, were almost empty. Tiger was an undemanding companion, and the countryside was restful after the bustle of London streets.

The house, when he reached it, looked forlorn; there were no open windows, no signs of life. He got out of the car with Tiger and walked round the side of the house; he found the back door open.

Amabel looked up as he paused at the door. He thought that she looked like a small bedraggled brown hen. He said, 'Hello, may we come in?' and bent to fondle the two dogs, giving her time to wipe her wet cheeks with the back of her hand. 'Tiger's quite safe with Cyril, and he likes cats.'

Amabel stood up, found a handkerchief and blew her nose. She said in a social kind of voice, 'Do come in. Isn't it an awful day? I expect you're on your way to Glastonbury. Would you like a cup of tea? I was just going to make one.'

'Thank you, that would be nice.' He had come into the kitchen now, reaching up to tickle a belligerent Oscar under the chin. 'I'm sorry Tiger's frightened your cat. I don't suppose there are many people about on a day like this—and your mother isn't back yet?'

She said in a bleak little voice, 'No...' and then to her shame and horror burst into floods of tears.

Dr Fforde sat her down in the chair again. He said comfortably, 'I'll make the tea and you shall tell me all about it. Have a good cry; you'll feel better. Is there any cake?'

Amabel said in a small wailing voice, 'But I've been crying and I don't feel any better.' She gave a hiccough before adding, 'And now I've started again.' She took the large white handkerchief he offered her. 'The cake's in a tin in the cupboard in the corner.'

He put the tea things on the table and cut the cake, found biscuits for the dogs and spooned cat food onto a saucer for Oscar, who was still on top of a cupboard. Then he sat down opposite Amabel and put a cup of tea before her.

'Drink some of that and then tell me why you are crying. Don't leave anything out, for I'm merely a ship which is passing in the night, so you can say what you like and it will be forgotten—rather like having a bag of rubbish and finding an empty dustbin...'

She smiled then. 'You make it sound so—so normal...' She sipped her tea. 'I'm sorry I'm behaving so badly.'

He cut the cake and gave her a piece, before saying matter-of-factly, 'Is your mother's absence the reason? Is she ill?'

'Ill? No, no. She's married someone in Canada...'

It was such a relief to talk to someone about it. It all came tumbling out: a hotch-potch of market gardens, plans for coming back and the need for her to be independent as soon as possible.

He listened quietly, refilling their cups, his eyes on her blotched face, and when she had at last finished her muddled story, he said, 'And now you have told me you feel better about it, don't you? It has all been bottled up inside you, hasn't it? Going round inside your head like butter in a churn. It has been a great shock to you, and shocks should be shared. I won't offer you advice, but I will suggest that you do nothing—make no plans, ignore your future—until your mother is home. I think that you may well find that you have been included in their plans and that you need no worries about your future. I can see that you might like to become independent, but don't rush into it. You're young enough to stay at home while they settle in, and that will give you time to decide what you want to do.'

When she nodded, he added, 'Now, go and put your hair up and wash your face. We're going to Castle Cary for supper.'

She gaped at him. 'I can't possibly...'

'Fifteen minutes should be time enough.'

She did her best with her face, and piled her hair neatly, then got into a jersey dress, which was an off the peg model, but of a pleasing shade of cranberry-red, stuck her feet into her best shoes and went back into the kitchen. Her winter coat was out of date and shabby, and for once she blessed the rain, for it meant that she could wear her mac.

Their stomachs nicely filled, Cyril and Oscar were already half asleep, and Tiger was standing by his master, eager to be off.

'I've locked everything up,' observed the doctor, and ushered Amabel out of the kitchen, turned the key in the lock and put it in his pocket, and urged her into the car. He hadn't appeared to look at her at all, but all the same he saw that she had done her best with her appearance. And the restaurant he had in mind had shaded rose lamps on its tables, if he remembered aright...

There weren't many people there on a wet Sunday evening,

but the place was welcoming, and the rosy shades were kind to Amabel's still faintly blotchy face. Moreover, the food was good. He watched the pink come back into her cheeks as they ate their mushrooms in garlic sauce, local trout and a salad fit for the Queen. And the puddings were satisfyingly shrouded in thick clotted cream...

The doctor kept up a gentle stream of undemanding talk, and Amabel, soothed by it, was unaware of time passing until she caught sight of the clock.

She said in a shocked voice, 'It's almost nine. You will be so late at Glastonbury...'

'I'm going back to town,' he told her easily, but he made no effort to keep her, driving her back without more ado, seeing her safely into the house and driving off again with a friendly if casual goodbye.

The house, when he had gone, was empty—and too quiet. Amabel settled Cyril and Oscar for the night and went to bed.

It had been a lovely evening, and it had been such a relief to talk to someone about her worries, but now she had the uneasy feeling that she had made a fool of herself, crying and pouring out her problems like a hysterical woman. Because he was a doctor, and was used to dealing with awkward patients, he had listened to her, given her a splendid meal and offered sensible suggestions as to her future. Probably he dealt with dozens like her...

She woke to a bright morning, and around noon a party of four knocked on the door and asked for rooms for the night, so Amabel was kept busy. By the end of the day she was tired enough to fall into bed and sleep at once.

There was no one for the next few days but there was plenty for her to do. The long summer days were over, and a cold wet autumn was predicted.

She collected the windfalls from the orchard, picked the last of the beans for the freezer, saw to beetroots, carrots and winter cabbage and dug the rest of the potatoes. She went to the rickety old greenhouse to pick tomatoes. She supposed that when her stepfather came he would build a new one; she and her mother had made do with it, and the quite large plot they used for vegetables grew just enough to keep them supplied throughout the year, but he was bound to make improvements.

It took her most of the week to get the garden in some sort of order, and at the weekend a party of six stayed for two nights, so on Monday morning she walked to the villager to stock up on groceries, post a letter to her mother and, on an impulse, bought the local paper again.

Back home, studying the jobs page, she saw with regret that the likely offers of work were no longer in it. There would be others, she told herself stoutly, and she must remember what Dr Fforde had told her—not to rush into anything. She must be patient; her mother had said that they hoped to be home before Christmas, but that was still weeks away, and even so he had advised her to do nothing hastily...

It was two days later, while she was putting away sheets and pillowcases in the landing cupboard, when she heard Cyril barking. He sounded excited, and she hurried downstairs; she had left the front door unlocked and someone might have walked in...

Her mother was standing in the hall, and there was a tall thickset man beside her. She was laughing and stooping to pat Cyril, then she looked up and saw Amabel.

'Darling, aren't we a lovely surprise? Keith sold the business, so there was no reason why we shouldn't come back here.'

She embraced Amabel, and Amabel, hugging her back, said, 'Oh, Mother—how lovely to see you.'

She looked at the man and smiled—and knew immediately that she didn't like him and that he didn't like her. But she held out a hand and said, 'How nice to meet you. It's all very exciting, isn't it?'

Cyril had pushed his nose into Keith's hand and she saw his impatient hand push it away. Her heart sank.

Her mother was talking and laughing, looking into the rooms, exclaiming how delightful everything looked. 'And there's Oscar.' She turned to her husband. 'Our cat, Keith. I know you don't like cats, but he's one of the family.'

He made some non-committal remark and went to fetch the luggage. Mrs Parsons, now Mrs Graham, ran upstairs to her room, and Amabel went to the kitchen to get tea. Cyril and Oscar went with her and arranged themselves tidily in a corner of the kitchen, aware that this man with the heavy tread didn't like them.

They had tea in the sitting room and the talk was of Canada and their journey and their plans to establish a market garden.

'No more bed and breakfast,' said Mrs Graham. 'Keith wants to get the place going as soon as possible. If we can get a glasshouse up quickly we could pick up some of the Christmas trade.'

'Where will you put it?' asked Amabel. 'There's plenty of ground beyond the orchard.'

Keith had been out to look around before tea, and now he observed, 'I'll get that ploughed and dug over for spring crops, and I'll put the glasshouse in the orchard. There's no money in apples, and some of the trees look past it. We'll finish picking and then get rid of them. There's plenty of ground there—fine for peas and beans.'

He glanced at Amabel. 'Your mother tells me you're pretty handy around the house and garden. The two of us ought to be able to manage to get something started—I'll hire a man with a rotavator who'll do the rough digging; the lighter jobs you'll be able to manage.'

Amabel didn't say anything. For one thing she was too surprised and shocked; for another, it was early days to be making such sweeping plans. And what about her mother's suggestion that she might like to train for something? If her stepfather might be certain of his plans, but why was he so sure that she would agree to them? And she didn't agree with them. The orchard had always been there, long before she was born. It still produced a good crop of apples and in the spring it was so beautiful with the blossom…

She glanced at her mother, who looked happy and content and was nodding admiringly at her new husband.

It was later, as she was getting the supper that he came into the kitchen.

'Have to get rid of that cat,' he told her briskly. 'Can't abide them, and the dog's getting on a bit, isn't he? Animals don't go well with market gardens. Not to my reckoning, anyway.'

'Oscar is no trouble at all,' said Amabel, and tried hard to sound friendly. 'And Cyril is a good guard dog; he never lets anyone near the house.'

She had spoken quietly, but he looked at her face and said quickly, 'Oh, well, no hurry about them. It'll take a month or two to get things going how I want them.'

He in his turn essayed friendliness. 'We'll make a success of it, too. Your mother can manage the house and you can work full-time in the garden. We might even take on casual labour after a bit—give you time to spend with your young friends.'

He sounded as though he was conferring a favour upon her, and her dislike deepened, but she mustn't allow it to show. He was a man who liked his own way and intended to have it. Probably he was a good husband to her mother, but he wasn't going to be a good stepfather…

Nothing much happened for a few days; there was a good deal of unpacking to do, letters to write and trips to the bank. Quite a substantial sum of money had been transferred from Canada and Mr Graham lost no time in making enquiries about local labour. He also went up to London to meet men who had been recommended as likely to give him financial backing, should he require it.

In the meantime Amabel helped her mother around the house, and tried to discover if her mother had meant her to have training of some sort and then changed her mind at her husband's insistence.

Mrs Graham was a loving parent, but easily dominated by anyone with a stronger will than her own. What was the hurry? she wanted to know. A few more months at home were neither here nor there, and she would be such a help to Keith.

'He's such a marvellous man, Amabel, he's bound to make a success of whatever he does.'

Amabel said cautiously, 'It's a pity he doesn't like Cyril and Oscar…'

Her mother laughed. 'Oh, darling, he would never be unkind to them.'

Perhaps not unkind, but as the weeks slipped by it was apparent that they were no longer to be regarded as pets around the house. Cyril spent a good deal of time outside, roaming the orchard, puzzled as to why the kitchen door was so often shut. As for Oscar, he only came in for his meals, looking carefully around to make sure that there was no one about.

Amabel did what she could, but her days were full, and it was obvious that Mr Graham was a man who rode roughshod over anyone who stood in his way. For the sake of her mother's happiness Amabel held her tongue; there was no denying that he was devoted to her mother, and she to him, but there was equally no denying that he found Amabel, Cyril and Oscar superfluous to his life.

It wasn't until she came upon him hitting Cyril and then turning on an unwary Oscar and kicking him aside that Amabel knew that she would have to do something about it.

She scooped up a trembling Oscar and bent to put an arm round Cyril's elderly neck. 'How dare you? Whatever have they done to you? They're my friends and I love them,' she added heatedly, 'and they have lived here all their lives.'

Her stepfather stared at her. 'Well, they won't live here much longer if I have my way. I'm the boss here. I don't like animals around the place so you'd best make up your mind to that.'

He walked off without another word and Amabel, watching

his retreating back, knew that she had to do something—and quickly.

She went out to the orchard—there were piles of bricks and bags of cement already heaped near the bench, ready to start building the glasshouse—and with Oscar on her lap and Cyril pressed against her she reviewed and discarded several plans, most of them too far-fetched to be of any use. Finally she had the nucleus of a sensible idea. But first she must have some money, and secondly the right opportunity...

As though a kindly providence approved of her efforts, she was able to have both. That very evening her stepfather declared that he would have to go to London in the morning. A useful acquaintance had phoned to say that he would meet him and introduce him to a wholesaler who would consider doing business with him once he was established. He would go to London early in the morning, and since he had a long day ahead of him he went to bed early.

Presently, alone with her mother, Amabel seized what seemed to be a golden opportunity.

'I wondered if I might have some money for clothes, Mother. I haven't bought anything since you went away...'

'Of course, love. I should have thought of that myself. And you did so well with the bed and breakfast business. Is there any money in the tea caddy? If there is take whatever you want from it. I'll ask Keith to make you an allowance; he's so generous...'

'No, don't do that, Mother. He has enough to think about without bothering him about that; there'll be enough in the tea caddy. Don't bother him.' She looked across at her mother. 'You're very happy with him, aren't you, Mother?'

'Oh, yes, Amabel. I never told you, but I hated living here, just the two of us, making ends meet, no man around the place. When I went to your sister's I realised what I was missing. And I've been thinking that perhaps it would be a good idea if you started some sort of training...'

Amabel agreed quietly, reflecting that her mother wouldn't miss her...

Her mother went to bed presently, and Amabel made Oscar and Cyril comfortable for the night and counted the money in the tea caddy. There was more than enough for her plan.

She went to her room and, quiet as a mouse, got her hold-all out of the wardrobe and packed it, including undies and a jersey skirt and a couple of woollies; autumn would soon turn to winter...

She thought over her plan when she was in bed; there seemed no way of improving upon it, so she closed her eyes and went to sleep.

She got up early, to prepare breakfast for her stepfather, having first of all made sure that Oscar and Cyril weren't in the kitchen. Once he had driven away she got her own breakfast, fed both animals and got dressed. Her mother came down, and over her coffee suggested that she might get the postman to give her a lift to Castle Cary.

'I've time to dress before he comes, and I can get my hair done. You'll be all right, love?'

It's as though I'm meant to be leaving, reflected Amabel. And when her mother was ready, and waiting for the postman, reminded her to take a key with her—'For I might go for a walk.'

Amabel had washed the breakfast dishes, tidied the house, and made the beds by the time her mother got into the post van, and if she gave her mother a sudden warm hug and kiss Mrs Graham didn't notice.

Half an hour later Amabel, with Oscar in his basket, Cyril on a lead, and encumbered by her holdall and a shoulder bag, was getting into the taxi she had requested. She had written to her mother explaining that it was high time she became independent and that she would write, but that she was not to worry. *You will both make a great success of the market garden and it will be easier for you both if Oscar, Cyril and myself aren't getting under your feet,* she had ended.

The taxi took them to Gillingham where—fortune still smiling—they got on the London train and, once there, took a taxi to Victoria bus station. By now Amabel realised her plans, so simple in theory, were fraught with possible disaster. But she had cooked her goose. She bought a ticket to York, had a cup of tea, got water for Cyril and put milk in her saucer for Oscar and then climbed into the long-distance bus.

It was half empty, and the driver was friendly. Amabel perched on a seat with Cyril at her feet and Oscar in his basket on her lap. She was a bit cramped, but at least they were still altogether...

It was three o'clock in the afternoon by now, and it was a hundred and ninety-three miles to York, where they would arrive at about half past eight. The end of the journey was in sight, and it only remained for Great-Aunt Thisbe to offer them a roof over their heads. A moot point since she was unaware of them coming...

'I should have phoned her,' muttered Amabel, 'but there was so much to think about in such a hurry.'

It was only now that the holes in her hare-brained scheme began to show, but it was too late to worry about it. She still had a little money, she was young, she could work and, most important of all, Oscar and Cyril were still alive...

Amabel, a sensible level-headed girl, had thrown her bonnet over the windmill with a vengeance.

She went straight to the nearest phone box at the bus station in York; she was too tired and light-headed from her impetuous journey to worry about Great-Aunt Thisbe's reaction.

When she heard that lady's firm, unhurried voice she said without preamble, 'It's me—Amabel, Aunt Thisbe. I'm at the bus station in York.'

She had done her best to keep her voice quiet and steady, but it held a squeak of panic. Supposing Aunt Thisbe put down the phone...

Miss Parsons did no such thing. When she had been told

of her dead nephew's wife's remarriage she had disapproved, strongly but silently. Such an upheaval: a strange man taking over from her nephew's loved memory, and what about Amabel? She hadn't seen the girl for some years—what of her? Had her mother considered her?

She said now, 'Go and sit down on the nearest seat, Amabel. I'll be with you in half an hour.'

'I've got Oscar and Cyril with me.'

'You are all welcome,' said Aunt Thisbe, and rang off.

Much heartened by these words, Amabel found a bench and, with a patient Cyril crouching beside her and Oscar eyeing her miserably from the little window in his basket, sat down to wait.

Half an hour, when you're not very happy, can seem a very long time, but Amabel forgot that when she saw Great-Aunt Thisbe walking briskly towards her, clad in a coat and skirt which hadn't altered in style for the last few decades, her white hair crowned by what could best be described as a sensible hat. There was a youngish man with her, short and sturdy with weatherbeaten features.

Great-Aunt Thisbe kissed Amabel briskly. 'I am so glad you have come to visit me, my dear. Now we will go home and you shall tell me all about it. This is Josh, my right hand. He'll take your luggage to the car and drive us home.'

Amabel had got to her feet. She couldn't think of anything to say that wouldn't need a long explanation, so she held out a hand for Josh to shake, picked up Oscar's basket and Cyril's lead and walked obediently out into the street and got into the back of the car while Aunt Thisbe settled herself beside Josh.

It was dark now, and the road was almost empty of traffic. There was nothing to see from the car's window but Amabel remembered Bolton Percy was where her aunt lived, a medieval village some fifteen miles from York and tucked away from the main roads. It must be ten years since she was last here, she reflected; she had been sixteen and her father had died a few months earlier...

The village, when they reached it, was in darkness, but her aunt's house, standing a little apart from the row of brick and plaster cottages near the church, welcomed them with lighted windows.

Josh got out and helped her with the animals and she followed him up the path to the front door, which Great-Aunt Thisbe had opened.

'Welcome to my home, child,' she said. 'And yours for as long as you need it.'

CHAPTER THREE

THE NEXT HOUR or two were a blur to Amabel; her coat was taken from her and she was sat in a chair in Aunt Thisbe's kitchen, bidden to sit there, drink the tea she was given and say nothing—something she was only too glad to do while Josh and her aunt dealt with Cyril and Oscar. In fact, quite worn out, she dozed off, to wake and find Oscar curled up on her lap, washing himself, and Cyril's head pressed against her knee.

Great-Aunt Thisbe spoke before she could utter a word.

'Stay there for a few minutes. Your room's ready, but you must have something to eat first.'

'Aunt Thisbe—' began Amabel.

'Later, child. Supper and a good night's sleep first. Do you want your mother to know you are here?'

'No, no. I'll explain...'

'Tomorrow.' Great-Aunt Thisbe, still wearing her hat, put a bowl of fragrant stew into Amabel's hands. 'Now eat your supper.'

Presently Amabel was ushered upstairs to a small room with a sloping ceiling and a lattice window. She didn't remember getting undressed, nor did she feel surprised to find both Oscar and Cyril with her. It had been a day like no other and she was beyond surprise or questioning; it seemed quite right that Cyril and Oscar should share her bed. They were still all together, she thought with satisfaction. It was like waking up after a particularly nasty nightmare.

When she woke in the morning she lay for a moment, staring up at the unfamiliar ceiling, but in seconds memory came flooding back and she sat up in bed, hampered by Cyril's weight on her feet and Oscar curled up near him. In the light of early morning yesterday's journey was something unbelievably foolhardy—and she would have to explain to Great-Aunt Thisbe.

The sooner the better.

She got up, went quietly to the bathroom, dressed and the three of them crept downstairs.

The house wasn't large, but it was solidly built, and had been added to over the years, and its small garden had a high stone wall. Amabel opened the stout door and went outside. Oscar and Cyril, old and wise enough to know what was wanted of them, followed her cautiously.

It was a fine morning but there was a nip in the air, and the three of them went back indoors just as Great-Aunt Thisbe came into the kitchen.

Her good morning was brisk and kind. 'You slept well? Good. Now, my dear, there's porridge on the Aga; I dare say these two will eat it. Josh will bring suitable food when he comes presently. And you and I will have a cup of tea before I get our breakfast.'

'I must explain...'

'Of course. But over a cup of tea.'

So presently Amabel sat opposite her aunt at the kitchen table, drank her tea and gave her a carefully accurate account of her journey. 'Now I've thought about it, I can see how silly I was. I didn't stop to think, you see—only that I had to get away because my—my stepfather was going to kill...' She faltered. 'And he doesn't like me.'

'Your mother? She is happy with him?'

'Yes—yes, she is, and he is very good to her. They don't need me. I shouldn't have come here, only I had to think of something quickly. I'm so grateful to you, Aunt Thisbe, for letting me stay last night. I wondered if you would let me leave Oscar and Cyril here today, while I go into York and find work. I'm not trained, but there's always work in hotels and people's houses.'

The sound which issued from Miss Parsons' lips would have been called a snort from a lesser mortal.

'Your father was my brother, child. You will make this your home as long as you wish to stay. As to work—it will be a godsend to me to have someone young about the place. I'm well served by Josh and Mrs Josh, who cleans the place for me, but I could do with company, and in a week or two you can decide what you want to do.

'York is a big city; there are museums, historical houses, a wealth of interest to the visitor in Roman remains—all of which employ guides, curators, helpers of all kinds. There should be choice enough when it comes to looking for a job. The only qualifications needed are intelligence, the Queen's English and a pleasant voice and appearance. Now go and get dressed, and after breakfast you shall telephone your mother.'

'They will want me to go back—they don't want me, but he expects me to work for him in the garden.'

'You are under no obligation to your stepfather, Amabel, and your mother is welcome to come and visit you at any time. You are not afraid of your stepfather?'

'No—but I'm afraid of what he would do to Oscar and Cyril. And I don't like him.'

The phone conversation with her mother wasn't entirely satisfactory—Mrs Graham, at first relieved and glad to hear from Amabel, began to complain bitterly at what she described as Amabel's ingratitude.

'Keith will have to hire help,' she pointed out. 'He's very vexed about it, and really, Amabel, you have shown us a lack of consideration, going off like that. Of course we shall always be glad to see you, but don't expect any financial help—you've chosen to stand on your own two feet. Still, you're a sensible girl, and I've no doubt that you will find work—I don't suppose Aunt Thisbe will want you to stay for more than a week or two.' There was a pause. 'And you've got Oscar and Cyril with you?'

'Yes, Mother.'

'They'll hamper you when you look for work. Really, it would have been better if Keith had had them put down.'

'Mother! They have lived with us for years. They don't deserve to die.'

'Oh, well, but they're neither of them young. Will you phone again?'

Amabel said that she would and put down the phone. Despite Great-Aunt Thisbe's sensible words, she viewed the future with something like panic.

Her aunt took one look at her face, and said, 'Will you walk down to the shop and get me one or two things, child? Take Cyril with you—Oscar will be all right here—and we will have coffee when you get back.'

It was only a few minutes' walk to the stores in the centre of the village, and although it was drizzling and windy it was nice to be out of doors. It was a small village, but the church was magnificent and the narrow main street was lined with small solid houses and crowned at its end by a large brick and plaster pub.

Amabel did her shopping, surprised to discover that the stern-looking lady who served her knew who she was.

'Come to visit your auntie? She'll be glad of a bit of company for a week or two. A good thing she's spending the winter with that friend of hers in Italy...'

Two or three weeks, decided Amabel, walking back, should be enough time to find some kind of work and a place to live. Aunt Thisbe had told her that she was welcome to stay as long as she wanted to, but if she did that would mean her aunt would put off her holiday. Which would never do... She would probably mention it in a day or two—especially if Amabel lost no time in looking for work.

But a few days went by, and although Amabel reiterated her intention of finding work as soon as possible her aunt made no mention of her holiday; indeed she insisted that Amabel did nothing about it.

'You need a week or two to settle down,' she pointed out, 'and I won't hear of you leaving until you have decided what you want to do. It won't hurt you to spend the winter here.'

Which gave Amabel the chance to ask, 'But you may have made plans...'

Aunt Thisbe put down her knitting. 'And what plans would I be making at my age, child? Now, let us say no more for the moment. Tell me about your mother's wedding?'

So Amabel, with Oscar on her lap and Cyril sitting between them, told all she knew, and presently they fell to talking about her father, still remembered with love by both of them.

Dr Fforde, immersed in his work though he was, nevertheless found his thoughts wandering, rather to his surprise, towards Amabel. It was some two weeks after she had left home that he decided to go and see her again. By now her mother and stepfather would be back and she would have settled down with them and be perfectly happy, all her doubts and fears forgotten.

He told himself that was his reason for going: to reassure himself that, knowing her to be happy again, he could dismiss her from his mind.

It was mid-afternoon when he got there, and as he parked the car he saw signs of activity at the back of the house. Instead of knocking on the front door he walked round the side of the house to the back. Most of the orchard had disappeared, and there was a large concrete foundation where the trees had been. Beyond the orchard the ground had been ploughed up; the bench had gone, and the fruit bushes. Only the view beyond was still beautiful.

He went to the kitchen door and knocked.

Amabel's mother stood in the doorway, and before she could speak he said, 'I came to see Amabel.' He held out a hand. 'Dr Fforde.'

Mrs Graham shook hands. She said doubtfully, 'Oh, did you meet her when she was doing bed and breakfasts? She's not here; she's left.'

She held the door wide. 'Come in. My husband will be back very shortly. Would you like a cup of tea?'

'Thank you.' He looked around him. 'There was a dog...'

'She's taken him with her—and the cat. My husband won't have animals around the place. He's starting up a market garden. The silly girl didn't like the idea of them being put down—left us in the lurch too; she was going to work for Keith, help with the place once we get started—we are having a big greenhouse built.'

'Yes, there was an orchard there.'

He accepted his tea and, when she sat down, took a chair opposite her.

'Where has Amabel gone?' The question was put so casually that Mrs Graham answered at once.

'Yorkshire, of all places—and heaven knows how she got there. My first husband's sister lives near York—a small village called Bolton Percy. Amabel went there—well, there wasn't anywhere else she could have gone without a job. We did wonder where she was, but she phoned when she got there... Here's my husband.'

The two men shook hands, exchanged a few minutes' conversation, then Dr Fforde got up to go.

He had expected his visit to Amabel's home to reassure him as to her future; it had done nothing of the sort. Her mother might be fond of her but obviously this overbearing man she had married would discourage her from keeping close ties with Amabel—he had made no attempt to disguise his dislike of her.

Driving himself back home, the doctor reflected that Amabel had been wise to leave. It seemed a bit drastic to go as far away as Yorkshire, but if she had family there they would have arranged her journey. He reminded himself that he had no need to concern himself about her; she had obviously dealt with her own future in a sensible manner. After all, she had seemed a sensible girl...

Bates greeted him with the news that Mrs Potter-Stokes had telephoned. 'Enquiring if you would take her to an art exhibition tomorrow evening which she had already mentioned.'

And why not? reflected Dr Fforde. He no longer needed to worry about Amabel. The art exhibition turned out to be very avant-garde, and Dr Fforde, escorting Miriam Potter-Stokes, listening to her rather vapid remarks, trying to make sense of the childish daubs acclaimed as genius, allowed his thoughts to wander. It was time he took a few days off, he decided. He would clear his desk of urgent cases and leave London for a while. He enjoyed driving and the roads were less busy now.

So when Miriam suggested that he might like to spend the weekend at her parents' home, he declined firmly, saying, 'I really can't spare the time, and I shall be out of London for a few days.'

'You poor man; you work far too hard. You need a wife to make sure that you don't do too much.'

She smiled up at him and then wished that she hadn't said that. Oliver had made some rejoinder dictated by good manners, but he had glanced at her with indifference from cold blue eyes. She must be careful, she reflected; she had set her heart on him for a husband...

Dr Fforde left London a week later. He had allowed himself three days: ample time to drive to York, seek out the village where Amabel was living and make sure that she was happy with this aunt and that she had some definite plans for her future. Although why he should concern himself with that he didn't go into too deeply.

A silly impetuous girl, he told himself, not meaning a word of it.

He left after an early breakfast, taking Tiger with him, sitting erect and watchful beside him, sliding through the morning traffic until at last he reached the M1. After a while he stopped at a service station, allowed Tiger a short run, drank a cup of coffee and drove on until, mindful of Tiger's heavy sighs, he stopped in a village north of Chesterfield.

The pub was almost empty and Tiger, his urgent needs dealt with, was made welcome, with a bowl of water and biscuits, while the doctor sat down before a plate of beef sandwiches, home-made pickles and half a pint of real ale.

Much refreshed, they got back into the car presently, their journey nearing its end. The doctor, a man who, having looked at the map before he started a journey, never needed to look at it again, turned off the motorway and made his way through country roads until he was rewarded by the sight of Bolton Percy's main street.

He stopped before the village stores and went in. The village was a small one; Amabel's whereabouts would be known...

As well as the severe-looking lady behind the counter there were several customers, none of whom appeared to be shopping with any urgency. They all turned to look at him as he went in, and even the severe-looking lady smiled at his pleasant greeting.

An elderly woman at the counter spoke up. 'Wanting to know the way? I'm in no hurry. Mrs Bluett—' she indicated the severe lady '—she'll help you.'

Dr Fforde smiled his thanks. 'I'm looking for a Miss Amabel Parsons.'

He was eyed with even greater interest.

'Staying with her aunt—Miss Parsons up at the End House. End of this street; house stands on its own beyond the row of cottages. You can't miss it. They'll be home.' She glanced at the clock. 'They sit down to high tea around six o'clock, but drink a cup around half past three. Expecting you, is she?'

'No...' Mrs Bluett looked at him so fiercely that he felt obliged to add, 'We have known each other for some time.' She smiled then, and he took his leave, followed by interested looks.

Stopping once more a hundred yards or so down the street, he got out of the car slowly and stood just for a moment looking at the house. It was red brick and plaster, solid and welcoming with its lighted windows. He crossed the pavement, walked up the short path to the front door and knocked.

Miss Parsons opened it. She stood looking at him with a severity which might have daunted a lesser man.

'I have come to see Amabel,' observed the doctor mildly. He held out a hand. 'Fforde—Oliver Fforde. Her mother gave me this address.'

Miss Parsons took his hand and shook it. 'Thisbe Parsons. Amabel's aunt. She has spoken of you.' She looked round his great shoulder. 'Your car? It will be safe there. And a dog?'

She took another good luck at him and liked what she saw. 'We're just about to have a cup of tea. Do bring the dog in— he's not aggressive? Amabel's Cyril is here...'

'They are already acquainted.' He smiled. 'Thank you.'

He let Tiger out of the car and the pair of them followed her into the narrow hallway.

Miss Parsons marched ahead of them, opened a door and led the way into the room, long and low, with windows at each end and an old-fashioned fireplace at its centre. The furniture was old-fashioned too, beautifully kept and largely covered by photos in silver frames and small china ornaments, some of them valuable, and a quantity of pot plants. It was a very pleasant room, lived in and loved and very welcoming.

The doctor, treading carefully between an occasional table and a Victorian spoon-back chair, watched Amabel get to her feet and heaved a sigh of relief at the pleased surprise on her face.

He said, carefully casual, 'Amabel...' and shook her hand, smiling down at her face. 'I called at your home and your mother gave me this address. I have to be in York for a day or two and it seemed a good idea to renew our acquaintance.'

She stared up into his kind face. 'I've left home...'

'So your stepfather told me. You are looking very well.'

'Oh, I am. Aunt Thisbe is so good to me, and Cyril and Oscar are happy.'

Miss Parsons lifted the teapot. 'Sit down and have your tea and tell me what brings you to York, Dr Fforde. It's a long way from London—you live there, I presume?'

The doctor had aunts of his own, so he sat down, drank his tea meekly and answered her questions without telling her a great deal. Tiger was sitting beside him, a model of canine obedience, while Cyril settled near him. Oscar, of course, had settled himself on top of the bookcase. Presently the talk became general, and he made no effort to ask Amabel how she came to be so far from her home. She would tell him in her own good time, and he had two days before he needed to return to London.

Miss Parsons said briskly, 'We have high tea at six o'clock. We hope you will join us. Unless you have some commitments in York?'

'Not until tomorrow morning. I should very much like to accept.'

'In that case you and Amabel had better take the dogs for a run while I see to a meal.'

It was dark by now, and chilly. Amabel got into her mac, put Cyril's lead on and led the way out of the house, telling him, 'We can go to the top of the village and come back along the back lane.'

The doctor took her arm and, with a dog at either side of them, they set off. 'Tell me what happened,' he suggested.

His gentle voice would have persuaded the most unwilling to confide in him and Amabel, her arm tucked under his, was only too willing. Aunt Thisbe was a dear, loving and kind under her brusque manner, but she hadn't been there; Dr Fforde had, so there was no need to explain about Cyril and Oscar or her stepfather...

She said slowly, 'I did try, really I did—to like him and stay at home until they'd settled in and I could suggest that I might train for something. But he didn't like me, although he expected me to work for him, and he hated Cyril and Oscar.'

She took a breath and began again, not leaving anything out, trying to keep to the facts and not colouring them with her feelings.

When she had finished the doctor said firmly, 'You did quite right. It was rather hazardous of you to undertake the long journey here, but it was a risk worth taking.'

They were making their way back to the house, and although it was too dark to see he sensed that she was crying. He reminded himself that he had adopted the role of advisor and impersonal friend. That had been his intention and still was. Moreover, her aunt had offered her a home. He resisted a desire to take her in his arms and kiss her, something which, while giving him satisfaction would possibly complicate matters. Instead he said cheerfully, 'Will you spend the afternoon with me tomorrow? We might drive to the coast.'

Amabel swallowed tears. 'That would be very nice,' she told him. 'Thank you.' And, anxious to match his casual friendliness, she added, 'I don't know this part of the world, do you?'

For the rest of the way back they discussed Yorkshire and its beauties.

Aunt Thisbe was old-fashioned; the younger generation might like their dinner in the evening, but she had remained faithful to high tea. The table was elegantly laid, the teapot at one end, a covered dish of buttered eggs at the other, with racks of toast, a dish of butter and a home-made pâté. There was jam too, and a pot of honey, and sandwiches, and in the centre of the table a cakestand bearing scones, fruitcake, oatcakes and small cakes from the local baker, known as fancies.

The doctor, a large and hungry man, found everything to his

satisfaction and made a good meal, something which endeared him to Aunt Thisbe's heart, so that when he suggested he might take Amabel for a drive the following day she said at once that it was a splendid idea. Here was a man very much to her liking; it was a pity that it was obvious that his interest in Amabel was only one of impersonal kindness. The girl had been glad to see him, and heaven knew the child needed friends. A pity that he was only in York for a few days and lived so far away...

He washed the dishes and Amabel dried them after their meal. Aunt Thisbe, sitting in the drawing room, could hear them talking and laughing in the kitchen. Something would have to be done, thought the old lady. Amabel needed young friends, a chance to go out and enjoy herself; life would be dull for her during the winter. A job must be found for her where she would meet other people.

Aunt Thisbe felt sharp regret at the thought of the holiday she would have to forego: something which Amabel was never to be told about.

Dr Fforde went presently, making his goodbyes with beautiful manners, promising to be back the following afternoon. Driving to York with Tiger beside him, he spoke his thoughts aloud. 'Well, we can put our minds at rest, can we not, Tiger? She will make a new life for herself with this delightful aunt, probably find a pleasant job and meet a suitable young man and marry him.' He added, 'Most satisfactory.' So why did he feel so dissatisfied about it?

He drove to a hotel close to the Minster—a Regency townhouse, quiet and elegant, and with the unobtrusive service which its guests took for granted. Tiger, accommodated in the corner of his master's room, settled down for the night, leaving his master to go down to the bar for a nightcap and a study of the city.

The pair of them explored its streets after their breakfast. It was a fine day, and the doctor intended to drive to the coast that afternoon, but exploring the city would give him the opportunity of getting to know it. After all, it would probably be in York where Amabel would find a job.

He lunched in an ancient pub, where Tiger was welcomed with water and biscuits, and then went back to the hotel, got into his car and drove to Bolton Percy.

Amabel had spent the morning doing the small chores Aunt Thisbe allowed her to do, attending to Oscar's needs and taking Cyril for a walk, but there was still time to worry about what she should wear for her outing. Her wardrobe was so scanty that it was really a waste of time to worry about it.

It would have to be the pleated skirt and the short coat she had travelled in; they would pass muster for driving around the country, and Dr Fforde never looked at her as though he actually saw her. It had been lovely to see him again, like meeting an old friend—one who listened without interrupting and offered suggestions, never advice, in the friendliest impersonal manner of a good doctor. He was a doctor, of course, she reminded herself.

He came punctually, spent ten minutes talking to Miss Parsons, suggested that Cyril might like to share the back seat with Tiger, popped Amabel into the car and took the road to the coast.

Flamborough stood high on cliffs above the North Sea, and down at sea level boats sheltered in the harbour. Dr Fforde parked the car, put the dogs on their leads and walked Amabel briskly towards the peninsula. It was breezy, but the air was exhilarating, and they seemed to be the only people around.

When they stopped to look out to sea, Amabel said happily, 'Oh, this is marvellous; so grand and beautiful—fancy living here and waking up each morning and seeing the sea.'

They walked a long way, and as they turned to go back Dr Fforde said, carefully casual, 'Do you want to talk about your plans, Amabel? Perhaps your aunt has already suggested something? Or do you plan to stay with her indefinitely?'

'I wanted to ask you about that. There's a problem. You won't mind if I tell you about it, and perhaps you could give me some advice. You see I was told quite unwittingly, by Mrs Bluett who owns the village shop, that Aunt Thisbe had plans to spend the winter in Italy with a friend. I haven't liked to ask her, and she hasn't said anything, but I can't allow her to lose a lovely holiday like that because I'm here. After all, she didn't expect me, but she's so kind and she might feel that she should stay here so that I've got a home, if you see what I mean.'

They were standing facing each other, and she stared up into his face. 'You can see that I must get a job very quickly, but I'm not sure how to set about it. I mean, should I answer advertisements in the paper or visit an agency? There's not much I can do, and it has to be somewhere Cyril and Oscar can come too.'

He said slowly, 'Well, first you must convince your aunt that you want a job—and better not say that you know of her holiday. Go to York, put your name down at any agencies you can find...' He paused, frowning. 'What can you do, Amabel?'

'Nothing, really,' she said cheerfully. 'Housework, cooking—or I expect I could be a waitress or work in a shop. They're not the sort of jobs people want, are they? And they aren't well paid. But if I could get a start somewhere, and also somewhere to live...'

'Do you suppose your aunt would allow you to live at her house while she was away?'

'Perhaps. But how would I get to work? The bus service is only twice weekly, and there is nowhere in the village where I could work.' She added fiercely, 'I must be independent.'

He took her arm and they walked on. 'Of course. Now, I can't promise anything, Amabel, but I know a lot of people and I might hear of something. Do you mind where you go?'

'No, as long as I can have Cyril and Oscar with me.'

'There is no question of your returning home?'

'None whatever. I'm being a nuisance to everyone, aren't I?'

He agreed silently to that, but he didn't say so. She was determined to be independent, and for some reason which he didn't understand he wanted to help her.

He asked, 'Have you some money? Enough to pay the rent and so on?'

'Yes, thank you. Mother let me have the money in the tea caddy, and there is still some left.'

He decided it wasn't worth while asking about the tea caddy. 'Good. Now we are going to the village; I noticed a pub as we came through it—the Royal Dog and Duck. If it is open they might give us tea.'

They had a splendid meal in the snug behind the bar: a great pot of tea, scones and butter, cream and jam, great wedges of fruitcake and, in case that wasn't enough, a dish of buttered toast. Tiger and Cyril, sitting under the table, provided with water and any tidbits which came their way, were tired after their walk, and dozed quietly.

He drove back presently through the dusk of late autumn, taking side roads through charming villages—Burton Agnes, with its haunted manor and Norman church, through Lund, with its once-upon-a-time cockpit, on to Bishop Burton, with its village pond and little black and white cottages, and finally along country roads to Bolton Percy.

The doctor stayed only as long as good manners dictated, although he asked if he might call to wish them goodbye the following morning.

'Come for coffee?' invited Miss Parsons.

The stiff breeze from yesterday had turned into a gale in the morning, and he made that his excuse for not staying long over his coffee. When Amabel had opened the door to him he had handed her a list of agencies in York, and now he wanted to be gone; he had done what he could for her. She had a home, this aunt who was obviously fond of her, and she was young and healthy and sensible, even if she had no looks to speak of. He had no further reason to be concerned about her.

All the same, driving down the M1, he was finding it difficult to forget her. She had bidden him goodbye in a quiet voice, her small hand in his, wished him a safe journey and thanked him. 'It's been very nice knowing you,' she had told him.

It had been nice knowing her, he conceded, and it was a pity that their paths were unlikely to cross in the future.

That evening Amabel broached the subject of her future to her aunt. She was careful not to mention Aunt Thisbe's holiday in Italy, pointing out with enthusiasm her great wish to become independent.

'I'll never be grateful enough to you,' she assured her aunt, 'for giving me a home—and I love being here with you. But I must get started somewhere, mustn't I? I know I shall like York, and there must be any number of jobs for someone like me—I mean, unskilled labour. And I won't stop at that. You do understand, don't you, Aunt?'

'Yes, of course I do, child. You must go to York and see what there is there for you. Only you must promise me that if you fall on hard times you will come here.' She hesitated, then, 'And if I am not here, go to Josh and Mrs Josh.'

'I promise, Aunt Thisbe. There's a bus to York tomorrow morning, isn't there? Shall I go and have a look round—spy out the land...?'

'Josh has to take the car in tomorrow morning; you shall go with him. The bus leaves York in the afternoon around four o'clock, but if you miss it phone here and Josh will fetch you.'

It was a disappointing day. Amabel went from one agency to the next, and was entered on their books, but there were no jobs which would suit her; she wasn't a trained lady's maid, or a cashier as needed at a café, she had neither the training nor the experience to work at a crêche, nor was she suitable as a saleslady at any of the large stores—lack of experience. But how did one get experience unless one had a chance to learn in the first place?

She presented a brave face when she got back to her aunt's

house in the late afternoon. After all, this was only the first day, and her name was down on several agencies' books.

Back in London, Dr Fforde immersed himself in his work, assuring Bates that he had had a most enjoyable break.

'So why is he so gloomy?' Bates enquired of Tiger. 'Too much work. He needs a bit of the bright lights—needs to get out and about a bit.'

So it pleased Bates when his master told him that he would be going out one evening. Taking Mrs Potter-Stokes to the theatre, and supper afterwards.

It should have been a delightful evening; Miriam was a charming companion, beautifully dressed, aware of how very attractive she was, sure of herself, and amusing him with anecdotes of their mutual friends, asking intelligent questions about his work. But she was aware that she hadn't got his full attention. Over supper she exerted herself to gain his interest, and asked him prettily if he had enjoyed his few days off. 'Where did you go?' she added.

'York...'

'York?' She seized on that. 'My dear Oliver, I wish I'd known; you could have called on a great friend of mine—Dolores Trent. She has one of those shops in the Shambles—you know, sells dried flowers and pots and expensive glass. But she's hopeless at it—so impractical, breaking things and getting all the money wrong. I had a letter from her only a few days ago—she thinks she had better get someone to help her.'

She glanced at the doctor and saw with satisfaction that he was smiling at her. 'How amusing. Is she as attractive as you, Miriam?'

Miriam smiled a little triumphant smile, the evening was a success after all.

Which was what the doctor was thinking...

CHAPTER FOUR

WHEN AMABEL CAME back from walking Cyril the next morning she was met at the door by her aunt.

'A pity. You have just missed a phone call from your nice Dr Fforde. He has heard of a job quite by chance from a friend and thought you might be interested. A lady who owns a shop in the Shambles in York—an arty-crafty place, I gather; she needs someone to help her. He told me her name—Dolores Trent—but he doesn't know the address. You might like to walk through the Shambles and see if you can find her shop. Most thoughtful of him to think of you.'

Josh drove her in after lunch. She was, her aunt had decreed, to spend as long as she wanted in York and phone when she was ready to return; Josh would fetch her.

She walked through the city, found the Shambles and started to walk its length. It was a narrow cobbled street, lined by old houses which overhung the lane, almost all of which were now shops: expensive shops, she saw at once, selling the kind of things people on holiday would take back home to display or give as presents to someone who needed to be impressed.

She walked down one side, looking at the names over the doors and windows, pausing once or twice to study some beautiful garment in a boutique or look at a display of jewellery. She reached the end and started back on the other side, and halfway down she found what she was looking for. It was a small shop, tucked between a bookshop and a mouthwatering patisserie, its small window displaying crystal vases, great baskets of dried silk flowers, delicate china and eye-catching pottery. Hung discreetly in one corner was a small card with 'Shop Assistant Required' written on it.

Amabel opened the door and went inside.

She supposed that the lady who came to meet her through the bead curtain at the back of the shop was Dolores Trent; she so exactly fitted her shop. Miss Trent was a tall person, slightly overweight, swathed in silky garments and wearing a good deal of jewellery, and she brought with her a cloud of some exotic perfume.

'You wish to browse?' she asked in a casual manner. 'Do feel free...'

'The card in the window?' said Amabel. 'You want an assistant. Would I do?'

Dolores Trent looked her over carefully. A dull little creature, she decided, but quite pleasant to look at, and she definitely didn't want some young glamorous girl who might distract customers from buying.

She said sharply, 'You live here? Have you references? Have you any experience?'

'I live with my aunt at Bolton Percy, and I can get references. I've no experience in working in a shop, but I'm used to people. I ran a bed and breakfast house...'

Miss Trent laughed. 'At least you sound honest. If you come here to work, how will you get here? Bolton Percy's a bit rural, isn't it?'

'Yes. I hope to find somewhere to live here.'

Several thoughts passed with quick succession through Dolores Trent's head. There was that empty room behind the shop, beyond the tiny kitchenette and the cloakroom; it could be furnished with odds and ends from the attic at home. The girl could live there, and since she would have rent-free accommodation there would be no need to pay her the wages she would be entitled to...

Miss Trent, mean by nature, liked the idea.

'I might consider you, if your references are satisfactory. Your hours would be from nine o'clock till five, free on Sundays. I'd expect you to keep the shop clean and dusted, unpack goods when they arrive, arrange shelves, serve the customers and deal with the cash. You'd do any errands, and look after the shop when I'm not here. You say you want to live here? There's a large room behind the shop, with windows and a door opening onto a tiny yard. Basic furniture and bedding. There's a kitchenette and a cloakroom which you can use. Of course you do understand that if I let you live here I won't be able to pay you the usual wages?'

She named a sum which Amabel knew was not much more than half what she should have expected. On the other hand, here was shelter and security and independence.

'I have a dog and a cat. Would you object to them?'

'Not if they stay out of sight. A dog would be quite a good idea; it's quiet here at night. You're not nervous?'

'No. Might I see the room?'

It was a pleasant surprise, quite large and airy, with two windows and a small door opening onto a tiny square of neglected grass. But there were high walls surrounding it; Cyril and Oscar would be safe there.

Dolores Trent watched Amabel's face. The girl needed the job and somewhere to live, so she wasn't likely to leave at a moment's notice if she found the work too hard or the hours too long. Especially with a dog and a cat...

She said, 'Provided your references are okay, you can come on a month's trial. You'll be paid weekly. After the month it will be a week's notice on either side.' As they went back to the shop she said, 'I'll phone you when I've checked the references.'

Amabel, waiting for Josh to fetch her in answer to her phone call, was full of hope. It would be a start: somewhere to live, a chance to gain the experience which was so necessary if she wanted to get a better job. She would have the chance to look around her, make friends, perhaps find a room where Cyril and Oscar would be welcome, and find work which was better paid. But that would be later, she conceded. In the meantime she was grateful to Dr Fforde for his help. It was a pity she couldn't see him and tell him how grateful she was. But he had disappeared back into his world, somewhere in London, and London was vast...

Convincing Aunt Thisbe that the offer of work from Miss Trent was exactly what she had hoped for was no easy task. Aunt Thisbe had said no word of her holiday, only reiterating her advice that Amabel should spend the next few weeks with her, wait until after Christmas before looking for work...

It was only after Amabel had painted a somewhat over-blown picture of her work at Miss Trent's shop, the advantages of getting one foot in the door of future prospects, and her wish to become independent, that Miss Parsons agreed reluctantly that it might be the chance of a lifetime. There was the added advantage that, once in York, the chance of finding an even better job was much greater than if Amabel stayed at Bolton Percy.

So Amabel sent off her references and within a day or so the job was hers, if she chose to take it. Amabel showed her aunt the letter and it was then that Aunt Thisbe said, 'I shall be sorry to see you go, child. You must spend your Sundays here, of course, and any free time you have.' She hesitated. 'If I am away then you must go to Josh and Mrs Josh, who will look after you. Josh will have a key, and you must treat the house as your home. If you need the car you have only to ask...'

'Will you be away for long?' asked Amabel.

'Well, dear, I have been invited to spend a few weeks with an old friend who has an apartment in Italy. I hadn't made up my mind whether to go, but since you have this job and are determined to be independent...'

'Oh, Aunt Thisbe, how lovely for you—and hasn't everything worked out well? I'll be fine in York and I'll love to come here, if Mrs Josh won't mind. When are you going?'

'You are to start work next Monday? I shall probably go during that week.'

'I thought I'd ask Miss Trent if I could move in on Sunday...'

'A good idea. Josh can drive you there and make sure that everything is all right. Presumably the shop will be empty?'

'I suppose so. I'd have all day to settle in, and if it's quiet Cyril and Oscar won't find it so strange. They're very adaptable.'

So everything was settled. Miss Trent had no objection to Amabel moving in on Sunday. The key would be next door at the patisserie, which was open on Sundays, and the room had been furnished; she could go in and out as she wished and she was to be ready to open the shop at nine o'clock on Monday morning. Miss Trent sounded friendly enough, if a trifle impatient.

Amabel packed her case and Miss Parsons, with brisk efficiency, filled a large box with food: tins of soup, cheese, eggs, butter, bread, biscuits, tea and coffee and plastic bottles of milk and, tucked away out of sight, a small radio. Amabel, for all her brave face, would be lonely.

Aunt Thisbe decided that she would put off her holiday until the following week; Amabel would spend Sunday with her and she would see for herself if she could go away with a clear conscience... She would miss Amabel, but the young shouldn't be held back.

She would have liked to have seen the room where Amabel was to live, but she sensed that Amabel didn't want that—at least not until she had transformed it into a place of which her aunt would approve. And there were one or two things she must tell Josh—that nice Dr Fforde might return. It wasn't very likely, but Aunt Thisbe believed that one should never overlook a chance.

Saying goodbye to Aunt Thisbe wasn't easy. Amabel had

been happy living with her; she had a real affection for the rather dour old lady, and knew that the affection was reciprocated, but she felt in her bones that she was doing the right thing. Her aunt's life had been disrupted by her sudden arrival and that must not be made permanent. She got into the car beside Josh and turned to smile and wave; she would be back on Sunday, but this was the real parting.

There were few people about on an early Sunday morning: tourists strolling along the Shambles, peering into shop windows, church goers. Josh parked the car away from the city centre and they walked, Amabel with the cat basket and Cyril on his lead, Josh burdened with her case and the box of food.

They knew about her at the patisserie; she fetched the key and opened the shop door, led the way through the shop and opened the door to her new home.

Miss Trent had said that she would furnish it, and indeed there was a divan bed against one wall, a small table by the window with an upright chair, a shabby easy chair by the small electric fire and a worn rug on the wooden floor. There was a pile of bedding and a box of cutlery, and a small table lamp with an ugly plastic shade.

Josh put the box down on the table without saying a word, and Amabel said, too brightly, 'Of course it will look quite different once I've arranged things and put up the curtains.'

Josh said, 'Yes, miss,' in a wooden voice. 'Miss Parsons said we were to go next door and have a cup of coffee. I'll help you sort out your things.'

'I'd love some coffee, but after that you don't need to bother, Josh. I've all the rest of the day to get things how I want. And I must take Cyril for a walk later. There's that park by St Mary Abbot's Church, and then I must take a look round the shop.'

They had their coffee and Josh went away, promising to return on the Sunday morning, bidding her to be sure and phone if she needed him or her aunt. She sensed that he didn't approve of her bid for independence and made haste to assure him that everything was fine...

In her room presently, with the door open and Cyril and Oscar going cautiously around the neglected patch of grass, Amabel paused in her bedmaking to reflect that Miss Trent was certainly a trusting kind of person. 'You would have thought,' said Amabel to Oscar, peering round the open door to make sure that she was there, 'that she would have wanted to make sure that I had come. I might have stolen whatever I fancied from the shop.'

Well, it was nice to be trusted; it augered well for the future...

Dolores Trent had in fact gone to Harrogate for the weekend, with only the briefest of thoughts about Amabel. The girl would find her own way around. It had been tiresome enough finding someone to help out in the shop. Really, she didn't know why she kept the place on. It had been fun when she had first had it, but she hadn't realised all the bookwork there would be, and the tiresome ordering and unpacking...

If this girl needed a job as badly as she had hinted, then she could take over the uninteresting parts and leave Dolores to do the selling. It might even be possible to take more time for herself; the shop was a great hindrance to her social life...

Amabel arranged the odds and ends of furniture to their best advantage, switched on the fire, settled her two companions before it and unpacked the box of food. Aunt Thisbe had been generous and practical. There were tins of soup and a tin opener with them, tins of food for Oscar and Cyril, and there was a fruitcake—one of Mrs Josh's. She stowed them away, together with the other stores, in an empty cupboard she found in the tiny kitchenette.

She also found a saucepan, a kettle, some mugs and plates and a tin of biscuits. Presumably Miss Trent made herself elevenses each morning. Amabel opened a tin of soup and put the saucepan on the gas ring, then went to poke her nose into the tiny cloakroom next to the kitchenette. There was a small geyser over the washbasin; at least there would be plenty of hot water.

She made a list while she ate her soup. A cheap rug for the floor, a pretty lampshade, a couple of cushions, a vase—for she must have flowers—and a couple of hooks so that she could hang her few clothes. There was no cupboard, nowhere to put her undies. She added an orange box to the list, with a question mark behind it. She had no idea when she would have the chance to go shopping. She supposed that the shop would close for the usual half-day during the week, though Miss Trent hadn't mentioned that.

She made Oscar comfortable in his basket, switched off the fire, got Cyril's lead and her coat and left the shop, locking the door carefully behind her. It was mid-afternoon by now, and there was no one about. She walked briskly through the streets to St Mary's, where there was a park, and thought there would be time each morning to take Cyril for a quick run before the shop opened. They could go again after the shop closed. There was the grass for him and Oscar during the day; she could leave the door open...

And there were Sundays to look forward to...

On the way back she wondered about Dr Fforde; she tried not to think about him too often, for that was a waste of time. He had come into her life but now he had gone again. She would always be grateful to him, of course, but she was sensible enough to see that he had no place in it.

When she reached the shop she saw that the patisserie was closing its doors, and presently, when she went to look, the shop lights had been turned out. It seemed very quiet and dark outside, but there were lights here and there above the shops. She took heart from the sight of them.

After she had had her tea she went into the shop, turned on the lights and went slowly from shelf to shelf, not touching but noting their order. She looked to see where the wrapping paper, string and labels were kept, for she felt sure Miss Trent would expect her to know that. She wasn't going to be much use for a few days, but there were some things she would be expected to discover for herself.

She had her supper then, let Oscar and Cyril out for the last time, and got ready for bed. Doing the best she could with a basin of hot water in the cloakroom, she pondered the question of baths—or even showers. The girl at the patisserie had been friendly; she might be able to help. Amabel got into her bed, closely followed by her two companions, and fell instantly asleep.

She was up early—and that was another thing, an alarm clock, she thought as she dressed—opened the door onto the grass patch and then left the shop with Cyril. The streets were empty, save for postmen and milkmen, but there were signs of life when she returned after Cyril's run in the park. The shops were still closed, but curtains were being drawn above them and there was a delicious smell of baking bread from the patisserie.

Amabel made her bed, tidied the room, fed the animals and sat down to her own breakfast—a boiled egg, bread and butter and a pot of tea. Tomorrow, she promised herself, she would buy a newspaper when she went out with Cyril, and, since the patisserie opened at half past eight, she could get croissants or rolls for her lunch.

She tidied away her meal, bade the animals be good and shut and locked the door to the shop. They could go outside if they wanted, and the sun was shining…

She was waiting in the shop when Miss Trent arrived. Beyond a nod she didn't reply to Amabel's good morning, but took off her coat, took out a small mirror and inspected her face.

'I don't always get here as early as this,' she said finally. 'Open the shop if I'm not here, and if I'm not here at lunchtime just close the shop for half an hour and get yourself something. Have you had a look round? Yes? Then put the "Open" sign on the door. There's a feather duster under the counter; dust off the window display then unpack that box under the shelves. Be careful, they are china figures. Arrange them on the bottom shelf and mark the price. That will be on the invoice inside the box.'

She put away the mirror and unlocked the drawer in the counter. 'What was your name?' When Amabel reminded her, she said, 'Yes, well, I shall call you Amabel—and you'd better call me Dolores. There probably won't be any customers until ten o'clock. I'm going next door for a cup of coffee. You can have yours when I get back.'

Which was half an hour later, by which time Amabel had dealt with the china figures, praying silently that there would be no customers.

'You can have fifteen minutes,' said Dolores. 'There's coffee and milk in the kitchenette; take it into your room if you want to.'

Cyril and Oscar were glad to have her company, even if only for a few minutes, and it made a pleasant break in the morning.

There were people in the shop by now, picking things up and putting them down again, taking their time choosing what they would buy. Dolores sat behind the counter, paying little attention to them and leaving Amabel to wrap up their purchases. Only occasionally she would advise a customer in a languid manner.

At one o'clock she told Amabel to close the door and lock it.

'Open up again in half an hour if I'm not back,' she said. 'Did I tell you that I close on Wednesday for a half-day? I shall probably go a bit earlier, but you can shut the shop and then do what you like.'

Amabel, while glad to hear about the half-day, thought that her employer seemed rather unbusinesslike. She closed the shop and made herself a sandwich before going to sit on the patch of grass with Oscar and Cyril for company.

She was glad when it was one o'clock on Wednesday; standing about in the shop was surprisingly tiring and, although Dolores was kind in a vague way, she expected Amabel to stay after the shop shut so that she could unpack any new goods or rearrange the windows. Dolores herself did very little, beyond sitting behind the counter holding long conversations over the phone. Only when a customer showed signs of serious buying did she exert herself.

She was good at persuading someone to buy the more expensive glass and china, laughing and chatting in an animated way until the sale was completed, then made no effort to tell Amabel how to go on, seeming content to let her find things out for herself. Amabel supposed that she must make a living from the shop, although it was obvious that she had very little interest in it.

It was a temptation to phone Aunt Thisbe and ask if Josh would fetch her for her half-day, but there were things she wished to do. Shopping for food and material for a window curtain, a new lampshade, flowers... Next week, when she had been paid, she would find a cheerful bedspread for the bed and a cloth for the table.

She did her shopping and took Cyril for a walk, and then spent the rest of her day rearranging her room, sitting by the electric fire eating crumpets for her tea and reading the magazine Dolores had left behind the counter.

Not very exciting, reflected Amabel, but it was early days, and there was Sunday to look forward to. She wrote a letter to her mother, read the magazine from end to end and allowed her thoughts to wander to Dr Fforde.

Sunday came at last, bringing Josh and the prospect of a lovely day and the reality of a warm welcome from Aunt Thisbe.

Warm as well as practical. Amabel was despatched to the bathroom to lie in a pine-scented bath—'For that is something you must miss,' said Miss Parsons. 'Come down when you are ready and we will have coffee and you shall tell me everything.'

Amabel, pink from her bath, settled before the fire in her aunt's drawing room with Oscar and Cyril beside her, and gave a detailed account of her week. She made it light-hearted.

'It's delightful working in such a pleasant place,' she pointed out. 'There are some lovely things in the shop, and Miss Trent—she likes to be called Dolores—is very kind and easygoing.'

'You are able to cook proper meals?'

'Yes, and I do—and the room looks so nice now that I have cushions and flowers.'

'You are happy there, Amabel? Really happy? You have enough free time and she pays you well?'

'Yes, Aunt. York is such a lovely city, and the people in the other shops in the Shambles are so friendly...'

Which was rather an exaggeration, but Aunt Thisbe must be convinced that there was no reason why she shouldn't go to Italy...

She would go during the following week, Miss Parsons told Amabel, and Amabel was to continue to spend her Sundays at End House; Josh would see to everything...

Amabel, back in her room with another box of food and a duvet her aunt had declared she didn't want, was content that she had convinced the old lady that she was perfectly happy; they would write to each other, and when Aunt Thisbe came back in the New Year they would review the future.

A week or two went by. Amabel bought a winter coat, a pretty cover for the duvet, a basket for Cyril and a cheap rug. She also saved some money—but not much.

After the first two weeks Dolores spent less and less time at the shop. She would pop in at opening time and then go and have her hair done, or go shopping or meet friends for coffee. Amabel found it odd, but there weren't many customers. Trade would pick up again at Christmas, Dolores told her.

Amabel, aware that she was being underpaid and overworked, was nonetheless glad to have her days filled. The few hours she spent in her room once the shop was closed were lonely enough. Later, she promised herself, once she felt secure in her job, she would join a club or go to night school. In the meantime she read and knitted and wrote cheerful letters home.

And when she wasn't doing that she thought about Dr Fforde.

Such a waste of time, she told herself. But there again, did that matter? It was pleasant to remember... She wondered what he was doing and wished she knew more about him. Wondered too if he ever thought of her...

To be truthful, he thought of her very seldom; he led a busy life and time was never quite his own. He had driven to Glastonbury once or twice to see his mother, and since the road took him past Amabel's home he had slowed the car to note the work being carried out there. He had thought briefly of calling to see Mrs Graham, but decided against it. There was no point now that Amabel was in York and happy. He hoped that she had settled down by now. Perhaps when he had time to spare he would drive up and go to see her...

He was seeing a good deal of Miriam, and friends were beginning to invite them together to dinner parties. He often spent evenings with her at the theatre when he would much rather have been at home, but she was amusing, and clever enough to appear to have a sincere interest in his work. Hardly aware of it, he was being drawn into her future plans...

It wasn't until one evening, returning home after a long day at the hospital to be met by Bates with a message from Miriam—she—and he—were to join a party of theatregoers that evening, he was to call for her at seven-thirty and after the theatre he would take her out to supper—that he realised what was happening.

He stood for a moment without speaking, fighting down sudden anger, but when he spoke there was nothing of it in his voice.

'Phone Mrs Potter-Stokes, please, and tell her that I am unable to go out this evening.' He smiled suddenly as an idea drowned the anger. 'And, Bates, tell her that I shall be going away.'

There was no expression on Bates's foxy face, but he felt a deep satisfaction. He didn't like Mrs Potter-Stokes and, unlike the doctor, had known for some time that she was set on becoming Mrs Fforde. His 'Very good, Doctor,' was the model of discretion.

As for Dr Fforde, he ate a splendid supper and spent the rest of the evening going through his diary to see how soon he could get away for a couple of days. He would go first to Miss Parsons' house, for Amabel might have chosen to ignore the chance of working in a shop in York. In any case her aunt would know where she was. It would be interesting to meet again...

Almost a week later he set off for York, Tiger beside him. It was a sullen morning, but once he was clear of the endless suburbs the motorway was fairly clear and the Rolls ate up the miles. He stopped for a snack lunch and Tiger's need for a quick trot, and four hours after he had left his home he stopped before Miss Parsons' house.

Of course no one answered his knock, and after a moment he walked down the narrow path beside the house to the garden at the back. It appeared to be empty, but as he stood there Josh came out of the shed by the bottom hedge. He put down the spade he was carrying and walked up the path to meet him.

'Seeking Miss Amabel, are you? House is shut up. Miss Parsons is off to foreign parts for the winter and Miss Amabel's got herself a job in York—comes here of a Sunday; that's her day off.'

He studied the doctor's face. 'You'll want to know where she's working. A fancy shop in the Shambles. Lives in a room at the back with those two animals of hers. Brings them here of a Sunday, spends the day at End House, opens the windows and such, airs the place, has a bath and does her washing and has her dinner with us. Very independent young lady, anxious not to be a nuisance. Says everything is fine at her job but she doesn't look quite the thing, somehow...'

Dr Fforde frowned. 'She got on well with her aunt? They seemed the best of friends...'

'And so they are. I'm not knowing, mind, but I fancy Miss

Amabel took herself off so's Miss Parsons didn't have to alter her plans about her holiday.'

'I think you may be right. I'll go and see her, make sure everything is as it should be.'

'You do that, sir. Me and the missus aren't quite easy. But not knowing anyone to talk to about it...'

'I'm here for a day or two, so I'll come and see you again if I may?'

'You're welcome, sir. You and your dog.' Josh bent to stroke Tiger. 'Miss Amabel does know to come here if needful.'

'I'm glad she has a good friend in you, Josh.'

Dr Fforde got back into his car. It was mid afternoon and drizzling; he was hungry, and he must book in at the hotel where he had stayed before, but before doing so he must see Amabel.

She was on her hands and knees at the back of the shop, unpacking dozens of miniature Father Christmases intended for the Christmas market. Dolores was at the hairdresser and would return only in time to lock the till, tell her to close the shop and lock up.

She was tired and grubby, and there hadn't been time to make tea. Dolores expected everything to be cleared away before she got back. At least there had been no customers for a while, but Amabel was becoming increasingly worried at the amount of work Dolores expected her to do. It had been fine for the first few weeks, but Dolores's interest was dwindling. She was in the shop less, and dealing with the customers and sorting out the stock was becoming increasingly difficult. To talk to her about it was risky; she might so easily give Amabel a week's notice, and although she might find work easily enough there were Oscar and Cyril to consider...

She unwrapped the last of the little figures and looked up as someone came into the shop.

Dr Fforde stood in the doorway looking at her. His instant

impression was that she wasn't happy, but then she smiled, her whole face alight with pleasure.

He said easily, 'Josh told me where you were. He also told me that Miss Parsons is away.' He glanced round him. 'You live here? Surely you don't run the place on your own?'

She had got to her feet, dusting off her hands, brushing down her skirt.

'No. Dolores—that is, Miss Trent—is at the hairdresser. Are you just passing through?'

'I'm here for a couple of days. When do you close this shop?'

'Five o'clock. But I tidy up after that.'

'Will you spend the evening with me?'

She had bent to stroke Tiger's head. 'I'd like that, thank you. Only I have to see to Oscar and Cyril, and take Cyril for a walk, so I won't be ready until about six o'clock.'

'I'll be here soon after five...'

Dolores came in then, assuming her charming manner at the sight of a customer. 'Have you found something you like? Do take a look round.'

She smiled at him, wondering where he came from; if he was on his own she might suggest showing him what was worth seeing in the city—the patisserie wasn't closed yet...

'I came to see Amabel,' he told her. 'We have known each other for some time, and since I am here for a day or two...'

'You're old friends?' Dolores asked artlessly. 'I expect you know York well? You don't live here?'

'No, but I have been here before. We met some time ago, in the West Country.'

Still artless, Dolores said, 'Oh, I thought you might be from London—I've friends there.' An idea—an unlikely idea—had entered her head. 'But I don't suppose you would know them. I came up here after my divorce, and it was an old schoolfriend—Miriam Potter-Stokes—who persuaded me to do something instead of sitting aimlessly around...'

She knew her wild guess had been successful when he said

quietly, 'Yes, I know Miriam. I must tell her how successful you are.'

'Do, please. I must be off. Amabel, close at five o'clock. There'll be a delivery of those candlesticks before nine o'clock tomorrow morning, so be sure to be ready for it.' She gave the doctor a smiling nod. 'Nice to have met you. I hope you enjoy your stay here.'

She wasted no time when she reached her home, but poured herself a drink and picked up the phone.

'Miriam, listen and don't interrupt. Do you know where this Oliver of yours is? You don't? He's a big man, handsome, rather a slow voice, with a black dog? He's in my shop. On the best of terms with Amabel, the girl who works for me. It seems they've known each other for some time.' She gave a spiteful little laugh. 'Don't be too sure that Oliver is yours, Miriam.'

She listened to Miriam's outraged voice, smiling to herself. Miriam was an old schoolfriend, but it wouldn't hurt her to be taken down a peg. Dolores said soothingly, 'Don't get so upset, darling. He's here for a few days; I'll keep an eye on things and let you know if there's anything for you to worry about. Most unlikely, I should think. She's a small dull creature and she wears the most appalling clothes. I'll give you a ring tomorrow some time.'

When Dolores had gone the doctor said, 'Where do you live, Amabel? Surely not here?'

'Oh, but I do. I have a room behind the shop.'

'You shall show it to me when I come back.' He glanced at his watch. 'In half an hour.'

She said uncertainly, 'Well...'

'You're glad to see me, Amabel?'

She said without hesitating, 'Oh, yes, I am.'

'Then don't dither,' he said.

He came closer, and, looking down into her face, took her

hands in his. 'There is a Nigerian proverb which says, "Hold a true friend with both your hands,"' he said. He smiled and added gently, 'I'm your true friend, Amabel.'

CHAPTER FIVE

CLOSING THE SHOP, tidying up, feeding Oscar and Cyril, doing her face and hair, Amabel was conscious of a warm glow deep inside her person. She had a friend, a real friend. She was going to spend the evening with him and they would talk. There was so much she wanted to talk about...

He had said that he would be back at half past five, so at that time she shut her room door and went back into the shop to let him in, stooping to pat Tiger. 'I still have to take Cyril for a walk,' she told him as she led the way to her room.

He stood in the middle of it, looking round him, absently fondling Cyril. He didn't allow his thoughts to show on his face, but remarked placidly, 'Having access to space for Oscar and Cyril is an advantage, isn't it? They're happy here with you?'

'Well, yes. It's not ideal, but I'm lucky to have found it. And I have you to thank for that. I couldn't thank you before because I didn't know where you lived.'

'A lucky chance. Can we leave Oscar for a few hours?'

'Yes, he knows I take Cyril out in the evening. I'll get my coat.'

She was longing for a cup of tea; the afternoon had been long and she hadn't had the chance to make one. She was hungry too. He had told her that they were true friends, but she didn't know him well enough to suggest going to a café, and besides, Cyril needed his run.

They set off, talking of nothing much at first, but presently, walking briskly through the park, she began to answer his carefully put questions with equally careful answers.

They had been walking steadily for half an hour when he stopped and caught her by the arm. 'Tea,' he said. 'Have you had your tea? What a thoughtless fool I am.'

She said quickly, 'Oh, it doesn't matter, really it doesn't,' and added, 'It was such a lovely surprise when you came into the shop.'

He turned her round smartly. 'There must be somewhere we can get a pot of tea.'

So she got her tea, sitting at a very small table in a chintzy teashop where shoppers on their way home were still lingering. Since she was hungry, and the doctor seemed hungry too, she tucked into hot buttered toast, hot mince pies and a slice of the delicious walnut cake he insisted that she have.

'I thought we'd have dinner at my hotel,' he told her. 'But if you're not too tired we might take a walk through the streets. York is such a splendid place, and I'd like to know more of it.'

'Oh, so would I. But about going to the hotel for dinner—I think it would be better if I didn't. I mean, there's Cyril, and I'm not—that is—I didn't stop to change my dress.'

'The hotel people are very helpful about dogs. They'll both be allowed to stay in my room while we dine. And you look very nice as you are, Amabel.'

He sounded so matter-of-fact that her doubts melted away, and presently they continued with their walk.

None of the museums or historical buildings was open, but they wouldn't have visited them anyway; they walked the streets—Lendal Street, Davey Gate, Parliament Street and Coppergate, to stare up at Clifford's Tower, then back through Coppergate and Fosse Gate and Pavement and so to the Shambles again, this time from the opposite end to Dolores's shop. They lingered for a while so that she could show him the little medieval church where she sometimes went, before going on to the Minster, which they agreed would need leisurely hours of viewing in the daylight.

The hotel was close by, and while Amabel went away to leave her coat and do the best she could with her face and hair the doctor went with the dogs. He was waiting for her when she got back to the lounge.

'We deserve a drink,' he told her, 'and I hope you are as hungry as I am.'

It wasn't a large hotel, but it had all the unobtrusive perfection of service and comfort. They dined in a softly lit restaurant, served by deft waiters. The *maître d'* had ushered them to one of the best tables, and no one so much as glanced at Amabel's dowdy dress.

They dined on tiny cheese soufflés followed by roast beef, Yorkshire pudding, light as a feather, crisp baked potatoes and baby sprouts, as gently suggested by the doctor. Amabel looked as though a good meal wouldn't do her any harm, and she certainly enjoyed every mouthful—even managing a morsel of the lemon mousse which followed.

Her enjoyment was unselfconscious, and the glass of claret he ordered gave her face a pretty flush as well as loosening her tongue. They talked with the ease of two people who knew each other well—something which Amabel, thinking about it later, found rather surprising—and presently, after a leisurely coffee, the doctor went to fetch the dogs and Amabel her coat and they walked back to the shop.

The clocks were striking eleven as they reached the shop door. He took the key from her, opened the door and handed her Cyril's lead.

'Tomorrow is Wednesday—you have a half-day?' When she nodded he said, 'Good. Could you be ready by half past one? We'll take the dogs to the sea, shall we? Don't bother with lunch; we'll go next door and have coffee and a roll.'

She beamed up at him. 'Oh, that would be lovely. Dolores almost always goes about twelve o'clock on Wednesdays, so I can close punctually, then there'll only be Oscar to see to.' She added anxiously, 'I don't need to dress up?'

'No, no. Wear that coat, and a scarf for your head; it may be chilly by the sea.'

She offered a hand. 'Thank you for a lovely evening: I have enjoyed it.'

'So have I.' He sounded friendly, and as though he meant it—which of course he did. 'I'll wait until you're inside and locked up. Goodnight, Amabel.'

She went through the shop and turned to lift a hand to him as she opened the door to her room and switched on the light. After a moment he went back to his hotel. He would have to return to London tomorrow, but he could leave late and travel through the early part of the night so that they could have dinner together again.

'Am I being a fool?' he enquired of Tiger, whose gruff rumble could have been either yes or no...

It was halfway through the busy morning when Dolores asked casually, 'Did you have a pleasant evening with your friend, Amabel?'

Amabel warmed to her friendly tone. 'Oh, yes, thank you. We went for a walk through the city and had dinner at his hotel. And this afternoon we're going to the sea.'

'I dare say you found plenty to talk about?'

'Yes, yes, we did. His visit was quite unexpected. I really didn't expect to see him again...'

'Does he come this way often? It's quite a long journey from London.'

'Well, yes. He came just before I started work here—my mother told him where I was and he looked me up.'

She had answered readily enough, but Dolores was prudent enough not to ask any more questions. She said casually, 'You must wrap up; it will be cold by the sea. And you can go as soon as he comes for you; I've some work I want to do in the shop.'

She's nicer than I thought, reflected Amabel, going back to her careful polishing of a row of silver photo frames.

Sure enough, when the doctor's large person came striding towards the shop, Dolores said, 'Off you go, Amabel. He can spend ten minutes in the shop while you get ready.'

While Amabel fed Oscar, got Cyril's lead and got into her coat, tidied her hair and made sure that she had everything in her handbag, Dolores invited the doctor to look round him. 'We're showing our Christmas stock,' she told him. 'It's always a busy time, but we close for four days over the holiday. Amabel will be able to go to her aunt's house. She's away at present, Amabel told me, but I'm sure she'll be back by then.' She gave him a sly glance. 'I dare say you'll manage to get a few days off?'

'Yes, I dare say.'

'Well, if you see Miriam give her my love, won't you? Are you staying here long?'

'I'm going back tonight. But I intend to return before Christmas.'

Amabel came then, with Cyril on his lead. She looked so happy that just for a moment Dolores had a quite unusual pang of remorse. But it was only a pang, and the moment they had gone she picked up the phone.

'Miriam—I promised to ring you. Your Oliver has just left the shop with Amabel. He's driving her to the sea and spending the rest of the day with her. What is more, he told me that he intends returning to York before Christmas. You had better find yourself another man, darling!'

She listened to Miriam raging for a few minutes. 'I shouldn't waste your breath getting into a temper. If you want him as badly as all that then you must think of something. When you have, let me know if I can help.'

Miriam thought of something at once. When Dolores heard

it she said, 'Oh, no, I can't do that.' For all her mischief-making she wasn't deliberately unkind. 'The girl works very well, and I can't just sack her at a moment's notice.'

'Of course you can; she's well able to find another job—plenty of work around before Christmas. When he comes tell Oliver she's found a better job and you don't know where it is. Tell him you'll let him know if you hear anything of her; he won't be able to stay away from his work for more than a couple of days at a time. The girl won't come to any harm, and out of sight is out of mind...'

Miriam, most unusually for her burst into tears, and Dolores gave in; after all, she and Miriam were very old friends...

The doctor and his little party had to walk to where he had parked the car, and on the way he marshalled them into a small pub in a quiet street to lunch upon a sustaining soup, hot crusty bread and a pot of coffee—for, as he explained, they couldn't walk on empty stomachs. That done, he drove out of the city, north through the Yorkshire Moors, until he reached Staithes, a fishing village between two headlands.

He parked the car, tucked Amabel's hand under his arm and marched her off into the teeth of a strong wind, the dogs trotting happily on either side of them. They didn't talk; the wind made that difficult and really there was no need. They were quite satisfied with each other's company without the need of words.

The sea was rough, grey under a grey sky, and once away from the village there was no one about. Presently they turned round, and back in the village explored its streets. The houses were a mixture of cottages and handsome Georgian houses, churches and shops. They lingered at the antiques shops and the doctor bought a pretty little plate Amabel admired before they walked on beside the Beck and finally turned back to have tea at the Cod and Lobster pub.

It was a splendid tea; Amabel, her cheeks pink, her hair all over the place and glowing with the exercise, ate the hot buttered parkin, the toast and home-made jam and the fruit cake with a splendid appetite.

She was happy—the shop, her miserable little room, her loneliness and lack of friends didn't matter. Here she was, deeply content, with someone who had said that he was her friend.

They didn't talk about themselves or their lives; there were so many other things to discuss. The time flew by and they got up to go reluctantly.

Tiger and Cyril, nicely replete with the morsels they had been offered from time to time, climbed into the car, went to sleep and didn't wake until they were back in York. The doctor parked the car at his hotel, led the dogs away to his room and left Amabel to tidy herself. It was no easy task, and she hardly felt at her best, but it was still early evening and the restaurant was almost empty.

They dined off chicken *à la king* and lemon tart which was swimming in cream, and the doctor talked comfortably of this and that. Amabel wished that the evening would go on for ever.

It didn't of course. It was not quite nine o'clock when they left the hotel to walk back to the shop. The girl who worked in the patisserie was still there, getting ready to leave. She waved as they passed and then stood watching them. She liked Amabel, who seemed to lead a very dull and lonely life, and now this handsome giant of a man had turned up...

The doctor took the key from Amabel, opened the shop door and then gave it back to her.

'Thank you for a lovely afternoon—Oliver. I feel full of fresh air and lovely food.'

He smiled down at her earnest face. 'Good. We must do it again, some time.' When she looked uncertain, he added, 'I'm going back to London tonight, Amabel. But I'll be back.'

He opened the door and pushed her inside, but not before he had given her a quick kiss. The girl in the patisserie saw that, and smiled. Amabel didn't smile, but she glowed from the top of her head to the soles of her feet.

He had said that he would come back...

* * *

Dolores was in a friendly mood in the morning; she wanted to know where Amabel had gone, if she had had a good dinner, and was her friend coming to see her again?

Amabel, surprised at the friendliness, saw no reason to be secretive. She gave a cheerful account of her afternoon, and when Dolores observed casually, 'I dare say he'll be back again?' Amabel assured her readily enough that he would.

Any niggardly doubts Dolores might have had about Miriam's scheme were doused by the girl in the patisserie who served her coffee.

'Nice to see Amabel with a man,' she observed chattily. 'Quite gone on her, I shouldn't doubt. Kissed her goodbye and all. Stood outside the shop for ages, making sure she was safely inside. He'll be back, mark my words! Funny, isn't it? She's such a plain little thing, too...'

This was something Miriam had to know, so Dolores sent Amabel to the post office to collect a parcel and picked up the phone.

She had expected rage, perhaps tears from Miriam, but not silence. After a moment she said, 'Miriam?'

Miriam was thinking fast; the girl must be got rid of, and quickly. Any doubts Dolores had about that must be quashed at once. She said in a small broken voice, 'Dolores, you must help me. I'm sure it's just a passing infatuation—only a few days ago we spent the evening together.' That there wasn't an atom of truth in that didn't worry her; she had to keep Dolores's sympathy.

She managed a sob. 'If he goes back to see her and she's gone he can't do anything about it. I know he's got commitments at the hospital he can't miss.' Another convincing lie. 'Please tell him that she's got another job but you don't know where? Or that she's got a boyfriend? Better still tell him that she said she would join her aunt in Italy. He wouldn't worry about her then. In fact that's what she will probably do...'

'That cat and dog of hers—' began Dolores.

'Didn't you tell me that there was a kind of handyman who does odd jobs for the aunt? They'll go to him.'

Put like that, it sounded a reasonable solution. 'You think she might do that?' Dolores was still doubtful, but too lazy to worry about it. She said, 'All right, I'll sack her—but not for a day or two. There's more Christmas stock to be unpacked and I can't do that on my own.'

Miriam gave a convincing sob. 'I'll never be able to thank you enough. I'm longing to see Oliver again; I'm sure everything will be all right once he's back here and I can be with him.'

Which was unduly optimistic of her. Oliver, once back home, made no attempt to contact her. When she phoned his house it was to be told by a wooden-voiced Bates that the doctor was unavailable.

In desperation she went to his consulting rooms, where she told his receptionist that he was expecting her when he had seen his last patient, and when presently he came into the waiting room from his consulting room she went to meet him.

'Oliver—I know I shouldn't be here. Don't blame your receptionist; I said you expected me. Only it is such a long time since we saw each other.'

She lifted her faced to his, aware that she was at her most attractive. 'Have I done something to annoy you? You are never at home when I phone; that man of yours says you're not available.' She put a hand on his sleeve and smiled the sad little smile she had practised before her mirror.

'I've been busy—am still. I'm sorry I haven't been free to see you, but I think you must cross me off your list, Miriam.' He smiled at her. 'I'm sure there are half a dozen men waiting for the chance to take you out.'

'But they aren't you, Oliver.' She laughed lightly. 'I don't mean to give you up, Oliver.' She realised her mistake when she saw the lift of his eyebrows, and added quickly, 'You are a perfect companion for an evening out, you know.'

She wished him a light-hearted goodbye then, adding, 'But you'll be at the Sawyers' dinner party, won't you? I'll see you then.'

'Yes, of course.' His goodbye was friendly, but she was aware that only good manners prevented him from showing impatience.

The sooner Dolores got rid of that girl the better, thought Miriam savagely. Once she was out of the way she would set about the serious business of capturing Oliver.

But Dolores had done nothing about sacking Amabel. For one thing she was too useful at this busy time of the year, and for another Dolores's indolence prevented her from making decisions. She was going to have to do something about it, because she had said she would, but later.

Then an ill-tempered and agitated phone call from Miriam put an end to indecision. A friend of Miriam's had mentioned casually that it was a pity that Oliver would be away for her small daughter's—his goddaughter's—birthday party. He'd be gone for several days, he had told her. The birthday was in three days' time...

'You must do something quickly—you promised.' Miriam managed to sound desperately unhappy, although what she really felt was rage. But it wouldn't do to lose Dolores's sympathy. She gave a sob. 'Oh, my dear, I'm so unhappy.'

And Dolores, her decision made for her, promised. 'The minute I get to the shop in the morning.'

Amabel was already hard at work, unwrapping Christmas tree fairies, shaking out their gauze wings and silky skirts, arranging them on a small glass shelf. She wished Dolores good morning, the last of the fairies in her hand.

Dolores didn't bother with good morning. She disliked unpleasantness if it involved herself, and the quicker it was dealt with the better.

'I'm giving you notice,' she said, relieved to find that once she had said it it wasn't so difficult. 'There's not enough work for you, and besides, I need the room at the back. You can go this evening, as soon as you've packed up. Leave your bits and pieces; someone can collect them. You'll get your wages, of course.'

Amabel put the last fairy down very carefully on the shelf. Then she said in a small shocked voice, 'What have I done wrong?'

Dolores picked up a vase and inspected it carefully. 'Nothing. I've just told you; I want the room and I've no further use for you in the shop.' She looked away from Amabel. 'You can go back to your aunt, and if you want work there'll be plenty of casual jobs before Christmas.'

Amabel didn't speak. Of what use? Dolores had made herself plain enough; to tell her that her aunt was still away, and that she had had a card from Josh that morning saying that he and Mrs Josh would be away for the next ten days and would she please not go and visit them as usual next Sunday, would be useless.

Dolores said sharply, 'And it's no use saying anything. My mind's made up. I don't want to hear another word.'

She went to the patisserie then, to have her coffee, and when she came back told Amabel that she could have an hour off to start her packing.

Amabel got out her case and began to pack it, explaining to Cyril and Oscar as she did so. She had no idea where she would go; she had enough money to pay for a bed and breakfast place, but would they take kindly to the animals? There wouldn't be much time to find somewhere once she left the shop at five o'clock. She stripped the bed, packed what food she had in a box and went back to the shop.

When five o'clock came Dolores was still in the shop.

She gave Amabel a week's wages, told her that she could give her name for a reference if she needed to, and went back to sit behind the counter.

'Don't hang about,' she said. 'I want to get home.'

But Amabel wasn't going to hurry. She fed Oscar and Cyril

and had a wash, made a cup of tea and a sandwich, for she wasn't sure where the next meal would come from, and then, neatly dressed in her new winter coat, with Cyril on his lead, Oscar in his basket and carrying her case, she left the shop.

She didn't say anything. Good evening would have been a mockery; the evening was anything but good. She closed the shop door behind her, picked up her case, waved to the girl in the patisserie, and started off at a brisk pace, past the still lighted shops.

She didn't know York well, but she knew that she wasn't likely to find anywhere cheap in and around the main streets. If she could manage until Josh and his wife got back...

She reached the narrow side streets and presently saw a café on a street corner. It was a shabby place, but it had a sign in its window saying 'Rooms to Let'. She went inside and went to the counter, where a girl lounged reading a magazine.

The place was almost empty; it smelled of fried food and wasn't too clean, but to Amabel it was the answer to her prayers.

The girl was friendly enough. Yes, there was a room, and she could have it, but she didn't know about the dog and cat. She went away to ask and came back to say that there was a room on the ground floor where the animals could stay with her, but only at night; during the day she would have to take them with her. 'And since we're doing you a favour we'll have to charge more.'

A lot more. But at least it was a roof over their heads. It was a shabby roof, and a small ill-furnished room, but there was a wash handbasin and a window opening onto a window box which had been covered by wire netting, and that solved Oscar's problems.

Amabel handed over the money, left her case, locked the door and went out again, intent on finding a cafeteria. Presently, feeling all the better for a meal, still accompanied by Oscar in his basket and Cyril, she bought a take away meat pie and milk, carrying them to her room.

Oscar, let out of his basket at last, made a beeline for the window box, and then settled down to eat the meat in the pie while Cyril wolfed the crust, washing it down with the milk before climbing onto the bed.

Amabel washed in tepid water, cleaned her teeth, got into her nightie and then into bed. She was tired, too tired to think rationally, so she closed her eyes and went to sleep.

She was up early, asked for tea and toast from the girl at the counter and took Cyril out for five minutes. Since she didn't dare to leave Oscar he went too, grumbling in his basket.

Assuring the girl they would be back in the evening, she locked the door and set off into the cold bright morning.

It was apparent by midday that a job which would admit Cyril and Oscar was going to be hard to find. Amabel bought a carton of milk and a ham roll and found a quiet corner by St Mary's, where she fed Oscar and Cyril from the tin she had in her shoulder bag before letting a timid Oscar out to explore the flowerbeds. With a cat's good sense he stayed close to her, and soon got back into his basket and settled down again. He was a wise beast and he was aware that they were, the three of them, going through a sticky patch...

The afternoon was as disappointing as the morning, and the café, when Amabel got back to it, looked uninviting. But it spelled security of a sort, and tomorrow was another day.

Which turned out to be most unfortunately, just like the previous one. The following morning, when Amabel went to her frugal breakfast in the café, the girl at the counter leaned across to say, 'Can't put you up any longer. Got a regular booked the room for a week.'

Amabel chewed toast in a dry mouth. 'But there's another room I can rent?'

'Not with them animals. Be out by ten o'clock, will you? So's I can get the bed changed.'

'But just for a few nights?'

'Not a hope. The boss turned a blind eye for a couple of

nights but that's it. Tried the Salvation Army, have you? There's beds there, but you'd have to find somewhere for that dog and cat.'

It was another fine morning, but cold. Amabel found a sheltered seat in the park and sat down to think. She discarded the idea of going home. She had escaped once; it might not be as easy again, and nothing was going to make her abandon Cyril and Oscar.

It was a question of waiting for eight days before Josh and his wife returned, and, however careful she was, there wasn't enough money in her purse to buy them bed and board for that time. She would try the Salvation Army—after five o'clock the girl had said—and hope that they would allow Cyril and Oscar to stay with her.

She had bought a local paper, so now she scanned the vacancies in the jobs columns. She ticked off the most promising, and set off to find the first of them. It was a tiresome business, for her suitcase was quite heavy and Oscar's basket got in the way. Each time she was rejected. Not unkindly, but with an indifference which hurt.

It was after four o'clock when she finally gave up and started on her way to the Salvation Army shelter. She had to pass the end of the Shambles to reach it, and on an impulse she turned aside and went through the half-open door of the little church she had sometimes visited. It was quiet inside and there was no one there. It was cold too, and dimly lighted, but there was peace there...

Amabel sat down in one of the old-fashioned high-backed pews, put Oscar's basket beside her, and, with her case on the other side and Cyril at her feet, allowed the tranquillity of the little church to soothe her.

She said aloud, 'Things are never as bad as they seem,' and Cyril thumped his tail in agreement. Presently, tired from all the walking, he went to sleep. So did Oscar, but Amabel sat without moving, trying to make plans in her tired head which, despite her efforts, was full of thoughts of Oliver. If he were there, she thought dreamily, he would know exactly what to do...

The doctor had reached York shortly after lunch, booked a room at the hotel and, with the faithful Tiger loping beside him, made his way to Dolores's shop. She was sitting behind the counter, reading, but she looked up as he went in and got to her feet. She had known that sooner or later he would come, but she still felt a momentary panic at the sight of him. Which was silly of her; he stood there in the doorway, large and placid, and his quiet greeting was reassuring.

'I've come to see Amabel,' he told her. 'Will you allow her to have an hour or two off? Or perhaps the rest of the afternoon? I can't stay in York long...'

'She's not here...'

'Oh, not ill, I hope?'

'She's gone. I didn't need her any more.' There was no expression on his face, but she took a step backwards. 'She's got an aunt to go to.'

'When was this? She had a week's notice, presumably?'

Dolores picked up a vase on the counter and put it down again. She said again, 'There's this aunt...'

'You sent her packing at a moment's notice?' The doctor's voice was quiet, but she shivered at the sound of it. 'She took the cat and dog with her?'

'Of course she did.'

'Did you know that her aunt was away from home?'

Dolores shrugged. 'She did mention it.' She would have to tell him something to make him see that it was useless looking for the girl. 'Amabel said something about going to stay with friends of her mother—somewhere near...' She paused for a moment, conjuring up names out of the back of her head. 'I think she said Nottingham—a Mrs Skinner...'

She heaved a sigh of relief; she had done that rather well.

He stood looking at her, his face inscrutable, his eyes cold.

'I don't believe you. And if any harm comes to Amabel I shall hold you responsible.'

He left the shop, closing the door quietly behind him, and Dolores flew to the kitchenette and reached for the bottle of whisky she kept hidden away there. Which meant that she missed seeing the girl at the patisserie go to the door and call to the doctor.

'Hi—you looking for Amabel? Poor kid got the sack at a moment's notice—told she wasn't wanted by that Dolores, I suppose...'

'You spoke to her?'

'Didn't have a chance. Had me hands full of customers. She waved though—had her case and that dog and cat, going heaven knows where. Haven't seen hair nor hide of her since...'

'How long ago?'

'Two days?'

'Dolores said that she had gone away to friends.'

The girl sniffed. 'Don't you believe it—that woman will tell you anything she thinks you want to hear.'

'Yes. You think Amabel is still in York? I'm going to drive to her aunt's house now; there's a man, Josh...'

'I've seen 'im once or twice of a Sunday—brings her back here—she goes there on her free day.'

The doctor thanked her. 'Probably she is there—and thank you. I'll let you know if I find her.'

'You do that—I liked her.'

She watched him go. He was a man to satisfy any girl's dreams, not to mention the money. That was a cashmere coat, and a silk tie costing as much as one of her dresses...

Of course there was no one at Miss Parsons' house, and no response from Josh's cottage when he knocked. He was equally unsuccessful at the village shop—Josh was away, he was told, and there had been no sign of Amabel.

The doctor drove back to York, parked the car once more at the hotel and set off with Tiger to scour the city. He was worried, desperately concerned as to Amabel's whereabouts. He forced himself to think calmly as he systematically combed the streets of the inner city.

He didn't believe for one moment that Amabel had left York, and he thought it unlikely that she would have had enough money to get her home. And to go home was the most unlikely thing she would do. She was here, still in York. It was just a question of finding her...

He stopped at several of the smaller shops to ask if anyone had seen her and was told in one of them—a shabby little café—that there had been a girl with a dog. She had bought a roll and had coffee two days ago. A slender clue, but enough to take the doctor through the streets once more.

It was as he reached the lower end of the Shambles for the second time that his eye lighted on the little church close by. He remembered then that Amabel had told him that she had gone there from time to time. He went through its open door and stood just inside, aware of the quiet and the cold, and he saw Amabel, a small vague figure in the distance.

He heaved a great sigh and went quietly to where she was sitting. 'Hello, Amabel,' he said in a calm voice, 'I thought I might find you here.'

She turned her head slowly as Cyril got to his feet, wagging his tail and whining with pleasure. 'Oliver—Oliver, is it really you?'

She stopped because she was crying, and he went and sat down beside her and put a great arm around her shoulders. He sat quietly and let her weep, and when her sobs became sniffs offered a handkerchief.

'So sorry,' said Amabel. 'You were a surprise—at least, I was thinking about you, and there you were.'

He was relieved to hear that her voice, while still watery, was quite steady.

'Are you staying in York?' she asked politely. 'It's nice to see you again. But don't let me keep you.'

The doctor choked back a laugh. Even in dire circumstances,

Amabel, he felt sure, would always be polite. He said gently, 'Amabel, I went to the shop and that woman—Dolores—told me what she had done. I've spent hours looking for you, but we aren't going to talk about it now. We are going to the hotel, and after a meal and a good night's sleep we will talk.'

'No,' said Amabel quite forcibly. 'I won't. What I mean is, thank you, but no. Tomorrow...'

He had Oscar's basket, and her case. Now he said, 'One day at a time, Amabel.'

CHAPTER SIX

SEVERAL HOURS LATER AMABEL, fed and bathed and in bed, with Cyril curled up on the floor and Oscar stretched out on her feet, tried to sort out the evening so that it made sense. As it was, it had been a fairy tale dream. In no other way could she account for the last few hours.

How had Oliver been able to conjure a private sitting room out of thin air? A tray of tea, food for Oscar and Cyril? Her case had been unpacked and its contents whisked away to be washed and pressed, she was in a bedroom with a balcony where Oscar could feel free, had had a delicious meal and a glass of wine, and Oliver urging her to eat and drink and not ask questions but to go to bed since they must leave early in the morning.

She had obeyed sleepily, thanked him for her supper and said goodnight, then spent ages in the bath. And it had all seemed perfectly normal—just as a dream was always normal. In the morning she must find a way of leaving, but now she would just close her eyes...

She opened them to thin sunshine through the drawn curtains and a cheerful girl with a tray of tea.

'Dr Fforde asks that you dress quickly and meet him in the sitting room in twenty minutes—and I'm to take the dog with me so that he can have a run with the doctor's dog.'

Amabel drank her tea, put Oscar on the balcony and went into the sitting room. She showered and dressed with all speed, anxious not to keep Oliver waiting, so her hair didn't look its best and her make-up was perfunctory, but she looked rested and ready for anything.

The doctor was at a window, looking out onto the street below. He turned round as she went in and studied her. 'That's better. You slept well?'

'Yes. Oh, yes, I did. It was like heaven.' She bent to stroke Cyril's head. 'Thank you for taking him out. And thank you for letting me stay here. It's like a dream.'

Breakfast was brought in then, and when they had sat down at the table she said, 'I expect you are in a hurry. The maid asked me to be quick. I'm very grateful, Oliver, for your kindness.' She added, 'There are several jobs I shall go and see about this morning.'

The doctor loaded toast with marmalade. 'Amabel, we are friends, so let us not talk nonsense to each other. You are a brave girl, but enough is enough. In half an hour or so we are leaving York. I have written to Josh so that he will know what has happened when he comes back home, and we will let Miss Parsons know as soon as possible.'

'Know what?'

'Where you will be and what you will be doing.'

'I'm not going home.'

'No, no, of course not. I am hoping that you will agree to do something for me. I have a great-aunt recovering from a slight stroke. Her one wish is to return to her home, but my mother hasn't been able to find someone who will live with her for a time. No nursing is needed, but a willingness to talk and be talked to, join in any small amusement she may fancy, help her to make life enjoyable. She is old, in her eighties, but she loves her garden and her home. She has a housekeeper and a housemaid who have both been with her for years. And don't think that I'm asking you to do this because you happen to be between jobs...'

Which sounded so much better, reflected Amabel, than being out of work, or even destitute. He was asking for her help and she owed him a great deal. Besides, he was her friend, and friends help each other when they were needed.

She said, 'If your great-aunt would like me to be with her, then I'll go to her. But what about Cyril and Oscar?'

'She has a house in the country; she likes animals and they will be welcome there. I should point out that she is a very old lady and liable to have another stroke, so the prospect for you is not a permanent one.'

Amabel drank the last of her coffee. 'Well, I expect for someone like me, with no special skills, it would be hard to find permanent work. But I must write to Aunt Thisbe and tell her.'

'Better still, if you have her phone number you can ring her up.'

'May I? When we get to wherever we are going?'

He crossed the room to the telephone on a side table. 'You have the number with you?' He held out a hand and she handed him the grubby slip of paper she had carried everywhere with her. He got the receptionist and waited for her to get the number, then handed Amabel the phone.

Aunt Thisbe's voice was loud and clear, demanding to know who it was.

'It's me. Amabel. There's nothing wrong, but I must tell you—that is, I must explain—'

The phone was taken from her. 'Miss Parsons? Oliver Fforde. Perhaps I can set your mind at rest. Amabel is with me and quite safe. She will explain everything to you, but I promise you that you have no need to worry about her.' He handed the phone back. 'I'll take the dogs for a quick walk—tell Miss Parsons that you will phone again this evening.'

Aunt Thisbe's firm voice begging her to take her time and tell her what had happened collected Amabel's wits for her. She gave a fairly coherent account of what had been happening. 'And Oliver has told me that he has a job waiting for me with an old aunt and has asked me to take it. And I've said I would because I should like to repay his kindness.'

'A sensible decision, child. An opportunity to express your thanks and at the same time give you a chance to decide what you intend to do. I heard Oliver saying that you will phone again this evening. This has changed things, of course. I was thinking of returning for Christmas, so that you would have somewhere to come over the holiday period, but now that there is no need of that and so I shall stay here for another few weeks. But remember, Amabel, if you need me I will return at once. I am very relieved that Oliver has come to your aid. A good man, Amabel, and one to be trusted.'

Amabel put down the phone as Oliver returned. He said briskly, 'I've put the dogs in the car. If you will get your coat, we'll be off.'

He shovelled Oscar into his basket. 'I must be back at the hospital by three o'clock, so I'll drop you off on the way.' He added impatiently, 'I'll explain as we go.'

Since it was obvious to her that he had no intention of saying anything more until it suited him, Amabel did as she was told.

Consumed by curiosity, and a feeling of uncertainty about her future, Amabel had to wait until they were travelling fast down the M1 before the doctor had anything to say other than enquiries as to her comfort.

'We are going to Aldbury in Hertfordshire. It's a small village a few miles from Berkhamsted. My mother is there, arranging for my aunt's return, and she will explain everything to you—time off, salary and so on—and stay overnight to see you settled in. She is very relieved that you have agreed to take the job and you will be very welcomed, both by her and by Mrs Twitchett, the housekeeper, and Nelly.'

Amabel said, 'Your great-aunt might not like me.'

'There is nothing about you to dislike, Amabel.'

A remark which did nothing for her ego. She had never had delusions about herself, but now she felt a nonentity...

The doctor glanced at her as he spoke, at her unassuming profile as she looked steadily ahead. She looked completely unfazed, accepting the way in which he had bulldozed her into an unknown future. He had had no chance to do otherwise; there had been no time, and to have left her there alone in York would have been unthinkable. He said, 'I've rushed you, haven't I? But sometimes one has to take a chance!'

Amabel smiled. 'A lucky chance for me. I'm so grateful, and I'll do my best with your great-aunt. Would you tell me her name?'

'Lady Haleford. Eighty-seven years old, widowed for ten years. No children. Loves her garden, birds, the country and animals. She likes to play cards and cheats. Since her stroke she has become fretful and forgetful and at times rather peevish.' He added, 'No young society, I'm afraid.'

'Well, I have never gone out much, so that doesn't matter.'

When he could spare the time, he reflected, he would take her out. Dinner and dancing, a theatre or concert. He didn't feel sorry for her, Amabel wasn't a girl one could pity, but she deserved some fun and he liked her. He was even, he had to admit, becoming a little fond of her in a brotherly sort of way. He wanted to see her safely embarked on the life she wanted so that she would have the chance to meet people of her own age, marry... He frowned. Time enough for that...

They travelled on in silence, comfortable in each other's company, and after a while he asked, 'Do you want to stop? There's a quiet pub about ten miles ahead; we can let the dogs out there.'

The pub stood back from the road and the car park was almost empty. 'Go on inside,' the doctor told her. 'I'll see to the dogs and make sure Oscar's all right. We can't stay long.'

As long as it's long enough to find the Ladies' thought Amabel, wasting no time.

They had beef sandwiches and coffee, saw to the dogs and

got back into the car. Oscar, snoozing in his basket, was hardly disturbed. Life for him had had its ups and downs lately, but now he was snug and safe and Amabel's voice reassured him.

Travelling in a Rolls-Royce was very pleasant, reflected Amabel, warm and comfortable and sliding past everything else on the road. And Oliver drove with relaxed skill. She supposed that he was a man who wasn't easily put out.

When he turned off the motorway he said, 'Not long now,' and sure enough, a few miles past Berkhamsted, he took a side turning and then a narrow lane and slowed as they reached Aldbury. It was a charming village, having its origin in Saxon times. There was a village green, a duck pond and a pub close by, and standing a little apart was the church, and beyond the village there was a pleasing vista of parkland and woods. Amabel, staring round her, knew that she would like living here, and hoped that it might be in one of the brick and timber cottages they were passing.

The doctor drove to the far side of the pond and stopped before a house standing on its own. Its front door opened directly onto the pavement—and it was brick and timber, as the others. It had a thatched roof, just as those did, but it was considerably larger and yet looked just as cosy.

He got out and opened Amabel's door. 'Come in and meet my mother again,' he invited. 'I'll come for the dogs and Oscar in a moment.'

The house door had been opened and a short stout woman stood there, smiling. She said comfortably, 'So here you are, Master Oliver, and the young lady...'

'Miss Amabel Parsons. Amabel, this is Mrs Twitchett.'

He bent to kiss her cheek and Amabel offered a hand, aware that as it was being shaken she was being studied closely. She hoped that Mrs Twitchett's smiling nod was a good sign.

The hall was wide with a wood floor, handsomely carpeted, but Amabel had no time to look around her for a door was thrust open and Mrs Fforde came to meet them.

The doctor bent to kiss her. 'No need to introduce you,' he said cheerfully. 'I'll leave you for a moment and see to the dogs and Oscar.'

'Yes, dear. Can you stay?'

'Ten minutes. I've a clinic in a couple of hours.'

'Coffee? It'll be here when you've seen to the dogs. What about the cat?'

'Oscar is a much-travelled beast; he'll present no problems and the garden is walled.'

He went away and Mrs Fforde took Amabel's arm. 'Come and sit down for a moment. Mrs Twitchett will bring the coffee; I'm sure you must need it. I don't suppose Oliver stopped much on the way?'

'Once—we had coffee and sandwiches.'

'But it's quite a drive, even at his speed. Take off your coat and come and sit down.'

'My husband's aunt, Lady Haleford, is old and frail. I expect Oliver has told you that. The stroke has left her in need of a good deal of assistance. Nothing that requires nursing, you understand, just someone to be there. I hope you won't find it too arduous, for you are young and elderly people can be so trying! She is a charming old lady, though, and despite the fact that she can be forgetful she is otherwise mentally alert. I do hope that Oliver made that clear to you?'

Mrs Fforde looked so anxious that Amabel said at once, 'Yes, he did. I'll do my best to keep Lady Haleford happy, indeed I will.'

'You don't mind a country life? I'm afraid you won't have much freedom.'

'Mrs Fforde, I am so grateful to have a job where Cyril and Oscar can be with me—and I love the country.'

'You will want to let your mother know where you are?' asked Mrs Fforde gently. 'Presently, when you are settled in, phone her. I shall be staying here overnight and will fetch Lady Haleford in the morning.'

The doctor joined them then, and Mrs Twitchett followed him in with a tray of coffee, Tiger and Cyril sidling in behind her.

'Oscar is in the kitchen,' he observed. 'What a sensible animal he is. Mrs Twitchett and Nelly have already fallen for his charms.' He smiled at Amabel and turned to his mother. 'You'll go home tomorrow? I'll try and get down next weekend. You will discuss everything with Amabel before you go? Good.' He drank his coffee and bent to kiss her cheek. 'I'll phone you...'

He laid a hand on Amabel's shoulder. 'I hope you will be happy with my aunt, Amabel. If there are any problems, don't hesitate to tell my mother.'

'All right—but I don't expect any. And thank you, Oliver.'

He was going again out of her life, and this time it was probably for the last time. He had come to her aid, rescued her with speed and a lack of fuss, set her back on her feet once more and was now perfectly justified in forgetting all about her. She offered her hand and her smile lighted up her face. 'Goodbye, Oliver.'

He didn't reply, only patted her shoulder and a moment later he was gone.

'We will go upstairs,' said Mrs Fforde briskly. 'I'll show you your room, and then we will go over the rest of the house so that you will feel quite at home before Lady Haleford arrives. We should be back in time for lunch and I'll leave soon after that. You're sure you can manage?'

'Yes,' said Amabel gravely. 'I'm sure, Mrs Fforde.' It might not be easy at first, but she owed Oliver so much...

They went up the staircase, with its worn oak treads, to the landing above, with several doors on either side and a passage leading to the back of the house.

'I've put you next to my aunt's room,' said Mrs Fforde. 'There's a bathroom between—hers. Yours is on the other side of your room. I hope you won't have to get up in the night, but if you are close by it will make that easier.'

She opened a door and they went in together. It was a large

room, with a small balcony overlooking the side of the house, and most comfortably furnished. It was pretty chintz curtains matching the bedspread, thick carpeting and a dear little easy chair beside a small table close to the window. The small dressing table had a stool before it and there was a pink-shaded lamp on the bedside table.

Mrs Fforde led the way across the room and opened a door. 'This is your bathroom—rather small, I'm afraid...'

Amabel thought of the washbasin behind the shop. 'It's perfect,' she said.

'And here's the door to my aunt's bathroom...' They went through it, and on into Lady Haleford's room at the front of the house. It was magnificently furnished, its windows draped in damask, the four-poster bed hung with the same damask, the massive dressing table loaded with silver-backed brushes and mirror, little cut-glass bottles and trinkets.

'Has Lady Haleford always lived here?'

'Yes—at least since her husband died. They lived in the manor house before that, of course, but when her son inherited he moved there with his wife and children and she came here. That was ten years ago. She has often told me that she prefers this house to the manor. For one thing the garden here is beautiful and the rooms aren't too large. And, being in the village, she can still see her friends without having to go too far. Until she had her stroke she drove herself, but of course that won't be possible now. Do you drive?'

'Yes,' said Amabel. 'But I'm not used to driving in large towns.'

'It would be driving Lady Haleford to church and back, and perhaps to call on local friends.'

'I could manage that,' said Amabel.

They went round the house in a leisurely manner. It was, she considered, rather large for one old lady and her two staff, but it was comfortable, rather old-fashioned, and it felt like home. Downstairs, beside the drawing room, there was a dining room, the morning room and a small sitting room—all immaculate. The kind of rooms, reflected Amabel, in which one could sit all day.

The last room they went into was the kitchen, as old-fashioned as the rest of the house. Something smelled delicious as they went in, and Mrs Twitchett turned from the Aga to warn them that dinner would be on the table in half an hour. Nelly was doing something at the table, and sitting before the Aga, for all the world as though they had lived there for ever, were Cyril and Oscar, pleased to see her but making no effort to rouse themselves.

'Happen they're tired out,' said Mrs Twitchett. 'They've eaten their fill and given no trouble.'

Amabel stooped to pat them. 'You really don't mind them being here?'

'Glad to have them. Nelly dotes on them. They'll always be welcome in here.'

Amabel had a sudden urge to burst into tears, a foolishness she supposed, but the relief to have a kind home for her two companions was great. They deserved peace and quiet after the last few months...

She smiled uncertainly at Mrs Twitchett and said thank you, then followed Mrs Fforde out of the kitchen.

Over dinner she was told her duties—not onerous but, as Mrs Fforde pointed out, probably boring and tiring. She was to take her free time when and where she could, and if it wasn't possible to have a day off each week she was to have two half-days. She might have to get up at night occasionally, and, as Mrs Fforde pointed out, the job at times might be demanding. But the wages she suggested were twice as much as Dolores had paid her. Living quietly, thought Amabel, I shall be able to save almost all of them. With a little money behind her she would have a chance to train for a career which would give her future security.

The next morning, buoyed up by high hopes, she waited for Mrs Fforde's return with Lady Haleford. All the same she was nervous.

* * *

It was a pity that she couldn't know that the doctor, sitting at his desk in his consulting rooms, had spared a moment to think of her as he studied his next patient's notes. He hoped that she would be happy with his great-aunt; the whole thing had been hurriedly arranged and even now she might be regretting it. But something had had to be done to help her.

He stood up to greet his patient and dismissed her from his thoughts.

Mrs Fforde's elderly Rover stopped in front of the door and Amabel went into the hall, standing discreetly at a distance from Mrs Twitchett and Nelly, waiting at the door. She and Cyril had been out early that morning for a walk through the country lanes; now he stood quietly beside her, and Oscar had perched himself close by, anxious not to be overlooked.

Lady Haleford was small and thin, and walked with a stick and the support of Mrs Fforde's arm, but although she walked slowly and hesitantly there was nothing invalidish about her.

She returned Mrs Twitchett's and Nelly's greetings in a brisk manner and asked at once, 'Well, where's this girl Oliver has found to look after me?'

Mrs Fforde guided her into the drawing room and sat her in a high-backed chair. 'Here, waiting for you.' She said over her shoulder, 'Amabel, come and meet Lady Haleford.'

Amabel put a cautionary finger on Cyril's head and went to stand before the old lady.

'How do you do, Lady Haleford?'

Lady Haleford studied her at some length. She had dark eyes, very bright in her wrinkled face, a small beaky nose and a mouth which, because of her stroke, drooped sideways.

'A plain girl,' she observed to no one in particular. 'But looks are only skin-deep, so they say. Nice eyes and pretty hair, though, and young...' She added peevishly, 'Too young.

Old people are boring to the young. You'll be gone within a week. I'm peevish and I forget things and I wake in the night.'

Amabel said gently, 'I shall be happy here, Lady Haleford. I hope you will let me stay and keep you company. This is such a lovely old house, you must be glad to be home again, you will get well again now that you are home.'

Lady Haleford said, 'Pooh,' and then added, 'I suppose I shall have to put up with you.'

'Only for as long as you want to, Lady Haleford,' said Amabel briskly.

'Well, at least you've a tongue in your head,' said the old lady. 'Where's my lunch?'

Her eye fell on Cyril. 'And what's this? The dog Oliver told me about? And there's a cat?'

'Yes. They are both elderly and well-behaved, and I promise you they won't disturb you.'

Lady Haleford said tartly, 'I like animals. Come here, dog.'

Cyril advanced obediently, not much liking to be called dog when he had a perfectly good name. But he stood politely while the old lady looked him over and then patted his head.

Mrs Fforde went home after lunch, leaving Amabel to cope with the rest of the day. Oliver had advised her to let Amabel find her own feet. 'She's quite capable of dealing with any hiccoughs,' he had pointed out, 'and the sooner they get to know each other the better.'

A remark which hadn't prevented him from thinking that perhaps he had made a mistake pitching Amabel into a job she might dislike. She was an independent girl, determined to make a good future for herself; she had only accepted the job with his great-aunt because she had to have a roof over her head and money in her pocket. But he had done his best, he reflected and need waste no more time thinking about her.

But as he had decided not to think any more about Amabel, so Miriam was equally determined to think about him. Dolores had phoned her and told her of his visit. 'I told him that she had left York—I invented an aunt somewhere or other, a friend of her mother's...' She didn't mention that he hadn't believed her. 'He went away and I didn't see him again. Is he back in London? Have you seen him?'

'No, not yet, but I know he's back. I rang his consulting rooms and said I wanted an appointment. He's been back for days. He can't have wasted much time in looking for her. You've been an angel, Dolores, and so clever to fob him off.'

'Anything for a friend, darling. I'll keep my eyes and ears open just in case she's still around.' She giggled. 'Good hunting!'

As far as she was concerned she didn't intend to do any more about it, although she did once ask idly if anyone had seen Amabel or her visitor when she had her coffee in the patisserie. But the girl behind the counter didn't like Dolores; she had treated Amabel shabbily and she had no need to know that that nice man had gone back one evening and told her that Amabel and her companions were safe with him.

Miriam had phoned Oliver's house several times to be told by Bates that his master was not home.

'He's gone away again?' she'd asked sharply.

'No. No, miss. I assume that he's very busy at the hospital.'

He told the doctor when he returned in the evening. 'Mrs Potter-Stokes, sir, has been ringing up on several occasions. I took it upon myself to say that you were at the hospital. She didn't wish to leave a message.' He lowered his eyes. 'I should have told you sooner, sir, but you have been away from home a good deal.'

'Quite right, Bates. If she should phone again, will you tell her that I'm very busy at the moment? Put it nicely.'

Bates murmured assent, concealing satisfaction; he disliked Mrs Potter-Stokes.

It was entirely by chance that Miriam met a friend of her mother's one morning. A pleasant lady who enjoyed a gossip.

'My dear, I don't seem to have seen you lately. You and Oliver Fforde are usually together...' She frowned. 'He is coming to dinner on Thursday, but someone or other told me that you were away.'

'Away? No, I shall be at home for the next few weeks.' Miriam contrived to look wistful. 'Oliver and I have been trying to meet for days—he's so busy; you would never believe how difficult it is to snatch an hour or two together.'

Her companion, a woman without guile and not expecting it in others, said at once, 'My dear Miriam, you must come to dinner. At least you can sit with each other and have a little time together. I'll get another man to make up the numbers.'

Miriam laid a hand on her arm. 'Oh, how kind of you; if only we can see each other for a while we can arrange to meet.'

Miriam went home well satisfied, so sure of her charm and looks that she was positive that Oliver, seeing her again, would resume their friendship and forget that silly girl.

But she was to be disappointed. He greeted her with his usual friendly smile, listened to her entertaining chatter, and with his usual beautiful manners evaded her questions as to where he had been. It was vexing that despite all her efforts he was still no more than one of her many friends.

At the end of the evening he drove her home, but he didn't accept her invitation to go in for a drink.

'I must be up early,' he told her, and wished her a pleasantly cool goodnight.

Miriam went angrily to her bed. She could find no fault in his manner towards her, but she had lost whatever hold she'd thought she had on him. Which made her all the more determined to do something about it. She had always had everything she wanted since she was a small girl, and now she wanted Oliver.

It was several days later that, an unwilling fourth at one of her mother's bridge parties, she heard someone remark, 'Such a pity he cannot spare the time to join us; he's going away for the weekend...'

The speaker turned to Miriam. 'I expect you knew that already, my dear?'

Miriam stopped herself just in time from trumping her partner's ace.

'Yes, yes, I do. He's very fond of his mother...'

'She lives at such a pleasant place. He's going to see an old aunt as well.' She laughed. 'Not a very exciting weekend for him. You won't be with him, Miriam?' The speaker glanced at her slyly.

'No, I'd already promised to visit an old schoolfriend.'

Miriam thought about that later. There was no reason why Oliver shouldn't visit an old aunt; there was no reason why she should feel uneasy about it. But she did.

She waited for a day or two and then phoned him, keeping her voice deliberately light and understanding. There was rather a good film on; how about them going to see it together at the weekend?

'I'll be away,' he told her.

'Oh, well, another time. Visiting your mother?'

'Yes. It will be nice to get out of London for a couple of days.'

He was as pleasant and friendly as he always had been, but she knew that she was making no headway with him. There was someone else—surely not that girl still?

She gave the matter a good deal of thought, and finally telephoned Mrs Fforde's home; if she was home, she would hang up, say 'wrong number', or make some excuse, but if she was lucky enough to find her out and the housekeeper, a garrulous woman, answered, she might learn something...

She was in luck, and the housekeeper, told that this was an old friend of the doctor's, was quite ready to offer the information that he would be staying for the weekend and leaving early on Sunday to visit Lady Haleford.

'Ah, yes,' said Miriam encouragingly, 'his great-aunt. Such a charming old lady.'

The housekeeper went on, 'Back home after a stroke, madam told me. But they've got someone to live with her—a young lady, but very competent.'

'I must give Lady Haleford a ring. Will you let me have her number?'

It was an easy matter to phone and, under the pretext of getting a wrong number, discover that Lady Haleford lived at Aldbury. It would be wise to wait until after Oliver had been there, but then she would find some reason for calling on the old lady and see for herself what it was about this girl that held Oliver's interest.

Satisfied that she had coped well with what she considered a threat to her future, Miriam relaxed.

Amabel, aware that fate was treating her kindly, set about being as nearly a perfect companion as possible. No easy task, for Lady Haleford was difficult. Not only was she old, she was accustomed to living her life as she wished—an impossibility after her stroke—so that for the first few days nothing was right, although she tolerated Cyril and Oscar, declaring that no one else understood her.

For several days Amabel was to be thoroughly dispirited; she had done nothing right, said nothing right, remained silent when she should have spoken, spoken when she was meant to be silent. It was disheartening, but she liked the old lady and guessed that underneath the peevishness and ill-temper there was a frightened old lady lurking.

There had been no chance to establish any kind of routine. She had had no free time other than brief walks round the garden with Cyril. But Mrs Twitchett and Nelly had done all they could to help her, and she told herself that things would improve.

She had coaxed Lady Haleford one afternoon, swathed in shawls, to sit in the drawing room, and had set up a card table beside her, intent on getting her to play two-handed whist. Her doctor had been that morning, pronounced himself satisfied with her progress and suggested that she might begin to take an interest in life once more.

He was a hearty man, middle-aged and clearly an old friend. He had taken no notice of Lady Haleford's peevishness, told her how lucky she was to have someone so young and cheerful to be with her and had gone away, urging Amabel at the same time to get out into the fresh air.

'Nothing like a good walk when you're young,' he had observed, and Mabel, pining for just that, had agreed with him silently.

Lady Haleford went to sleep over her cards and Amabel sat quietly, waiting for her to rouse herself again. And while she sat, she thought. Her job wasn't easy, she had no freedom and almost no leisure, but on the other hand she had a roof—a comfortable one—over her head, Oscar and Cyril had insinuated themselves into the household and become household pets, and she would be able to save money. Besides, she liked Lady Haleford, she loved the old house and the garden, and she had so much to be thankful for she didn't know where to begin.

With the doctor, she supposed, who had made it all possible. If only she knew where he lived she could write and tell him how grateful she was...

The drawing room door opened soundlessly and he walked in.

Amabel gaped at him, her mouth open. Then she shut it and put a finger to it. 'She's asleep,' she whispered unnecessarily, and felt a warm wave of delight and content at the sight of him.

He dropped a kiss on her cheek, having crossed the room and sat down.

'I've come to tea,' he told her, 'and if my aunt will invite me, I'll stay for supper.'

He sounded matter-of-fact, as though dropping in for tea was something he did often, and he was careful to hide his pleasure at seeing Amabel again. Still plain, but good food was producing some gentle curves and there were no longer shadows under her eyes.

Beautiful eyes, thought the doctor, and smiled, feeling content in her company.

CHAPTER SEVEN

LADY HALEFORD GAVE a small snort and woke up.

'Oliver—how delightful. You'll stay for tea? Amabel, go and tell Mrs Twitchett. You know Amabel, of course?'

'I saw her as I came in, and yes, I know Amabel. How do you find life now that you are back home, Aunt?'

The old lady said fretfully, 'I get tired and I forget things. But it is good to be home again. Amabel is a good girl and not impatient. Some of the nurses were impatient. You could feel them seething under their calm faces and I can sympathise with them.'

'You sleep well?'

'I suppose so. The nights are long, but Amabel makes tea and we sit and gossip.' She added in an anxious voice, 'I shall get better, Oliver?'

He said gently, 'You will improve slowly, but getting well after illness is sometimes harder than being ill.'

'Yes, it is. How I hate that wheelchair and that horrible thing to help me walk. I won't use it, you know. Amabel gives me an arm...'

The old lady closed her eyes and nodded off for a moment, before adding, 'It was clever of you to find her, Oliver. She's a plain girl, isn't she? Dresses in such dull clothes too, but her voice is pleasant and she's gentle.' She spoke as though Amabel wasn't there, sitting close to her. 'You made a good choice, Oliver.'

The doctor didn't look at Amabel. 'Yes, indeed I did, Aunt.'

Nelly came in with the tea tray then, and he began a casual conversation about his mother and his work and the people they knew, giving Amabel time to get over her discomfort. She was too sensible to be upset by Lady Haleford's remarks, but he guessed that she felt embarrassed...

Tea over, Lady Haleford declared that she would take a nap. 'You'll stay for dinner?' she wanted to know. 'I see you very seldom.' She sounded peevish.

'Yes, I'll stay with pleasure,' he told her. 'While you doze Amabel and I will take the dogs for a quick run.'

'And I shall have a glass of sherry before we dine,' said the old lady defiantly.

'Why not? We'll be back in half an hour or so. Come along, Amabel.'

Amabel got up. 'Is there anything you want before we go, Lady Haleford?' she asked.

'Yes, fetch Oscar to keep me company.'

Oscar, that astute cat, knew on which side his bread was buttered, for he settled down primly on the old lady's lap and went to sleep.

It was cold outside, but there was a bright moon in a starry sky. The doctor took Amabel's arm and walked her briskly through the village, past the church and along a lane out of the village. They each held a dog lead and the beasts trotted beside them, glad of the unexpected walk.

'Well,' said the doctor, 'how do you find your job? Have you settled in? My aunt can be difficult, and now, after her stroke, I expect she is often querulous.'

'Yes, but so should I be. Wouldn't you? And I'm very happy here. It's not hard work, and you know everyone is so kind.'

'But you have to get up during the night?'

'Well, now and then.' She didn't tell him that Lady Haleford woke up during the early hours most nights and demanded company. Fearful of further probing questions, she asked, 'Have you been busy? You haven't needed to go to York again?'

'No, that is a matter happily dealt with. You hear from your mother and Miss Parsons?'

'Yes, Aunt Thisbe is coming home at the end of January, and my mother seems very happy. The market garden is planted and they have plenty of help.' She faltered for a moment. 'Mother said not to go home and see her yet, Mr Graham is still rather—well, I think he'd rather that I didn't visit them...'

'You would like to see your mother?' he asked gently.

'Yes, but if she thinks it is best for me to stay away then I will. Perhaps later...'

'And what do you intend to do later?'

They turned for home and he tucked her hand under his arm.

'Well, I shall be able to save a lot of money. It's all computers these days, isn't it? So I'll take a course in them and get a good job and somewhere to live.' She added anxiously, 'Your aunt does want me to stay for a while?'

'Oh, most certainly. I've talked to her doctor and he thinks that she needs six weeks or two months living as she does at present, and probably longer.'

They had reached the house again.

'You have very little freedom,' he told her.

She said soberly, 'I'm content.'

They had supper early, for Lady Haleford became easily tired, and as soon as the meal was finished the doctor got up to go.

'You'll come again?' demanded his aunt. 'I like visitors, and next time you will tell me about yourself. Haven't you found a girl to marry yet? You are thirty-four, Oliver. You've enough money and a splendid home and the work you love; now you need a wife.'

He bent to kiss her. 'You shall be the first to know when I find her.' And to Amabel he said, 'No, don't get up. Mrs Twitchett will see me out.' He put a hand on Amabel's shoulder as he passed her chair, and with Tiger at his heels was gone.

His visit had aroused the old lady; she had no wish to go to bed, she said pettishly. And it was a pity that Oliver could visit her so seldom. She observed, 'He is a busy man, and I dare say has many friends. But he needs to settle down. There are plenty of nice girls for him to choose from, and there is that Miriam...' She was rambling a bit. 'The Potter-Stokes widow—been angling for him for an age. If he's not careful she'll have him.' She closed her eyes. 'Not a nice young woman...'

Lady Haleford dozed for a while so Amabel thought about Oliver and the prospect of him marrying. She found the idea depressing, although it was the obvious thing for a man in his position to do. Anyway, it was none of her business.

A week went by, almost unnoticed in the gentle routine of the old house. Lady Haleford improved a little, but not much. Some days her testiness was enough to cast a blight over the entire household, so that Mrs Twitchett burnt the soup and Nelly dropped plates and Amabel had to listen to a diatribe of her many faults. Only Cyril and Oscar weathered the storm and her fierce little rages, sitting by her chair and allowing her peevish words to fly over their heads.

But there were days when she was placid, wanting to talk, play at cards, and walk slowly round the house, carefully hitched up under Amabel's arm.

Her doctor came, assured her that she was making steady progress, warned Amabel to humour her as much as possible and went away again.

Since humouring her meant getting up in the small hours to read to the old lady, or simply to talk until she drowsed off to a light sleep, Amabel had very little time for herself. At least each morning she took Cyril for a walk while Lady Haleford rested in her bed after breakfast before getting up, and she looked forward to her half-hour's freedom each day, even when it was cold and wet.

On this particular morning it was colder and wetter than it had been for several days, and Amabel, trudging back down the village street with Cyril beside her, looked rather as though she had fallen into a ditch and been pulled out backwards. Her head down against the wind and rain, she didn't see the elegant little sports car outside Lady Haleford's gate until she was beside it.

Even then she would have opened the door and gone inside if the woman in the car hadn't wound down the window and said in an anxious voice, 'Excuse me—if you could spare a moment? Is this Lady Haleford's house? My mother is a friend of hers and asked me to look her up as I was coming this way. But it's too early to call. Could I leave a message with someone?'

She smiled charmingly while at the same time studying Amabel's person. *This must be the girl*, reflected Miriam. *Plain as a pikestaff and looks like a drowned rat. I can't believe that Oliver is in the least bit interested in her. Dolores has been tricking me...* She spent a moment thinking of how she would repay her for that, then said aloud, at her most charming, 'Are you her granddaughter or niece? Perhaps you could tell her?'

'I'm Lady Haleford's companion,' said Amabel, and saw how cold the lovely blue eyes were. 'But I'll give her a message if you like. Would you like to come back later, or come and wait indoors? She has been ill and doesn't get up early.'

'I'll call on my way back,' said Miriam. She smiled sweetly. 'I'm sorry you're so wet standing there; I am thoughtless. But perhaps you don't mind the country in winter. I don't like this part of England. I've been in York for a while, and after that this village looks so forlorn.'

'It's very nice here,' said Amabel. 'But York is lovely; I was there recently.'

Her face ringed by strands of wet hair, she broke into a smile she couldn't suppress at the remembrance of the doctor.

Miriam said sharply, 'You have happy memories of it?'

Amabel, lost in a momentary dream, didn't notice the sharpness. 'Yes.'

'Well, I won't keep you.' Miriam smiled and made an effort to sound friendly. 'I'll call again.'

She drove away and Amabel went indoors. She spent the next ten minutes drying herself and Cyril and then went to tidy herself before going to Lady Haleford's room.

The old lady was in a placid mood, not wanting to talk much and apt to doze off from time to time. It wasn't until she was dressed and downstairs in her normal chair by the drawing room fire that she asked, 'Well, what have you been doing with yourself, Amabel?'

Glad of something to talk about, Amabel told her of her morning's encounter. 'And I'm so sorry but she didn't tell me her name, and I forgot to ask, but she said that she'll be back.'

Lady Haleford said worriedly, 'I do have trouble remembering people... What was she like? Dark? Fair? Pretty?'

'Fair and beautiful, very large blue eyes. She was driving a little red car.'

Lady Haleford closed her eyes. 'Well, she'll be back. I don't feel like visitors today, Amabel, so if she does call make my apologies—and ask her name.'

But of course Miriam didn't go back, and after a few days they forgot about her.

Miriam found it just impossible to believe that Oliver could possibly have any interest in such a dull plain girl, but all the same it was a matter which needed to be dealt with. She had begun to take it for granted that he would take her to the theatre, out to dine, to visit picture galleries, and even when he had refused on account of his work she had been so sure of him...

Her vanity prevented her from realising that he had merely been fulfilling social obligations, that he had no real interest in her.

She would have to change her tactics. She stopped phoning him with suggestions that they should go to the theatre or dine out, but she took care to be there at a mutual friend's house if he were to be there, too. Since Christmas was approaching, there were dinner parties and social gatherings enough.

Not that he was always to be found at them. Oliver had many friends, but his social life depended very much on his work so that, much to Miriam's annoyance, she only saw him from time to time, and when they did meet he was his usual friendly self, but that was all. Her pretty face and charm, her lovely clothes and witty talk were wasted on him.

When they had met at a friend's dinner party, and she'd asked casually what he intended to do for Christmas, he'd told her pleasantly that he was far too busy to make plans.

'Well, you mustn't miss our dinner party,' she'd told him. 'Mother will send you an invitation.'

The days passed peacefully enough at Aldbury. Lady Haleford had her ups and downs—indeed it seemed to Amabel that she was slowly losing ground. Although perhaps the dark days of the winter made the old lady loath to leave her bed. Since her doctor came regularly, and assured Amabel that things were taking their course, she spent a good many hours sitting in Lady Haleford's room, reading to her or playing two-handed patience.

All the same she was glad when Mrs Fforde phoned to say that she would be coming to spend a day or two. 'And I'm bringing two of my grandchildren with me—Katie and James. We will stay for a couple of days before I take them to London to do the Christmas shopping. Lady Haleford is very fond of them and it may please her to see them. Will you ask Mrs Twitchett to come to the phone, Amabel? I leave it to you to tell my aunt that we shall be coming.'

It was a piece of news which pleased the old lady mightily. 'Two nice children,' she told Amabel. 'They must be twelve years old—twins, you know. Their mother is Oliver's sister.' She closed her eyes for a moment and presently added, 'He has two sisters; they're both married, younger than he.'

They came two days later; Katie was thin and fair, with big

blue eyes and a long plait of pale hair and James was the taller of the two, quiet and serious. Mrs Fforde greeted Amabel briskly.

'Amabel—how nice to see you again. You're rather pale— I dare say that you don't get out enough. Here are Katie and James. Why not take them into the garden for a while and I will visit Lady Haleford? Only put on something warm.' Her eyes lighted on Cyril, standing unexpectedly between the children.

'They are happy, your cat and dog?'

'Yes, very happy.'

'And you, Amabel?'

'I'm happy too, Mrs Fforde.'

Oscar, wishing for a share of the attention, went into the garden too, and, although it was cold, it was a clear day with no wind. They walked along its paths while the children told Amabel at some length about their shopping trip to London.

'We spend Christmas at Granny's,' they explained. 'Our aunt and uncle and cousins will be there, and Uncle Oliver. We have a lovely time and Christmas is always the same each year. Will you go home for Christmas, Amabel?'

'Oh, I expect so,' said Amabel, and before they could ask any more questions added, 'Christmas is such fun, isn't it?'

They stayed for two days, and Amabel was sorry to see them go, but even such a brief visit had tired Lady Haleford, and they quickly slipped back into the placid pattern of their days.

Now that Christmas was near Amabel couldn't help wishing that she might enjoy some of the festivities, so it was a delightful surprise when Lady Haleford, rather more alert than she had been, told her that she wanted her to go to Berkhamstead and do some Christmas shopping. 'Sit down,' she commanded, 'and get a pen and some paper and write down my list.'

The list took several days to complete, for Lady Haleford tended to doze off a good deal, but finally Amabel caught the village bus, her ears ringing with advice and instructions from Mrs Twitchett, the list in her purse and a wad of banknotes tucked away safely.

It was really rather exciting, and shopping for presents was fun even if it was for someone else. It was a long list, for Lady Haleford's family was a large one: books, jigsaw puzzles, games for the younger members, apricots in brandy, a special blend of coffee, Stilton cheese in jars, a case of wine, boxes of candied fruits, and mouthwatering chocolates for the older ones.

Amabel, prowling round the small grocer's shop which seemed to stock every luxury imaginable, had enjoyed every minute of her shopping. She had stopped only briefly for a sandwich and coffee, and now, with an hour to spare before the bus left, she did a little shopping for herself.

High time too, she thought, stocking up on soap and toiletries, stockings and a thick sweater, shampoos and toothpaste. And then presents: patience cards for Lady Haleford, a scarf for Mrs Twitchett, a necklace for Nelly, a new collar for Cyril and a catnip mouse for Oscar. It was hard to find a present for her mother; she chose a blouse, in pink silk, and, since she couldn't ignore him, a book token for her stepfather.

At the very last minute she saw a dress, silvery grey in some soft material—the kind of dress, she told herself, which would be useful for an occasion, and after all it was Christmas... She bought it and, laden with parcels, went back to Aldbury.

The old lady, refreshed by a nap, wanted to see everything. Amabel drank a much needed cup of tea in the kitchen and spent the next hour or so carefully unwrapping parcels and wrapping them up again. Tomorrow, said Lady Haleford, Amabel must go into the village shop and get coloured wrapping paper and labels and write appropriate names on them.

The village shop was a treasure store of Christmas goods. Amabel spent a happy half-hour choosing suitably festive paper and bore it back for the old lady's approval. Later, kneeling on the floor under Lady Haleford's eyes, she was glad of her experience in Dolores's shop, for the gifts were all shapes and sizes. Frequently it was necessary to unwrap something and repack it because Lady Haleford had dozed off and got muddled...

The doctor, coming quietly into the room, unnoticed by a dozing Lady Haleford and, since she had her back to the door, by Amabel, stood in the doorway and watched her. She wasn't quite as tidy as usual, and half obscured by sheets of wrapping paper and reels of satin ribbon. Even from the back, he considered, she looked flustered...

The old lady opened her eyes and saw him and said, 'Oliver, how nice. Amabel, I've changed my mind. Unwrap the Stilton cheese and find a box for it.'

Amabel put down the cheese and looked over her shoulder. Oliver smiled at her and she smiled back, a smile of pure delight because she was so happy to see him again.

Lady Haleford said with a touch of peevishness, 'Amabel—the cheese...'

Amabel picked it up again and clasped it to her bosom, still smiling, and the doctor crossed the room and took it from her.

'Stilton—who is it for, Aunt?' He eyed the growing pile of gaily coloured packages. 'I see you've done your Christmas shopping.'

'You'll stay for lunch?' said Lady Haleford. 'Amabel, go and tell Mrs Twitchett.' When Amabel had gone she said, 'Oliver, will you take Amabel out? A drive, or tea, or something? She has no fun and she never complains.'

'Yes, of course. I came partly to suggest that we had dinner together one evening.'

'Good. Mrs Twitchett told me that the child has bought a new dress. Because it's Christmas, she told her. Perhaps I don't pay her enough...'

'I believe she is saving her money so that she can train for some career or other.'

'She would make a good wife...' The old lady dozed off again.

It was after lunch, when Lady Haleford had been tucked up for her afternoon nap, that the doctor asked Amabel if she would have dinner with him one evening. They were walking the dogs, arm-in-arm, talking easily like two old friends, comfortable with each other, but she stopped to look up at him.

'Oh, that would be lovely. But I can't, you know. It would mean leaving Lady Haleford for a whole evening, and Nelly goes to her mother's house in the village after dinner—she's got rheumatism, her mother, you know—and that means Mrs Twitchett would be alone...'

'I think that something might be arranged if you would leave that to me.'

'And then,' continued Amabel, 'I've only one dress. I bought it the other day, but it's not very fashionable. I only bought it because it's Christmas, and I...really, it was a silly thing to do.'

'Since you are going to wear it when we go out I don't find it in the least silly.' He spoke gently. 'Is it a pretty dress?'

'Pale grey. Very plain. It won't look out of date for several years.'

'It sounds just the thing for an evening out. I'll come for you next Saturday evening—half past seven.'

They walked back then, and presently he went away, giving her a casual nod. 'Saturday,' he reminded her, and bent to kiss her cheek. Such a quick kiss that she wasn't sure if she had imagined it.

She supposed that she wasn't in the least surprised to find that Lady Haleford had no objection to her going out with the doctor. Indeed, she seemed to find nothing out of the ordinary in it, and when Amabel enquired anxiously about Nelly going to her mother, she was told that an old friend of Mrs Twitchett's would be spending the evening with her.

'Go and enjoy yourself,' said that lady. 'Eat a good dinner and dance a bit.'

So when Saturday came Amabel got into the grey dress, took pains with her face and her hair and went downstairs to where the doctor was waiting. Lady Haleford had refused to go to bed early; Mrs Twitchett would help her, she had told Amabel, but

Amabel was to look in on her when she got home later. 'In case I am still awake and need something.'

Amabel, the grey dress concealed by her coat, greeted the doctor gravely, pronounced herself ready, bade the old lady goodnight, bade Oscar and Cyril to be good and got into the car beside Oliver.

It was a cold clear night with a bright moon. There would be a heavy frost by morning, but now everything was silvery in the moonlight.

'We're not going far,' said the doctor. 'There's rather a nice country hotel—we can dance if we feel like it.'

He began to talk about this and that, and Amabel, who had been feeling rather shy, lost her shyness and began to enjoy herself. She couldn't think why she should have felt suddenly awkward with him; after all, he was a friend—an old friend by now...

He had chosen the hotel carefully and it was just right. The grey dress, unassuming and simple but having style, was absorbed into the quiet luxury of the restaurant.

The place was festive, without being overpoweringly so, and the food was delicious. Amabel ate prawns and Caesar salad, grilled sole and straw potatoes and, since it was almost Christmas, mouthwatering mince pies with chantilly cream. But not all at once.

The place was full and people were dancing. When the doctor suggested that she might like to dance she got up at once. Only as they reached the dance floor she hesitated. 'It's ages since I danced,' she told him.

He smiled down at her. 'Then it's high time you did now,' he told her.

She was very light on her feet, and she hadn't forgotten how to dance. Oliver looked down onto her neat head of hair and wondered how long it would be before she discovered that she was in love with him. He was prepared to wait, but he hoped that it wouldn't be too long...!

The good food, the champagne and dancing had transformed a rather plain girl in a grey dress into someone quite different. When at length it was time to leave, Amabel, very pink in the cheeks and bright of the eye, her tongue loosened by the champagne, told him that she had never had such a lovely evening in her life before.

'York seems like a bad dream,' she told him, 'and supposing you hadn't happened to see me, what would I have done? You're my guardian angel, Oliver.'

The doctor, who had no wish to be her guardian angel but something much more interesting, said cheerfully, 'Oh, you would have fallen on your feet, Amabel, you're a sensible girl.'

And all the things she suddenly wanted to say to him shrivelled on her tongue.

'I've had too much champagne,' she told him, and talked about the pleasures of the evening until they were back at Lady Haleford's house.

He went in with her, to switch on lights and make sure all was well, but he didn't stay. She went to the door with him and thanked him once again for her lovely evening.

'I'll remember it,' she told him.

He put his arms round her then, and kissed her hard, but before she could say anything he had gone, closing the door quietly behind him.

She stood for a long time thinking about that kiss, but presently she took off her shoes and crept upstairs to her room. There, was no sound from Lady Haleford's bedroom and all was still when she peeped through the door; she undressed and prepared for bed, and was just getting into bed when she heard the gentle tinkling of the old lady's bell. So she got out of bed again and went quietly to see what was the matter.

Lady Haleford was now wide awake, and wanted an account of the evening.

'Sit down and tell me about it,' she commanded. 'Where did you go and what did you eat?'

So Amabel stifled a yawn and curled up in a chair by the bed to recount the events of the evening. Not the kiss, of course.

When she had finished Lady Haleford said smugly, 'So you had a good time. It was my suggestion, you know—that Oliver should take you out for the evening. He's so kind, you know— always willing to do a good turn. Such a busy man, too. I'm sure he could ill spare the time.' She gave a satisfied sigh. 'Now go to bed, Amabel. We have to see to the rest of those Christmas presents tomorrow.'

So Amabel turned the pillow, offered a drink, turned the night light low and went back to her room. In her room she got into bed and closed her eyes, but she didn't go to sleep.

Her lovely evening had been a mockery, a charitable action undertaken from a sense of duty by someone whom she had thought was her friend. He was still her friend, she reminded herself, but his friendship was mixed with pity.

Not to be borne, decided Amabel, and at last fell asleep as the tears dried on her cheeks.

Lady Haleford had a good deal more to say about the evening out in the morning; Amabel had to repeat everything she had already told her and listen to the old lady's satisfied comments while she tied up the rest of the parcels.

'I told Oliver that you had bought a dress...'

Amabel cringed. Bad enough that he had consented to take her out; he probably thought that she had bought it in the hope that he might invite her.

She said quickly, 'We shall need some more paper. I'll go and buy some...'

In the shop, surrounded by the village ladies doing their weekly shopping, she felt better. She was being silly, she told herself. What did it matter what reason Oliver had had for asking her out for the evening? It had been a lovely surprise and she had enjoyed herself, and what had she expected, anyway?

She went back and tied up the rest of the presents, and recounted, once again, the previous evening's events, for the old lady protested that she had been told nothing.

'Oh, you spent five minutes with me when you came in last night, but I want to know what you talked about. You're a nice girl, Amabel, but I can't think of you as an amusing companion. Men do like to be amused, but I dare say Oliver found you pleasant enough; he can take his pick of pretty women in London.'

All of which did nothing to improve Amabel's spirits.

Not being given to self-pity, she told herself to remember that Lady Haleford was old and had been ill and didn't mean half of what she said. As for her evening out, well, that was a pleasant memory and nothing more. If she should see the doctor again she would take care to let him see that, while they were still friends, she neither expected nor wanted to be more than that.

I'll be a little cool, reflected Amabel, and in a few weeks I expect I'll be gone from here. Being a sensible girl, she fell to planning her future...

This was a waste of time, actually, for Oliver was planning it for her; she would be with his aunt for several weeks yet—time enough to think of a way in which they might see each other frequently and let her discover for herself that he was in love with her and wanted to marry her. He had friends enough; there must be one amongst them who needed a companion or something of that sort, where Cyril and Oscar would be acceptable. And where he would be able to see her as frequently as possible...

The simplest thing would be for her to stay at his house. Impossible—but he lingered over the delightful idea...

He wasn't the only one thinking about Amabel's future. Miriam, determined to marry Oliver, saw Amabel as a real threat to her plans.

She was careful to be casually friendly when she and Oliver met occasionally, and she took care not to ask him any but the vaguest questions about his days. She had tried once or twice to get information from Bates, but he professed ignorance of his employer's comings and goings. He told her stolidly that the doctor was either at his consulting room or at the hospital, and if she phoned and wanted to speak to him at the weekend Bates informed her that he was out with the dog.

Oliver, immersed in his work and thoughts of Amabel, dismissed Miriam's various invitations and suggestions that they might spend an evening together with good-mannered friendliness; he didn't believe seriously that Miriam wanted anything more than his company from time to time; she had men-friends enough.

He underestimated her, though. Miriam drove herself to Aldbury, parked the car away from the centre of the village and found her way to the church. The village shop would have been ideal ground from which to glean information, but there was the risk of meeting Amabel. Besides, people in the village might talk.

The church was old and beautiful, but she didn't waste time on it. Someone—the vicar, she supposed—was coming down the aisle towards her, wanting to know if he could help her...

He was a nice elderly man, willing to talk to this charming lady who was so interested in the village. 'Oh, yes,' he told her, 'there are several old families living in the village, their history going back for many years.'

'And those lovely cottages with thatched roofs—one of them seems a good deal larger than the rest?'

'Ah, yes, that would be Lady Haleford's house. A very old family. She has been ill and is very elderly. She was in hospital for some time, but now I'm glad to say she is at home again. There is a very charming young woman who is her companion. We see her seldom, for she has little spare time, although Lady Haleford's nephew comes to visit his aunt and I have seen the pair of them walking the dogs. He was here recently, so I'm told, and took her out for the evening...! How I do ramble on, but living in a small village we tend to be interested in each other's doings. You are touring this part of the country?'

'Yes, this is a good time of year to drive around the countryside. I shall work my way west to the Cotswolds,' said Miriam, untruthfully. 'It's been delightful talking to you, Vicar, and now I must get back to my car and drive on.'

She shook hands and walked quickly back to her car, watched by several ladies in the village shop, whose sharp eyes took in every inch of her appearance.

She drove away quickly and presently pulled up on the grass verge the better to think. At first she was too angry to put two thoughts together. This was no passing attraction on Oliver's part; he had been seeing this girl for some time now and his interest was deep enough to cause him to seek her out. Miriam seethed quietly. She didn't love Oliver; she liked him enough to marry him and she wanted the things the marriage would bring to her: a handsome husband, money, a lovely home and the social standing his name and profession would give her.

She thumped the driving wheel in rage. Something would have to be done, but what?

CHAPTER EIGHT

QUIET THOUGH THE routine of Lady Haleford's household was, Christmas, so near now, was not to be ignored. Cards were delivered, gifts arrived, visitors called to spend ten minutes with the old lady, and Amabel trotted round the house arranging and rearranging the variety of pot plants they brought with them.

It was all mildly exciting, but tiring for the invalid, so that Amabel needed to use all her tact and patience, coaxing callers to leave after the briefest of visits, and even then Lady Haleford exhibited a mixture of lethargy and testiness which prompted her to get the doctor to call.

He was a rather solemn man who had looked after the old lady for years, and he now gave it as his opinion that, Christmas or no Christmas, his patient must revert to total peace and quiet.

'The occasional visitor,' he allowed, and Amabel was to use her discretion in turning away more than that.

Amabel said, 'Lady Haleford likes to know who calls. She gets upset if someone she wishes to see is asked not to visit her. I've tried that once or twice and she gets rather uptight.'

Dr Carr looked at her thoughtfully. 'Yes, well, I must leave that to your discretion, Miss Parsons. Probably to go against her wishes would do more harm than good. She sleeps well?'

'No,' said Amabel. 'Although she dozes a lot during the day.'

'But at night—she is restless? Worried...?'

'No. Just awake. She likes to talk, and sometimes I read to her.'

He looked at her as though he hadn't really seen her before.

'You get sufficient recreation, Miss Parsons?'

Amabel said that, yes, thank you, she did. Because if she didn't he might decide that she wasn't capable enough for the job and arrange for a nurse. Her insides trembled at the thought.

So Amabel met visitors as they were ushered into the hall and, unless they were very close old friends or remote members of Lady Haleford's family, persuaded them that she wasn't well enough to have a visitor, then offered notepaper and a pen in case they wanted to write a little note and plied them with coffee and one of Mrs Twitchett's mince pies.

Hard work, but it left both parties satisfied.

Though it was quite quiet in the house, the village at its doorstep was full of life. There was a lighted Christmas tree, the village shop was a blaze of fairy lights, and carol singers—ranging from small children roaring out the first line of 'Good King Wenceslas' to the harmonious church choir—were a nightly event. And Mrs Twitchett, while making sure that Lady Haleford was served the dainty little meals she picked at, dished up festive food suitable to the season for the other three of them.

Amabel counted her blessings and tried not to think about Oliver.

Dr Fforde was going to Glastonbury to spend Christmas with his mother and the rest of his family. Two days which he could ill spare. He had satisfied himself that his patients were making progress, presented the theatre staff with sherry, his ward sister and his receptionist and the nurse at the consulting rooms with similar bottles, made sure that Bates and his wife would enjoy a good Christmas, loaded the car boot with suitable presents and, accompanied by Tiger, was ready to leave home.

He was looking forward to the long drive, and, more than

that, he was looking forward to seeing Amabel, for he intended to call on his aunt on his way.

He had been working hard for the last week or so, and on top of that there had been the obligatory social events. Many of them he had enjoyed, but not all of them. He had found the dinner party given by Miriam's parents particularly tedious, but he had had no good reason to refuse the invitation—although he had been relieved to find that Miriam seemed no longer to look upon him as her future. She had been as amusing and attractive as always, but she had made no demands on his time, merely saying with apparent sincerity that he must be glad to get away from his work for a few days.

It was beginning to snow when he left, very early on the morning of Christmas Eve. Tiger, sitting very upright beside him, watched the heavy traffic. It took some time to get away from London but the doctor remained patient, thinking about Amabel, knowing that he would be seeing her in an hour or so.

The village looked charming as he drove through it and there was a small lighted Christmas tree in the cottage's drawing room window. He got out of the car, opened the door for Tiger, and saw Amabel and Cyril at the far end of the village street. Tiger, scenting friends, was already on his way to meet them. Oliver saw Amabel stop, and for a moment he thought she was going to turn round and hurry away. But she bent to greet Tiger and came towards him. He met her halfway.

There was snow powdering her woolly cap and her coat, and her face was rosy with cold. He thought she looked beautiful, though he was puzzled by her prim greeting.

He said cheerfully, 'Hello. I'm on my way to spend Christmas with the family. How is my aunt?'

'A bit tired,' she told him seriously. 'There have been a great many visitors, although she has seen only a handful of them.'

They were walking back towards the house. 'I expect you'd like to see her? She'll be finishing her breakfast.' Since he didn't speak, the silence got rather long. 'I expect you've been busy?' Annabel finally ventured.

'Yes, I'll go back on Boxing Day.' They had reached the front door when he said, 'What's the matter, Amabel?'

She said, too quickly, 'Nothing. Everything is fine.' And as she opened the door added, 'Would you mind going up to Lady Haleford? I'll dry the dogs and tidy myself.'

Mrs Twitchett came bustling into the hall then, and Amabel slipped away. Oliver wouldn't stay long and she could keep out of his way...

The dogs made themselves comfortable on either side of Oscar in front of the Aga, and when Nelly came in to say that Mr Oliver would have a cup of coffee before he went away Amabel slipped upstairs. Lady Haleford would be ready to start the slow business of dressing.

'Go away,' said the old lady as Amabel went into her room. 'Go and have coffee with Oliver. I'll dress later.' When Amabel looked reluctant, she added, 'Well, run along. Surely you want to wish him a happy Christmas?'

So Amabel went downstairs again, as slowly as possible, and into the drawing room. The dogs and Oscar had gone there with the coffee, sitting before the fire, and the doctor was sitting in one of the big wing chairs.

He got up as she went in, drew a balloon-backed chair closer to his own and invited her to pour their coffee.

'And now tell me what is wrong,' he said kindly. 'For there is something, isn't there? Surely we are friends enough for you to tell me? Something I have done, Amabel?'

She took a gulp of coffee. 'Well, yes, but it's silly of me to mind. So if it's all the same to you I'd rather not talk about it.'

He resisted the urge to scoop her out of her chair and wrap her in his arms. 'It isn't all the same to me...'

She put down her cup and saucer. 'Well, you didn't have to take me out to dinner just because Lady Haleford said that you should—I wouldn't have gone if I'd known...' She choked with sudden temper. 'Like giving a biscuit to a dog...'

Oliver bit back a laugh, not of amusement but of tenderness and relief. If that was all...

But she hadn't finished. 'And I didn't buy a dress because I hoped you would take me out.' She looked at him then. 'You are my friend, Oliver, and that is how I think of you—a friend.'

He said gently, 'I came to take you out for the evening, Amabel. Anything my aunt said didn't influence me in any way. And as for your new dress, that was something I hadn't considered. It was a pretty dress, but you look nice whatever you are wearing.' He would have liked to have said a great deal more, but it was obviously not the right moment. When she didn't speak, he said, 'Still friends, Amabel?'

'Yes—oh, yes, Oliver. I'm sorry I've been so silly.'

'We'll have another evening out after Christmas. I think that you will be here for some time yet.'

'I'm very happy here. Everyone in the village is so friendly, and really I have nothing to do.'

'You have very little time to yourself. Do you get the chance to go out—meet people—young people?'

'Well, no, but I don't mind.'

He got up to go presently. It was still snowing and he had some way to drive still. She went with him to the door, and Tiger, reluctant to leave Cyril and Oscar, pushed between them. Amabel bent to stroke him.

'Go carefully,' she said, 'and I hope that you and your family have a lovely Christmas.'

He stood looking down at her. 'Next year will be different!' He fished a small packet from a pocket. 'Happy Christmas, Amabel,' he said, and kissed her.

He didn't wait to hear her surprised thanks. She stood watching the car until it was out of sight, her mouth slightly open in surprise, clutching the little gaily wrapped box.

The delightful thought that he might come again on his way back to London sent a pleasant glow through her person.

She waited until Christmas morning before she opened the box, sitting up in bed early in the darkness. The box contained a brooch, a true lover's knot, in gold and turquoise—a dainty thing, but one she could wear with her very ordinary clothes.

She got up dressed in the grey dress and pinned the brooch onto it before getting into her coat and slipping out of the house to go to church.

It was dark and cold, and although the snow had stopped it lay thick on the ground. The church was cold too, but it smelled of evergreens and flowers, and the Christmas tree shone with its twinkling lights. There weren't many people at the service, for almost everyone would be at Matins during the morning, but as they left the church there was a pleasant flurry of cheerful talk and good wishes.

Amabel made sure that Lady Haleford was still asleep, had a quick breakfast with Mrs Twitchett and Nelly and took Cyril for his walk. The weather didn't suit his elderly bones and the walk was brief. She settled him next to Oscar by the Aga and went to bid Lady Haleford good morning.

The old lady wasn't in a festive mood. She had no wish to get out of her bed, no wish to eat her breakfast, and she said that she was too tired to look at the gifts Amabel assured her were waiting for her downstairs.

'You can read to me,' she said peevishly.

So Amabel sat down and read. *Little Women* was a soothing book, and very old-fashioned. She found the chapter describing Christmas and the simple pleasures of the four girls and their mother was a sharp contrast to the comfortable life Lady Haleford had always lived.

Presently Lady Haleford said, 'What a horrid old woman I am...'

'You're one of the nicest people I know,' said Amabel, and,

quite forgetting that she was a paid companion, she got up and hugged the old lady.

So Christmas was Christmas after all, with presents being opened, and turkey and Christmas pudding and mince pies, suitably interposed between refreshing naps, and Amabel, having tucked Lady Haleford into her bed, went early to bed herself. There was nothing else to do, but that didn't matter. Oliver would be returning to London the next day, and perhaps he would come and see them again...

But he didn't. It was snowing again, and he couldn't risk a hold-up on the way back to London.

The weather stayed wintry until New Year's Day, when Amabel woke to a bright winter's sun and blue sky. It was still snowy underfoot, and as she sloshed through it with a reluctant Cyril she wondered what the New Year would bring...

As for the doctor, he hardly noticed which day of the week it was, for the New Year had brought with it the usual surge of bad chests, tired hearts and the beginnings of a flu epidemic. He left home early and came home late, and ate whatever food Bates put before him. He was tired, and often frustrated, but it was his life and his work, and presently, when things had settled down again, he would go to Amabel...

Miriam waited for a few days before phoning Oliver. He had just got home after a long day and he was tired, but that was something she hadn't considered. There was a new play, she told him, would he get tickets? 'And we could have supper afterwards. I want to hear all about Christmas...'

He didn't tell her that he was working all day and every day, and sometimes into the night as well. He said mildly, 'I'm very busy, Miriam, I can't spare the time. There is a flu epidemic...'

'Oh, is there? I didn't know. There must be plenty of junior doctors...'

'Not enough.'

She said with a flash of temper, 'Then I'll get someone who will enjoy my company.'

The doctor, reading the first of a pile of reports on his desk, said absent-mindedly, 'Yes, do. I hope you will have a pleasant evening.'

He put the phone down and then picked it up again. He wanted to hear Amabel's voice. He put it down again. Phone conversations were unsatisfactory, for either one said too much or not enough. He would go and see her just as soon as he could spare the time. He ignored the pile of work before him and sat back and thought about Amabel, in her grey dress, wearing, he hoped, the true lover's knot.

Miriam had put down the phone and sat down to think. If Oliver was busy then he wouldn't have time to go to Aldbury. It was a chance for her to go, talk to the girl, convince her that he had no interest in her, that his future and hers were as far apart as two poles. It would be helpful if she could get Amabel away from this aunt of his, but she could see no way of doing that. She would have to convince Amabel that she had become an embarrassment to him...

There was no knowing when Oliver would go to Aldbury again, and Miriam waited with impatience for the snow to clear away. On a cold bright day, armed with a bouquet of flowers purporting to come from her mother, she set out.

The church clock was striking eleven as she stopped before Lady Haleford's cottage. Nelly answered the door, listened politely to Miriam's tale of her mother's friendship with Lady Haleford and bade her come in and wait. Lady Haleford was still in her room, but she would fetch Miss Parsons down. She left Miriam in the drawing room and went away, and presently Amabel came in.

Miriam said at once, 'Oh, hello—we've met before, haven't we? I came at the wrong time. Am I more fortunate today? Mother asked me to let Lady Haleford have these flowers...'

'Lady Haleford will be coming down in a few minutes,' said Amabel, and wondered why she didn't like this visitor.

She was being friendly enough, almost gushing, and Lady Haleford, when Nelly had mentioned Miriam's name, had said, 'That young woman—very pushy. And I haven't met her mother for years.' She had added, 'But I'll come down.'

Which she did, some ten minutes later, leaving Amabel to make polite conversation that Miriam made no effort to sustain.

But with the old lady she was at her most charming, giving her the flowers with a mythical message from her mother, asking about her health with apparent concern.

The old lady, normally a lady of perfect manners, broke into her chatter. 'I am going to take a nap. Amabel, fetch your coat and take Mrs Potter-Stokes to look round the village or the church if she chooses. Mrs Twitchett will give you coffee in half an hour's time. I will say goodbye now; please thank your mother for the flowers.'

She sat back in her chair and closed her eyes, leaving Amabel to usher an affronted Miriam out of the room. In the hall Amabel said, 'Lady Haleford has been very ill and she tires easily. Would you like to see round the church?'

Miriam said no, in a snappy voice, and then, mindful of why she had come, added with a smile, 'But perhaps we could walk a little way out of the village? The country looks very pretty.'

Amabel got into her coat, tied a scarf over her head and, with Cyril on his lead, led the way past the church and into the narrow lane beyond. Being a friendly girl, with nice manners, she made small talk about the village and the people who lived in it, aware that her companion hadn't really wanted to go walking—she was wearing the wrong shoes for a start.

Annoyed though Miriam was, she saw that this was her chance—if only there was a suitable opening. She stepped into a puddle and splashed her shoe and her tights and the hem of her long coat, and saw the opening...

'Oh, dear. Just look at that. I'm afraid I'm not a country girl.

It's a good thing that I live in London and always shall. I'm getting married soon, and Oliver lives and works there too...'

'Oliver?' asked Amabel in a careful voice.

'A nice name, isn't it? He's a medical man, always frightfully busy, although we manage to get quite a lot of time together. He has a lovely house; I shall love living there.'

She turned to smile at Amabel. 'He's such a dear—very kind and considerate. All his patients dote on him. And he's always ready to help any lame dog over a stile. There's some poor girl he's saved from a most miserable life—gone out of his way to find her a job. I hope she's grateful. She has no idea where he lives, of course. I mean, she isn't the kind of person one would want to become too familiar with, and it wouldn't do for her to get silly ideas into her head, would it?'

Amabel said quickly, 'I shouldn't think that would be very likely, but I'm sure she must be grateful.'

Miriam tucked a hand under Amabel's arm. 'Oh, I dare say— and if she appeals to him again for any reason I'll talk to her. I won't have him badgered; heaven knows how many he's helped without telling me. Once we're married, of course, things will be different.'

She gave Amabel a smiling nod, noting with satisfaction that the girl looked pale. 'Could we go back? I'm longing for a cup of coffee...'

Over coffee she had a great deal to say about the approaching wedding. 'Of course, Oliver and I have so many friends, and he's well known in the medical profession. I shall wear white, of course...' Miriam allowed her imagination full rein.

Amabel ordered more coffee, agreed that four bridesmaids would be very suitable, and longed for her unwelcome visitor to go. Which, presently, she did.

Lady Haleford, half dozing in her room, opened her eyes long enough to ask if the caller had gone and nodded off again, for which Amabel was thankful. She had no wish to repeat their conversation—besides, Oliver's private life was none of her business. She hadn't liked Miriam, but it had never entered her head that the woman was lying. It all made sense; Oliver had never talked about his home or his work or his friends. And why should he? Mrs Twitchett had remarked on several occasions that he had given unobtrusive help to people. 'He's a very private person,' she had told Amabel. 'Lord knows what goes on in that clever head of his.'

There was no hope of going to see Amabel for the moment; the flu epidemic had swollen to a disquieting level. The doctor treated his patients with seeming tirelessness, sleeping when he could, sustained by Mrs Bates's excellent food and Bates's dignified support. But Amabel was always at the back of his mind, and from time to time he allowed himself to think about her, living her quiet life and, he hoped, sometimes thinking about him.

Of Miriam he saw nothing; she had prudently gone to stay with friends in the country, where there was less danger of getting the flu. She phoned him, leaving nicely calculated messages to let him see that she was concerned about him, content to bide her time, pleased with herself that she had sewn the seeds of doubt in Amabel's mind. Amabel was the kind of silly little fool, she reflected, who would believe every word of what she had said. Head over heels in love with him, thought Miriam, and doesn't even know it.

But here she was wrong; Amabel, left unhappy and worried, thought about Oliver a good deal. In fact he was never out of her thoughts. She *had* believed Miriam when she had told her that she and Oliver were to marry. If Lady Haleford hadn't been particularly testy for the next few days she might have mentioned it to her, but it wasn't until two o'clock one morning, when the old lady was sitting up in her bed wide awake and feeling chatty, that she began to talk about Oliver.

'Time he settled down. I only hope he doesn't marry that

Potter-Stokes woman. Can't stand her—but there's no denying that she's got looks and plenty of ambition. He'd be knighted in no time if she married him, for she knows all the right people. But he'd have a fashionable practice and turn into an embittered man. He needs to be loved...'

Amabel, curled up in a chair by the bed, wrapped in her sensible dressing gown, her hair neatly plaited, murmured soothingly, anxious that the old lady should settle down. Now was certainly not the time to tell her about Miriam's news.

Lady Haleford dozed off and Amabel was left with her thoughts. They were sad, for she agreed wholeheartedly with the old lady that Miriam would not do for Oliver. He does need someone to love him, reflected Amabel, and surprised herself by adding *me*.

Once over her surprise at the thought, she allowed herself to daydream a little. She had no idea where Oliver lived—somewhere in London—and she knew almost nothing about his work, but she would love him, and care for him, and look after his house, and there would be children...

'I fancy a drop of hot milk,' said Lady Haleford. 'And you'd better go to bed, Amabel. You looked washed out...'

Which effectively put an end to daydreams, although it didn't stop her chaotic thoughts. Waiting for the milk to heat, she decided that she had been in love with Oliver for a long time, accepting him into her life as naturally as drawing breath. But there was nothing to be done about it; Miriam had made it plain that he wouldn't welcome the prospect of seeing her again.

If he did come to see his aunt, thought Amabel, pouring the milk carefully into Lady Haleford's special mug, then she, Amabel, would keep out of his way, be coolly pleasant, let him see that she quite understood.

These elevating thoughts lasted until she was back in her own bed, where she could cry her eyes out in peace and quiet.

The thoughts stood her in good stead, for Oliver came two days later. It being a Sunday, and Lady Haleford being in a good mood, Amabel had been told that she might go to Matins, and it was on leaving the church that she saw the car outside the cottage. She stopped in the porch, trying to think of a means of escape. If she went back into the church she could go out through the side door and up the lane and stay away for as long as possible. He probably wasn't staying long...

She felt a large heavy arm on her shoulders and turned her head.

'Didn't expect me, did you?' asked the doctor cheerfully. 'I've come to lunch.'

Amabel found her voice and willed her heart to stop thumping. She said, 'Lady Haleford will be pleased to see you.'

He gave her a quick, all-seeing look. Something wasn't quite right...

'I've had orders to take you for a brisk walk before lunch. Up the lane by the church?'

Being with him, she discovered, was the height of happiness. Her high-minded intentions could surely be delayed until he had gone again? While he was there, they didn't make sense. As long as she remembered that they were friends and nothing more.

She said, 'Where's Tiger?'

'Being spoilt in the kitchen. Wait here. I'll fetch him and Cyril.'

He was gone before she could utter, and soon back again with the dogs, tucking an arm in hers and walking her briskly past the church and up the lane. The last time she had walked along it, she reflected, Miriam had been with her.

Very conscious of the arm, she asked, 'Have you been busy?'

'Very busy. There's not been much flu here?'

'Only one or two cases.' She sought for something to talk about. 'Have you seen Lady Haleford yet? She's better—at least I think so. Once the spring is here, perhaps I could drive her out sometimes—just for an hour—and she's looking forward to going into the garden.'

'I spent a few minutes with her. Yes, she is making progress, but it's a long business. I should think you will be here for some weeks. Do you want to leave, Amabel?'

'No, no, of course not. Unless Lady Haleford would like me to go?'

'That is most unlikely. Have you thought about the future?'

'Yes, quite a lot. I—I know what I want to do. I'll go and see Aunt Thisbe and then I'll enrol at one of those places where I can train to use a computer. There's a good one at Manchester; I saw it advertised in Lady Haleford's paper.' She added, to make it sound more convincing, 'I've saved my money, so I can find somewhere to live.'

The doctor, quite rightly, took this to be a spur-of-the-moment idea, but he didn't say so.

'Very sensible. You don't wish to go home?'

'Yes. I'd like to see Mother, but she wrote to me just after Christmas and said that my stepfather still wasn't keen for me to pay a visit.'

'She could come here...'

'I don't think he would like that. I did suggest it.' She added, 'Mother is very happy. I wouldn't want to disturb that.'

They had been walking briskly and had passed the last of the cottages in the lane. The doctor came to a halt and turned her round to face him.

'Amabel, there is a great deal I wish to say to you...'

'No,' she said fiercely. 'Not now—not ever. I quite understand, but I don't want to know. Oh, can't you see that? We're friends, and I hope we always will be, but when I leave here it's most unlikely that we shall meet again.'

He said slowly, 'What makes you think that we shall never meet again?'

'It wouldn't do,' said Amabel. 'And now please don't let's talk about it any more.'

He nodded, his blue eyes suddenly cold. 'Very well.' He turned her round. 'We had better go back, or Mrs Twitchett will be worried about a spoilt lunch.'

He began to talk about the dogs and the weather, and was she interested in paintings? He had been to see a rather interesting exhibition of an early Victorian artist...

His gentle flow of talk lasted until they reached the cottage again and she could escape on the pretext of seeing if the old lady needed anything before lunch. The fresh air had given her face a pleasing colour, but it still looked plain in her mirror. She flung powder onto her nose, dragged a comb through her hair and went downstairs.

Lady Haleford, delighted to have Oliver's company, asked endless questions. She knew many of the doctor's friends and demanded news of them.

'And what about you, Oliver? I know you're a busy man, but surely you must have some kind of social life?'

'Not a great deal—I've been too busy.'

'That Potter-Stokes woman called—brought flowers from her mother. Heaven knows why; I hardly know her. She tired me out in ten minutes. I sent her out for a walk with Amabel...'

'Miriam came here?' asked Oliver slowly, and looked at Amabel, sitting at the other side of the table.

She speared a morsel of chicken onto her fork and glanced at him quickly. 'She's very beautiful, isn't she? We had a pleasant walk and a cup of coffee—she couldn't stay long; she was on her way to visit someone. She thought the village was delightful. She was driving one of those little sports cars...' She stopped talking, aware that she was babbling.

She put the chicken in her mouth and chewed it. It tasted like ashes.

'Miriam is very beautiful,' agreed the doctor, staring at her, and then said to his aunt, 'I'm sure you must enjoy visitors from time to time, Aunt, but don't tire yourself.'

'I don't. Besides, Amabel may look like a mouse, but she can be a dragon in my defence. Bless the girl! I don't know what I would do without her.' After a moment she added, 'But of course she will go soon.'

'Not until you want me to,' said Amabel. 'And by then you will have become so much better that you won't need anyone.' She smiled across the table at the old lady. 'Mrs Twitchett has made your favourite pudding. Now, there is someone you would never wish to be without!'

'She has been with me for years. Oliver, your Mrs Bates is a splendid cook, is she not? And Bates? He still runs the place for you?'

'My right hand,' said the doctor. 'And as soon as you are well enough I shall drive you up to town and you can sample some of Mrs Bates's cooking.'

Lady Haleford needed her after-lunch nap.

'Stay for tea?' she begged him. 'Keep Amabel company. I'm sure you'll have plenty to talk about...'

'I'm afraid that I must get back.' He glanced at his watch. 'I'll say goodbye now.'

When Amabel came downstairs again he had gone.

Which was only to be expected, Amabel told herself, but she would have liked to have said goodbye. To have explained...

But how did one explain that, since one had fallen in love with someone already engaged to someone else, meeting again would be pointless. And she had lost a friend...

Later that day Lady Haleford, much refreshed by her nap, observed, 'A pity Oliver had to return so soon.' She darted a sharp glance at Amabel. 'You get on well together?'

'Yes,' said Amabel, and tried to think of something to add but couldn't.

'He's a good man.'

'Yes,' said Amabel again. 'Shall I unpick that knitting for you, Lady Haleford?'

The old lady gave her a thoughtful look. 'Yes, Amabel, and then we will have a game of cards. That will distract our thoughts.'

Amabel, surveying her future during a wakeful night, wondered what she should do, but as events turned out she had no need to concern herself with that.

It was several days after Oliver's visit that she had a phone call. She had just come in with Cyril, after his early-morning walk, and, since Nelly and Mrs Twitchett were both in the kitchen, she answered it from the phone in the hall.

'Is that you, Amabel?' Her stepfather's voice was agitated. 'Listen, you must come home at once. Your mother's ill—she's been in hospital and they've sent her home and there's no one to look after her.'

'What was wrong? Why didn't you let me know that she was ill?'

'It was only pneumonia. I thought they'd keep her there until she was back to normal. But here she is, in bed most of the day, and I've enough to do without nursing her as well.'

'Haven't you any help?'

'Oh, there's a woman who comes in to clean and cook. Don't tell me to hire a nurse; it's your duty to come home and care for your mother. And I don't want any excuses. You're her daughter, remember.'

'I'll come as soon as I can,' said Amabel, and took Cyril to the kitchen.

Mrs Twitchett looked at her pale face. 'Something wrong? Best tell us.'

It was a great relief to tell someone. Mrs Twitchett and Nelly heard her out.

'Have to go, won't you love?' Nelly's eye fell on Cyril and Oscar, side by side in front of the Aga. 'Will you take them with you?'

'Oh, Nelly, I can't. He wanted to kill them both; that's why I left home.' Amabel sniffed back tears. 'I'll have to take them to a kennel and a cattery.'

'No need,' Mrs Twitchett said comfortably. 'They'll stay here until you know what's what. Lady Haleford loves them both, and Nelly will see to Cyril's walks. Now, just you go and tell my lady what it's all about.'

Lady Haleford, sitting up in bed, sipping her early-morning tea and wide awake for once, said immediately, 'Of course you must go home immediately. Don't worry about Cyril and Oscar. Get your mother well again and then come back to us. Will she want you to stay at home for good?'

Amabel shook her head. 'No, I don't think so. You see, my stepfather doesn't like me.'

'Then go and pack, and arrange your journey.'

CHAPTER NINE

THE DOCTOR HAD driven himself back to London, deep in thought. It was obvious that Miriam had said something to Amabel which had upset her and caused her to retire into her shell of coolness. But she hadn't sounded cool in the lane. The only way to discover the reason for this was to go and see Miriam. She had probably said something as a joke and Amabel had misunderstood her...

He had gone to see her the very next evening and found her entertaining friends. As she had come to meet him he had said, 'I want to talk to you, Miriam.'

She, looking into his bland face and cold eyes, said at once, 'Oh, impossible, Oliver—we're just about to go out for the evening.'

'You can join your friends later. It is time we had a talk, Miriam, and what better time than now?'

She pouted. 'Oh, very well.' Then she smiled enchantingly. 'I was beginning to think that you had forgotten me.'

Presently, when everyone had gone, she sat down on a sofa and patted the cushion beside her. 'My dear, this is nice—just the two of us.'

The doctor sat down in a chair opposite her.

'Miriam, I have never been your dear. We have been out together, seen each other frequently at friends' houses, visited the theatre, but I must have made it plain to you that that was the extent of our friendship.' He asked abruptly, 'What did you say to Amabel?'

Miriam's beautiful face didn't look beautiful any more. 'So that's it—you've fallen in love with that dull girl! I guessed it weeks ago, when Dolores saw you in York. Her and her silly pets. Well, anyway, I've cooked your goose. I told her you were going to marry me, that you had helped her out of kindness and the sooner she disappeared the better...'

She stopped, because Oliver's expressionless face frightened her, and then when he got to his feet said, 'Oliver, don't go. She's no wife for you; you need someone like me, who knows everyone worth knowing, entertains all the right people, dresses well.'

Oliver walked to the door. 'I need a wife who loves me and whom I love.' And he went away.

It was a pity, he reflected that his next few days were so crammed with patients, clinics and theatre lists that it was impossible for him to go and see Amabel. It was a temptation to phone her, but he knew that would be unsatisfactory. Besides, he wanted to see her face while they talked.

He drove back home and went to his study and started on the case notes piled on his desk, dismissing Amabel firmly from his thoughts.

Lady Haleford had summoned Mrs Twitchett to her bedroom and demanded to know how Amabel was to go home. 'I don't know where the girl lives. Didn't someone tell me that she came from York?'

'And so she did, my lady; she's got an aunt there. Left home when her mother brought in a stepfather who don't like her. Somewhere near Castle Cary—she'll need to get the train to the nearest station and get a taxi or a bus, if there is one.'

Mrs Twitchett hesitated. 'And, my lady, could we keep Oscar and Cyril here while she's away? Seeing that her stepfather won't have them? Going to put them down, he was, so she left home.'

'The poor child. Arrange for William down at the village garage to drive her home. I've already told her that of course the animals must stay.'

So Amabel was driven away in the village taxi, which was just as well, for the journey home otherwise would have been long and tedious and she had had no time to plan it.

It was late afternoon when William drew up with a flourish at her home.

There were lights shining from several windows, and she could see a large greenhouse at the side of the house. As they got out of the car she glimpsed another beyond it, where the orchard had been.

The front door opened under her touch and they went into the hall as she saw her stepfather come from the kitchen.

'And about time too,' he said roughly. 'Your mother's in the sitting room, waiting to be helped to bed.'

'This is William, who brought me here by taxi,' said Amabel. 'He's going back to Aldbury, but he would like a cup of tea first.'

'I've no time to make tea...'

Amabel turned to William. 'If you'll come with me to the kitchen, I'll make it. I'll just see Mother first.'

Her mother looked up as she went into the sitting room.

'There you are, Amabel. Lovely to see you again, dear, and have you here to look after me.' She lifted her face for Amabel's kiss. 'Keith is quite prepared to let bygones be bygones and let you live here...'

'Mother, I must give the taxi driver a cup of tea. I'll be back presently and we can have a talk.'

There was no sign of her stepfather. William, waiting patiently in the kitchen, said, 'Not much of a welcome home, miss.'

Amabel warmed the teapot. 'Well, it all happened rather suddenly. Do you want a sandwich?'

William went very soon, feeling all the better for the tea and sandwiches, and the tip he had accepted reluctantly, and Amabel went back to the sitting room.

'Tell me what has been wrong with you, Mother. Do you stay up all day? The doctor visits you?'

'Pneumonia, love, and I went to hospital because Keith couldn't possibly manage on his own.'

'Have you no help?'

'Oh, yes, of course. Mrs Twist has been coming each day, to see to the house and do some of the cooking, and the hospital said a nurse would come each day once I was back home. She came for a day or two, but she and Keith had an argument and he told them that you would be looking after me. Not that I need much attention. In fact he's told Mrs Twist that she need not come any more, now that you are back home.'

'My stepfather told me that there was no one to look after you, that he had no help...'

Her mother said lightly, 'Oh, well, dear, you know what men are—and it does seem absurd for him to pay for a nurse and Mrs Twist when we have you...'

'Mother, I don't think you understand. I've got a job. I came because I thought there was no one to help you. I'll stay until you are better, but you must get Mrs Twist back and have a nurse on call if it's necessary. I'd like to go back to Aldbury as soon as possible. You see, dear, Keith doesn't like me—but you're happy with him, aren't you?'

'Yes, Amabel, I am, and I can't think why you can't get on, the pair of you. But now you are here the least you can do is make me comfortable. I'm still rather an invalid, having breakfast in bed and then a quiet day here by the fire. My appetite isn't good, but you were always a good cook. Keith likes his breakfast early, so you'll have all day to see to the house.'

She added complacently, 'Keith is doing very well already, and now he won't need to pay Mrs Twist and that nurse he can plough the money back. You'll want to unpack your things, dear. Your old room, of course. I'm not sure if the bed is made up, but you know where everything is. And when you come down we'll decide what we'll have for supper.'

Of course the bed wasn't made up; the room was chilly and unwelcoming and Amabel sat down on the bed to get her thoughts sorted out. She wouldn't stay longer than it took to get Mrs Twist back, see the doctor and arrange for a nurse to visit, whatever her stepfather said. She loved her mother, but she was aware that she wasn't really welcome, that she was just being used as a convenience by her stepfather.

She made the bed, unpacked, and went back downstairs to the kitchen. There was plenty of food in the fridge. At least she wouldn't need to go to the shops for a few days...

Her mother fancied an omelette. 'But that won't do for Keith. There's a gammon steak, and you might do some potatoes and leeks. You won't have time to make a pudding, but there's plenty of cheese and biscuits...'

'Have you been cooking, Mother?'

Her mother said fretfully, 'Well, Keith can't cook, and Mrs Twist wasn't here. Now you're home I don't need to do anything.'

The next morning Amabel went to the village to the doctor's surgery. He was a nice man, but elderly and overworked.

'You're mother is almost fit again,' he assured Amabel. 'There is no reason why she shouldn't do a little housework, as long as she rests during the day. She needs some tests done, of course, and pills, and a check-up by the practice nurse. It is a pity that her husband refuses to let her visit; he told me that you would be coming home to live and that you would see to your mother.'

'Has Mother been very ill?'

'No, no. Pneumonia is a nasty thing, but if it's dealt with promptly anyone as fit as your mother makes a quick recovery.'

'I understood from what my stepfather told me on the phone that Mother was very ill and he was without help.' She sighed. 'I came as quickly as I could, but I have a job...'

'Well, I shouldn't worry too much about that. I imagine that a few days of help from you will enable your mother to lead her usual life again. She has help, I believe?'

'My stepfather gave Mrs Twist notice...'

'Oh, dear, then you must get her back. Someone local?'

'Yes.'

'Well, it shouldn't be too difficult to persuade Mr Graham to change his mind. Once she is reinstated, you won't need to stay.'

Something which she pointed out to her stepfather later that day. 'And do please understand that I must go back to my job at the end of week. The doctor told me that Mother should be well by then. You will have to get Mrs Twist to come every day.'

'You unnatural girl.' Keith Graham's face was red with bad temper. 'It's your duty to stay here...'

'You didn't want me to stay before,' Amabel pointed out quietly. 'I'll stay for a week, so that you have time to make arrangements to find someone to help Mother.' She nodded her neat head at him. 'There was no need for me to come home. I love Mother, but you know as well as I do that you hate having me here. I can't think why you decided to ask me to come.'

'Why should I pay for a woman to come and do the housework when I've a stepdaughter I can get for nothing?'

Amabel got to her feet. If there had been something suitable to throw at him she would have thrown it, but since there wasn't she merely said, 'I shall go back at the end of the week.'

But there were several days to live through first, and although her mother consented to be more active there was a great deal to do—the cooking, fires to clean and light, coal to fetch from the shed, beds to make and the house to tidy. Her stepfather didn't lift a finger, only coming in for his meals, and when he wasn't out and about he was sitting by the fire, reading his paper.

Amabel said nothing, for eventually there was only one more day to go...

She was up early on the last morning, her bag packed, and

she went down to cook the breakfast Keith demanded. He came into the kitchen as she dished up his bacon and eggs.

'Your mother's ill,' he told her. 'Not had a wink of sleep—nor me neither. You'd better go and see to her.'

'At what time is Mrs Twist coming?'

'She isn't. Haven't had time to do anything about her...'

Amabel went upstairs and found her mother in bed.

'I'm not well, Amabel. I feel awful. My chest hurts and I've got a headache. You can't leave me.'

She moaned as Amabel sat her gently against her pillows.

'I'll bring you a cup of tea, Mother, and phone the doctor.'

She went downstairs to phone and leave a message at the surgery. Her stepfather said angrily, 'No need for him. All she needs is a few days in bed. You can stay on a bit.'

'I'll stay until you get Mrs Twist back. Today, if possible.'

Her mother would eat no breakfast, so Amabel helped her to the bathroom, made the bed and tidied the room and then went back downstairs to cancel the taxi which was to have fetched her in an hour's time. She had no choice but to stay until the doctor had been and Mrs Twist was reinstated.

There was nothing much wrong with her mother, the doctor told her when he came. She was complaining about her chest, but he could find nothing wrong there, and her headache was probably due to the sleepless nights she said she was having.

He said slowly, 'She has worked herself up because you are going away. I think it would be best if you could arrange to stay for another day or two. Has Mr Graham got Mrs Twist to come in?'

'No. He told me that he had had no time. I thought I might go and see her myself. You don't think that Mother is going to be ill again?'

'As far as I can see she has recovered completely from the pneumonia, but, as I say, she has worked herself up into a state—afraid of being ill again. So if you could stay...'

'Of course I'll stay until Mother feels better.' She smiled at him. 'Thank you for coming, Doctor.'

He gave her a fatherly pat. He thought she looked a bit under the weather herself he must remember to call in again in a day or two.

Amabel unpacked her bag, assured her mother that she would stay until Mrs Twist could come, and went to see that lady...

Mrs Twist was a comfortable body with a cheerful face. She listened to Amabel in silence and then said, 'Well, I'm sorry to disoblige you, but I've got my old mum coming today for a week. Once she's gone home again I'll go each day, same as before. Staying long, are you?'

'I meant to go back to my job this morning, but Mother asked me to stay until you could arrange to come back.' She couldn't help adding, 'You will come, won't you?'

'Course I will, love. And a week goes by quick enough. Nice having your ma to chat to.'

Amabel said, yes, it was, and thought how nice that would have been. Only there was precious little time to chat, and when she did sit down for an hour to talk it was her mother who did the talking: about how good Keith was to her, the new clothes she had bought, the holiday they intended to take before the spring brought all the extra work in the greenhouses, how happy she was... But she asked no questions of Amabel.

She said, 'I expect you've got a good job, darling. You were always an independent girl. You must tell me about it one day... I was telling you about our holiday...'

It was strange how the days seemed endless, despite the fact that she had little leisure. She had written a note to Lady Haleford, saying that she would return as soon as she could arrange help for her mother. Since her mother seemed quite well again, it was now just a question of waiting for Mrs Twist's mother to go home. Her mother, however, was disinclined to do much.

'There's no need for me to do anything,' she had said, half laughing, 'while you're here.'

'Mrs Twist does everything when she comes?'

'Oh, yes. Although I do the cooking. But you're such a good cook, love, and it gives you something to do.'

One more day, thought Amabel. She had missed Cyril and Oscar. She had missed Oliver too, but she tried not to think of him—and how could she miss someone she hardly ever saw?

Amabel had been gone for almost two weeks before the doctor felt free to take time off and go to Aldbury. His aunt greeted him with pleasure. 'But you've come to see Amabel? Well, she's not here. The child had to go home; her mother was ill. She expected to be gone for a week. Indeed, she wrote and told me she would be coming back. And then I had another letter saying that she would have to stay another week. Can't think why she didn't telephone.' She added, 'Mrs Twitchett phoned and a man answered her. Very abrupt, she said, told her that Amabel wasn't available.'

It was already late afternoon, and the doctor had a list early on the following morning, a clinic in the afternoon and private patients to see. To get into his car and go to Amabel was something he wanted to do very much, but that wasn't possible; it wouldn't be possible for two days.

He thought about phoning her, but it might make matters worse and in any case there was a great deal he could do. He went back home, sat down at his desk and picked up the phone; he could find out what was happening...

Mrs Graham's doctor was helpful. There was no reason, he said over the phone, why Amabel should stay at home. She had told him very little, but he sensed that her mother's illness had been used to get her to return there. 'If there is anything I can do?' he offered.

'No, no, thanks. I wanted to be sure that her mother really needs her.'

'There's no reason why she shouldn't walk out of the house, but there may be circumstances which prevent her doing that.'

The doctor picked up the phone and heard Miss Parsons' firm voice at the other end.

'I hoped that you might be back...' He talked at some length and finally put the phone down and went in search of Bates. After that, all he had to do was to possess his soul in patience until he could go to Amabel.

He set off early in the morning two days later, with Tiger beside him and Bates to see him on his way.

Life was going to be quite interesting, Bates thought as he went in search of his wife.

Once free of London and the suburbs, Oliver drove fast. He hoped that he had thought of everything. A lot was going to happen during the next few hours, and nothing must go wrong.

It was raining when he reached the house, and now that the apple orchard had gone the house looked bare and lonely and the greenhouses looked alien. He drove round the side of the house, got out with Tiger, opened the kitchen door and went in.

Amabel was standing at the sink, peeling potatoes. She was wearing an apron several sizes too large for her and her hair hung in a plait over one shoulder. She looked pale and tired and utterly forlorn.

This was no time for explanations; the doctor strode to the sink, removed the potato and the knife from her hands and folded his arms around her. He didn't speak, he didn't kiss her, just held her close. He was holding her when Mr Graham came in.

'Who are you?' he demanded.

Oliver gave Amabel a gentle push. 'Go and get your coat and pack your things.' Something in his voice made her disentangle herself from his embrace and look up at his quiet face. He smiled down at her. 'Run along, darling.'

She went upstairs and all she could think of then was that he had called her darling. She should have taken him into the sitting room, where her mother was... Instead she got her case from the wardrobe and began to pack it, and, that done, picked up her coat and went downstairs.

The doctor had watched her go and then turned to Mr Graham, who began in a blustering voice, 'I don't know why you're here, whoever you are—'

'I'll tell you,' said Oliver gently. 'And when I've finished perhaps you will take me to Amabel's mother.'

She looked up in surprise as they went into the sitting room.

'He's come for Amabel,' said Mr Graham, looking daggers at Oliver. 'I don't know what things are coming to when your daughter's snatched away and you so poorly, my dear.'

'Your doctor tells me that you are fully recovered, Mrs Graham, and I understand that you have adequate help in the house...'

'I'm very upset—' began Mrs Graham. Glancing at the quiet man standing there, she decided that a show of tears wouldn't help. 'After all, a daughter should take care of her mother...'

'And do the housework and the cooking?' From the look of her Amabel has been doing that, and much more besides.

'She ought to be grateful,' growled Mr Graham, 'having a home to come to.'

'Where she is expected to do the chores, cook and clean and shop?' asked Oliver coolly. 'Mr Graham, you make me tired—and extremely angry.'

'Who is going to see to things when she's gone?'

'I'm sure there is adequate help to be had in the village.' He turned away as Amabel came into the room. 'Everything is satisfactorily arranged,' he told her smoothly. 'If you will say goodbye, we will go.'

Amabel supposed that presently she would come to her senses and ask a few sensible questions, even ask for an explanation of the unexpected events taking place around her, but all she said was, 'Yes, Oliver,' in a meek voice, and went to kiss her mother and bid her stepfather a frosty goodbye.

She said tartly, 'There's a lot I could say to you, but I won't,' and she walked out of the room with Oliver. Tiger was in the kitchen, and somehow the sight of him brought her to her senses.

'Oliver—' she began.

'We'll talk as we go,' he told her comfortably, and popped her into the car, settled Tiger in the back seat and got in beside her. Presently he said in a matter-of-fact voice, 'We shall be home in time for supper. We'll stop at Aldbury and get Oscar and Cyril.'

'But where are we going?'

'Home.'

'I haven't got a home,' said Amabel wildly.

'Yes, you have.' He rested a hand on her knee for a moment. 'Darling, *our* home.'

And after that he said nothing for quite some time, which left Amabel all the time in the world to think. Chaotic thoughts which were interrupted by him saying in a matter-of-fact voice, 'Shall we stop for a meal?' and, so saying, stopping before a small pub, well back from the road, with a lane on one side of it.

It was dim and cosy inside, with a handful of people at the bar, and they had their sandwiches and coffee against a background of cheerful talk, not speaking much themselves.

When they had finished the doctor said, 'Shall we walk a little way up the lane with Tiger?'

They walked arm in arm and Amabel tried to think of something to say—then decided that there was no need; it was as though they had everything that mattered.

But not quite all, it seemed, for presently, when they stopped to look at the view over a gate, Oliver turned her round to face him.

'I love you. You must know that, my dear. I've loved you since I first saw you, although I didn't know it at once. And then you seemed so young, and anxious to make a life for yourself; I'm so much older than you...'

Amabel said fiercely, 'Rubbish. You're just the right age. I don't quite understand what has happened, but that doesn't matter...' She looked up into his face. 'You have always been there, and I can't imagine a world without you...'

He kissed her then, and the wintry little lane was no longer a lane but heaven.

In a little while they got back into the car, and Amabel, with a little gentle prompting, told Oliver of her two weeks with her mother.

'How did you know I was there?' she wanted to know, and when he had told her she said, 'Oliver, Miriam Potter-Stokes said that you were going to marry her. I know now that wasn't true, but why did she say that?' She paused. 'Did you think that you would before you met me?'

'No, my darling. I took her out once or twice, and we met often at friends' houses. But it never entered my head to want to marry her. I think that she looked upon me, as she would look upon any other man in my position, as a possible source of a comfortable life.'

'That's all right, then,' said Amabel.

She looked so radiantly happy that he said, 'My dearest, if you continue to look like that I shall have to stop and kiss you.'

An unfulfilled wish since they were on a motorway.

There was no doubt about the warmth of their welcome at Lady Haleford's cottage. They were met in the hall by Mrs Twitchett, Nelly, Oscar and Cyril, and swept into the drawing room, where Lady Haleford was sitting.

She said at once, 'Amabel, I am so happy to see you again, although I understand from Oliver that this visit is a brief one. Still, we shall see more of each other, I have no doubt. I shall miss you and Oscar and Cyril. Oliver shall bring you here whenever he has the time, but of course first of all he must take you to see his mother. You'll marry soon?'

Amabel went pink and Oliver answered for her. 'Just as soon as it can be arranged, Aunt.'

'Good. I shall come to the wedding, and so will Mrs Twitchett and Nelly. Now we will have tea...'

An hour later, once more in the car, Amabel said, 'You haven't asked me...'

He glanced at her briefly, smiling. 'Oh, but I will. Once we are alone and quiet. I've waited a long time, dear love, but I'm not going to propose to you driving along a motorway.'

'I don't know where you live...'

'In a quiet street of Regency houses. There's a garden with a high wall, just right for Oscar and Cyril, and Bates and his wife look after me and Tiger, and now they will look after you three as well.'

'Oh—is it a big house?'

'No, no, just a nice size for a man and his wife and children to live in comfortably.'

Which gave Amabel plenty to think about, staring out of the window into the dark evening through rose-coloured spectacles, soothed by Oliver's quiet voice from time to time and the gentle fidgets of the three animals on the back seat.

She hadn't been sure of what to expect, and when she got out of the car the terrace of houses looked elegant and dignified, with handsome front doors and steps leading to their basements. But Oliver gave her time to do no more than glimpse at them. Light streamed from an open door and someone stood waiting by it.

'We're home,' said Oliver, and took her arm and tucked it under his.

She had been feeling anxious about Bates, but there was no need; he beamed at her like a kindly uncle, and Mrs Bates behind him shook her hand, her smile as wide as her husband's.

'You will wish to go straight to the drawing room, sir,' said Bates, and opened a door with a flourish.

As they went in, Aunt Thisbe came to meet them.

'Didn't expect to see me, did you, Amabel?' she asked briskly. 'But Oliver is a stickler for the conventions, and quite right too. You will have to bear with me until you are married.'

She offered a cheek to be kissed, and then again for Oliver.

'You two will want to talk, but just for a moment there is something I need to do...' he murmured.

Aunt Thisbe made for the door. 'I'll see about those animals of yours,' she said, and closed the door firmly behind her.

The doctor unbuttoned Amabel's coat, tossed it on a chair and took her in his arms. 'This is a proposal—but first, this...' He bent his head and kissed her, taking his time about it.

'Will you marry me, Amabel?' he asked her.

'Will you always kiss me like that?' she asked him.

'Always and for ever, dearest.'

'Then I'll marry you,' said Amabel, 'because I like being kissed like that. Besides, I love you.'

There was only one answer to that...

* * * * *